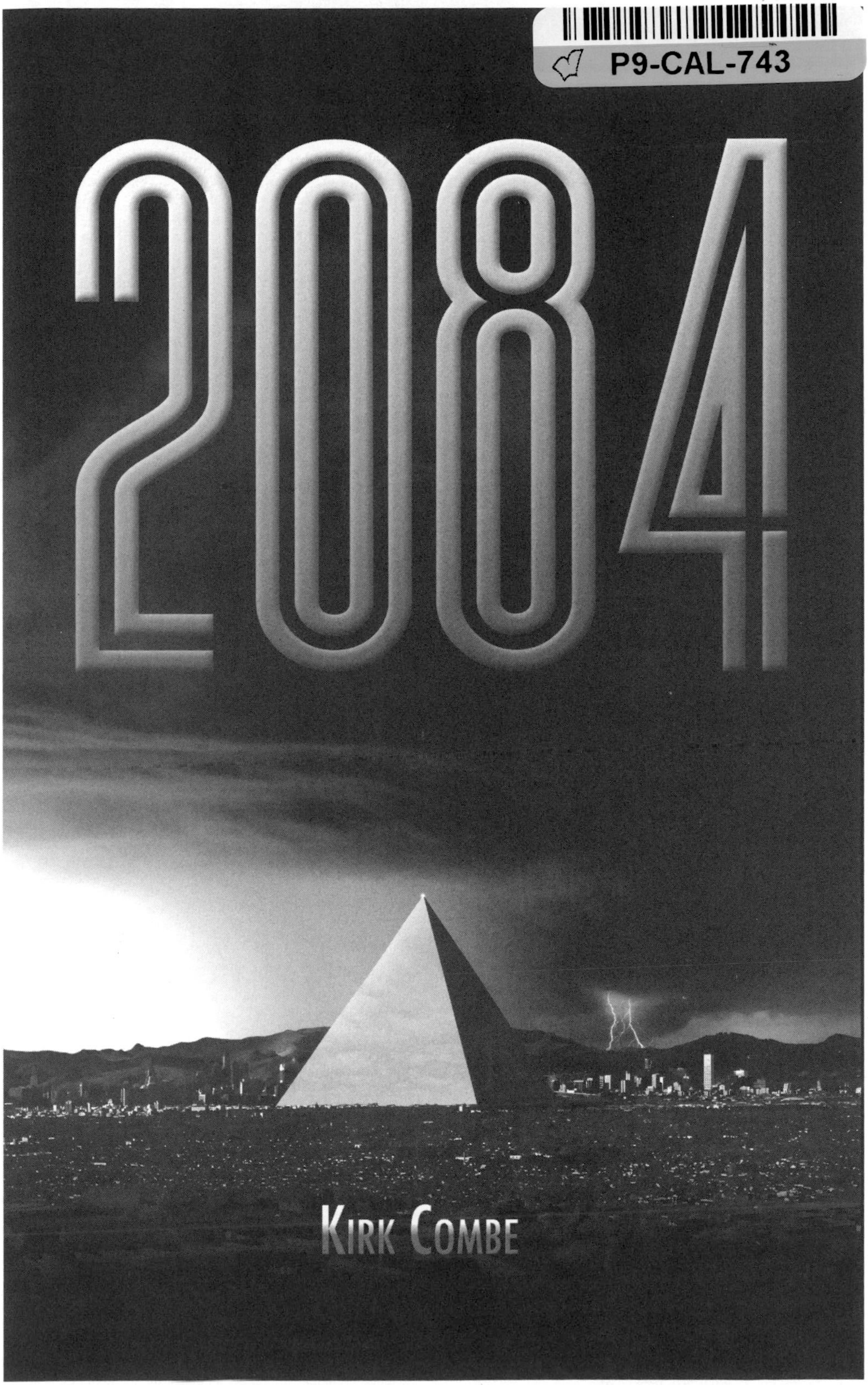
2084
KIRK COMBE

2084

Kirk Combe

Mayhaven Publishing, Inc.
P O Box 557
Mahomet, IL 61853
USA

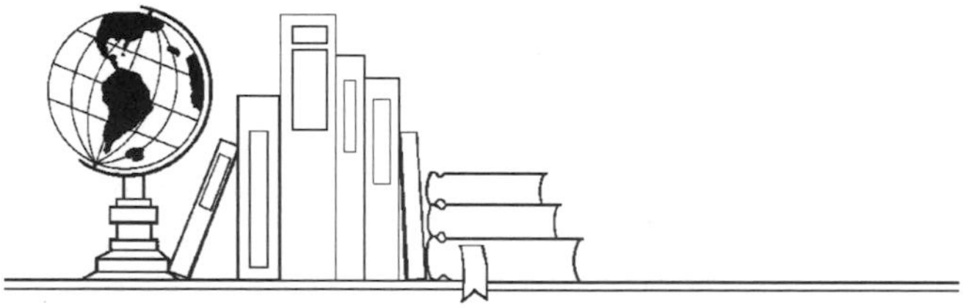

First Edition—First Printing 2009

Library of Congress Control Number: 2009924417
ISBN 13: 978 1932278637
ISBN 10 193227863X

Dedication

To my favorite people in the world:
Hannah, Olivia, Clayton, Bren

Memorial

In memory of Bettie Carter Combe, 1929-2000;
teacher, art historian, mother

“I think that all in all, the manufacturing aristocracy that we see rising before our eyes is one of the hardest that has appeared on earth; but it is at the same time one of the most restrained and least dangerous.

Still, the friends of democracy ought constantly to turn their regard with anxiety in this direction; for if ever permanent inequality of conditions and aristocracy are introduced anew into the world, one can predict that they will enter by this door.”

—Alexis De Tocqueville, 1835

“Modern industry has established the world-market, for which the discovery of America paved the way.”

—Karl Marx,1848

“If the step were not being taken, if the stumbling-forward ache were not alive, the bombs would not fall, the throats would not be cut.

Fear the time when the bombs stop falling while the bombers live—for every bomb is proof that the spirit has not died.”

—John Steinbeck, 1939

“When Europe and America are divided,
history tends to tragedy.”

—George W. Bush, 2001

CONTENTS

PART ONE

TAT FOR TIT

The Elevator to Outer Space

Announced by an amusing hermetic farting sound, Bleached Wheat steps, smiling to himself, from between the sliding outer doors of the double airlock. He's always relieved to disembark a shuttle. Cramped and vile things, if you really want to know. Their stale air gives him headaches. As he'd ordered, the executive platform is deserted, as he likes it for this kind of things. On the wall to his right is the big white star inside a thin red circle against the deep blue background. In fact the whole interior of the execplat is deep blue. Walls, deck, ceiling. People like color—dynamic color. It helps them enjoy their space. He puts a kiss on the fingertips of his right hand and plants it with a brisk slap in the center of the star. Then, with anticipation in his step, he makes his way across the forty meters of polished blue floor to the curved bank of observation windows.

"Top80," he says as he goes.

An agreeable, faintly militaristic tune begins to play. *Just right*, he thinks. *Motivating*. One hand sweeps the lank, blond forelock from his eyes. His other hand brings his gold Rolex watchwrist up for him to see. Time to catch Vieworld. Another thin smile stretches over his bluish lips. As those talkheads constantly blurt out: "Time To Know!" Yes indeed. How sweet it is to *be* the know.

He stops a few meters short of the windows to concentrate on the little flatscreen. Nothing newsbig running at the moment—as he'd ordered—just the drone. Happy financial indicators. Sentimental tales of miraculous good fortune or heinous crime. The usual brainslow fare. Satisfied, he buries his hands in his pockets and slowly takes the last few steps toward the windows. The panes extend floor-to-ceiling, thick and convex—all but invisible. He places his toes right at their edge before allowing himself to focus. When he does, the base of his scrotum tingles, deliciously. Far, far below is the Big Blue, soon to be his. All his. But enough of the selfoblidge.

He swivels his head toward the east and narrows his eyes. It takes some moments, but finally there it is. A glint of nearly black light along the immense brim. Their Glassea. In a normal speaking voice—for something like this it's always better not to risk miscom with whispers—Bleached Wheat delivers a series of words he has contrived and only he knows: "Six slashback thirty slashback fifty-four legislate basal."

☆ ☆ ☆ ☆ ☆ ☆

Enron can tell the second they're in his head, especially when guard-posted on their Glassea. Something about the brute flat of the place, the dull sheen rising off all horizons—like living on a silver platter—gives him a sideways kick whenever the yankers patch through. Not that he much minds the patch any more. That's so issue he got used to it his first year in. But the jolt to the head when he's wrapped so tight in his nukesuit...well, plaintalk, it makes Enron crap his chaps. You take a tumble in this exteme, on this particular Indian country, and your ass *is* glass. That's why they say in Ground and, as a branch, Ground is all about the hotseat humor. How else can you deal? One year walking the line in Fosfuelville saws three to five off your span, no matter how many layers of lead rootboot you pull over your yanker. Quadprofit or no quadprofit, yank that. But it ain't like you got a choice. They send you where they like—what corping is all about. They corvée your butt. Well, look your fill, whoever the fuck you are. Nothing the hell to see out here anyway, unless you're stiff for big stretches of zero.

CorpTroops learn to accept standing at attention while the head executes the initial orienting sweep. Accept is too voluntary a word. They soon learn to put up with their bodies going through certain involuntary motions, no matter how inconvenient circumstances might be. Hell, you could be growling on the blowpot after a feed, or in the middle of yanking a throb sweetpuss, when all of a sudden you're up-and-see. Terds don't give a shit when they jerk your chain, and if they don't, Crats sure as hell don't. This time at least Enron doesn't have to pirouette around like a fruitcake. Must be seeing just what they want—BigRig19, the mother of all petroxtraction towers. Pumps up megabarrels per second. Enron is standing guard about a demi-klick away from it. Then he feels the hair standing up on the back of his neck.

"Shit no," he murmurs.

His voice sounds hollow inside his mask and hood. His stagnant breath bounces back in his face. A fierce twitch stabs its way up his spine. A CorpTroop tastes the surge order. There's the routine three-second delay, then the dull detonation. BigRig19 goes up in a spectacular ball of fire, and—big surprise—Enron's got the ringside seat—the perf camang. Fuckmothers. *Yanking fuckmothers.* The second before the shockwave smacks him down, he slaps hard with the palm of his glove on his right thigh just above the knee. It might kill him, but why not bang in every drop of poppy and epinephrine his nukesuit has?

☆ ☆ ☆ ☆ ☆ ☆

In geosynch orbit, 36,000km above the surface, Bleached Wheat speaks aloud again, "Telcast primal."

Jitney, Ponzi, Yupcap, and Java can be heard rushing to emerge from the shuttle, Jitney practically clawing open the outermost airlock doors. Bleached Wheat knew they'd be coming on the scamper. Their distress always captivates him. They're such buttsuckers. Each one dresses exactly like him: loose-fit trousers, flamboyant shirts, gelsole runners. Everything casual. They all sport trim goatees and standout cuts. Each one of them looks as agreeable and successful as the next. In person, they're often meddlesome and preening louts, in particular the senior two. Much like he was, at their age. But their on-air look is not to be underestimated—especially Java's, the most semidark of them. All four are fit. All four are ice. All rangy like rock climbers. All doublego and ballsy like sharebrokers. They reek risktaker but are averagejoe. Crats, to be sure, but you just have to like them, *trust* them. After all, they're working for *you*. Bleached Wheat is still crux, too. He's let his goat spread into a sandy fringe along his razor jaw line. He, too, keeps lean. His signature hair is like flax—not a dash of gray—and his irises...his irises. Are there a more famous pair in TexArc? Around the globe? Pure fox. Glacial in hue. Zero glassy. Such eyes never before seen.

"I know," Bleached Wheat says, without bothering to turn. What he likes best about these four is their not speaking unless spoken to. "Get back to the shuttle," he orders, remembering from his own subceo days just how disappointing it was not to be allowed to relate a choice chip of breakingnews to the bossman. He adds, "We'll be on our way in a moment." His tone is not without a touch of ridicule.

Once they're gone, and the execplat is completely still, Bleached Wheat appreciates the perfectly modulated Top80 tunes for awhile. He directs his gaze between his feet, down the colossal shaft of the elevator. They decided, in the end, to anchor the first one in the Atlantic instead of the Pacific. It's still along the equator, but strategic advantage outweighs the enormous expense and elaborate nuisance of having to veer the elevator's floating base platform out of the path of developing hurricanes. Fortunately, that's a perfectly safe, if never completely routine, procedure. Nanotubes are now incorruptible, and the whole skeleton of the elevator is snapped taut by centripetal force. It's also tended 24/7 by the best of

ArcSea, ArcAir, and ArcSpace. That makes the Atlantic location a choice plan. The staging platforms at multiple levels along the column are like having a dozen operational space stations in orbit at once. You just have to push a button to ascend to them all. TexArc keeps its entire shuttle fleet, military and commercial, at doublego—all the time. *All* the time. Their elevator to outer space is a damn monopolization miracle, and now about to pay dividends to boot. Bleached Wheat spots the Highclimber lumbering upcolumn, right on schedule. Six metric tons, with a payload of twelve more. The cargocar is goosed upward by the freelectron lasers beaming upsky into its photocells. *Marvelous capitalserve*, he thinks, *compared to shuttle launches costing an arm and a leg*. He decides to trigger before it climbs too close. There's no real danger. Drynano Selfassemble Support runs up and down the shaft. The vid, though, from this slant, will showstop. Dmega primetime.

Bleached Wheat listens a last moment to the shouts coming over his watchwrist. Still the gratifying soprano of fevernews. *BigRig19! Glassea!* He spreads his feet slightly more apart to establish a solid base, and arches his eyebrows to remind himself not to blink.

"Three one five," he says deliberately.

One hundred meters below him a generous explosion erupts soundlessly outward from the side of the glossy white shaft. Bleached Wheat feels the tremor through his feet. Instantly, the tunes stop, replaced by a baritone, gut-rumbling, rhythmic alarm. Three Servs on routine maintenance in bubbly evasuits float not far below the execplat. Naturally, before descending on their tethers to investigate the blast breach, they hesitate.

"Come on, boys," Bleached Wheat says impatiently to himself. He's on something of a tight schedule. "Don't go thinking on me."

Stupid Parkers always slowing protocol. Yet dutifully, by-and-by and one-by-one, the three glide down cautiously to the rupture. Their actions create a good bit of drama. The moment they're assembled like sitting ducks, a second blast flares out, producing three small, but quite spectacular and very unmistakable, purple puffs the approximate color of bruising flesh. Paf! Paf! Paf! These little wisps appear stark, even beautiful, against the pure white backdrop of the cloud cover thousands of meters below.

“Telcast subsidiary.”

Has Vieworld ever provided more agog?

<<Wherever you go, there we are!>>

<<More ‘you-decide’ breakingnews!>>

<<A second staggering terror attack!>>

<<Coming just minutes after the first!>>

<<Well-coordinated assaults on our freedom!>>

<<First death on our Glassea!>>

<<Now death in our sky!>>

<<Horrifying vidfeed up to the second!>>

<<Taste more heroes making the ultimate sacrifice!>>

<<Boosting today’s gruesome deadcount to seventy-six!>>

The vid plays the initial elevator blast, slightly slowed to exaggerate detail and without aud. The silence of space is uncanny, the huge luminous shaft inspirational, despite its wounding.

<<What cowards are behind this atrocity to progress?>>

The three maintenance Servs drift down into frame–and are immediately blown sideways out of it.

<<Which rogue state now is jealous enough to kill?>>

Ah, for spectacle, you can’t beat the Simulacrum. Bleached Wheat never ceases to marvel at the consummate professionalism. Now let the imagesense sink in thoroughly before rolling out the talkheads to advocate blame. Rerun each targetstrike, at least four or five times, in increasing slowdown. That’s paradigm. Bleached Wheat makes a savoring hmmm sound while he bobs his head in approval. Right now, every upleft in TexArc is fixed, dancing with flickerlights. Every mot-sen/corband is getting torqued and seared with pure universal impact value, right down to the acerbic whiff of scalding flesh. Not enough to sicken, but enough to give pause. He ordered the unprecedented technique of voiding the shopdrop at the upright for one entire minute, to punctuate exactly the magnitude of everything taking place. Extraordinary measures for extraordinary times.

Bleached Wheat looks up from his watchwrist. He's surrounded by Netsmen—materialized out of thin, sterile air, as he knew they must. Two burly ones press roughly against him, their exoshoulders butting up against his shoulders, on either side. Both are at hyper, with their misters up and ready, facing the interior of the platform and set to doublego. Bleached Wheat so admires their smart military bearing. With the Netsmen comes, inevitably, the anxious presence of Jitney, Ponzi, Yupcap, and Java, once more. He senses them standing, Dmega concerned, somewhere behind him. He's in the mood to get it over with quickly.

"Yes?" he says.

"Sir!"

It's Jitney. He almost always speaks too emphatically. He's subceo boss of Security, and, accordingly, going mindfuck. Their elevator's been terrorstruck.

"We should be back to shuttle and away by now!"

Bleached Wheat replies indifferently. "Should we really?"

"Sir!" Jitney's word is a plea. He can be a federal pain in the ass.

Showing no sign of hurry, Bleached Wheat watches the Highclimber complete its catastrophe stop in time. *That's profit. No outlay of DollArcs more than the minimum. This has all gone quite well*, he thinks. *Quite well*. Smiling to himself, Bleached Wheat, looking east, scans the curve of the earth on a northerly line, high, where he estimates EVe to be. He widens his strange eyes and whispers his jeer, not worried the two closest Netsmen can hear. "Take that, you old bitch. You and your fancy wine. You and your stinking cheese. You and your yanksucking public ownership of alienable productive assets."

Corpfeud versus Marksoc. High noon. High time they come to blows. This world ain't big enough for the two of us. That's the TexArc way.

"Backward and Upward!" Bleached Wheat shouts as he turns on his heels.

All, to a company man, repeat, "Backward and Upward!" and follow him doublequick back toward the airlock.

Pessimism of the Intellect

Frame One: Point-of-view. Driver's side of a MiniSol approaching a busy roundabout a short ways off. Street is urban but tree-lined. Traffic is moderate. Day is sunny. The hood of the Mini is neongreen and decorated with white-and-yellow Daisy 3/Decals. Reggae music plays on the entertainment deck. The peep of birds floats occasionally through the open windows. The soft mew of an electromotor purrs. A young woman's hands are on the steering wheel. Her nails painted neon-green. She wears many rings, all of them in the shape of white-and-yellow daisies. Her forearms are festooned with loose and jangly bracelets.

Frame Two: Same point-of-view. Same soundscape. Slight elapse of time. The Mini slows to stop at the edge of the roundabout, allowing several small electrautos already within the roundabout pass by. Then it enters the flow of traffic.

Frame Three: Same point-of-view. Same soundscape. Slight elapse of time. The Mini is within the roundabout. The young woman's hand thumbs the signal pad in preparation to exit at the next turning. The flashing amber panel light and the intermittent chime flick on.

Frame Four: Same point-of-view. All sound suddenly absent. Slight elapse of time. As Mini begins to exit, an oldways Cadillac convertible careens into the roundabout from the left. The driver of the Mini is forced to brake hard. The Cadillac is a shimmering gold, unimaginably long, sporting huge tail fins, like dual sharks. Its engine roars. Its fat tires squeal. Its dangling and rattling tailpipe belches clouds of white smoke. Behind the wheel is a man wearing a checkered blazer, a bolo tie, a white ten-gallon cowboy hat. Paying no mind to surrounding traffic, he yips, "Yee-haa!" barreling right through the roundabout.

Final Frame: Point-of-view. Several meters above the roundabout and behind the Mini. Slight elapse of time. A Vauxhall 'Lectro has rear-ended the Mini. A milk lorry now rear-ends the Vauxhall, sending crates of milk crashing and spilling onto the road. All other electrautos screech to a halt, reducing the roundabout to a dead still. The Cadillac is out of frame, its engine still heard roaring, billows of white exhaust still hanging in the air. Text appears across the bottom of the frame: THOSE WERE THE DAYS?

Underminister Harrods clears his throat before speaking, this vocal gesture seemingly indicating approval. "Very nice as well," he remarks. "Once more, quite clever and on message. Are there others, dear boy?"

"Scads, Underminister," Provost Weetabix replies. "Simply scads."

He pads another. He has good experience dealing with ministry types. Never, though, with one of such high level. It's ruffled him. The Underminister insists viewing outdoors and on an isolated unit. Quite unheard of. Negates all their lovely core fixtures, that does, and denies the Provost the chance fully to display the prowess of his Committee. On the other hand, the eccentric request has given Weetabix the opportunity to show off Worcester grounds a bit—a performance he savors. They had strolled out of the quad areas and along shaded footpaths to the wide cricket pitch, not uncomfortable in their never-wrinkle muslin suits, largely evading the beastly heat of the direct morning sun, and allowing them to discuss their particular business.

Weetabix had settled them onto an ancient stone bench overlooking Worcester's well-known duck pond. They sit in deep shade, more than adequate cover for their conversation. Just to their right is the stone frame of an old portal, the endpoint, at pond's edge, of all that remains of an antediluvian bulwark. A functioning wrought-iron gate squeaks on its hinges whenever one passes through this meaningless survival. *Surely there's a metaphor to be found*, thinks Weetabix, but he isn't confident enough to hazard a metaphysical observation. Metaphysics is, after all, what the Provost leaves to the signers under his charge.

Before them is the goodly-sized empty pool. The coot ducks that adorn the Worcester coat-of-arms have long since vanished, and the aquamirror only creates the semblance of water. Even so, the setting is marked by scholastic serenity. Precisely the effect the Provost had hoped to accomplish. The palm trees overhanging the pond's edge are just slightly browned by the current drought.

"Oxford is simply lovely in the winter, don't you think, Underminister?"

Weetabix immediately regrets his remark—so commonplace. The Underminister obviously has not come up from London on a holiday. Generously, Underminister Harrods makes no acknowledgment. Instead, he finishes watching the new spot on the palmbook, leans back against the hard stone, and clears his throat. "Once more, Provost Weetabix, wry and insightful. No doubt this is a person of considerable talent and intelligence. We may well be onto something."

"But?"

The Underminister raises an eyebrow. With such an intuitive question, Weetabix feels as though he's redeemed himself. "But has she that *edge*?" the Underminister asks.

"What edge, Underminister, might that be?"

Underminister Harrods considers his words before clearing his throat. "Passion," he says deliberately, "of a variety of sorts. And anger."

"Ah yes," replies Weetabix.

He pads in a series of numbers. Both men watch the display. A medley of brief spots run, none above twenty seconds. One opens with a trombone shot of a line worker in a dingy and noisy factory. Once the frame stabilizes, the shot begins to zoom over the worker's shoulder. What the worker is manufacturing with his or her repetitive movements is impossible to determine. With every pull downward on a long lever, a stamp press bangs down onto a small lump of what looks like clay. When the press lifts again, a tiny figure is left, only to be whisked away on a conveyor belt and replaced with a new lump. Zooming closer and closer to these manufactured forms, at last they are evident: little figures, engaged in pulling downward on a long lever over and over again. Once close enough to one of these figures, the entire frame jolts to the right, as though caught on the conveyor belt. Then the process begins anew. While zooming over the duplicated figure's shoulder, another line of tiny workers is endlessly being stamped out—and on and on.

Another spot opens with a blank screen, the sound of a telly advert playing at extreme volume. An obnoxiously happy voice hawks unidentifiable wares. The shot rises to reveal what looks to be a teenage boy watching a huge flatscreen before him. The young man's head draws our attention. It is shaved, resembling a light bulb. As the shot moves closer on the boy's head, we notice perpendicular lines of a commodities bancode tatooed across the base of his skull, just above the neck.

There are four or five more spots, all punctuated with the same three words appearing at the bottom of the screen just when the frame starts to fade, and remaining visible for a short time after no image is left:

Social Reproduction. Questions?

Underminister Harrods has both his eyebrows raised and is nodding. "I had no idea she was responsible for these," he comments.

Provost Weetabix holds up a finger to indicate there's one more, but of a different ilk. He brings his finger down onto a pad of the palmbook.

A very attractive woman and man are in bed together—naked. There is nothing coy about the shot. Both people are frankly displayed. The lights are low, the music is soft, an inverted bottle of champagne is speared into a silver ice bucket, two half-filled, long-stemmed glasses sit on the night table. However, the woman and the man are relegated to different halves of the bed, sitting isolated, motionless, staring straight ahead, as though ignorant of each another's company. After a moment they both glance down into their respective laps, simultaneously heave a plaintive sigh, then look back up. A moment later and quite suddenly, as if thinking of something altogether brilliant, they look at one another.

"You take care of me?" the woman asks breathlessly of the man.

"And you of me?" the man returns. They both nod eagerly, turn and embace in a long kiss. As the shot begins to fade, we hear gentle moans of gratification. A female voiceover says, "Alterity. Think what love would be without it." The moans start to crest toward the throes of ecstacy. "Think what we can achieve with it."

The Underminister's jaw, quite uncharacteristically, has dropped.

"I take it you've no need to see more?" Weetabix asks.

"Indeed not," Underminister Harrods replies.

"Love Week" had been promoted less than a year ago and proved to be the most unmitigated success in EVe telecast history. "Socialism makes good sex" was its primary slogan—a send up of an earlier, drier, not very successful campaign mounted around the motto "Socialism makes good sense." Weetabix shows the Underminister several more adverts from the advocacy project collectively known as: "What's good in the sack is good in the state." Never before had anyone linked those two meanings of Love—physical and emotional passion with social solidarity. Never before had anyone thought to equate liberty, equality, and alterity with mutual orgasm. Simply quite brilliant. Yet Provost Weetabix cannot resist placing a bit of icing on the cake. "A year prior to 'Love Week,' she came up with the 'Bourgeois Moment'. You recall that cycle, of course. The first really effective counter-greed spots ever cast?"

Indeed, Underminister Harrods knew the series well. Everyone did. "Having a bourgeois moment, are we?" had become embedded in popular culture. His personal favorite had been the one about the man impatiently waiting for his physician's appointment at the Wellness Centre. Who doesn't experience the occasional me/other moment now and again?

Clearing his throat, the Underminister suggests earnestly, "Tell me more about her."

Provost Weetabix smiles. "At age thirty, she is the single best signer we have here at Committee. Probably the best we have *ever* had. Not unlikely the best we ever *will* have. No one grasps signification better."

"She's a purist, then? An idealist?"

Weetabix scoffs. "Hardly. She curses like a submariner, and there's not a sentimental bone in her body. No, she loathes the oversimplification of the classic purist. Mere sloganeering is anathema to her. She will not compromise on the difficult concepts. She believes people can handle anything if it is explained to them adequately and within their own cultural moment. Ah, but that's the real trick of the cultural worker, is it not? Kenning the true cultural moment. How does one tell the difference between inhabiting the culture and manipulating the culture? Not an easy matter, that. She and I have gone many rounds on this topic. I always find myself backing down. She seems quite convinced she can tell the difference."

"Headstrong then, is she?"

"In the extreme."

"Difficult to work with?"

Weetabix only smiles.

"Perhaps all the better," Underminister Harrods says to himself and nods. He wrinkles his brow. "This business about her heritage."

"What of it?" asks Weetabix.

"It's never given you worry?"

"Not in the least. Why should it? In fact, I believe it just might be the ultimate source of her peculiar talent."

The Underminister is unconvinced. "First generation, though," he points out.

"Second, technically," Weetabix corrects him. "Interestingly, she had a great grandfather who was an overseas doctoral student in last century, at this very college, in fact."

"Oh really?"

"Indeed. At some point he likely sat on this very bench, contemplating actual ducks swimming in actual water."

The Underminister arches his eyebrow and clears his throat. "So her grandfather was born here, moved back overseas, then subsequently his family line emigrated back? It that it?"

"His daughter, yes. Her mother. Sometime in the '30s, during the first great flee before the Canadian Wars. I'm sure she settled in Oxford because of the former connection. She was an academic as well. Semiotics, I believe. She eventually married an economics don at Oriel. So you see, not only is cultural work in her blood, she's practically a local girl."

"That is interesting." The Underminister pulls out his handpad and tabs a note to himself.

"Anything else I should know about her before we meet?"

Provost Weetabix hesitates. Regardless of the consequences, he feels it important enough to mention. "She's an abstainant."

"My." Underminister Harrods purses then unpurses his lips several times. "Perhaps that's to the better."

☆ ☆ ☆ ☆ ☆ ☆

Mall sits at her core fixture console trying to resist padding in the directions, in the end, she knows she'll pad in. Every time, her morbid curiosity gets the better of her. The thought of these images signaling an actual reality, of their being more than just flatpics on her signscreen, conjures up titillation and terror. Still, it's precisely that unnameable shiver, this morning like most mornings, that will make her gawk at those lurid pix.

She must make a better show of resistance!

Mall nudges up the volume of audioAmbient. She checks the program playlist. "Solar Bubo" by "Technophobic Monkeyboys." Amusing, but meaning little to her. Ambient is the thinking person's elevator music. It helps her focus without occupying much brain space. She glances upward at her two credos stickied to the wall above her signscreen. The uppermost reads: *Structure determines agency*. The lowermost reads: *Don't mistake the dominant for the universal*. The top one her father had taught her. The bottom one, her mother. It strikes her to wonder if there's some kind of sexual meaning to their positioning. Sod it. She's thinking of those nasty pix.

Mall's been at her console since before first light, working on a large and ongoing advocacy project. Sketches and mockups about the glory of co-ops and workteams, the very bedrock of Marksoc, hang everywhere on the walls, focusing on Worker-owned enterprise paying workers according to their levels of knowledge, skills, and experience. Team members vote on leadership positions all the way to the very top. "Alterity in action." Affirmation spots always strike Mall as inherently preachy, though, and boring. That's why she looks for a borderline of ridicule that turns out to be, in the end, ripe with celebration. Sex works well. She's been toying with the idea of creating a Norwegian orgy as a farcical objective correlative for workteams, giving new meaning to supporting and embracing your fellow worker, coming on time, mastering innovative techniques, not to mention climbing your way to the top of the heap. The cultural allusion to the historical origins of EVe's fundamental workplace model might be a touch too obscure. Mall still must think about that. She likes the basic whimsy of the whole notion. She likes it very much, indeed.

She breakfasts at her signstation. She'll likely lunch there, too. She'll go home well after last light to take a run across Port Meadow and along the Isis towing path, wearing her personal navilamp, an exerciser's contraption, practical for her needs. It's far too hot to run during the day. Occasionally in January or February, with heavy overcast, she can run in late afternoon, but rarely in recent years. She's aware how manic she is about her fitness. Something else she's inherited, evidently, from her mother's family. They were athletes in the old country. Now, she's thoroughly addicted to her regimen and can't imagine herself without it. Later she'll dine at one of the pubs or restaurants along her street. Afterwards she'll study in her flat until sleep overtakes her. Or she'll watch films—Mall loves films—this century's or the last's, native or imported. Rich terrain for signification. In particular she favors films from early century, just prior to realignment. Passion ran high, then, and symbolism deep. Mall watches over and over, for example, the three surviving films made by her somewhat famous grandfather, the foreign one she never knew. They are oddly a mix of popular and intellectual themes. He also pioneered the significant mix of digital and live-shot. Clucus was his name—Yeoman Clucus. Any film enthusiast has heard of him. For some reason, he chose to stay behind, an unlucky choice. Her mother was never able to discover what became of him. Some nights, while sipping her favorite beaujolais-today, Mall will watch all three of his films in a row. She fancies her austere existence matches her forebear's filmic vision. She also believes, given how hard she works, she deserves to have a few quirks, a few vices. Just one pad touch separates her from... *Not quite yet. Must make a little braver show.*

Mall looks out the thick, tinted windows of her rooms. Her console is housed in one of the medieval row cottages. Across a sun-washed quad an imposing ocher edifice, a neoclassical building, sits on slightly higher ground—the result of college founders and benefactors from the eighteenth century. The artificial grass of the quad glistens vibrant green in the heat. Awhile back Mall noticed the Provost walking the quad, escorting a glum, abstracted older man. Looked a ministry type. For a moment the two sauntered as though bound for her door. Happily, they disappeared from her window frame and no one knocked. Provost Weetabix is a benign and astute enough superior, but the less one has to do with administrators, the better. Perhaps her attitude is not in the best spirit of commonweal, but, bugger all, she can bloody well think what she likes. Individuals make up community as much as community sustains individuals. She doesn't allow purists to convince her otherwise.

With that combative thought in mind, Mall presses hard the fatal pad. Her console rides EVeWave to the pre-set address and in microseconds the pix appear on her broad, rectangular signscreen. Mall feels certain Benedictine monks, the original occupants of her digs, would have fallen on their knees, absolutely rapturous, if they could have seen what she sees: fantastically bloated willies engorging fabulously shimmering cunnies. Willies perforating, in fact, all the various female portals, even inventing a few new ones to invade, between pairs of breasts or twixt the arching soles of talented feet. The images pop up in scores of angles and positions, in twosome and threesome, combinations limited only by what camangles can register and the rather pedestrian minds of the smut masters can visualize. They must all be men, and panting wankers at that. Not an original take on the world among them. Sometimes Mall thinks she's missed her true calling. Waveporn just might have been her forte. The pix arrive conveniently sorted into vast selections of thumbnails. No category is neglected; no penchant goes unsated. There's amateur, facial, backdoor, interracial, fetish, sado, farmyard, extreme. There's intergenerational, mature, lesbian, hardcore, erotica, african, voyeur, toys, homo, barely legal, outdoor, bondage, feet, exhibitionist. And one can't forget multicultural, shaved, closeup, blond, cumshot, peeping tom, dressup, midget, lovely bum, jumbo knockers, hairy crack, giant, pipsqueak, asian, public, dirt, animé, peniscam, upskirt, lavatory, quim-lick, plump, french pastry, weird tricks, rope burn, begging, latina, first time, redhead, orgy, onanism, she-male, food, bizarre, petite, rubber suit—and on and on. To her embarrassment, Mall likes to wander this maze of digigraph links. She's driven not by guilty pleasure, but by guilty fascination. Not caring to touch does *not* mean not caring to gape—practically the reverse. She can go days, perhaps as much as a week or more, without giving in to the urge, but always her discipline breaks down. She finds herself padding up the wavesite again, then looking and looking and looking until finally she feels disgust from all the voyeuristic goggling.

Mall's not sure what she's after. It's obviously not sex. From what she's seen, sex in the flesh is all too easy to find. No need for waveporn if mere physical gratification is what one's after. In fact, it strikes her that smut is about the last place to look for sex. Frustration would seem to be all that's available. It's just that amid the ocean of mannequins having it off, she runs across a moment, a freezeframe, every once in awhile, of unguarded human interaction that impresses her as being a facet of the quintessential. A twinkling of collaboration between two people—not posed, not planned, not intended—that denotes actual pleasure. Even love. Mall imagines such pix to be, in fact, mistakes. Probably segue shots slipped by an inattentive bonk editor in his hurry to fill the Wave with indecency. Usually they involve expressions of surprise on the faces of the participants, eyes gingerly shut or a gasp digitally arrested. In the same vein, bodily contortions are unselfconscious, betraying deep sensation, ardently seeking more. These moments make Mall sit and stare and ache—not in her groin, but in her being.

In her own defense, she has formulated some Wave ethics for her vice. She links only on WorldSex, for example, a site that panders solely to relatively healthy displays of erectile functioning. There's no brutality on WorldSex, no truly sick material from the realms of violence or mutilation.

During some early voyages into waveporn she'd stumbled across unimaginably disturbing images, especially on sites patched in from outside EVeWave. The southern hemispheres are rich in famine sites and necrophilia. From across the Atlantic, on the rare occasion any patch at all can be captured, thumbnails include such categories as snuff, gangbang, humiliation, and powertool. A truly appalling inventory that Mall never has opened. She won't play movies, either. They seem particularly numb to her, unimaginative and mechanical, and she never will attempt any of the stimulation simulators. Not only does the gear look tedious, but the very idea of mechstim is, to her, hypocrisy in the extreme. Pure cowardice. When she'd first started exploring smut links, she self-justified it as research. Understanding the popular mind was basic to effective signification. To a degree, that's turned out to be so. But she no longer lies to herself about why she keeps logging back on. She's addicted. Mall knows she's in the grips of a gnawing hunger that only produces more gnawing hunger.

Her message display flashes. It's the Provost calling. For a bit of fun Mall situates Weetabix's message to appear at the tip end of a long, thick, tally whacker. She can't hide her wicked smile when his face comes over live. Weetabix notices her flippancy immediately.

"Goodness me. Not again, Mall. What the deuce do you have to smirk at practically every time I message you?"

"Nothing, sir. Really."

"Get clear of your silliness, for pity's sake. I've got someone here for you to meet. Someone important. Someone, in fact, who's keen to meet you."

"Is it that misery guts I saw you strolling the grounds with earlier?"

"Stop it, Mall. Stop it. I'm telling you, there's nothing amusing in this. You'll soon see." She's making the wank bob up and down, the Provost's face bobbing along with it. "And stop whatever it is you're doing. Good lord, start your growing up, Mall. Get yourself over to the Linbury Building straight away. We're here waiting for you."

"Why on earth meet in the Linbury Building? Important visitors are always taken to the Morley Fletcher Room."

"I'm well aware of that. This comes at our visitor's express request. Something about how they don't monitor outbuildings as closely as they do central complexes."

The information takes some of the air out of Mall's giddiness.

"That does sound serious," she admits.

"You don't know the half of it, Mall. Be on your way."

☆ ☆ ☆ ☆ ☆ ☆

Underminister Harrods quickly estimates the young woman who steps into the reception hall. She's already removed her wide-brimmed hat and darkglasses. She's tall and a deep brunette with a long, comely, slightly oval face, accentuated by hair cut into a short bob. Quite practical, yet not at all unbecoming. Her eyes are dark hazel and quite alert. He expected no less. Her general coloring, in fact, seems Mediterranean, probably old Italia. Dressed, he notices, for some kind of action, wearing a sleeveless white Tshirt and French combat fatigues, sand-colored ones with the various pockets running along each thigh. Her shoes are athletic trainers. Indeed, she looks extraordinarily fit. She's trim at the waist and small at the bosom like a distance runner, her shoulders and arms showing evidence of machine-weight training. The Underminister speculates how this laudable physical conditioning could prove immeasurably useful at some point down the road. Quite a little bonus, really, that surely will do her no harm.

Uncharacteristically, Provost Weetabix makes the briefest of introductions, "Mall, please meet Underminister Harrods."

The two meet eyes and nod to one another. Mall asks the visitor, "Underminister of...?"

"Countermeasures."

He now has Mall's complete attention.

"Let's go into the meeting room and sit, shall we?" Provost Weetabix suggests.

"No," says the Underminister. "If we remain in the reception area, it will appear as though we are merely chatting."

"Does this business really call for that degree of precaution?" Mall asks.

The Provost answers her, hoping to check her incredulous tone of voice. "Mall," he counsels, "just listen."

Underminister Harrods clears his throat. "I'm afraid it has finally begun, Mall."

Gnosis

Underminister Harrods recently has turned sixty-five. That milestone brings him to an unanticipated late-life crisis, one of teleology. He suddenly understands the state of the world will not improve before his time to die. It will instead, in all likelihood, deteriorate—possibly devastatingly. He understands, everything he has worked so diligently toward his entire adult life—pareto optimality, land and technological monotonicity, limited self-ownership, protection of the infirm—will not come to pass in anything like the degree he always reasonably believed they would—in his own lifetime. Instead, if all goes quite well, these things might barely keep their proverbial heads above water. Far more likely, he fears, such ideas will fade entirely. Fade is a kind way of putting it. They will be overwhelmed—eradicated, erased—by far less responsible ways of behaving in this world. They will be swept aside and away, probably forever. That means his long career in Countermeasures will have gone completely for naught. That means he will not leave behind a legacy of a better social construct for his children and grandchildren. That means, quite starkly, he will have failed in his life's endeavor. The personal crisis Underminister Harrods faces, then, is this: can he make do with the final knowledge that at least he has fought the good fight? Can the good fight conceivably be enough?

Unequivocally, Harrods has decided. No.

He sees the same crisis dawning on this young and obviously brilliant woman. How unfair, he thinks, to be brought to this well before your time, while still in the bloom of your professional life. It's far too early to be teleologically confronted, but she must be thoroughly prepared for what she will be asked to face—inasmuch as Harrods knows what she will be facing. He has confessed to her, the great majority of this is guesswork.

For the best part of the last three days Mall has done nothing but read Countermeasures portfolios, all of them marked "Urgency" and "Privy." They've been so important, in fact, they are committed to paper, not consoles or palmbooks, so as to emit no electronic trace. The mental exertion of her forced study has not worn on her half so much as its subject matter. As with all constituents of EVe, Mall knows well the broad strokes: the long-standing stalemate, the fundamental clash of fiscal doctrine and civic formation, the cultural cold war. Schoolbook matters, these, and common knowledge. As a signer with Signification Committee, though, Mall understands better exactly what is at stake. Liberty, equality, alterity. Marksoc itself. She has spent her life immersed in this philosophical struggle. She lives and breathes it every day in her work, but it would seem, in her day-to-day life, she has gone under informed about the magnitude and precariousness of this physical struggle, about the know war. Nothing could have prepared her for the enormity of the information contained in these portfolios. Reading them has made her feel quite the babe in the woods. It all yet seems unreal to her, even though she's seen these matters committed to printed word. For instance, everyone knows of the Labor Day Massacre of 2033, but Mall was quite unaware of the extensive pogroms that followed. Of the AFL-CIO, the UAW, the ACLU, the NAACP, the Greens, the AAUP, the DNC, and so many more. She had been always under the impression the libflee of the '30s had been something of an elective, almost quixotic affair. More of a life choice than a life-or-death decision. Not so, it seems. Nothing remotely like it. She's forced to rethink her mother. What did she have to go through to get out? Why did she never speak of it to Mall? What became of Mall's grandparents left behind? Why hadn't they tried to escape? Or had they—but were prevented? In lyceum, everyone also studies the Canadian Wars of the '40s, a set piece for nasty, ongoing conflict between a superior invading force and an occupied resistance that refused to give over. Yet no one knows that the mini-nuking of Montréal in 2047—what brought the conflict to its sudden close—was *not* the terrorist act of the Parti Québécois or the Front de Libération du Québec, as the official story line runs. In fact, it was a frank display of—how was this said in the portfolios—calculated brutality by Lower North America, one that then served as the catalyst for the bloodless fall of the central isthmus all the way south to the Panamanian Canal. It would seem, reasonably enough, the people of la Ciudad de México had no desire to suffer a similar fate. Thus was the extent of immediate empire established, not via a grand, corporate accord to shield against irrational acts of jealous extremists and unchecked roguestates—but by the crude, hegemonic, and vicious act of blackmail. Archetypal hostile takeover. After these events, of course, came the reorganization, the downsizing, the renaming, the great closing off. Then their never-ending campaign for The New North American Century. The world creeps in its shadow, now more than ever, like living between the feet of an elephant, some global regions managing to fare less horribly than others. What the Countermeasures portfolios have shown Mall most of all, though, is just how dark the shadow has become. Very soon, it strikes her, no one will be able to manage to fare at all.

Mall and the Underminister sit at a rickety table in the gardens of the Trout Inn. The public house sits along the Isis, upriver from Oxford City Centre, two kilometers or so near the village of Wolvercote. They walked along the well-trod towing path to arrive there, across Port Meadow and eventually past the ruins of the Godstow Nunnery. Mall is surprised at the older man's stamina in the heat. She never imagined he'd make it. It's just gone two, and the luncheon crowd has dissipated. Mall and the Underminister make certain to sit under a wide sunbrella at the far end of the garden. New pints of the yeasty local bitter have been set before them. They each take a grateful sip and settle into their chairs. On the walk up, as a routine matter of precaution, they only chatted, commenting on the weather, the scenery, the level of the river. Before either speaks, Underminister Harrods pulls a small, roundish devise out of his jacket pocket, rotates its base to switch it on, and places the object on the table between them. It's tan and resembles a farm egg. Mall raises her eyebrows.

"I thought blockers only alert them more," she says.

"Don't forego all hope quite yet, my dear." He picks his pint up but waits to drink. "We still have tricks up our sleeve." The Underminister notes with interest how his quip causes Mall to frown. "I take it then, you did not find your reading," he pauses to select a word, "enjoyable."

Mall frowns harder. "Edifying, yes," she replies, "but hardly enjoyable."

The Underminister nods sympathetically. "Given your heritage, I was sure that would be the case. I am sorry."

"It's not your fault, Underminister."

"Indeed not," he answers.

Mall glances up at the thatched roof on The Trout, at its moss-covered stone walls, its small square windows with glass too thick to see through. So much care to preserve the outdated. The effort comforts her. That's why she chose this place. She tastes her bitter again. She prefers lager, but so much is ersatz anymore. At least with bitter one can taste the outdated, knowing on your tongue that some worthwhile traditions can be maintained. Not that she, by any means, is a rabid traditionist. She admires craft, is all. On the other side of the stone retaining wall next to them, the Isis flows slowly by. Its waters roil only a bit from under the Godstow Bridge and the Kings Weir, but enough to create a natural background noise to help mask their conversation–the reason Underminister Harrods agreed to walk all the way here. It's their first of many compromises. He had insisted on a noisy, public venue. She had wanted to get out into the countryside.

"So where do we go from here?" Mall asks, appreciating the setting.

Underminister Harrods clears his throat.

"I thought it might be best if you pose questions to me. Anything that comes to mind based on your reading. Anything you feel you must know before you get yourself any deeper into this muddle." He pauses to sip his glass of bitter, then re-emphasizes, "Anything at all."

Mall finds his statements curious since, at this point, she hasn't a bloody clue as to what "this muddle" refers. At the same time, she understands his must be an extraordinary offer. An Underminister, of Countermeasures no less, inviting her, a mid level signer at Sr/Sd, to ask whatever it is she would like to know about the current geopolitical situation. That's not an occasion one runs into every day. In an odd way, Mall wishes she'd been offered this opportunity *before* reading all those dossiers. In her ignorance, she would have had an assortment of questions to fire confidently at him. Now she sees that most of them would have been immaterial. In her newly acquired state of knowledge, she is having difficulty knowing what it is she still needs to know—what it is she doesn't understand. She does, though, take a stab at it. "Why hide their tactics from us?"

Underminister Harrods endorses her question, "I think it is a mistake. The policy was adopted some time ago. I'm not sure why. Perhaps it was believed, if the reality of things were made known, we would, in effect, be doing their nasty work for them. Since the turn of the century they've operated on the intimidation of brute force. I suppose it might have been reasoned, if we weren't aware of that brute force, we would have no cause to be intimidated by it."

"Dodgy reasoning, that."

"Probably so, if that was the reasoning behind the decision."

"You don't know?"

"I am an *under*minister," Harrods stresses.

Mall is unsure whether to believe in his innocence or not. "Based on the papers you gave me," she tries again, "I imagine Caucus has decided it cannot hide the facts any longer. Is that why you're here? To ask me to devise an advocacy project to inform the constituency?"

The Underminister delights in Mall's deduction, but he shakes his head. "Not at all, I'm afraid. You see, Caucus has decided no such thing. What I'm here to ask of you is considerably more involved than that."

Mall dislikes his answer. It boxes her back into a blind corner. "Look," she says, and not in the tone of a request, "why don't we stop playing our charade? Why don't you just tell me what we're on about, here?"

Underminister Harrods does not nod or clear his throat or hesitate in any way. "No," he replies, "I don't believe I will. I want to hear more of your questions."

Mall is not prepared for such a blunt rebuff. The Underminister smiles cordially at her. Clearly, he is no Provost Weetabix she can lead about. Whatever this man wants to tell her will be on his schedule, not hers. Right enough. Best just to play this along. If she can't make him budge, perhaps she can make him twitch.

"Very well, then," she says, gesturing toward a sky hidden by the sunbrella. "So the bastards control the lot of it, eh? And we haven't a prayer?"

"No, not a prayer, " Underminister Harrods answers her candidly. He knows exactly what she suggests. "We're bested."

Mall did not expect to be answered, let alone so plainly. "The skies are theirs?" she asks, disbelieving. "We're buggered?"

"Ah, it's more than just the skies. It extends to outer space as well. Low orbit, high orbit. To the moon and back. To infinity and beyond, if you will. We've had no stake up there for some decades."

"How is that possible?"

The Underminister shrugs.

"The terrible potency of technological advantage."

"Then we *are* done for."

"Not entirely. As I said, we still have some tricks left to us. If they control outer space, we dominate inner space."

"Inner space?"

"Underseas, for one. Old Soviet submarine technology was not inconsiderable. We've advanced it immeasurably. And brute force brings with it a certain hamfistedness. They haven't often the need to be careful. We hold the distinct edge on them in stealth technology."

"So we can skulk about better than they underseas? Is that supposed to comfort me?"

"As the bard says, comfort's in heaven, and we are on the earth. Your finding comfort was not the aim of your reading, Mall. Tactical knowledge of our current moment is."

"But their Star Wars system," she protests out of frustration.

"Quite right," the Underminister acknowledges. "The ultimate foundation of their power. Not impenetrable until the '60s. Even now, our deep-sloops can lie up close to their coastal shelves undetected. A launch from there renders their anti-missile system as conventional as our own. They simply haven't the time, and they have been hit in living memory, Mall. Make no mistake. They may be bullies, but they've had their nose bloodied on more than one occasion. I expect a good nuking causes them a spot of internal turmoil just as much as anyone else."

The North Koreans managed to strike Honolulu in 2053. The Chinese reached Los Angeles in 2057. Both were exceptionally messy bombs. There had been rumors of these events in EVe, of course, but they were dismissed as wild speculation. No one heard of the District of Columbia being razed in 2061—not even rumors of the event, which was likely a satchel nuke. Not enormous, but sufficient to the purpose. It had the effect, however, of stimulating the completion of their space-based missile defenses once and for all—their global array of satellites and lasers and mirrors. They moved their capital city inland, as well. No one knows where.

"I don't see why they don't just obliterate us and have done with it. From what I gather in your narratives, they certainly have the means and, for whatever reason, the perverse motivation. What's been keeping them off?"

"That *is* the really interesting question, is it not?"

This underminister is verging on annoying Mall.

The facts—insofar as she is willing to accept that concept, even when committed to paper—of the century's awful history crowd Mall's head like the fog of derivative calculus. Only a few circumstances stand out to her as being more horrendous than others. Unmistakably, the two political entities have had no formal, and scant informal, contact for some forty years. The crucial rift came about over what the portfolios termed "The Final Solution," but what apparently became known popularly as "The Glass Sea." Mall vaguely remembered hearing the expression as a child. Lower North America—termed LNA in the portfolios—had pressured the trans-Atlantic treaty organization of the day to reposition force concentration to the southeast, to the Balkans. Evidently, stability in lower Europe meant increased strategic control of a region even further to the south, the area then known as The Middle East. From all Mall read, that territory was the raison d'être of the early century. The ne plus ultra. What all rows were for. Pétrole brut. Decades-old incursion-democratization programs by the Lower North Americans stubbornly had failed to take hold in old Iraq, old Afghanistan, old Syria, old Jordan. LNA was looking to strengthen further its military hand. However, as is so often the case with chronicles, what Mall read was an intelligible story of how human action produces results other than intended. With the LNA military withdrawing from the old UK and the old FRG, the fledgling European Union began to develop a defense identity of its own, one corresponding to the civil and financial goals of its new commonwealth. Stretching back into the previous century, Europeans and Lower North Americans had not seen eye-to-eye on any number of affairs, and the Balkans policy placed a fatal strain on the last Atlantic alliance. European leaders realized tolerating LNA ignorance-cum-arrogance-cum-avarice, in order to benefit from their martial protection, was a wrongheaded strategy destined for catastrophe. The EU was being "protected" straight toward assimilation. The final straw came in December 2039. The former Iran at last proved too resistant to invasion. It was willing to use its battlefield nuclear weapons. That devastating blow against LNA forces crossing the border in order to, as the catch-all phrase had become, "liberate an oppressed people from a brutal dictatorship" ignited new resistance throughout the region. Within a week, the long-corrupt Saudi monarchy collapsed. Reinvigorated insurgencies popped up in every former sovereign state. Middle East stability, for years a cruel illusion, was inexorably shattered.

The consequences were horrific.

"If Star Wars became their shield," Underminister Harrods explains events, "then the tactical nuclear missile became their sword, their political weapon of choice."

"How do you mean?"

"They applied it liberally in the region."

"You must be joking."

"I'm afraid not. They began with Tehran, naturally enough, then went on to Hamadan and Tabriz, for good measure. Then apparently someone in their hierarchy snapped. Things snowballed, to use a much outdated phrase, and the situation got completely out of hand. Photos we've managed to smuggle out of the Arabian Peninsula recently show vast tracks of land resembling fused sand. Miles and miles of it."

"The Glass Sea," Mall murmurs the strange name, "was their final solution."

"Indeed. It seems they were careful to calculate throw-weights well under that necessary to bring about nuclear winter." The Underminister shakes his head and laughs. "I've heard it rumored, though, some among their directors argued a mild nuclear winter might be just the thing to offset greenhouse gases." The Underminister's smile quickly fades. "Primarily they employed so-called 'bunker busters' designed to detonate below ground after a brief penetration. These produce lethal but quite localized radiation. As I said, their weapon of choice."

"Good God."

"Not only were the major population centers hit, but many of the giant fields as well: Tuba, Saddam, Naft Safid, Aboozar, Jaladi, Abu Sa'fah, Ratqa, Bul Hanine, Saih Rawl, and some dozens more. It was as if to say, simply, 'Get out. Further human presence is not required. We have no use for any of you.'"

"And I take it they have been there ever since?"

The Underminister nods, finishes his bitter, motions to the waitress kindly to bring them two more, then remarks, "Harvesting."

Mall shudders in the heat. When the new pints arrive, she absentmindedly samples hers. "So we broke away from the bastards over this," she decides. "The old EU, I mean."

"We did more than just break with them, Mall. We fought a brief war with them."

Mall widens her hazel eyes, looking the color of moss at the moment. "Impossible," she says.

"A series of tentative, but quite violent skirmishes—all in the Balkans. Our immediate ground forces matched up well with theirs. We had no supply line difficulties to speak of."

"You're telling me they withdrew?"

"Yes."

"But why? Why not use their tactical nukes on us?"

"At that point they couldn't really, could they? They had no failsafe anti-missile umbrella in place. We had any number of creditable military threats, most notably an abundance of nuclear warheads of our own—and the intercontinental ballistics to deliver them. Nor had they consolidated hegemony in their own hemisphere. No, they simply weren't prepared for us to spurn their authority. I think it took them unawares. We had been taken very much for granted."

What followed was radical realignment. The Lower North Americans accomplished their corporatization with the Canadian Wars. The EU slowly negotiated itself into the latinatized EV, a hopeful nod to the puissance of ancient republic and empire. Their bloc became Europe and the western third of Russia, from the Arctic and Atlantic oceans to the Mediterranean and Black seas. The former Turkey remained under LNA control, and the Black Sea and the Caspian Sea are still disputed waters due to the scurry for natural gas in former Turkmenistan and Uzbekistan. Africa has become a forsaken continent. East of the Urals, Siberia now seems a land more wild than usual. What the rest of the globe is up to has become very difficult to tell. With the new corpstate of TexArc aggressively in the ascendancy, EVe has been forced to concentrate on self-sufficiency–on raw survival–in this new world order.

"In other words," Mall observes accusingly, "we've buried our heads in the sand."

Underminister Harrods promptly corrects her, "More like we had sand heaped atop our heads, Mall." He keeps his voice even, "You must learn to keep the TexArcan modus operandi forever in view. They make certain *never* to operate on a level playing field, and yet they *always* feign they do. We can only surmise they are playing to an internal audience, and hence have domestic considerations of at least some delicacy to consider. Potentially that presents a vulnerability for us to explore. They certainly do not care a jot for public relations outside of their corpborders." The Underminister runs a thoughtful hand back through his limp gray hair. His eyes are sad like a hound's. His face kind with a broad forehead and a narrow jaw. "In fact," he brings himself to say, "it is their peculiar manipulation of reality and appearance that has prompted my visit to Oxford to confer first with Weetabix, and now with you."

Mall smiles at the Underminister. "So at last you are ready to tell me something concrete?"

"Perhaps." The Underminister sips his bitter and returns her smile. *This Mall creature is not so difficult to deal with as the Provost made out.* "But first there must be one or two questions you yet need to ask."

Mall accepts the small test. What would be vital to know at the moment? She takes some deeper breaths of the countryside air. They're fresh with the slight spray put up by the weir, as after a rare rainstorm.

"After they obliterated Arabia, but before they had their Star Wars entirely in place," she begins, "must have been a touch-and-go time for them. How exactly did they manage to consolidate their global monopoly?"

"With a blend of military terror added to their well-established methods of economic coercion and cultural invasion. They'd had no true competitor state since the old Soviet Union fell, and they worked hard to deter the rise of a new superpower to take its place. With Islam 'stabilized,' as they smugly liked to say, their immediate attention turned to the far east."

"Didn't they have to keep an eye on us?"

"They did. Your comment about having our head in the sand, though, is not altogether inappropriate. They were scrupulous about making their actions appear, at least to the less mindful, justified, no matter in what twisted or extenuated way. That appears to be how they kept most domestic protest at bay. World opinion, of course, was not fooled, but, unhappily, was content with only grousing about matters. Europeans, for instance, seemed more enamored with arguing about the predicament than dealing with it." The Underminister sighs. "That could well have been our tragic flaw. Practically speaking, though, we had little recourse. Even before the United Nations building was bombed to the ground to start off the Labor Day Massacre, that world body was impotent, and none replaced it. Although we possessed the world's most capable military force, our assets were defensive and not nearly extensive enough to challenge them on a global scale. It was all we could do to establish a viable defense posture. Along with establishing our new union was all Europe could manage."

"And so what became of Asia?"

"The foremost LNA concern became with what they term 'rogue states,' meaning anyone having nuclear missile capacity. On the Korean peninsula TexArc staged an enemy incursion of the demilitarized zone as an excuse to invade the North. When the North Koreans wouldn't give way to conventional force, two or three mini-nukes were used to smash their resolve. It's in that exchange Hawaii was hit."

"And China was dealt with in the same way?" More and more of Mall's reading is beginning to make sense to her.

"Fundamentally. That was a bigger and more problematic operation. They concocted a Chinese air attack on Taiwan in order to live up to a mutual defense treaty in place at the time. After a few navel skirmishes to make it seem as though they were exercising restraint, they had only to flatten a city or two on the mainland. They spared Hong Kong, of course, and Beijing, portraying their selection of targets as benevolent, seeing how China had hit the LNA west coast. TexArc knew it was impossible to subdue China. They wanted merely to keep it in check, to blunt its growth into a great power for another fifty years or so. Another trait you should keep in mind about them is their basic short-sightedness. If nothing else, they are creatures of immediate gratification."

"And," Mall adds reflectively, chin resting in her hand, "they have perfected the basic strategy of appearing the victim in order to mask their own unilateral aggression. Rather elemental signification, but it can be quite effective with the right type of narratee."

Underminister Harrods' involuntarily dour features brighten. At last he is sure this young woman is right for the job. "They've set for themselves the task of managing a variety of small theater wars throughout the globe and confronting any number of distinct adversaries pursuing separate goals. Playing the role of good sheriff seems to be what they've settled on, to be sure."

"Then they are quite the shits, aren't they, sir?"

The Underminister, not used to people cursing in his presence, searches for words, "Um...quite."

Mall enjoys his evident discomfort. "I suppose my last question, then, Underminister, other than what brings us here, is how do things stand at the moment? How well or poorly are we doing?"

Harrods looks out over the river before speaking. "Surprisingly well, until just recently. Considering what we've been facing for the past half century, EVe has been holding her own. Based on the old Swiss model, we've turned ourselves into a bunker one would do well to think twice before assaulting. We certainly cannot hope to challenge them militarily around the globe, but our borders and contiguous seas are amply guarded by conventional force." He turns back to table hoping to meet her eyes, to offer some degree of reassurance, but her eyes are averted, so he continues to elaborate. "We maintain a dependable ground-based nuclear defense shield of anti-missiles and lasers. Of course, that is only capable of intercepting incoming missiles at late-stage flight and we could be overwhelmed. That's why we let them see we keep our intercontinental ballistic missiles at the ready. A barrage from us would put a strain even on their Star Wars system. And we permit them to play a certain amount of cat-and-mouse with some of our submarines, just to keep them wary. That's likely what keeps them off us, the obscurity of our submariner fleet. They are aware of its presence but not of the extent of its capabilities."

Mall has been staring at the table while listening. She looks up into the Underminister's pale blue, slightly moist eyes.

"So effectively we are hemmed in. We're in a bit of a tight spot. Is that what you're telling me?"

He clears his throat. He's heard the irony and the gravity of her tone. In the main, it seems to be her habit to speak in that combination. "Yes. If you want to look at it in that way."

"So why don't they just leave us alone? Why even take the risk of attacking us? Why bother? It makes little sense."

"There are only theories at this point."

"Just tell me yours."

Underminister Harrods approves of Mall's desire for relevant detail. He takes a moment to decide how to put things.

"I believe they fear two of our possessions. One is Marksoc. Against great odds, we have managed to put in place a social order based on the old Scandinavian model that embraces self-ownership while at the same time preventing the primitivism of exploitation. That has never been accomplished before. It flies in the face of everything they are about. We've flattened managerial hierarchies, promoted trade unionism, narrowed income disparity, made omnipresent both health services and education, and carefully stewarded our land and limited natural resources." He looks at Mall. "But I have no need to tell you any of this."

Indeed not. "This" is what Mall advocates as a signer.

"And our second possession?"

"KME."

Mall has seen the acronym used in the portfolios, but not the definition. "And that is?" she asks for clarification's sake.

"Sorry," apologizes the Underminister. "It's a term we throw about at the ministry. It stands for Knowledge of Mass Enablement."

Mall's expression indicates she is waiting for more information.

"The controversial technologies, don't you know. Genetic engineering and nano-technology, that sort of thing." Harrods watches the look of disapproval gradually come over her face. "Look, whatever you may think of it, such technologies have enabled us to survive. Dry nanotech, for example, has rendered solar cells to be truly viable alternatives to our nearly depleted access to oil and gas reserves. And genetically hearty crops and livestock have staved off hunger. I know some think we're playing at God with such techniques—"

"Bugger all God," Mall interrupts. "You're playing at potential human self-annihilation."

"Do you suppose for a moment they are not?" demands the Underminister.

Mall tightens her mouth and looks across the Isis.

"Look here, Mall. The simple fact is, God seems to have taken His bucket full of fossil fuels and poured it over the North Pole. They've dripped down primarily over the Northern Hemisphere, and we've been fortunate to have the technology to extract a goodly portion of it from the polar region and our subarctic territories of old Russia, but as TexArc's little stunt of the Glass Sea should make most plain, oil is an immanently finite possession. Whatever the risks of KME—"

"Of KMD," Mall corrects. Knowledge of Mass Destruction is a common term used among constituents. The debate in EVe is a factious one.

"Of KM*E*," the Underminister insists, "it is unavoidable, and potentially the single greatest threat to them. Enablement and autonomy destroy their economic stranglehold. I would have thought you, above all people, would appreciate that. I believe they will stop at nothing to put an end to it."

He's right, of course, she admits to herself, but Mall's life work has been in promoting Marksoc, in making socialistic political economy sexy. She never has been able to bring herself to trust these new and mind-boggling technologies, no matter their utility or inevitability. *Bugger all.*

As a peace offering, the Underminister suggests they order lunch, his treat on ministry budget. He well knows this means Mall can then order *God's Own*, the line of wholly natural foods untouched by genetics which is otherwise, he surmises correctly, too dear for her to purchase. Grudgingly, Mall accepts his offer of lunch and his persistent suggestion she get her preferred brand. When queried by the waitperson, she asks for a sprout-and-bean salad with a demi-loaf of rustic bread and a thimble of creamery butter. The Underminister orders his accustomed ploughman's lunch, of the synthetic variety. While eating, he discovers a rather plump slug among its lettuce. He wraps the beast up in a leaf and pops it into his mouth. He jokes to Mall that this really is *God's Own* and genuine protein is deucedly hard to come by. She cannot help being amused by the sight of an underminister consuming a slug roll-up. As a sign, it epitomizes EVe's current state.

"Look here, Mall," Underminister Harrods returns to their serious conversation, "you asked me to speculate on the source of our new troubles, and I have. Some in Countermeasures think it's just the march of power. Others hypothesize they have had bigger fish to fry, more pressing geopolitical problems to address, and now it has come around at last simply to being our turn. I cannot disagree with those viewpoints. I believe they hold large elements of the truth. But this time I also sense something novel in the machinations of TexArc. There's an anxiety to them, an edge of fear, hitherto absent from the way they conduct their business. People at the ministry tell me I'm imagining things, that I'm projecting. Perhaps they're right. If I am right, however, I believe that renders our current defense strategy moot."

"And that strategy is?"

"To be a poison pill to them. To represent a Pyrrhic victory. Traditionally, we have always proceeded on the assumption, if our conquest will come at too high a price for them, we will be left alone. It's old cold war standoff mentality."

"And what is it that has you feeling differently now, sir? I don't mean to be rude in reminding you, but you've yet to tell me anything at all about what you've just called our 'new' troubles. What is it, exactly, that's happened?"

"Ah." Harrods lifts his unruly eyebrows. "Quite right you are."

In succinct terms, the Underminister, after clearing his throat, describes to Mall the incidents of recent days, TexArc's self-inflicted acts of terrorism on their Glass Sea and to their Space Elevator. Mall has heard the tattle of there being an elevator to outer space but always found it impossible to believe. Discovering such a thing exists jolts her. At greater length, the Underminister characterizes the clutter the ministry teeks have managed to slice from the ArcNet stream subsequent to these two violent propaganda stunts taking place. In all of them, official TexArc blame for the attacks falls squarely upon EVe, alone. On a small vidaud device, Harrods shows her some samples. The programming seems to be called Vieworld—or rather, *VIEWORLD!* The shouting, the bombast, the browbeating are appalling. These slices chill Mall. They also raise her professional hackles. What she is witnessing is signification at its most crude and manipulative.

"I believe what this all means," Harrods sums up, "is that TexArc will not be going away this time, as they did so many years ago when we fought them over the initial Glass Sea incident." He shakes his head sadly. "I believe they are convinced, this time around, they cannot afford to leave us alone. We are likely to represent to them all that is left that could plausibly put an end to their way of life. We might actually offer the world a glimmer of its only real alternative to Pax TexArcana. They want no one even to have a wisp of such a possibility."

"So it is as bad as all that? We've *no* potential allies?"

"That's difficult to say. With outside communication being so spotty, who really knows what the state of the rest of the world is nowadays? Japan seems an unlikely rescuer of the planet, and goodness knows enough of their island is underseas to give them ample internal headaches to contend with. From what we can tell, China, for all its vast resources, is as unsettled as ever. Australia has not fared too badly as a sparsely populated continent, but it seems content, as always, to remain essentially apart and down under." Harrods pauses to finish off his pint. "As for elsewhere around the globe, we get little more out of the southern American hemisphere than we do out of Africa. God knows what is transpiring on those ruined continents. Drought, famine, epidemic, and heat oppress us all. Those regions doubtlessly are feeling the brunt of it." Realizing the embarrassing incongruity, the Underminister rather guiltily lays down his fork. "No, my guess is, we are the last region stable enough and technologically advanced enough to take them on. And they well know it."

"Yet, as you've just made abundantly clear, we are effectively cornered."

"Um, quite right."

"So what different do you propose to do? What defense strategy can we possibly mount that is *not* moot right now?"

"None. That's been just my point."

"Then what, pray tell, dear Underminister, is your solution?"

"A strategy for offense."

Mall blinks as she inhales. "Good lord."

"Precisely."

Praxis

Sinalco had arrived in Oxford the previous day via the covered train up from Paddington. Toting the oversized rucksack of a student on an EVRail pass, she'd walked in from the station, down Park End Street and New Road, which turns into Queen Street before arriving at Carfax. At that busy roundabout she'd turned north up Cornmarket Street, making her way slowly along the pedestrian thoroughfare, looking into shop windows, ducking into the Golden Cross courtyard to buy a Cornish pasty at the small bakery for tourists, negotiating the crowds. As she strolled, Sinalco was careful always to stay underneath her wide sunbrella, one of the colorful new *Both Holes* model students tend to carry. Stenciled on its top, aimed skyward, is a large and bright yellow hand on a vivid red background giving the reversed Victory sign, a little message for the survey satellites. No one assumed anything but that she was trying to protect her curiously fresh, strawberry-fair complexion. Every passerby was struck, however, by her statuesque form. At the top of Magdalene Street, before the road widens into St. Giles, Sinalco tarried for a time at the Martyr's Memorial, reading all the plaques. Those poor souls had been burned not far from the spot, just around the corner on Broad Street. Scorch marks can still be seen on one of the buildings. Instead of going to inspect that nick of history, she turned west down Beaumont Street, where before getting very far she nipped into the Randolph Hotel–not the normal lodgings for rucksacked students on EVRail passes. Sinalco did not re-emerge from the building until very early the next morning, quickly turning left when her hikeboots reached the pavement. At the west end of Beaumont Street, where it terminates into Walton Street running north-south, stands the neoclassical front edifice and gate of Worcester College.

☆ ☆ ☆ ☆ ☆ ☆

The knock on her door at 6H startles Mall. Normally no one is at the college for hours yet, and she's more accustomed to collaborators simply barging in. *Who bothers to knock?* She sets down her mug of green tea and goes to answer. Upon swinging open her door she finds, barely framed by her doorway, an alarmingly immense young woman holding, in the predawn gloom, an enormous sunbrella over her head. The top of the sunbrella is above the doorframe and out of Mall's sight, but she hears its pinions scuffing up against the side of her row cottage, a signal she reads as this person's being keen to avert skyID.

"I am for you," the oddity speaks before Mall has time to conjure a greeting. The accent is Français, or perhaps Deutsche.

"I beg your pardon?"

The young woman pushes through the doorway and folds down her sunbrella in one swift motion. Mall can do nothing but step aside.

"This symbol," the woman points enthusiastically to the engraved Sr/Sd on Mall's door, "is everywhere here. It means what?"

Clenching the doorknob as though it is her last link to reality, Mall surprises herself by answering politely. "Signification," she says. "That's what we do here."

"This big S little r and then this big S and little d. Each means what?"

Mall explains a little less courteously this time as she points to each in turn. "Signifier. Signified."

"Ah, oui. A way to say the one thing and mean another. Like the shitbull. Nicht so?"

"'Bullshit,'" Mall corrects her. "The word is 'bullshit,'" she says again. "And no," Mall answers the woman's question, "not so. It's how one says anything—with signs."

The woman's accent seems a little contrived. Her eyes are too perfectly cornflower blue. She's significantly taller than Mall, who's tall, and considerably more fleshed out. Not chubby, just...larger overall, as though she were built to a slightly different scale. One up from humans. Her hair is a hardly-believable, massive tangle of strawberry blond curls haloing her head and face, making her look even taller. *With that mane,* Mall wagers, *the woman nears two meters.*

"So you do *not* approve of the bullshit?" the woman asks aggressively, as though throwing down a gauntlet. She also pinches her lips into a tiny rosebud and arches both eyebrows, making a quintessential French grimace. The expression places her prominent nose just on the proud side. She's faintly crossed the line of believability, but it also feels to Mall as though the giant woman intends it either as a joke or a test.

"Speaking of shitbull," Mall decides to have done with games, "who the bloody fucking hell are you?"

The woman's blast of laughter jars Mall.

"Nom de Dieu!" the woman cries out. "We will be so *fun*!" A heavy and familiar palm gets placed on Mall's shoulder, and she stiffens under its odd density. She does not like to be touched. Ignoring Mall's evident discomfort, the woman asserts eagerly, "I am Sinalco. I am from Harrods." She appears to presume Mall will understand perfectly.

Mall does not. "From Harrods?"

"Yes, yes," the woman nods. "I am your—how do you say?—*teek*." She pronounces the word quickly and with a rising pitch. She also wears a silly look of joy on her face, as though she were just now able to remember the name of some little furry animal.

"My tech-geek?" says Mall. "I don't understand."

"Si, si. Your *teek*," she asserts again. "For *you*. From Harrods. Yes." The woman continues to nod emphatically.

"I've no need of a teek. I've got my own." Mall simultaneously glances askance at the hand infringing on her personal space and commits the cardinal sin when speaking to off-islanders: she begins to talk louder and slower. "We've plenty of first-rate teeks here already, you see. No need for any more."

The woman deliberately sets her other meaty palm on Mall's other shoulder. Grinning knowingly, she pulls their faces closer together. She inspects Mall's eyes just long enough for the shorter woman to feel really uncomfortable. "I am better," she then says, speaking louder and slower. "I am from Harrods."

Mall enjoys being mocked even less than being touched. She clasps this weird person's thick wrists and removes from her shoulders the curious weight of those hands, letting them drop. "You seem to be loads of fun yourself," she tells the woman, the mannerly tone serving as warning, "but honestly, I've got my own teek. His name is Branston. He's utterly splendid."

"I am better," Sinalco informs her soberly.

"But—"

"I am for you. We can talk about this no more here." She glances upward, then looks back and giggles. "He is cute?"

Her question confuses Mall even more than her abrupt shifts in manner. "Who is cute? What on earth do you mean?"

"This Branston teek of yours. He is cute, I bet."

☆ ☆ ☆ ☆ ☆ ☆

Pairing Signification's best signer with Countermeasure's best teek had been Underminister Harrods proposed plan from the start. Their job would be to slice into ArcNet, deep into it, to see what could be discovered. Little solid information existed any longer about the workings of TexArcan society. As the millions around the world perished beginning mid-century, the lone superpower paradoxically projected its might while retreating behind its firewalls, geographically and virtually. For two generations, Countermeasures has been able to cull only bits and pieces of cultural detail off the ArcNet stream, drawing from the widely disseminated bands in amounts not enough to create an overall profile. The clutter was always dense and chaotic, a frenzied cacophony of image and voice. Never text, it had been noted often. TexArc seemed never to put anything in writing. Harrods' insight was that perhaps the crackerjack signer could make something of it all, could wade into the snarl of utterance and decipher it better than anyone from Countermeasures has been able to do. That assumed, of course, the crackerjack teek can embed the signer further in than anyone hitherto has been able to—no, willing to go. As a cyberenvirons, ArcNet is notoriously precarious. There, no one knows freak from foe.

The Underminister's project, submitted to the Headminister of Countermeasures, was founded on two clear-headed bits of reasoning. First Premise: despite its worldwide command, TexArc still must watch zealously over an unruly globe. At a given moment, any number of parochial conflicts promise to flare into challenges of its authority within a region. Such widespread crisis management compels scattered if not isolated and myopic thinking. Therefore, TexArc is constantly in a state of preoccupation and, as a result, likely to be vulnerable in ways EVe cannot imagine at the moment. Harrods feels it worthwhile to probe that core inattention for possible advantage. Perhaps EVe can locate a debility worth exploiting. Most analysts grant him these conjectures. Second Premise—this being the more controversial: TexArc experiences internal constraints of some kind. It must. Why else mount the mass inculcation efforts it does over its media? Time and again, Countermeasures witnessed the pattern in TexArc of fashioning a foreign enemy as a prelude to striking that enemy. ArcNet stream suddenly clogs with accusations and distortions of the wildest nature. This disinformational surge, believes Harrods, can only signal that discipline is crucial to their internal operation–crucial in a way, ironically, that ideology has become obsolete to their external behavior. Extramurally, mini-nukes do their talking. TexArc hasn't troubled to win hearts and minds for decades. Intramurally, it would seem to be a different story. Someone within their corpstate still wants persuading. Who? How many? And, most pressingly, why? If his surmise turns out to be correct, Harrods hopes that a signer not only can dismantle the demonization campaign now in motion against EVe, but plausibly reverse it, even turn the newspeak tide against the TexArcan directors. Moreover, if strategists are being honest with themselves, such a counter-advocacy project might represent EVe's best and only legitimate hope. History records that once TexArc identifies a state as "rogue" or an individual as "terrorist," both are destined for its dustbin. Military resistance is altogether futile. Hence, the Underminister fervently recommends what he terms "cultural insurgency" against them. Carry the fight to TexArc by waging a guerrilla culture war. Slice a signer far into ArcNet and give that society a taste of alterity and KME. See what might develop. In fact, Harrods has titled his very program *Gambit Culture War*.

A few in the ministry think the scheme inspired. Most think it rubbish. Notwithstanding, the Headminister carried it along with some two dozen more threat responses—all other plans being strictly military in nature—to Caucus, which, after lengthy debate, selected Harrods' as one of ten strategies to be put into action. Among the members of Caucus, several considered Harrods' deductions to be insights of genius, holding out great hopes for the project. The majority of communicants, though, upon first hearing of the strategy, waved their hands dismissively and made droll faces. What lunacy now? Signification is an accepted instrument within EVe, yes, but outside it there are just too many uncertainties. Why entrust the survival of the commonwealth to what amounts to little more than serene linguistic nihilism? In the end, though, "Harrods' Folly," as the proposal became renamed by detractors, was approved as an afterthought, as a wild hair. It wasn't expensive and what could it hurt?

Harrods had counted on no more.

☆ ☆ ☆ ☆ ☆ ☆

Mall and Sinalco, as directed by the Underminister, work exclusively out of public places: pubs, tearooms, restaurants, clubs and the like. Someplace different every couple of hours, just as long as the place is crowded and very noisy, and as long as it's located in the central part of the city.

From the beginning, Harrods cautioned them, "You don't want to be caught out in isolation."

Mall's not sure what to make of such a warning. The pair wander Oxford day and night, seeking public shielding. The *Yesbut* on George Street, the *Wheatsheaf* on High. *Bar Love* on King Edward, the *Coffee Republic* on New Inn Hall Street, *Po-Na-Na Souk Bar* on Magdalene Street, the *Eagle and Child* and then the *Lamb and Flag* opposite to it on St. Giles. Then there's *Freud* on Walton Street, the *Quod Bar & Grill* back on High, *The Kings Arms* on the corner of Holywell Street and Parks Road, *Purple Turtle Union Bar* in Frewin Court, *Jongleurs* on Hythe Bridge, and, Mall's favorite spot, the *Turf*, well hidden on Bath Place. Sinalco marvels ceaselessly at the architecture. In one square old mile there exists examples of buildings from every century stretching back to the eleventh. The grand colleges particularly impress her with their creamy facades and scores of dreamy spires, all looking as though they were poured with wet sand. Whenever possible, Sinalco asks that they prowl through a college's interior puzzleworks of passageways and quads.

"You know," she comments one day as they emerge from the gate under Tom Tower, "these colleges so dignified and majestic bought up much property left vacant by the Black Death." She tisks her tongue in the

French way. "Profiteur, ça."

On the busy streets, Sinalco saunters always beneath her broad sunbrella, even after dark, cutting a broad swath through her fellow pedestrians. The custom piques Mall no end. At her insistence, they soon stop frequenting pubs. Blokes chat them up endlessly, especially Sinalco, who is like a cod-and-bollocks magnet. It's bloody well useless for them to try to work in pubs or clubs. Sinalco considers all the attention "jolly good fun," but, as Mall soon discovers, she's a bleeding snogall. This continental trollop will yank anyone. The morning after their first meeting, Mall walked in on Sinalco astride Branston, who was sitting at his core fixture console looking, poor man, very much like his spine were about to snap. The fact is, Mall *had* thought Branston cute, and even though she had no intention of acting on things, this gigantic tart had no right waltzing in and straight away plucking him. *Sodding yankers, the both of them*. For her part, Sinalco has no qualms at all about anything. She is the most abandoned person Mall has ever met.

"Mall, my pet," Sinalco has taken to addressing her in such terms of endearment, "you really must bite off more than you can chew. Believe me. You must."

On more than one occasion, Mall catches Sinalco insinuating the curve of a colossal breast against Mall's upper arm while they lean closely together to work. If she can get away with it, she'll even start to rub tenderly back and forth. When Mall pulls startled away, Sinalco only laughs.

"My love," she finally inquires, "why you snog not anyone at all?" Sinalco loves this new expression.

Mall decides to have the conversation done with quickly and for good. "I'm an abstainant," she says flatly, expecting that to be the end of it.

"So?"

"That means a nonsexual. I've decided I will have no sex."

"I know what this means. Many people in EVe do this abstainant."

Sinalco shakes her head of curls. "I don't know why."

"That's my decision," Mall snips, "and my own bloody business, to boot."

"Not even wearing the full body condom?" goads Sinalco.

Mall must admit she's deliberated that option. But the thought of wriggling into such a layering, never mind how sheer, strikes her as both preposterous and repugnant. "Contagion and pregnancy. I don't fancy slow death or bringing a child into this fuck-all world. Or the combination of the two. Is that clear enough for you, then?"

Sinalco, thickening her accent to heighten her sarcasm, shrugs. "Yes. Very lucid."

"I can't believe you yank anything that bleeding well walks upright."

"Erect is very important," agrees Sinalco with a madwoman leer crossing her face. "Do not worry. I have my precautions, my sweet."

☆ ☆ ☆ ☆ ☆ ☆

Notwithstanding their differences in personal style, the two work brilliantly together. Harrods must have known something. During the midday rush at *The Nosebag* on St. Michael's Street, they have their breakthrough. While Mall eats her soy salad, Sinalco lifts her face suddenly from her palmbook—for all her size, she seems scarcely to eat a bite—and asks, "Dear girl, tell me please, what is it *exactly* that you do, at its core, its pith?"

Immediately, Mall perceives the intention behind the question. She stops chewing. "I suppose I play with the gap between the signifier and the signified, between what is indicated by utterance and what is conceptualized by awareness."

"So words do not mean what they mean?"

"Words don't have meaning at all. They have application."

"Ah," Sinalco makes a mental note, "Wittgenstein. Tell me more."

Mall has learned Sinalco cuts to the chase. No need to explain esoteric concepts. Just engage them. Mall adds, "Truths are illusions about which it has been forgotten that they *are* illusions."

"Yes. And Nietzsche." Sinalco pads some items, using only one hand, her fingers moving uncommonly fast. "Good. And of course you have moved beyond the modern with Saussure and Barthes and Derrida, non?"

"Right. People don't speak language, language speaks people. So you understand now?"

"These basics only. Plus, s'il tu plaît."

Mall sips her purged water to clear her palate.

"The history that gives birth to us, then disciplines us, is most intelligible as a chronicle of conflicts, as relations of force rather than relations of meaning."

Sinalco nods, still padding. "War, not the language."

"Power," Mall finally uses the crucial word in both their minds, "isn't simply a form of warlike domination, but continues in the peace of the state. Peace would then be a form of war, and the state a means of waging it."

"Mais, bien sûr." Sinalco completes some final pads, looks up from the flatscreen and smiles. "Monsieur Foucault."

"None other. So, in the end, I'm that specific intellectual, that cultural worker, engaged in the struggle between contending régimes of truth, between rival systems that produce truth by virtue of multiple forms of constraint. Perhaps that makes me a warrior of some kind."

Sinalco lets loose the prolonged Franco-ejaculation, "Ah!" that indicates great enlightenment. She pads furiously on a palmbook like nothing Mall has ever seen. So small, so compact—yet so dense. The one time Mall picked it up to hand to Sinalco, she nearly dropped it to the floor. Sinalco, though, brandishes it about like an evening purse.

"Courage, ma petite," she says at last, watching matters evolve on the flatscreen. "Now, what do you say is your battleground, ma soldat?"

That's simple. "Adverts," Mall answers.

Mall explains that advertizing is everything in the current culture. That for three centuries humans have fixated on the manufacture of an immense collection of commodities. More than capital, more than labor, commodity is what drives human lives, fuels human beliefs, determines human culture, shapes the physical planet, and will dictate human fate. When the problem of mass production was solved fairly early in the game, the new social economy faced the more serious problem of mass consumption. If consumption does not match output, everything grinds to a halt. There's no way around it, if we insist on founding our lives on the base of commodity. By way of a solution, advertizing was invented as a means to create a culture in which desire and personality become fused with commodities. Identity is begot by the commercial. Individual and citizens disappear, dwindling into customer and clients. Not: you are what you buy. Worse. You buy what you are.

Sinalco listens carefully through Mall's description. "Jhally," she says, slapping her forehead with the heel of her hand. "Nom de Dieu. And heading towards hooks et Chomsky, je suis sûr."

"Do you want the full account?" asks Mall. "It's long."

"Yes, yes. We must."

Mall tells how advertizing became modern mythology—the stories people tell about themselves as a society. From these stories, people learn how to behave, what is good and evil, moral and immoral. There were other storytelling mechanisms, but advertizing came to be the central one, and eventually the only one. It infiltrated all the others. It infiltrated every corner of life. Civil institutions, religion, education, the arts. The message of commodity became a single one: consumption brings happiness, freedom, and fulfillment; ownership of things leads to jubilant and emancipated and glorious singularity. The myth from the marketplace can be no other. "It's a right proper load of rubbish, too," Mall complains, "and bugger-all to dislodge from anyone's thinking who has been raised up and naturalized to its fairy tales."

"Go on."

"Goods, however, do *not* bring happiness with them, it turns out. Above a certain level of material comfort, merchandise cannot supply you with control over your own life, with a sense of self-worth, with a loving family, with close friends, with romance and love. Commodities and their buying and selling are certainly useful aspects of a society, but they cannot provide sociability."

"So all along this has been the grand lie, my lovely? Oui?"

"Yes. Since well back into last century, advert agencies stopped talking about the properties of commodities and started talking about the relationship of manufactured objects to the social life of people. They did everything they could to link their products with real sources of human happiness." Therein lies the falsity of advertizing: not in the real emotional appeal it makes, but in the solely commercial answer it provides. "Advertizing taps into our dreams and hopes for human social contact and then reconceptualizes and repackages them back to us connected to the world of marketed things." Mall sips at her water. "Advertizing is a dream, a bleeding fantasy factory. It translates our desires for love, and meaning, and sex, and adventure into our dreams of those things fulfilled by the purchase of sodding inventory."

Sinalco stops padding to reflect a moment. "So okay," she begins, "I will play the advocate of the devil now." She fixes eyes with Mall. "Et alors, quoi? Why is this so terrible a thing? So the advertizement reflects our dreams. So what?"

Mall shakes her head wearily, having heard this particular fallacy a thousand times. "Advertizing does fuck-all more than just *reflect* the dream-life of the culture," she says. "It helps *create* it. Don't you see? Fancy and gewgaw get tied neatly together with a pretty ribbon and then broadcast to us with all the authority of a bloody communiqué from God Herself on high. When you grow up in a society feeding you nothing but such prattle, you become a deep believer in the idea that money buys you love."

Sinalco, silent for a time, begins to pad again.

After a minute or two, Mall asks hopefully, "Are we done, then?"

"Non," Sinalco responds. "Tell me now about the battle itself."

That is simpler still. Advertizing is the invention of mammonism. Small wonder the chase after commodities produces the opposite of sociability: the fetishism of greed. Advertizing pitches its appeal to people as individuals, not as members of a community. Just so with mammonism. Individual needs and desires, therefore, come first and must be fulfilled while collective issues can go to hell. In this way we come to obsess about our own comfort and pleasure and craving and success while crucial societal matters get pushed to one side.

"We'll fret over what the size and the make of the cars we're driving says about us," Mall complains, "but have no concerns about who we're bombing to get the petrol to run the fucking things. Or I must have just the right formula shampoo to keep the soapy buildup out of my hair, but don't trouble me with the mundane bits about the workers manufacturing the stuff not having enough food or housing or healthcare or education—or if my shampoo runoff is mucking up the groundwater. Those little details just put a crimp in my otherwise nice and happy good-hair day."

A young mum with two small children at the adjacent table catches Mall's attention and nods agreement. Mall finds her gesture very gratifying.

"In the world of the mammonistic marketplace," she concludes for both audiences, "there is no such thing as society. Only *me*."

"You become very cute when you grow mad and proud."

"Piss off."

Sinalco laughs again while she attends to her padboard. "So I will make you mad some more, just to see your eyes twinkling." She completes a last few strokes, waits, then speaks as though reciting, "But we are just selling things. We are just doing the business. We must make a living. We are creating the jobs. We are just giving people what they want. We are serving the customer. What harm in this?"

Mall smiles and won't bite. "Now you're just being stupid," she says.

"Peut-être. But it is not bliss?"

"That's ignorance that's bliss, deary. Not stupidity."

"There is a différance?"

They come to the crux. To the contending régimes of truth. To EVe versus TexArc and Marksoc versus Corpfeud.

"Commercial culture is flash and easy, love, but it's also the culture of the anti-state, of privatized conglomeration founded on there being haves and have-nots. At face value it's hard to see that, and so commercialism *sells* much better than the dull doings of state. Now here's where we come to my job with Signification." Mall scoots forward her chair. "My task is to do away with gray and dismal statism, to make collectivity pleasurable and productive. To sell solidarity as fun and passionate and even a touch lusty. That's something I'm sure you can appreciate. As a signer, my voice mixes with the many voices that have access to EVe's communication channels, to EVe's marketplace of *ideas*–not just commodities. My work is to glamorize the culture and the leveling protection of the state, to meet fire with advertizing fire."

"So you are every bit the shitbuller as are they. Non?" Sinalco enjoys the role of troublemaker. "They mask their ideology as wares, and your merchandise is the ideology. N'est-ce pas? How is this not the same?"

Mall fills her mouth with a large forkload of salad then, with one canine, tears off a goodly wedge of her granary bread. While she chews she points out calmly, "What I sell does not require standing on anyone's throat. I promote democratic socialism. They promote despotic barbarism. And don't forget, in point of fact, I don't sell empty bloody promises. Alterity brings a sufficient life standard to everyone. Consumerism can neither satisfy the basic need for genuine human contact among its haves nor adequately feed, clothe, and house its have-nots. The first get fucked up, and the second get fucked over. Either bloody way, we're all bloody well fucked." Mall swallows. "Aren't we?" She tears off another piece of bread and looks out the restaurant window into the busy street. "Only thing good for business is the bottom line. Meantime, business has brought us to the bloody brink." Mall looks back at Sinalco. "Hasn't it now?"

"Yes, yes. Très bien. Très dramatique." Sinalco has been preoccupied tapping a few last pads. "I see I have been slicing in the wrong places. Much too deep in. The teek must not lead the signer. The signer must guide the teek. I see this now. C'est ma faute." She watches alertly while something transpires on the flatscreen. "Okay," she claps and rubs her palms together. "Now we go."

Sinalco turns the tiny palmbook halfway around on the tabletop so that they both can see. Mall peers at a three-dimensional sphere being represented on the flatscreen. The shape is hazy towards its edges, more clotted and bright nearer its center. She can see straight through some parts of it while other segments are solid. The entire interior of the sphere is ever shifting, at times looking like the random flux of airy vapor, at times flywheeling as might the tumble gears of a complex lock. Mall hasn't a clue what the image is. She can manipulate any number of intricate softwares expertly, but the deep programming of teeks is well beyond the range of her technological interest.

"And we are looking at?" she says.

"ArcNet."

"What it might look like?"

"Non," comes Sinalco's flat answer. "What it is."

"That's ArcNet?" Mall is skeptical. "For real?"

"Oui, c'est ça," Sinalco nods casually at the flatscreen. "And no matter what you do, touch no pads."

"Why not?"

"The ArcNet is very dangerous."

Mall scowls in deeper disbelief. "Bollocks," she says.

"I will make this rapid," Sinalco ignores her, "because I know you do not give the shit about technicité and I cannot keep them off for long."

"Keep who off?" Mall interrupts.

"The hunter-seekers mostly. There are also the tanks and the bouncers to watch for. The mines and the torpedoes are the attrape-nigaud only, so as long as we make no moves we are fine for those."

"Hold on." Mall puts a hand on Sinalco's forearm. "Are you telling me this is some kind of bleeding vidgame?"

"Yes. Why not? The principle is just the same. The seriousness is not."

Mall reconsiders the image filling the flatscreen. "Right," she says, not sure if her tone is suddenly more wary. "Carry on, then."

"ArcNet is like the onion. Many layers and the structure, but as well the organic and haphazard quality to it. I do not know how they achieve this, but it is there. ArcNet is also like the maze. Many, many avenues and barricades. All of them, you know, assembled by the rational thinking. So in principle there must be patterns that can unravel and then we do the navigation. Yes?" Sinalco shakes her head in frustration. "Mais alors, the maze is crazy. Incroyable."

"Yes, yes. A right nasty old labyrinth." Feeling oddly afraid of the flatscreen, Mall wants to hurry this along. "That's to be expected, isn't it?"

"Non. You don't understand. Organic onion stratification combined with multiple routing and cul-de-sac make it practically impenetrable to–"

"Not for an ace teek like yourself, right?"

Sinalco frowns. "Well, maybe not. With much time, and *if* the ArcNet wasn't always in movement."

"In movement? I don't follow." Sinalco gestures for Mall to re-inspect the flatscreen. She does. "You mean all that squirming about it's doing?"

"Justement. A temporal flow," Sinalco explains, "both organical *and* mechanical. I cannot make a way through this. I think even they do not know completely how this network they have functions. They have made it, yes, and they use it, yes, but it is not now in their absolute control. This makes security very, very good. Maybe impossible."

"So we're buggered? We can't get through? Is that what you're saying?"

"I think so, probably yes, up to just a little time ago. For these days I have been running the chinks in the firewalls and rucksacking along the signal lines that hide me well. But there is too much flow shift and too many things coming after me to get very far." She points to the bright center of the sphere, careful not to touch the flatscreen. "There is where I have been trying to get us, but I cannot go there from here."

Mall feels suddenly betrayed—by Harrods—not by Sinalco. She had convinced herself she was about to use her skills to make a difference, to fight back against these bastards, only to be told the doorway is blocked—there's no way in. Damn it all. "We *are* buggered then."

"No, no, we are not, because of what we just talked about." Sinalco nimbly taps one pad. "Regard."

The image shifts to a closer view of one quarter of the sphere's outer zone. Here there are ample gaps and few of the tumble-lock rotations. Mostly there are thin arms of the casual vapor fluctuations. Mall studies the flatscreen.

"What are we looking at?"

"Where they do not much care," Sinalco says. "At the center is all the purpose and so all their defense. Out here they are more blasé."

"That helps us?"

"If what you just tell me is so, yes. You tell me you work at the pivot of signal and idea. Yes? Where the sounds of words are fixed to meanings for the words? I am right? And that this place is also where the truths are forgotten to be the illusions. No? So I slice for some places where the big lies are made big truths in TexArc. Some micropoints where the power produces the réalité. There, I think maybe we can work. Yes? This is making sense to you?"

"Very much," Mall says. As a matter of fact, it's sodding textbook.

The problem is not changing people's consciousness—or what's in their heads—but the political, economic, institutional régime of the production of truth. It's not a matter of emancipating truth from every system of power—which would be a chimera, for truth is already power—but of detaching the power of truth from the forms of hegemony, social, economic and cultural, within which it operates at the present time.

"I slice us as deep through ArcNet as I dare and it only gets us here," she points again at the flatscreen, "but it is somewhere, I think, where we can work."

"Bloody brilliant. We'll give it a go."

A melodic hum sounds from the palmbook, nothing outwardly alarming. Quicker than Mall's eye can follow, Sinalco reaches out to change screens, causing the ArcNet sphere abruptly to vanish.

"What?" asks Mall.

"A spinner," Sinalco says. "Their most clever freak."

Mall shakes her head, unfamiliar with a lot of teek pidgin.

"Trick, Mall," Sinalco corrects herself. "You believe you are getting somewhere, but you are being led around a loop. You spin around it until they get you."

"Until what gets you?"

"I don't know," Sinalco smiles. "I have never been got."

Mall looks at the blank screen, which seems positively sinister now. Sinalco reaches across the table to take her hand. Her display is not a joke, not a faux seduction. "Your best protection inside ArcNet is speed. Be smarter than them, yes, but also be quicker than them." Sinalco gives Mall's leaner hand a squeeze. "Don't worry. No one is faster than me."

Mall reassesses the entire situation. For the first time she feels real fear. Apparently this will *not* be the same as coursing about EVeWave compulsively searching after smut. Mall squeezes Sinalco's hand in return. "Come on," she says brightly. "Let's go tell old misery guts we've located a place to sign."

☆ ☆ ☆ ☆ ☆ ☆

Underminister Harrods is elated but quite surprised at the positive report coming so soon from his team. Other Countermeasures teeks take weeks to venture a toe inside ArcNet, and once in, they are far too paranoid to move about much, even along its outermost tier. Never mind venturing into the interior. Without a firm destination in mind, merely stumbling about is much too nerve wrenching, or so the Underminister has been told. Now he'll have the opportunity to see if the signer he's selected turns out to be worth her salt. The three of them meet the next day in the tea room at the Oxford railway station. This way Harrods can train up from London, convene, and train back entirely covered and in public. Mall and Sinalco show him a sampling of the preliminary slices they've pulled from ArcNet. The vidclips are from deeper than anyone has penetrated before. While still confusing, the political nature of the vidclips is manifest. The Underminister grows quite animated. "My word, this is absolutely amazing," he stammers. "Fine work, you two. Fine work indeed! I imagine you can begin your counter-advocacy straight away."

Mall brims with ideas, but it's Sinalco who speaks up first. "Herr Harrods," as she's taken to addressing him, "our Mall, I am sure, can counter advocate all things, but I am thinking it might do no good here."

"Oh? And why is that?"

"We are not so deep in."

"Nonsense. No one has ever gotten this far."

"Perhaps so. Still, this place is too easy to get to. It is too little protected. We are someplace with some importance, yes. I believe so, too, but I do not think we are at a place where there are very many of their important types. You see? So who does Mall talk to here that can make a difference?"

Sinalco's question is legitimate. Underminister Harrods turns a hopeful face to Mall.

"We're peachy here," she says confidently. "What I'm hoping to do can't be done at a place they're worried enough about to guard tightly. We'll be just fine."

Harrods and Sinalco exchange a look, agreeing they must trust their signer. Happy with their response, Mall sets to work.

☆ ☆ ☆ ☆ ☆ ☆

Rather than slice off the ArcNet stream, a limited activity and one destined eventually to be detected, Mall creates a feed. Such a strategy has never been attempted, but it is in keeping, she feels, with Harrods' policy of offensive action. Sinalco worms Mall's creations into ArcNet and protects them while Mall works, but the team is frequently interrupted, making progress slow. Tanks of various kinds routinely patrol the neighborhood. Sinalco has no particular trouble gulling these, but as Mall patches in more and more of her feed, hunter-seekers begin to appear, a few at first, then in numbers, accompanied by spinners. Sinalco is not sure whether this enhancement is an automated network response or a live-operator consciously looking for intruders.

Inside of a week Mall feels as though she's making true headway. She's situated several spots within the queue of an autoloop which should be undiscoverable for some time. Now if only her themes can punch the clutter. Mall has crafted messages suiting the stream and heritage germane. Her research has been thorough, and her pitch lunges for the jugular. But it's like launching blind—a paper boat in mysterious seas. One simply hopes.

A few days later, she feels she's made at least one vital discovery. She messages to Harrods at ministry late one afternoon. "I doubt they're out to obliterate us, sir," she says over the safelink of her palmbook. She and Sinalco sit in a cramped, student quickeat near the Examination Schools.

"What makes you say that, Mall?"

"It does them no good. They hardly need more territory."

"And what about our resources?"

"Beneficial, yes, but, to be perfectly honest, sir—paltry really, considering they can range the entire rest of the planet at will. No, I think they need something else altogether from us."

"That being?"

"Why, our markets, sir."

There is a long silence from Harrods' end. Mall doesn't have this conversation on screen as so many people are nearby, but she can picture the tormented look on the Underminister's face as he digests this information. Market acquisition is described in the portfolios as the worst case scenario when engaged by TexArc. It means TexArc not only desires your heart—it wants your soul.

Finally the return. "You're quite sure?"

"Yes, quite."

"All right then."

"All right what? You'll pass this along," Mall insists.

"I'll pass it along to my Headminister," replies Harrods defensively. "Send me your data. What he decides to do with it, I can't say."

Sinalco taps Mall on the forearm and gestures with her hand, suggesting Mall drop the subject. Mall grimaces, wanting to press her findings all the way to Caucus. Instead, she says tersely, "Right," and pads off after relaying the documentation. "Officious turd," she mutters.

"Mein Herr is not so bad," Sinalco soothes her collaborator's feathers.

They get up and leave the quickeat. It's just 16.30H and the congestion is considerable on High Street. They must wend their way through the City Centre towards Mall's flat on North Parade. Sinalco has moved in with clear understanding that she conducts her snogging sessions elsewhere, as they can get rather boisterous. Over the course of the past week, the pair has followed a habit of returning home in the early evenings for Mall to take her run while Sinalco drinks a restorative glass of wine. Then they freshen up and go for drinks at the *Rose and Crown*—just across the way. Afterwards, they'll have a proper meal before returning to their work. Tonight they've planned for Mall's favorite restaurant, the *Luna Caprese*. As they come to the first crosswalk, Mall's messager hums. She stops to remove it from her top thigh pocket, checking the identification. "Weetabix," she announces. Almost forgetting she still works for the milksop Provost, Mall asks, "What could he possibly want?"

Under her wide sunbrella, an island in the coursing pedestrian stream, Sinalco uses their delay to look over heads and take stock of the traffic.

Mall brings the messager close to her face. On the tiny screen Weetabix's pinched features appear. He's flushed, his voice urgently high-pitched.

"Mall! I say, is that you?"

Please spare us all the thespianism, thinks Mall. Weetabix is jealous of her being singled out for such an important and indefinite leave of commonweal duty. "Yes, of course it's me!" she shouts back. "Dear God, sir, don't howl so. What*ever* is the matter?"

"Branston!"

Icily: "What of him, sir?" Mall pantomimes a cross look at Sinalco, who smiles shamelessly. Mall nearly sniggers.

"He's dead!"

Mall reinspects the diminutive face on the screen. "What?"

"Killed!"

"What *are* you on about?"

"Executed from the looks of it, Mall! Mall? Do you hear me? We found him just this minute—at his console! Draped backward over his chair! I tell you there's a hole in his forehead the diameter of a laserpencil!"

At that moment Mall's messager skids across the pavement, jerked loose from her hand as Sinalco seizes her wrist and drags her pell-mell out into traffic. They dodge through the rows of minis, lorries, buses, cyclists until they reach the opposite side of High where Sinalco abruptly drops Mall's arm. "Follow me!" she demands. "Be alert, but go like crazy people!"

Almost more unnerving is the sight of Sinalco without her sunbrella. She's abandoned it on the far side of the street. Sinalco then turns and runs. Mall is afraid not to follow. They duck into the narrow mouth of Queen's Lane, going full tilt. They race its walled alley north, between Teddy Hall and Queen's College, coming to a sharp left dogleg. Mall has focused her mind enough to wonder what in bloody hell they are doing and where in bloody hell they are going, when Sinalco dodges a student coming around the corner on a bicycle. Mall doesn't move quick enough and the student banks off her.

"You wankers!" he yells as he skids off to one side and close to the stone wall.

"Just run!" Sinalco calls without looking behind her.

Heading west, the lane widens a bit. Even when skirting people Sinalco manages to lengthen her stride. Greek deity fleet, she is. Mall's lucky to be equal to the test, and sprints not far behind. The buildings of New College loom to their right. Left, on the other side of the wall, Mall can sense the open grounds of All Souls. Queen's Lane becomes New College Lane with a series of veers—right, left, right, left again. Pedestrians come in clumps, and the porter at New College gate shouts an angry warning for them to watch themselves. It's just then that Mall sees Sinalco flinch slightly, as though dodging from something coming head-on at her. *Are they being shot at?* Then Weetabix's strange message hits her. Oh my God—Branston!

Mall runs like bloody hell. The lane becomes a narrow gorge, gray structures rising on either side. They rip right along behind Hertford and round the final turn to see the Bridge of Sighs looming ahead. Figures are crossing it, people moving dimly inside the windows of the ornate Venetian archway, and just before passing underneath Mall glances up to see if anyone is pointing anything down at them. She hears a loud crack and involuntarily cringes. The noise might have come from a delivery van knocking about ahead on Catte Street.

"Sinalco!" Mall shouts, her lungs starting to ache. "Where...?"

"Just move your blooming arse!" comes a prompt response.

Emerging from New College Lane, Sinalco cuts sharply left down Catte Street—as though veering out of a line of sight—and races diagonally across the road to the east entryway into the Old Bodleian, under the Tower of the Five Orders. The gate into the Schools Quadrangle is locked, as it's used only for ceremonial processions, but Sinalco kicks open the smaller sized portal and pushes her way through—Mall hard behind her. Students walking the broad and unevenly paved quadrangle freeze in place as the two sprint straight toward the library entrance, swerving around the statue of Pembroke. The maneuver saves their lives. As they barge through the glass doorway into the Bodleian, the Earl's bronze head explodes. Students scatter.

"Bloody hell!" Mall yowls, throwing her arms over her head.

They vault the security barrier and without so much as a "Sorry" knock to the floor the elderly porter who inspects all bags. Sinalco heads down the Proscholium entrance hall and at its end starts to lope her way up the seventeenth-century stairwell. Mall follows blindly. The first landing puts them one floor up at the Arts End. Knowing they must risk the bank of windows, Sinalco leads them catty corner across the reading room and into the Duke

Humfrey's Library, specifically toward the Reserve Desk where book deliveries are picked up. They leap the desk, librarians too shocked to protest, and wedge their way back into the private room. Mall can't be sure, but she hears shattering glass, and sees something splintering into oak shelving, thunking into ancient vellum. Sinalco quickly pulls Mall with her into the cramped manuscript elevator and pushes the button for the bottom level.

"Almost there," Sinalco calls reassuringly. She's not short of breath, not gleaming with perspiration. Mall's near collapse.

When the elevator door slides open, Sinalco leads, pushing between close shelves filled with old parchments. The musty odor is stunning, the air heavily damp. They run to one corner of the basement where Sinalco reaches behind a shelf to pad in, from touch only, a long series on an obscure panel face. The shelving slides aside, revealing a spiral metal staircase leading downward. "Cliché, je sais," Sinalco apologizes for the palpable skullduggery.

At the bottom of the staircase is a single-track, underground station—except there are no tracks. Waiting for them is something that might be a 22nd-century tube carriage. It's sleek but rounded, blunt-nosed at both ends, the top half entirely glass.

"What's all this?" Mall asks.

"Vacuum train," Sinalco tells her.

"Are we going somewhere?"

"Someplace safer."

They step on and immediately set off, traveling a round tunnel that looks to be coated with glass. Soon the sensation of great speed becomes disorienting. Others had been waiting for them on the car. Several look to be fighters, a vocation Mall has never been around. One who does not look martial, a man, maybe forty and exuding importance, steps forward and extends his hand. "Very sorry about the shenanigans, Mall. Sometimes such things cannot be helped."

Mall shakes his hand without replying.

"My name is Natwest," the man continues. "I'm the Headminister of Countermeasures."

Mall can't see this as a positive development. "And where is Underminister Harrods?" she asks.

"He's dead."

The blunt news shocks Mall. She looks questioningly at Sinalco and then back to Natwest. He nods.

"And so it's true then about Branston?"

"I'm afraid it is. Provost Weetabix as well, along with five more at Signification."

Mall sits down in one of the thick-cushioned seats lining the walls. She can't be sure if her distress comes from motion sickness or from what she's heard. "This is insane," she says softly to herself.

"It may seem so right now, Mall," Natwest answers, "but I can assure you we are dealing with people who do not mess about."

Mall eyes the Headminister more carefully. He is rather squat, round in all his features, his head bald and pale as a cue ball. Dressed crisply in his light muslims, everything about him reminds her of ice cream.

"But how could this possibly happen?" she asks, hoping for real answers.

"We're not sure," Natwest responds. "Obviously, they managed to get some people on the ground."

"How would they know where to go? What people to target?"

"Perhaps Branston plays with my slice routines," Sinalco suggests. "He asks me all the time about them. Maybe he wanders inside ArcNet and gets noticed."

"Perhaps," muses the Headminister. "We may never know."

Such an explanation sounds nonsensical to Mall. Branston was no meddler, and he was no oaf. He was a spot-on teek. He never would have sliced into ArcNet on a lark. *For Sinalco so casually to be tossing blame his way now...after what they...it was obscene*. "You know *bloody* well Branston *never* would have sliced where he wasn't *bloody* damn sure..." Mall's voice trails off. She first puts one hand to her forehead, then dips her head down between her knees. She's about to retch.

Watching her discomfort, the Headminister leans down: "It's *you* that has caught their attention, Mall. *You*. It would seem old Harrods was right on the mark, after all. That's quite extraordinary."

At Natwest's beckoning, a medic steps up to apply a patch to the exposed back of Mall's neck. Two fighters then stretch her out across the seats. One says, "She'll sleep for the rest of the passage." Natwest confers briefly with some of the others. Finally he talks with Sinalco alone, stepping to the very nose of the carriage. The endless tunnel of glass zips by.

"Do you think this wise?" says Sinalco.

"We knew this would be all cat and mouse."

"So when do we know which is who?"

Natwest snorts an uneasy laugh. "When one of us has a tail dangling out his mouth. That's when."

Sinalco nods and yawns, stretching her arms up over her head to touch the glass ceiling of the cabin. "At least I am no longer having to carry that ridiculous parapluie."

The Feed

This on upleft:

Wherever you go, there we are! [majestic sweepviews, inspiring leadmusic] See the world, be the world! [talkheads appear—stiff, grinning, perfect like adverbots] More youdecide breaking news! The newsbig of the day off our glassea: conclusive evidence now linking EVe strongman Adolph Stalin with the terrorbombing of BigRig19! [vidfeed: gaping sand crater, thick blackgusher rising high in stark bluesky] Unmistakable traces found of chemical explosives used by covert EVe havoc-and-assassination squads! [flashpic: EVe strongman Adolph Stalin—bearded, swarthy, turbaned, dark menacing eyes] Exclaims Stalin: "We will bury you!" [talkheads again] Meanwhile dangerous repair operations continue in our sky as the deadcount tragically mounts! Seventeen now have perished as workcrews fight to stabilize the structural integrity of our... [vidfeed: high-orbit meldpods floating alongside the colossal glossy white shaft, kilometers below cotton fluffs placid over deep bluesea]...

With this on upright:

Like a rock! [stirring sellmusic] Like a rock! [vidfeed: gargantuan pickup with terrain tires taller than a man scrambling to crest a boulder-strewn ridge] Like a rock! The all-new '84 'Nam! Bigger! Tougher! More firepower! Backing available! Zero DollArcs down! Twelve hours same as cash! Lowest credgrades in town! Hurry on down to Parker Motors today! [flashpic: meg sitemap underneath the Gmotors logo] Twelve hours same as cash! Zero DollArcs down! Backing available! Like a rock! Hurry on down to Parker Motors today! [hardcut; happy sellmusic, vidfeed: happers at The Arcs] In a hurry? Slurp a McSlurry! Feeling blurry? Make yours McSlurry! Got worry? Catch that McSlurry fury! [flashpic: Arcs logo] Just can't get off the dime? Well then it's McSlurrys time! [hardcut; soft sellmusic, vidfeed: Serv asleep ontheline] If you want to rock it up, you got to sock it up! Amp gets you there! [Serv patching back of his neck then launching into linejob] Amp gets you where you need to be! [flashpic: Amp logo] And ye shall know the Amp, and the Amp shall set you free! [hardcut; hard sellmusic]...

With this on downleft:

And as always we thank you for aligning in with Blood in the Face for Jesus! [soothmusic, serenesmile talkheads] Your personal pathway to righteousness and salvation! Right now we're going to our callers, and on the wireless from out Eagle way is Duchess! Duchess, hello? Are you there, Duchess? Hello? [vidfeed: fatfaced Serv tits'n'ass] Oh yes, Race, hello. I'm here! [talkheads] Well, hello there back to you, Duchess! May God bless you and keep you! [vidfeed: Duchess] Oh, and you, too, Race. [talkheads] Well, thank you! Thank you very much, Duchess! And what's your question for us today, dear sister in Christ? [vidfeed: Duchess] Well, Race, first off I just got to tell you how much I love you and your vidfeed. I just watch it all day every day so's I make sure never to set foot off my personal pathway to righteousness and salvation. [talkheads] Well praise Our Lord and Savior Jesus Christ for that, Duchess! Oh my goodness, all praise to Jesus for that small and wonderful miracle! [vidfeed: Duchess] Amen, Race! Praise His Name and Glory! And thanks be to God Almighty for you being here each and every day to do the Lord's work! [talkheads] Well I thank you, sister! I am only His humble servant, Duchess, doing what just one man can! Now Duchess, just what is your question for us today, dear sister? [vidfeed: Duchess] Oh, Race, well, I guess I'm just a little bit confused. I thought these folks way over yonder in EVe were supposed to be like us. You know, good God-fearing Blood-in-the-Face Christians. So's how come they're doing all these terrible things to us now and so out of the blue and all like this? [talkheads] Well, that's just it, Duchess! That just goes to show you what can happen if you stray from His pathway to righteousness and salvation! [soothmusic starts in] You see, these folks in EVe may have started out like us a long time back, God-fearing and all, but over the years they've slowly become corrupt! [flashpic: EVe strongman Adolph Stalin—bearded, swarthy, turbaned, dark menacing eyes] Yes sirree, some of them are as black as tar and as sick as sin, Duchess! In fact, most are now decadent unbelievers! They just don't stick no more to that old-timey religion, Duchess! Not like you and me! No sirree! They've let liberalism and unionism and bolshevism creep into their souls and infect their hearts! Am I right, Duchess? Am I right? Can I get an Amen from you, Duchess? [vidfeed: Duchess eyes rolled back ecstatic] Oh my lands, yes, Race! Yes! Yes! Amen to that, brother Race...

With this on downright:

[autovoice-flashpic: clear bluesea, clear bluesky, bump white sand island with three swaying palms, sailboat entering from left] Onehundred and twentyseven jobapps pending! Searchmode doublego! Recent jobhist: Simplot tatergunner, Brigade Corp chempools, Sawtooth Fluid tanktruck ops, HP linejob, BoiCity Hydro storm sewer ops, more data available! Workcreds pending: sevenhundredtwelve thousand sixhundred seventytwo! Current credgrades: fiftyeight and onehalf percent! Searchmode doublego! Onehundred and thirtyone jobapps pending! Jobfind likely at seventyfive percent! Daytrade options: VersaCorps fortyseven and oneeight down onehalf, NanoTech ninetythree and fiveeights up three, Simplot fifty and threequarters down onequarter—[hotflash in upleft of downright]–Hottip! Hottip! Sawtooth Fluid split! Buy at fourteen! Buy at fourteen! Doublego Dmega hottip at fourteen for Sawtooth Fluid...

Oak Wat has been feeling the glassy for some little time now. He can't quite remember when it set on hard. Maybe two weeks. Maybe a month. Hell, it could maybe be longer. Point is, he doesn't exactly know, and feeling hard the glassy isn't when you can't see through it, like most people expect. No, that ain't the glassy at all. If you stop to think on it, not seeing through it is norm. If most the time you think you're seeing through it and not letting it get to you, you're wrong. You're not seeing through it at all, and it's getting to you plenty. You think you're ignoring it, but you can't. That's the plain point. There's no goddamn ignoring this shit. So thinking you can, and you are, really only means you can't and you ain't. Only you don't know it. That means the more you feel free of it, the more you're really cornered by it, but all that's just if you *really* stop to think on it—which just about nobody does. Don't get Oak started on that one. No. Simple bottom-line is this: feeling hard's nothing like any of them brainfarts think it is. Nope. It's flat worse. The real deal glassy is when you see *neither*. Not through it. Not not through it. You see nothing—just the big zero. *That*, my friend, is when you are good and fucked. You end up staggering and stumbling around all day long, the big totoblank always in front of your face—and you don't give a flat fuck. That's what the scariest part of the whole damn thing is. You don't even care. Yep. Good and fucked.

Like everybody else, Oak's heard tell stories of old folks going glassy—more than just a few, in fact. After a rough thirty, forty years the shit can get to you, sure, but Oak's maybe only twenty-one, twenty-two—thereabouts. Parker tough as drynano born and bred. He's held down fifty, sixty jobs since coming of age at ten. Nothing out of line. So most would say there's no cause for him to be catching bad the glassy now, before his time. Maybe for a short spell, yeah. Lots of Parkers get the short spells of it, but you snap right out of them. Get hooting beerbent and yank a snatch and you're right as pain. Oak's glassy, though, has been hanging on for too damn long and for too damn hard. Hell, could be Oak's a wonderboy. Hell, we can't all be commonsense joes. Oak's been starting to suspect there's something more to the glassy than just the 24/7 of the all4s. No fooling. He's been thinking some mindfuck shit. Past couple of days he's been wondering if seeing the nothing doesn't have something to do with the goddamned yub from the hub. Why not? It's like this. The yub's always a bitch that blueballs you every time. Like now. Yub is—*again*—he's yanked good until his cred-spending hikes up to over eight-hundred-thow. Just no hiring for him until then. So—*again*—he's faced with the sameold: how to dig himself out of—and then keep himself clear of—that goddamned bottomless credspending shithole? Far as Oak's seen, there's just no beating that or the yub, not by him or by any Parker he's ever heard tell of. On the other hand, the feed off the all4s is always a virho. Feed'll fuck you eight ways to Sunday and tell you anything you like to hear all day, every day. No stopping the feed. What if them two, the yub and the feed, are in cahoots? What then? Like the feed feelgood blows in your ear while the yub credspend fucks you over—and you never know they're working it together. Something like that. What if *that's* the actual-fact glassy? Like a double whammy—what you *want* going on and what *is* going on. Just a notion Oak the wonderboy's been thinking on. Nothing's too clear in his own head. Hell, anymore Oak don't know if he's coming or going. He does know, though, that wonder-boys get into the deepshit if they're found out.

On upleft:

On the noonhour: this is Vieworld, your complete breaking news source, with our local lunch-time special feature on the IMS recall elections just getting underway, touting a variety of candidates looking to keep the taxman away from our doors and biggov off our backs, leaving us free to pursue...

On upright:

On the noonhour: this is Shopdrop, your complete consumer notification source, with our local lunchtime special feature on some hot new prods made just for the BoiCity meg: A SolarStove that can fry up that perfect deersteak, or The Mighty Duct Tape—guaranteed to keep unwanted wind, dust, and those pesky outbreak bugs out of your mobile...

On downleft:

On the noonhour: this is Youchoose, your complete idiversion source, with our local lunchtime special feature on Coyote Killing in the Cascade, showing you the latest to take out those howling nuisances, whether by bow, bullet, or fragbomb, plus how to treat that hide for maximum years of utility...

On downright:

On the noonhour: this is Brandyou, your complete employment and icommunication source, with our local lunchtime special feature on Jobbing It Up in the BoiCity Meg, letting you in on where the new hotjobs will be coming from, plus daytrade tips from our experts who can show you how, with just a little savtrade and insidertips, you too can earn...

Whichever vid Oak focuses on, the aud comes up a little louder, but with the others always in the background. As a kid you learn to pick your way through it. On the noonhour local lunchtime special feature his ass. Oak's stomach is growly something awful, but vit costs big creds and creds is what he *don't* want pending right now. But hell, you got to eat, right? He'd had a small bite, long gone, out at his mobile before heading in for the Brown Belt to report for demesne labor. Seems they always know just when he's down on work. That's right when they call him up. Never while he's jobbing. He's yet to be pulled *off* the job for demesne, instead. That'd be like killing two birds for him. No, they just get him when he's 'tween. Had him up to his chest this morning in the smelly river mud—levee work and flood control. Do it during winter when the water's extra low. There's been no bad flood in recent years, with the short snowfalls, but if a couple of good thunderboomers in a row come up in spring, all that can change in a hurry. BoiCity seems to get washed out pretty good every few years, so they want to keep ready, and the river does run through the Gater district.

Don't never forget that. Can't have nothing touching them nice homes with the cut lawns and the clipped hedges. Oak's always interested by going behind the wall, into Gaterville, up near The Pyramid. Fascinating to see how *that* half lives. By his math, though, half don't sound near right. Not by half. There's way more of us living out here in shitville than there is of them living in Gaterville. A whole shitload more.

That's another one of them, "If you really stop to think on it." To do that you got to stop the vidaud, the picvoice. Good fucking luck doing that.

Don't go thinking on me now! Everyone ought to be rich! God wants you to be rich! You're Brand You! Market! Upwards and Backwards!

Oak's walk back from the big T-184 Gate has been long and tiring, taking over an hour just to get him into the general vicinity of his Tiegs Corner ward. He was forced to credspend on a megbus this morning—infrequent and unreliable sons of bitches, them things—to report to riverside good and damn early—four in the fucking a.m. Coming back out he didn't want to credspend no more, so he hoofed it, walking out across Amity Road, then Lake Hazel Road, then Columbia Road. Hell, he's young yet, he figures. He can take the extra, and BoiCity's not like most megs, not quite so sprawl. Instead of The Pyramid being at the hub and the Gaters tight around, with the Parkers spread out all over hell's half acre around them, like a big wagon wheel, BoiCity butts up against the foothills, making a half circle around. The Gaterville Wall runs from Eagle, northwest, around down to Barber at the southeast. The real Parkerville commences south and west of T-84—always packjammed with traffic—spreading out over the scrubland, the way, Oak guesses, all Parkervilles do. Spreading out to Nampa due west, and to Melba southwest, and even out to the empty sageflats due south. Hell, the parks is almost sprawled to Cheney River. Be there soon now. Megs ain't small, even a half meg, and like all megs BoiCity's got The Pyramid sitting there at its hub, against the tan camelback foothills running a northwest-southeast line to the meg, like a backscreen or a barricade, the bigger pinetop peaks back beyond them. That's wild country way out there. The Pyramid gleams hard in the constant sun like a wedge of gold. You can see it for klicks, and klicks, and klicks. Oak turns around and looks to it, just to gauge how fucking far he's walked. By the ache of his feet and the rumble in his guts, too damn far. He turns and drops his head down and keeps plodding, readjusting his sungoggles and tugging the frayed bill of his jobcap against the sudden gritty gusts of wind. It's best to watch your feet. No straight, or level, or uncracked damn streets in the Parker district. All makeshift and potholes. Biggest roads mostly are paved, but with weeds coming up through every seam. The sideroads are dust-cloudy dirt, a thick powder, turning into slick bronze diarrhea mud the second it ever rains hard enough. It's all linemill, storedepot, manushop, stripmall, prefabs-on-slabs, parklot, and chainlink fence out here in the parks. Off the main arteries, it's mobile, after mobile, after mobile, staked out on small plots with scruff scratchgardens and jacked-up vehics. It's plain shit.

On upleft:

...so I say, bring it on, my friend! We in BoiCity are ready to meet any challenge...

On upright:

...what you really need is HydroPure, the drop-in tabs that kill anything...

On downleft:

...for urban control, the Coyote-Be-Gone minimister seems to work best in tight spaces...

On downright:

...so what you really want to do is diversify that parkport of yours...

Alright! Oak decides to try the bootstrap option as a way to put off lunch for as long as he can. He pushes through the grimy, glass doors of the next Downright DayTrade he comes to. Like all of them, it's crowded and noisy inside, packed with the smelly bodies of the noon-time swarm. Day laborers trying to get ahead for God, for Corp, for Market. Maybe Oak used to feel that way, back when downsizing felt like a small vacation and workcreds were just funnymoney to him. The cheap linoleum is worn to the concrete in the high traffic spots in front of each cubicle. He has to wait twenty minutes, stomach churning, for a carrel finally to open up. When at last he gets to sit down, Oak can't identify from which end the guy before him was passing gas. Smells all the same. Rotting potato, old roadkill, stagnant storm drain. Before long he can't smell it. Oak activates his parkport code and conducts a few standard deals. His markstrat keeps him mainly local, going only with corps and concerns he knows by his own work experience. Then for diversifying just a touch, he runs with a few Arcwide big boys—NanoTech, NRA. Old reliables. For the most part, Oak holds his own. He ain't ever crashed out yet, by God. He ain't struck the big DollArcs yet, neither. Not even close. But shit a brick, TexArc wasn't built in a day. *That* nestegg takes time. As usual, all the hottips on Downright sound like horseshit. He does pick up a few more shares of Sawtooth Fluid. Good corp, Sawtooth. He's worked stints for them a dozen times. And folks'll always need water, right? After about thirty minutes, Oak gets too dizzy to think shareprice anymore, so he shuts off, stands up, and elbows his way out of the shop. He's sweating heavy and the river mud has caked dry to his coveralls. He knocks off as many chunks as he can as soon as he steps outside. Back out on the street, the air is little fresher than inside. No weather has passed through in weeks. The current invert's getting pretty brownbutted up against the foothills. Winter's worst for air. At least the heat stays down most the time. Otherwise the oldsters would be dropping off like flies, like in summer. Winter keeps off some malaria, the breakbone, and the west nile, too. All them damn mex diseases they bring with them when they come north. The cholera's the constant worry. *Just be careful which hole you drink out of is all.*

On upleft:

...freedom ain't wage-slavery...

Traffic is thick on Ronald Boulevard. So's the exhaust, clouds of it trailing every vehic. Oak needs to cross six lanes and you can't trust nobody to pay attention to the lights. He takes off running, mid-block, and dodges his way out to the center line. There he gets stranded for a time and almost run down by some jackass in an old Desert Storm. Being the driver sits near three meters high, them damn things don't handle worth shit. He manages to ding the back of it good with a chunk of pavement as it tear-asses away, but no way the driver felt or even heard it. Thick and loud is how they build Storms.

On upright:

...I feel the need! The need for feed! Stop by SpeedFeed today! [hardcut; vidfeed: Serv standing dazed on his empty plot next to his scratchgarden with tire tracks running through it] Don't come home to no home! Mobile jacking is statistic crime one, these days! Get Iron Dick wheellocks for peace of mind! [hardcut; vidfeed: happers tubed on] Need to git some vit? Come to GitVit quick!...

The far sidewalk's crammed. Oak can barely bust his way onto it. Everyone's hurrying back to jobs after their lunchthirty. Things will lighten down in a bit. Lots of dogs are at the garbage, sometimes scrapping over it in packs. That's good. Less for the coyotes at night. Oak walks six slow blocks southwest and pops in at the showroom of Parker Motors. As usual, it's empty. Not a happer in sight. Hap Straw's standing there, though, drinking chickweed coffee and doing nothing. He's wearing his god-awful Terd collarshirt and tie. *Jesus H. Christ. Who the hell does he think he's fooling?* Hap and Oak have worked lots of crews together. You don't get much more Serv than Hap.

"You look a goddamned fool," Oak calls out.

Hap puts down his coffee and comes toward him, beaming. "You're the one head to toe in shit," Hap replies as they shadow hug, one fist of either man tapping his friend once between the shoulder blades.

"You ain't sold her yet, have you?"

Hap's face goes serious. "I told ya I wouldn't, Oak. But I can't hold off for good, ya know. They'll start breathing down my neck."

"I know." Oak rubs his brow with his dirty hand. This is his third repossess. "I appreciate what you're doing for me, Hap. Can I see her?"

Hap glances around. One other seller in the showroom, and he's pitching way over by the big windows to some happer who's just wandered in.

"Sure, but let's make it quick."

Hap leads Oak out to the back lot. Parked by a wall with no pricesign on the windshield is Oak's little Goblin, long and low with just the six mag wheels. It's been washed and polished up. Oak knows that's a bad sign.

"How long I got?" he asks.

"Couple days, most," Hap says. "Sorry, boss."

"Well shit on me."

"Like I told ya, Oak, we got this credsborrow plan. Everyone does it. Grades are a little steep, but I can get you back out on the road today if you like."

"You want me borrowing creds with more creds, Hap. How you figure that's going to work out?"

"Look, Oak. I just work the job, and all I earn's commissions. Let corp sweat the big stuff. Right? I don't know what else to tell ya."

"Job ain't on the horizon for me again until eight-hundred-thow. You know the yub."

"All the more reason to go with our plan, Oak. You know the show. Sooner you hit your creds mark, sooner the work comes open. You can't fight The Pyramid, buddy."

Workcreds to borrow workcreds to pay off shit you buy with workcreds. There ain't no end to it. Just a high pile of creds to work off before you ever start turning profit. Then when you do get back to jobbing they always size down your ass a week or two after you breakthrough to real earnings. Every goddamn time like clockwork. A goddamned yanktease.

"No offense, Hap. I know none of this is your doing. But fuck your plans. Just be careful you don't turn into a peckerneck yourself."

Oak kicks his way through the showroom double doors. If he's got to run up his workcreds to get back to job he's good and goddamn well going to do it on vit and not on getting his goddamn Goblin out of vend. To-and-fro around Parkerville without your zoomzoom is the true and honest shits, but they'll just end up pulling another repossess on the damn thing. Hell, Oak bought the vehic on a repovend in the first place. Hap's told him that's how Parker Motors generates most their cap. Just how fucking dumb do they think he is?

On upright:

...EasyCred, your all-in-one creds store! Friendly grades! No creds down! Come—[off hardcut; moment of feed disrupt]—friends, this is your fight. Good pay or bum work. You need to choose. Fight for the full product of your labor...

Four blocks west is the nearest McSlurrys. Around it is a SpeedFeed and a FeedSpeed, a VitGit and a GitVit, all with parklots full and thrudrives jammed 24/7. Oak heads straight for The Arcs. You are what you feed, so only the best for him. Pure shit in, pure shit out. Inside he goes through the joke of waiting in line to order, like their prod ain't all the same slurry. Oak's worked the killhouses more than once, them and the Simplot tater lines. He knows better. Gaters may get to chew their franchise food, but Parkers tube direct skin and bone, fat and flesh, tail and hoof, bowels and balls. He's seen it mixed live. The kid taking orders can't be eleven. He looks a bit bleary eyed. Fastfeed can profit the juniors pennies and work them any and as many hours as corp needs. McSlurrys was his first post as a junior. Oak knows the drill. Back then, Oak could smile the suckup better than any other counterjockey. He did it for the fun of bluffing the ninnies—like a game. All a big joke to Oak first coming to age and starting out. Managers used to give sell prizes to them, too, like a handful of real fries to eat. Those tasted damn good, too. Inside the shop only the McHappy jingle plays, over and over. On his upright, AutoShopdrop takes over on premises and reads out the menu while he waits his turn. Oak's got to smile. Same menu as way back. He's still got it memorized. When it comes his turn in line he recognizes the suck-up the kid behind the counter is giving him.

"Listen, junior. Just make mine a shitbritches." That's crewtalk for The Hurry Slurry, the quickest and cheapest tubefeed. The kid smiles for real at Oak, knowing an old hand when he sees one, and rings up his credscard. In Parker districts, McSlurrys don't even take DollArcs. The boy tells him Booth 75D. Oak makes his way down to the far end of the store and slides onto the shiny, yellow plastic bench. Only one of the other boothfeeders nods to him, a skinny blond who's been sucking on way too many tobaccosticks lately from the looks of her. Oak catches a glimpse of her right hooter just above the red ring of skin where her feedtube goes in. The titty's floppy and baggy and kind of blueish, see-through-skinned. It don't do much for him. He undoes the velcro of his coveralls down past his solar plexis and untapes his feedtube from his ribs. Before uncapping it, he reaches up and pulls down a feedtube dangling overhead. He brings the two ends together and screws them tight. Last thing you want is Slurry squirting all over the place. The shit smells like, well, shit. Once he's go, he pushes the big orange button marked D in front of him on the table. After a delay, the graybrown sludge comes inching down along the tube. It's hard getting started, being crusty on top, but it breaks through and Oak feels his gut fill up fast. In and out in fifteen minutes. On his way out, he gets his barrel of cokecola from the fountain. He's got to hold the plastic pail in both hands as he walks, and he sucks the drink down as fast as he can through the straw. Delivers the best rush that way, and the blow should kill his appetite for the rest of the day. When he's done he tosses the huge cup to some kids alongside the road. They use them to build and break hand-made damns and play with in the mud. Oak recalls how he used to.

Midafternoon and Oak figures he's started a minor spendspree. Might as well keep going with it. You got to get in debt to stay in debt. He decides to head over to Bullet Bobs to check out that new minimister. Can't kill a man, but fuck him up good. Pepper a damn coyote, though, and Oak's been hearing the critters sniffing around under his mobile for the past few nights. Can't fucking have that. Turns out old Bobs having a markdown. Oak knows damn well it's hype, but he figures to give his credspending a kick upward to see if he can't shake something loose. Why not creds for one of these? The minimister scattershots plastic pellets, a thousand or so at a go. Breaks the skin, but won't go through bone, so it ain't strictly lethal. The pistol's a nasty little fuck. Tucks neat into the palm of your hand. The seller at Bobs is only too happy to throw in extra ammopacks to sweeten the deal. Oak pretends he thinks he's getting a big break, just to watch the guy think he's smart as hell. Bullet Bobs is busy as Oak's ever seen. Automatics flying off the shelves. People getting spooked serious by this new EVe business. Far as Oak's concerned, that place is a long damn way off, but the drone on Vieworld is all about them embedded sleeper terror-cells. Can't be too careful. Shit like that. *Yank*, Oak thinks. EVe wants god-damn BoiCity that much, especially the parks, they can good and yanking well come and get the fuckmother. Welcome to her, too.

Downleft:

...comes only from God on high, Who I don't fear! No! I don't fear God! And do you know why, my friend? Because I know God loves me! And how do I know of God's great love? Because God so loves me that He gave His own Son to save me from my sins! Me! Can you imagine doing that yourself for anyone else—[off hardcut; moment of feed disrupt; vid-feed: kindly older man, tousled white-haired, round red cheeks]—and do

you imagine for a moment, friends, that the boss really cares a fig about you? About your kids at home? About the neighborhood your kids grow up in? About the kind of school they go to?...

Downright:

[autovoice-flashpic: clear bluesea, clear bluesky, bump white sand island with three swaying palms, sailboat entering from left] One hundred and sixtysix jobapps pending! Searchmode doublego! Recent jobhist: Simplot tatergunner, Brigade Corp chempools, Sawtooth Fluid tanktruck ops, HP linejob, BoiCity Hydro storm sewer ops, more data available! Workcreds pending: sevenhundredtwelve thousand eighthundred eleven! Current credgrades: sixtyone and onequarter percent! Searchmode doublego! Jobfind likely at eightytwo percent! Daytrade options...

A four-klick walk later, Oak's showing off his purchase to the boys at The Slop-Chute, and in particular to Jiplap Ball, who's plum nuts over any kind of firearms.

"How the holy hell you afford this little number, Oak? God in hell, I ain't never seen one of these before."

"They just come out with them, Jiplap. Pitching them as coyote killers. And I *can't* goddamn afford it. Just the fucking point, ain't it?"

Jiplap betrays no opinion about Oak's last remarks. He pretends to be busy admiring the multibarrels and the gas springaction for the pellets. "Damn clever design. These fucks must come out at about a thousand klicks an hour," he guesses. "A damn good clip." Besides, everybody knows Oak's been touched hard by the glassy.

"Yeah, ya think so, Jip?" Oak reacts harshly to his friend's casual observation. He grabs the minimister out of Jiplap's hands and points it at him. "Maybe we ought to time them out on your sorry ass."

Jiplap shrinks back on his barstool and covers his face. *Oak's just crazy enough to do stupid shit. Always has been since a kid.* Over the years Jiplap's seen him split wide open hundreds of dogs and coyotes with shot and blades of all description, and he knows Oak's killed at least one fella in a bad brawl a couple years back. He was there and saw it himself. Oak crushed the guy's skull with a long-handled pipe wrench. Bone and brain sprayed all over the worksite. Turns out Oak was right, though, about which bypass valve to shut down, so the super, instead of turning Oak in for altercation and work stoppage, just made up that the other guy experienced an unfortunate workplace accident. One simple report and that was that. Stories are, Oak's killed a few other guys since then, too, but Jiplap's only heard about them. "Jesus, Oak," Jiplap pleads, "you don't have to do that now. Come on, buddy."

Oak lowers the minimister and shakes his head a few times, hard, like he's trying to dislodge something in there. "Lord, it ain't even loaded, Jip," he says flatly. "Hold your damn water."

Oak turns to the barkeep and orders up a round of Oly for the whole damn bar. Got to be about a hundred guys, all of them smelling somewhere between sweat and shit. The keep asks Oak if he's sure, and Oak snarls back, "Yeah, damn sure, *and* make it a supersize for every last goddamned son-of-a-bitching one of them." That's like an entire bucket of suds for every Parker in the joint.

The keep smiles and holds up his hands. "Hey, no problem, Bud." He gets to siphoning out the beers.

When folks realize what's going on, a cheer rises up and turns into a chant, "Oak! Oak! Oak! Oak!"

Oak jumps up on the bar, waves his arms over his head, and starts shouting back, "Hey, it's the water, fellas! It's the fuckmothering water!"

While pouring, the barkeep laughs and tells Jiplap the Olympia sellrep will piss his pants with happy when he hears about all this free pitching. The bar flies drink steady for about thirty or forty minutes, with only some of the guys complaining about having to wait until after six for

Youchoose to open up for anything you want to watch, not just a choice of the daytime pantywaist godshows.

After springing for the big round, Oak keeps buying only for the four or five guys he's with at the bar. None of them worries much about it or thinks it strange. Free beer is free. Glassy or not, Oak's a big boy and can do what he likes. Oak's getting bent pretty good, too. Hell, they all are.

Then the totoblank. *God damn, that fucks you up.* Then over the all4s the taste. *Shit, not the fuckmother taste.* Total imagesense. Rocks your vieworld. The crown of every guy's head goes hot. Everyone freezes in his seat. It's like you're in someone else's eyes. In someone else's body.

You're running through some hallways, breathing hard, it's dark, there's lots of corners to go around, your guts feels like you've got to drop a load of mexvit. [Vieworld talkheads always describe the sensation as being "battle primed"; Oak thinks of it as being right on the edge of scared shitless.] *You go around one last corner and into a tight room—like a bunker, walls thick and concrete—and there's an odd flag pinned up and lots of maps of TexArc with target marks drawn all over them and at the far end, a big picture of that Adolph Stalin dude stuck on the wall staring back at you with them dead cold eyes of his. Then a scramble of guys in strange uniforms push back from a table in one corner, all of them reaching for weapons at once and you swing around and level your mister at them. In one quick pull they're all nothing—all five or six of the bastards—but a thick cloud of red after a deafening whoosh. You're hollering: "Yeah, fuck!" But then a stab like you never felt before pierces your left kidney and you're thrown up against a wall. All of a sudden your right elbow cracks and you're down twisting around on the cold, hard floor in pain—terrible bad. Out of nowhere a boot comes down on your throat—heavy—and you grab it with both your hands, but you're not strong enough to pry it off. A dark face, with a burly mustache and black eyes that look like they got no pupils, hovers over you, solemn, menacing, crazed looking. The bastard's wearing some kind of a nightblue beret with a strange insignia on it—a circle of gold stars or some damn thing—and he narrows his nasty eyes and bends forward to inspect your face up close. So close you can smell the stinking spices on his hot breath. Then the pressure on your adam's apple gets sharper and you just can't breathe. You flat can't, no matter what you do. A sick-assed smile comes to the bastard's plump, greasy lips, seeing you not being able to breathe. Then the business end of a pistol barrel brings your eyes into a close focus right above your forehead. Holy fuckmother! This shit's going to pop a rock into your skull! There's a sick smirk on this sick fuck's face—but right then he gets wiped by friendly fire coming from the doorway. At the same damn second the outcorp bastard manages to pull the trigger and blow your fucking head off.*

The taste terms.

Most guys in The Slop-Chute have pissed themselves bad. A few evacuated their bowels at the last. Once their scalps stop tingling and they can gain their feet, they push back in their chairs and make a mad dash for the pooper. Oak hasn't pissed himself during a taste in years, not since his own couple of months of CorpTroop training. Training for CorpTroop makes a taste seem tame as vidsex. A walk in the damn grass. Jiplap, on the other hand, still has whiz trickling down his leg once the feed cuts, plus he's spilled his beer all down the bar. "Fuck me!" he yells when coming out of it enough to see what he's done.

On the all4s:

Thirteen heroes make the ultimate sacrifice today when flushing out an EVe terrorcell just north of Atlanta in the BHC! [talkheads; flashpic: map of Atlanta meg vicinity] Holed up in the mountains and obviously preparing for subversive tactics...

Even while the talkheads are yubbing the routine jingofrenzy sets off. "Them goddamn EVe sons a bitches!" someone shouts out.

"Ought to just take their asses out!"

"Fuckmother gayboy libbies!"

"I say tacnuke them ragheads back to the goddamn stone age and be goddamn done with it!"

The barkeep reaches underneath the counter and flips the switch to get the light show going. Suddenly big, white hologram stars inside a thin, red circle float everywhere in the deep blue interior of The Slop-Chute. These symbols seem like you could grab hold of them but they can pass right through a guy, too. The all4s turn to corpanthem with cutshots and vidclips of ArcGround, ArcAir, ArcSea, and ArcSpace in action. Landwarriors gun down batches of ragheads storming over sand dunes. Wedge-shaped stealthwings shoot down rival box-shaped fighters with astonishing firepower and ease. Six stiletto cruisemissiles rise up off the deck of a narrow stealthdestroyer then streak off toward the ocean horizon. A highorbit HEL system charges up then lets fly a laser bolt down towards earth. With each Arc kill guys whoop and cheer. The booming overvoice starts up, too, shouting out messages like SUPPORT OUR CORP-TROOPS! and THE PRIDE OF POWER!

Before too long the whole damn place goes wild and breaks out into their one and favorite chant, "Tex-Arc! Tex-Arc! Tex-Arc! Tex-Arc!"

Jiplap notices Oak ain't chanting. He has to shout to be heard over the din, "Groundsmen or Netsmen you figure, Oak?" He's got that suck-up tone to his voice.

Before answering Oak looks down at his own joke of a pellet gun sitting before him on the bar. "Should be Groundsmen doing the dirty work like that, Jip," he says. "But they don't issue misters to regular Groundsmen. No damn way." Oak shakes his head. "Something ain't right."

"Netsmen, then," Jiplap shrugs, shaking his leg, but otherwise ignoring the mess he's sitting in. "Not worth pissing over."

ArcGround CorpTroops come direct from Servs, like themselves. Oak ought to know. A Parker can join up any old time he gets disgusted with ups and downs of jobbing. Then, if the bootcamp don't kill him, he can serve proud, doing the Arc gruntwork. And Ground is the grunt. No mistake about that. If there's shit to do, you know who. A Groundsman serves proud til he ends up dead. That's the only way Oak's ever heard of a guy retiring from the corps, except for the way Oak got himself out, but that sure as hell wasn't normal. Of course, the profit's better in than out of CorpTrooping, that much is true. Still, it seemed a natural fool's game to Oak. But it taught him shit. Shit he otherwise never could have known. Taught him how these damn ArcNet come from Terds, not Servs, and are special-trained, plain and simple killers you don't want to tangle with, no fucking matter what. A damn Netsman will just as soon thumb your eyeballs into the back of your skull and suck your feedtube dry as goddamn look at you. Mean psycho assholes, the Netsmen.

"Go the hell wash off, Jip," Oak tells him. "You're going to smell like coyote when that dries."

Jiplap sits still and orders up a fresh Oly. "Christ, I already smell like a damn dog, Oak. Don't see much difference to the matter."

A taste always sobers up everybody cruel, about like they got to start all over again. His boys sure do, and Oak still buying the rounds like he don't give a yank for all his tomorrows. The bar gets back to normal for a good while before Oak strikes it lucky. So does Jiplap and some eight or ten more guys around the place. At five-thirty, exact, the hotflash at the upleft of all of their downrights starts blinking crazy. Joboffer! Joboffer! Bingo! Bingo! Sawtooth Fluid a-calling!

"Makes sense what with them splitting today," Jiplap points out.

"Makes horseshit sense maybe," Oak says back.

Nothing's making real sense anymore, he says to himself. Oak even toys a minute at the idea of turning them down flat, just to see what would happen. Saying no to joboffers just ain't an option. Everybody knows that.

They flash you—you jump to. If you don't, the credsgoons will get all over your ass for not working off your credspending. And credsgoons might be a sight *worse* than yanking Netsmen. Even so, Oak gives it some serious consideration before the few specifics follow on the downright. Start next day. Report five in the a.m. for transit, George Station—outer Gater district, just south of the Brown Belt, corner of Beacon and Longmont. Pack bag. Overnights likely. General maintenance/troubleshooting at Arrowrock Dam, Anderson Ranch Dam, Cascade Dam, possible points further interior.

"That's wilderness area," says Jiplap, sounding iffy about it. "I ain't never been."

Oak's been quite a few times for jobs before this one, driving the super-wide water trucks along narrow, canyon roads.

"Scares you," he confirms. "Lots of quiet out there. Lots of open. At nighttime, there's lots and lots of dark."

"Lots of damn coyotes?" asks Jiplap, sounding even more worried than before.

"Hell, Jip, coyotes is the least of your damn worries out there."

☆ ☆ ☆ ☆ ☆ ☆

Oak's back at his mobile in the heart of the Tiegs Corner ward by seven. The walk over's a blur, what with being pretty good and bent on top of the glassy. The streets are caked dry and dusty with the no rain, so they don't smell so bad of shitwater, but the garbage piles is high and reeky, and the dogshit is everywhere underfoot in tall, turd heaps. Little ragbundles of kids run about like so many damn rabbits, shouting all to beat hell. The mobiles are parked tight on their small plots, acres and acres and acres of them, laid out like a huge graveyard for the living. On one side of Oak's little homestead is a big family of fat people all the time arguing with one another and a baby howling. On the other side is a young couple who like to throb yank all night through. *Working themselves toward becoming just like the fat family on his other side*, is all Oak can ever think about them. *That gal's an authentic screamer, she is*, which for some reason pisses him off more than the yowling baby. Lots of nights those two come at him in stereo. Oak waves back at some of the folks along his road, but he don't stop to talk like usual. Too bent, and he's got job tomorrow early. His mobile is dinky, silver, potato-bug shaped. Reflects off the sun good. It stands on four cinder blocks because he sold off the tires long ago. Hell, he ain't going anywhere soon. Out back in his scratchgarden—which he don't do a damn thing to grow—he climbs on and bikepedals up the generator for twenty minutes or so to give him enough battery electric for the evening. He goes inside to quick change and come back out to rinse his coveralls in a tub of tan water he gets from the one spigot across the road. They don't get anywhere near clean, but that does knock the rivermud off. Oak hangs the coveralls outside on the line hoping they might be dry enough come morning. Doesn't really matter if they are or not. He'll wear them anyway. He pours the tub water into his mobile's storetank and throws in a couple HydroPure tabs before relocking the cap. Once these chores are done, it's pretty much dark. Hunger starts to haunt him. He goes inside to finish off the last of his Nilla Wafers—them being sweet usually puts a stop to his hollow stomach for the night. Running nose-to-back in his mobile is the small liveroom, then the open-face kitchenette, a pooper the size of a storecloset, then the tiny sleeproom at the butt end of the potatobug. If Oak was any taller—and he ain't tall to begin with—he'd have to bend his neck to keep his head from scraping the ceiling. If he was to stretch his arms out full to either side, he could just about touch both flank walls of the mobile at once. In the summertime his tin can is like an oven and in wintertime can get like an icebox. ChannelWeather on downleft says it's not supposed to get too terrible cold tonight, so Oak won't waste the power heating her up. Besides, he's managed to get his hands on four or five good indian blankets over the years and doesn't mind at all wrapping up in them, even during the off blizzard that might still come through. Saves creds.

Oak settles down in his lollchair in the liveroom, putting the minimister handy in case he hears coyotes outside. *Wouldn't mind peppering one or two tonight, just to see how she works.* Past six o'clock all sorts of feeds come on the downleft. Total Youchoose idiversion, like they say. Nothing else like it in the world. Oak likes the sports best, either the NASVEHIC racing, WFW grappling, or the MeBall. All of them have lots of knocks. Tonight he picks MeBall. It's not playoff time, but teams are jockeying hard for slots in the late season. The MFL has five divisions, one for each of the regional corpents, with lots of teams in each division, so many Oak can't always keep track. Hell, some of the Dmega megs like BostonPhiladelphia or Atlanta might have three, four teams apiece. Tonight Oak's BoiCity Trappers are playing the Cleveland Browns from back east in the GLR. Huge game. Lots for the postseason riding on this one. He's ready in his chair, three plasticans of lukewarm Oly from the fridgeunit close to hand. He aligns in chan5457 for the pregame. The announcers run through the line-ups, review the records, and talk up the game's key match-ups. Tonight's contest is sponsored by GoodHands, running sametime on upright. Sometimes Oak can't help but pay it a bit of heed. *GoodHands, Your All-In-One Insurer: tornado, flood, lightening, drought, avalanche, flashfire, heatstroke, famine, pandemic, brownout, blackout, streetcrime, pettycrime, domesticrime, violentcrime, sexcrime, gunfight, roadrage, vehicjack, vehicstrip, vehicollide, mobilejack, terrorstrike, neural overload, mininuke, to name but a handful of your soundmind needs. Try our GoodHands. All at manageable terms. Standard credgrades apply.*

Oak's got to smile. Who's got the creds to throw after any of that? Besides, he's never heard of a Serv's claim getting paid off. Soundmind's for Terds, for Terds and for the damn Crats.

Comes at last to game time, and Oak has to make his select. That's never a hesitation. Any team he watches he goes with the QB, special with the Trappers, because that means Peyton Unitas—the best damn thrower in the league. Guy can chuck a pigskin eighty damn yards. Oak scrolls down the idiversion player menu and synchs in. Just like that, there he is, every inch of him total imagesensing Peyton Unitas right down there on the damn field. Oak Wat imagesenses himself/Unitas jogging out on the field, hearing the crowd roar, pacing along the sidelines, calling plays in the huddle, talking on the headphones with his coaches up in the watchboxes, taking snaps and making handoffs and hitting his receivers downfield.

Reclined in his lollchair, Oak jerks and twitches during the game, avoiding their blitz, sometimes getting his bell rung hard, sliding feet-first a couple of times for crucial first downs. Wat/Unitas is playing one hell of a game. At halftime Oak desynchs and has time enough to stick his yanker out his mobile's door to piss, then downs two of his beers. Second half is nip and tuck, the game coming down to a final two-minute drill for the Trappers. Down by four, they got to drive seventy yards for the win. Oak Unitas will get them there, by god. One play he scrambles for nineteen yards on a fourth-and-fifteen. Three times he hits quick down-and-outs for good short yardage. Twice he dares throwing down the gut, threading the needle both times for long gainers. The home Trapper crowd's going damn harebrained. Oak couldn't tell you where the BoiCity Municipal Stadium is located, though. He's sure never seen it, or knows any guy who has. Nobody he knows has ever been to a game for real. From the feed, the field looks to be indoors. Maybe it's underground, probably way into the Gater district somewhere. *That sounds the most likely.* With time run out, Oak finds himself dodging tacklers deep in the red zone, circling and backcircling, trying to find an open receiver in the endzone. Finally he spots his man and on the dead run rifles one of his patented Unitas bullets. Zam! Hits his man square between the numbers! Trappers beat the goddamn Browns!

Oak's sweaty and tired and cheerful in his chair as he savors the victory along with sipping down his last Oly. Yes sir, beer tastes good to a man. He knows he's got to get up extra early next morning, but like usual after a game, he flips over to chan69. Hell, he can't resist. Oak unbuckles and wiggles out of his work pants, kicking them off onto the floor. He checks to make sure he's got his roll of paper towels down alongside his chair. Then he sinks back and closes his eyes. Oak's hips are curiously narrow and his legs look like two scrawny cords of sinew, pale yellowy and their skin needing a good scouring, especially around the knees. He's taut but fragile, rubbery durable like a tendon but also right on the verge of snapping, maybe like one of them Chihuahua dogs. His preset is for the postgame cheerleader doublefuck, a chan69 classic. Tonight he menus up one mex and one squaw, the first being soft and seductive, the second wiry and aggressive. Like always, they grab him while he's walking off the field and through the tunnel toward the locker room. Giggling, and with their giant titties flopping around inside their tight sweaters with the Trappers logo stretched across them, they drag him off to some deserted equipment room, fondling him up stiffy as they go. Like always, he ain't Peyton Unitas, or Troy Namath, or any other damn MeBaller QB no more. He's him—Oak. For virtual. In his own virbod fixing to get his own virocks off with two peach virhos of his own ichoosing. Yep, nothing but the best for him. Pure yank throb Dmega selfoblige over the best damn virsex align on the feed. He's got the hardnob from the getgo, but don't even need to use his hand. That's the beauty of chan69. Does all the work for you, near good as a taste. In fact you can't hardly tell a difference. By the time the threesome shuts the door behind them in the sweat smell of the equipment room, Oak's got a liplock on the mexgal and tonguing furious while the squawho is down on her knees hoovering hard his dingdong. Not being a particular long laster, Oak quick turns her around and bends her over the jumbo pile of dirty uniforms always there in the middle of the floor. Lifting up the scant skirt and tugging down the thong panties and wham he's in her, pounding doggy for all he's worth. Everybody knows that's how them redskinhumps like it best.

Bow-wow. The mexho strips off and starts frenching the gasping squawgal. Then Oak switches things up and does the mex a few whichways, her shouting out fast and high-pitch in her frantic speak. Mainly he does her missionary, the way mexsluts like it best. The most honest gratifying part of the whole thing is the way chan69 makes out the heft of your viryank to be, both girthwise and reachwise, *much* improved over your actual. It gives you a bangbone the size of a billy club. Each virho yips and huffs out apt when it's her turn to get reamed, even flinching away some when Oak plies his mantool in extra deep. He breaks off after a while and has them do some lesy things to one another so's he can calm a bit. When he feels like he can last some more he joins back in. They end up as he lots of times has them ending up. Obligingly, the squaw spreads wide her own asscheeks while Oak cornholes her like nobody's business—just something to him about cornholing—while meantime the mexho kneels behind Oak spreading apart his own asscheeks so's she can lick his cornhole clean. Good Lord almighty. Just something about a mexgal doing that to him too. He's soon done for. The jet of his jism near touches the ceiling of his mobile, leaving his pink little yanker small, floppy, and slimy as a minnow.

☆ ☆ ☆ ☆ ☆ ☆

Lying on his mat back in the sleeproom a little later, Oak realizes, for all that time he spent in his lollchair, the glassy hadn't been bothering him. Not at all. As soon as he thinks that, though, it's right back on him, and hard. Goddamn upleft telling him to hate this; fucking upright telling him to buy that; fuckmother downleft telling him to believe this; yanksucking downright telling him to do that. 24/7/365. Either he's got to find a way to stay permanent-like in his lollchair, or else break off for good what causes the glassy—whatever in the goddamned fuckmothering hell that might turn out to be. Oak ain't been able to penetrate far into a root origin yet at all. Hell, not nearly. His mind's mainly too damn cluttered with shit to think square. Being his assigned sleepspan, the pitch on his feed, both vid and aud, has notched down a touch. This eases conditions in his head til morning comes around again anyway. The roar and quake of vehics charging by out front has backed off, too. People gone to their secondshifts by now. Strangest is his neighbors to both sides being still for once. Creates kind of a nice, lone moment for Oak where he can just wonder how many of his blankets to pile on top of him for the night. Along his floor, the sound of scratching comes to him. Too meek to be coyote. Probably only brown rats. Oak can't tell if the rustling comes above or below the flooring. He don't rightly care. Too damn tired to mess with it, now. It's been another long and pretty useless day.

Oak pulls his covers tighter around his shoulders and curls on his side into a ball. One good thing he supposes the glassy will do for you every now and again is slow you down enough to the point where you might focus on one particular thing for a time. The sleepspan can help with that, too, if he don't go too far and think on nothing at all. And that moment, right then, is when Oak finally hears it, sees it, and takes the trouble to watch it all, his eyes shut and him cozy in his mat, watch it all the way through fed to him on all of the four. Hold on now. On the all4s? Just how in the hell can *that* be? That would make it creed, like a taste. Ceo, like *Time to Know!* But it looks like just one of them damn recall spots for the fuckwad local votes they hold every so often. BoiCity candidates squawking and blowing yokel smoke up your ass is all. These ain't ever on all4s coming at you from onhigh. In fact, as Oak heeds it—as it slowly sucks him in—it strikes him as just the contrary to onhigh. The spot is soft, idle, near to the point where you got to strain to make it out. *That's* what draws Oak's notice so much in the first place. It's not trying to *shout* you in. Oak's never seen nothing like it. On his all4s, just a fella talking to him, with a tone in his voice like he might be making sense for you to think over. Not like he's decided what the sense is and you got to buy it. This time it's up to you. The guy's an older fella, respectful looking, dressed plain in a white, wrinkly suit and string tie, holding a worn widebrim white hat in his hands. He's got a headfull of stark, white hair with one wild lock curling down onto his forehead. Every once in a while he pushes it back up out of his way, but it's no use. The curl keeps falling down onto his forehead, funny like. His gray eyes are smart and easy, too. His cheeks, a little plumpy and rosy, make you imagine the fella's just puffed up a long flight of stairs to get to where he's standing, or else he just might of had himself a small nip of strong drink right before commencing to talk to you. Bottom line, this elder fella ain't out to tug your rope. Oak lies still and considers his every word.

My friends, call me Uncle Wobbly. I'm here to talk to you about the abolition of the wage system. About freedom from wage-slavery. About joining the one big union. You know, friends, freedom and democracy don't mean wage-slavery. It can't. How can things be free and democratic when you got a sourpuss boss all the time telling you what to do and how to do it, what to believe and how to behave, where to live and on how little pay you got to make do with? Seems like people ought to be able to write their own ticket in life on a fair and even playing field, not one where rich folks got all the big houses for their families to live in, got all the up-to-date schools for their children to go to, got all the good-paying jobs for themselves to enjoy. How can that be right? Plain folks work every bit as hard as rich folks do. Heck, friends, I bet if you stop and think about it, plain folks work a good bit harder. Don't you? So where are the just rewards for your labor? Huh? Where are they? Seems to me the only kind of freedom this rich-folks democracy leaves us plain folks is free to lose. Think it over what I mean by that. My friends, this is a class war going on. Don't be fooled otherwise. This is your fight. Don't be a slacker. Join the one big union. IWW is the International Workers of the World. IWW members are plain folks, working folks just like you and me, from all around the globe. IWW fights for more wages, better working conditions, shorter hours, emancipation—in short, friends, solidarity. IWW fights for the abolition of the wage system, for the abolition of unemployment, for shop democracy, for good pay instead of bum work. Think it over. Join the one big union. Fight for the full product of your labor. I'm running for the recall vote to put our voice out into the world. The voice of the worker. Only the voice of the one big union of all workers can change things for the better. You know that as well as I do. Think it over. Vote Wobbly. It's the greatest thing on earth.

☆ ☆ ☆ ☆ ☆ ☆

Bleached Wheat clenches between his teeth the fattest and the finest of hand-rolled cigars this country has to offer. He inhales, appreciates, then blows upward an extended puff of thick, ivory smoke that collides against the terrorproof glass of the long, ornate window, rounded at the top, from which he's gazing out over the broad and sun-soaked Plaza de la Relocalización. Rising high above the plaza is an odd X-shaped column, visible throughout the maxtropical city. At its base is an austere, white sculpture of a man with one elbow resting on his knee, depicted in the act, no doubt, of doing something important. Gazing into the future, say. José Sharon, is it? Bleached Wheat doesn't much try to keep his history straight. What good is history, anyway? What possible purpose can it serve? It's over and done with. Only invites unfavorable comparisons. Come to think of it, Bleached Wheat doesn't have much use for the concept of the future, either. That only prompts unreasonable longings. He does enjoy this yearly official state visit, however. The grandiose event feeds so well, reassuring his fellow TexArcans they have a ceo not only confident to travel abroad, but sagely abreast of global affairs. Yes, he likes how they do things down here. The slower pace. Their sense of color. The tall and exotic drinks. Behind him he hears what must be Ponzi entering sedately through the stateroom's double doors. A hushed squeak of gelsole runners comes across the polished parquetry of the Palacio de la Relocalización. Bleached Wheat asks without turning around, “What’s the news?”

“Sir, we’ve trailed the slice.”

“And?”

“Dispatched Countermeasures.”

“With what success?”

“Eight killed, two flushed.”

“And ours?”

“All deadcount, sir. One kia, two selfterm.”

Bleached Wheat puffs several times on his cigar to help him think. Such a risk to have taken. “Flushed where?”

“Uncertain at this time. They’re hunkered down or they’ve slipped out.”

“Slipped out?” Even the chance of that happening surprises Bleached Wheat. “How? Underground?”

“That’s the only way they could move, sir.”

Bleached Wheat flicks his ashes onto the shining floor. “If that’s the case, they certainly have become capable at this underground business. Have they *not*, Ponzi?”

The question is pointed, and Ponzi knows it. “Yes, they have, sir. *If* that’s the case.”

Bleached Wheat vaguely enjoys jousting with Ponzi. He and Jitney are the only two who will even hint at backtalk. That’s why they’re his top two subceos—at the moment. *Have to keep a close eye on these types to notice exactly when their toe goes over the line.* This underground business certainly is something new—and unanticipated. Maybe these old marxites have been busier than he thinks. “And this slice. Is it still running?”

“As far as we can tell, it is, sir. But we don’t know how. I’ve never seen anything quite like it.”

“More.”

“It’s a lowlevel embed, sir, opportunistic rather than invasive. Seems just to run wherever it can introduce itself without drawing attention. That makes it difficult to trail, backwards or forwards."

"Interesting."

As subceo boss of ArcNet, Ponzi is not permitted to find anything merely "interesting." The job doesn't afford him the luxury of idle curiosity, and Ponzi knows full well Bleached Wheat is never a tourist in anything he undertakes, not even during this sham state visit they make every year to The Promised Land. Nothing transpires without its reasons. The trouble is, the really critical reasons Bleached Wheat keeps to himself. That's what has Ponzi worried about this strange slice. The boss is after one thing, but simulating he's after another. Ponzi can feel the misdirection in his cortices. Coverup and dodge is what ArcNet does best, and Ponzi's extraordinarily adept at it. Bleached Wheat is just eerily better.

And here it comes. Bleached Wheat adds, "And also unacceptable."

"The hell of it is, sir," Ponzi knows he can't let this sound too much like excuse, "we can't tell how the slice is doing what it does."

"How do you mean?"

"It could be autocycle, but that seems unlikely to me, sir."

"Oh? And why?"

"It's too fast and too smart. It chinks our firewalls and rucksacks our signals without ever triggering a mine or a torp. That's impossible, but our hunter-seekers don't even seem to notice it's there. And weirdest of all..." Ponzi has to hesitate.

"And weirdest of all, what?"

"I know this sounds stupid, sir, but our spinners can't even freak it."

At this news Bleached Wheat tilts his head minimally to one side.

"I've watched it happen myself a half dozen times. When our spinner comes across it, it not only seems to know exactly what's coming, but it's got the zip to evade. No autocycle is intuitive enough for that, and no operator has that kind of reaction time. It's completely fruitcake."

Two, then three clouds of smoke rise against the window pane.

Bleached Wheat's response comes in careful, noncommittal tones, "Now that really is something."

Ponzi is not stupid enough to believe he's off the hook. He decides to probe, cautiously. "Should we keep trying to cleanse the slice, sir?"

The curious question, indicating a countermand of standard ArcNet protocol, makes Bleached Wheat raise an eyebrow. He deliberately drops it back in place before turning to face his subceo, whom he always finds as indistinguishably handsome as the other three bootlicks who staff his inner board of directors. "As a mater of fact, Ponzi, no." If his top subceo wants to play, he'll play. "Let's see where this takes us, shall we? Keep up your ineffectual show of trying to catch it." Bleached Wheat smiles. "ArcNet seems to be doing a fine job in that department, and we don't want whoever, or whatever, to get suspicious. But, yes, by all means make sure you don't really freak the slice."

Ponzi is taken aback. "That could be dangerous, sir. Very dangerous."

Bleached Wheat puffs on his cigar. "It's *all* dangerous, Ponzi."

Through the smoke, the two Crats inspect one another's eyes and facial expressions for a moment.

"And our trail, sir?"

"Oh, yes," Bleached Wheat waves his cigar while with his other hand reaches toward a glass bowl filled with bananas, that most phallic fruit. "Continue your trail, of course. Backwards and forwards—equally. To tell you the truth, Ponzi, I can't decide if I'm more intrigued by where this thing is coming from or by where it's going to."

Ponzi understands this is his cue to simper and comply, but his blood has been heated by their game. He remains stonefaced but courteous. "And when we find either, sir?"

When and not if, thinks Bleached Wheat. The guy's definitely got the rocks. Bleached Wheat now lets him see the raised eyebrow, just as a word to the wise. He needs Ponzi over the short haul, and isn't ready to reboot the job. Not yet. Evenly, even kindly, Bleached Wheat responds, “Bridges to cross, Ponzi. Bridges to cross.”

The gold inlay double doors close pertly behind the subceo. Yes, Bleached Wheat does love to keep his staffers on their toes. That way, they’re less likely to act behind his back. Upper management rule one. This slice, though, is turning out to be legitimately perturbing. Bleached Wheat resolves to get a good handle on it. When he does, it probably will be best to act promptly and belligerently. EVe must have no encouragement at all. At the same time, Bleached Wheat can’t help feeling pleased. A ceo knows, when things threaten to spiral out of hand, potential dividends grow highest. Upper management rule two. Always push the envelope.

Happily, Bleached Wheat has more relaxing duties to perform at the moment. First the majestic procession, then the state dinner, finally the gala commemorative ceremonies in historic Tel Aviv Vieja. Upleft vidops too numerous to calculate. Today marks the forty-fourth anniversary of The New Jerusalem when the children of Israel were airlifted off the Glassea to be resettled on their island—The Promised Land. The slow motorcade will begin within the hour, heading north along Avenida Rancho Boyeros, turning west onto Ben Yehuda which eventually becomes Avenida Simón Bolivar, then northward again up Derekh Ha-Ofel—to arrive at the Wailing Wall of Castillo de San Salvador de la Punta. On that dramatic site, first Bleached Wheat, then Prime Minister Che Horowitz, will deliver commemorative addresses. Later that evening The Fiesta of Lights along the Hayarkon waterfront, overlooking Caleta de San Lázaro, will outfeed most impressively over the all4s. When it’s all over, Bleached Wheat will be whisked off by armorvehic to Guantánamo for safekeeping and some normal vit—his usual burger and fries—before returning tomorrow to good old TexArc soil.

Jowler dans la Vieille Ville

Mall wakes in a sparse and strangely small room she knows immediately is underground. The scenery outside the window opposite her is too digitally bucolic. Somehow she can feel in her temples the deep pressure surrounding her. Sinalco sits beside her on the edge of the bunk. The patient look on her face tells Mall she's been sitting there for some time. The headache grabs hold of her as Mall tries to sit up. Sinalco moves a few strands of hair off Mall's forehead, then reaches for something on the bedside table. "Here. Drink this," she says softly. Sinalco holds out a huge, white, round-bottomed porcelain mug of steaming black coffee. "C'est la vrai chose aussi, ma chienne."

"Truly?"

Sinalco nods. Mall's never tasted real coffee before. Normally she'd object to such an act of privilege. Not in the right spirit of alterity and all that. Given recent events, though, she figures sod all. Best try a few things before she ends her days like poor Branston and Weetabix. Sinalco helps prop Mall up. She takes the mug and slowly sips. The rich, thick smell alone nearly overwhelms her. "So where the bloody fucking hell are we?"

"La Vieille Ville."

"Deary, there's lots and lots of bloody fucking Vieille Villes about."

Sinalco smiles. "Fribourg."

"Old Deutschland?"

"Nein. Alte Schweiz."

Mall blinks. That can't be right. She couldn't have been out for that long and, more to the point, why would someone like her be allowed into the heart of Maneuvers? But Sinalco nods, reading Mall's confusion, and helps her to more sips of the coffee, richly extraordinary. "Well bugger me blind," muses Mall, blowing ripple rings on the surface of her coffee.

"Now that is more like yourself," smiles Sinalco.

At first Mall returns the smile. Then the bizarre scene on the strange train comes back to her. She pushes the huge mug back into Sinalco's hands, suddenly distrusting the drink. Her tone changes to accusation. "Branston never would have mucked around inside ArcNet like that, and you know better than to say he had. No teek slices there on a sodding lark. Why did you say such nonsense?"

"To protect you, love. Even under the best circumstances, Headminister Natwest dislikes very much the surprises and distractions, and you, ma belle, have presented him with both when we are under the very worst circumstances."

From the very start Mall had decided to trust Sinalco only selectively. She finds this answer too vague. "Protect me from what?"

"From the very nasty world you have now entered. Countermeasures is filled with les sale type, my Mall, but Maneuvers is worse. So you see, things are not at all sympa toward you, here. And this is even before we consider the TexArc."

Maneuvers is the combat entity for EVe, as Countermeasures is its spy entity. Mall's always heard it rumored of Maneuvers that its fighters are lethal and slightly insane in their dedication to commonweal. "And so in which of these nasty orbits, Sinalco, do you operate exactly? Countermeasures or Maneuvers?"

"Countermeasures. As I explained you, I am from Harrods. Always. Or I was. But you must watch out for Maneuvers. They try to be even more the sons-of-a-bitch than TexArc."

With some reassuring coaxing, Sinalco tells her to get more coffee into Mall. She also points out the butter croissant and small pot of blackcurrant jam on the bedside table. Mall nods her appreciation.

"Now get yourself ready—quickly," Sinalco instructs her as she exits the tiny room. "We two have much explaining to do to many people."

Twenty minutes later Mall emerges from her room. She is directed by polite, black-uniformed guards down a long series of narrow hallways—tunnels actually, she supposes—towards the parley chamber. Everything about the complex strikes her as being aggressively military in nature, though, so far, she's seen none of the advanced weaponry or ultracomplex hardware with which she imagines Maneuvers would be brimming. Mall rounds a last, tight corner to find Sinalco waiting for her outside a vivid, red door. Sinalco takes hold of Mall's hand, gives it a firm squeeze, then drops it just before they enter the room.

Inside is a vast space. Immediately, they must descend steep and narrow stairs. Dominating the chamber are various holomaps suspended in the broad central darkness of what Mall makes out, once her eyes adjust, as an amphitheater. A holo of the globe is the largest thing visible, and hovers highest in the hall. Just below the holo globe is a detailed representation of the Atlantic hemisphere—obviously the topic for discussion. Her vision adapting, Mall realizes every seat in the arena is filled. Several hundred people are watching her and Sinalco make their way down to the core oval. The silence in the great room is still agitated with the echo of many voices, suddenly hushed. Mall follows Sinalco down the many stairs, mindful of her step. Once they set foot within the oval the lighting brightens and the amplified voice of a perturbed woman bites into the stillness.

"Headminister Natwest! So *this* is Harrods' folly?"

"Yes, Administer."

"Remarkable!"

Even with the aud distortion, Mall recognizes the voice of Administer

Movënpick, Chair-of-Caucus. Mall had seen her at a distance when she'd toured some of the Oxford committees—*not* Signification, though. The Administer didn't seem to care much for Signification. Mall remembers not being impressed with her. Movënpick struck Mall as a bossy, synGauloise chain-smoking Teuton, a touch too proud of her DDR heritage. "A purer form of alterity" had been her canvass pledge. Mall certainly hadn't balloted for her. Too lenin.

"One teek and one signer causing such a *fuss*!"

"Administer, let me assure you—"

"Headminister! Let me assure *you* that this escapade by your ministry has been nothing short of disastrous for..."

It dawns on Mall, *this is Caucus.* The rising circle of audience, the core oval, not being able to locate where the Chair's voice comes from—all administers being just one of a crowd. *Bloody hell. I've been called to the floor of Caucus.* "What's happened?" Mall shouts up into the darkness, once to get their attention, then again to be understood. Her upstart demand is met with a lengthy pause.

"What do you mean, what's *happened*?"

It's Movënpick herself answering.

"I mean, I don't know what's happened," Mall's voice echoes. "I was in Oxford. Then I was running. Then I was lead onto a kind of odd train. Then I was patched and I wake up here." Mall glances to Sinalco. "And I'm not even sure where 'here' is."

A prolonged mummer spreads around the parley chamber.

"Sit down, if you *please*!"

Mall sees Natwest is already seated in the central of three red swivel chairs situated at the heart of the oval. Sinalco moves to sit at Natwest's one hand, Mall at his other. She dislikes this symbolism.

"To dispense with your question," comes the acrid voice again, "Oxford was inserted! By *them*! This has never before taken place on EVe territory! Eight of your compeers were murdered at Worcester before the assassin was blown into small bits and made *useless* to us!"

Headminister Natwest shifts uneasily in his seat.

"The other two killed sixty-three constituents, most of them our fighters, in City Centre before they suddenly dropped dead where they stood! Apparently their heads spontaneously combusted to a char from the *inside*!"

Mall sees a sparker ignite a synGauloise near the outer rim of the seats. Embers glow intense orange for a moment, then calm. Maybe that's where Movënpick is seated. "That's all we know! Otherwise, as you might expect, bulletins of this insertion now have EVe in somewhat of a panic! We could probably use one of your sly advocacy projects, *Mall*, to help quell our collective fears!"

"That's *not* what Signification is about."

"Perhaps not, signer! But I am beginning to appreciate the rationale for implementing your craft for such purposes!"

"*Sodding cow*," Mall mutters to herself. Sinalco suppresses a laugh.

"Administer," Natwest steps in quickly, "if I may explain—"

"No you may *not*, Headminister! Now is our turn for questions! *Teek*! What have *you* done?"

Sinalco's answer is long and teched. The upshot is peripheral embed slice. Faux autocycle, maxevasive. There's complete silence while she explains every detail. When she's finished another voice—male, old Poland—asks two questions.

"And so what are they doing with it? Cleanse?"

"No," Sinalco answers. "Trail."

A profusion of small, animated conversations breaks out among the communicants. These continue for several minutes.

"They must be quite intrigued!" comes another amplified voice, this one female and old Greece.

"Tellement," agrees Sinalco.

"And which are they most likely to locate?" Female, old Ireland. "Backwards or forwards?"

"Backwards, évidemment," Sinalco answers with a hint of self-satisfaction, despite the fact seventy-one were killed in Oxford. Obscuring forward slice is thought to be impossible.

"We see then!" Movënpick again. She's through with the teek. "Now you, signer! Let me return *your* question! What's happened?"

"Do you mean what have I been up to?"

"Of course I mean what you have been up to! And the *short* version, if you please! You signers prattle on endlessly about your semantics!"

"Semiotics."

"Das macht nichts! Schnell! What did you *do*?"

"I created Uncle Wobbly." Mall says no more. After some moments, she murmurs, "*There*. Is *that* short and schnell enough for you, you commienazi frump?"

Once again, Sinalco struggles not to laugh. Natwest's pate flushes pinker and pinker the longer Mall refuses to volunteer any elaboration. Finally Movënpick blurts out: "And *who* in hell is this?"

"Recall candidate. Somewhere in TexArc called BoiCity."

Mall sits passively once more, awaiting the next question. Movënpick puts an end to their game with a wave of her synGauloise. "All right, then! Tell us the *medium* version, if you please! Prattle on a bit, by all means! Be my *guest*!"

Sinalco nods to Mall. *You have won. Go ahead.*

Mall begins, but is immediately interrupted. "Sinalco here—"

"You will refer to her as the *teek*!"

Mall takes her time swiveling her chair 360 degrees, looking the darkened spectators up and down in a show of searching out Movënpick. She's fairly certain it's the synsmoker she spotted earlier, but Mall is in no rush. Under his breath, Natwest tells her to bloody well get on with it. Sinalco whispers to him that real caffeine seems to agree with their signer. Mall finishes her slow tour and, deliberately, begins again. This time she is uninterrupted. “Sinalco, here, got me deep enough into ArcNet to work. We’re certainly not walking any virtual corridors of power, but we have wormed our way to a pressure point for local control. I’m afraid that’s the best we could do under the circumstances. It appears they do practice some form of decentralization, at least on the local level. I have my doubts, though, about its authenticity judging by what else I’ve seen.”

“*And* this Uncle Wobbly?” comes a caustic reminder.

“Yes, assuredly. Sorry.” Mall delays further by clearing her throat—like Harrods, it strikes her suddenly. “At any rate, I’m standing a candidate for local office in BoiCity. What office, exactly, I’m not entirely certain. Probably city council or some such. How their electoral system works, I haven’t been able to fathom. It seems as though they have no set elections, just a perpetual series of recall votes. Parts of their stream are thick with campaign adverts, all nominees doing nothing other than attacking the incumbent—remorselessly. When one of them finally gets voted in, all others begin instantly attacking him. Even the chap just voted out of office straight away dives in, stumping for the same office again. It’s very peculiar. As a matter of record, in this district it looks as though the same five or six blokes canvass year round, more or less taking turns being elected, then tossed out on their ears. Sinalco just plugged my man into the mix.”

“Mais, pourquoi?” Male voice, old France.

“Underminister Harrods told us to slice into ArcNet and have a good look around, then tell him what we think we’re seeing. He also told me, if I could, to toss a turd into their punch bowl, as it were—to stir things up a bit. To disrupt the normal functioning of their culture just to see what might come of it.” Mall points her tone. “TexArc would appear to use Signification for all the wrong reasons, Chair Movënpick. For disciplinarity. Uncle Wobbly is designed to give them a taste of its opposite—alterity.”

"Yes, yes!" comes a dour reply. "This we all *know*! Harrods' Folly! Yes! Just some details, *if* you please!"

"Wobbly from the Wobblies, old IWW from the outset of last century."

"IWW?"

"Industrial Workers of the World. Surely, Chair Movënpick, I would have thought *you* of all communicants–"

"Yes, *yes*! Continue!"

"I modified Uncle Wobbly's party to the *International* Workers of the World. His platform, however, remains historically the same. To countermand the two cardinal rules of mammonism: bust unions and deregulate."

"And just who do you imagine, my dear, is currently viewing your Uncle Wobbly spots?" Male, fellow old Brit.

"To be perfectly honest with you, I haven't a clue."

"And just what do you propose we do," female, old Portugal, "if you get your man elected and no one shows up to assume the office?"

"Again, I have no idea. My job was to construct, then feed an advocacy project into ArcNet that would break through their considerable clutter and introduce ideas radically different to their dominant culture. Uncle Wobbly was the only opportunity I saw for doing that."

Movënpick stands up. The amphitheater lighting notches brighter by a few degrees, the holomaps fading in their vividness. Indeed, the Administer is where Mall thought she was, up near the outer rim. She's a tall and angular woman with spiked hair tinted far too blonde.

"In *brief*, then, this is all rubbish!" the Administer calls down, her ampaud line now off. Peevishly, Movënpick reseats herself, the lights dim again, and she repeats harshly with ampaud back on: "*Rubbish*! A waste of our *time* at a moment when time is *critical*!"

No one dares speak for some moments. Then, quite casually, Sinalco stands, walks over behind Mall's chair, and rests her monstrous hands on the signer's shoulders. "Uncle Wobbly is currently polling at sixty-two percent," she announces to Caucus. "Somehow they manage to poll one hundred percent of the poor bastards over there. They poll them several times a week. So I take this number to be quite reliable. And this is after only a week and a half of Mall's Wobbly campaign."

Now there is a very lengthy silence in the parley chamber. Some whispers, at last, begin. Many of the communicants already are nodding to one another. Red hololetters suddenly hang over the oval, reading in multiple languages: SILENT VOTE. Pads get pushed. Then Movënpick herself is nodding her head, albeit reluctantly. "Head*minister*! It seems now this is officially Natwest's Folly! Do not *yank* it up!"

☆ ☆ ☆ ☆ ☆ ☆

A buzz coming from the center of his head, like an aud itch, wakes Enron from his twenty-five minute speedsleep. Time to doublego. Right away he's woozy. Yank space. Can't stand being above halfplat on the Elevator, and their shuttle de-docked from threequarters. That's way too far up the ladder for his stomach. High de-dock did give Enron a chance to peek at the repair work going on above them, though. Sure didn't look to him like anything vital was hit—and as a Groundsman he knows how the hell to terror. *Why even bother putting an eruptive there? And such a fuck dinky one? All for show,* Enron thought, shaking his head. Good waste of a clearshot. Made no commonsense joe at all. His shuttle had then thrust off north-by-east global, just a couple hours back.

He refuses any vit at the briefing. Why make his stomach feel any worse by tubing on? Besides, this will be short. He'll either be deadcount or pickup—probably deadcount—within an hour or two. If he needs a boost, he'll hit an adrenal patch. Vit just slows you up. Two standard issue ArcSpace Terds plus two dudes Enron suspects are Netsmen—a pair of real steely-eyed, flat-bellied types—run over the final insertion orientation with the kill squad. *Must be more than a routine urbpass if fucking Net's involved. Those fuckmothers love to send Groundsmen off to buy the firm.* And all ArcSpace ever does is float the fuck around up here. Ground gets all the shit jobs in indian country.

The mission is commonsense joe enough. Go down and kill ragheads. It seems two in particular need terming. Both tits'n'ass. Otherwise, term as many along the way as you like. "Knock yourself out," the squad is told.

At the end of the brief, one of the Netsmen looks square at Enron and says, "For revenge!" giving him, at the same time, the corndog double thumbs up—a signal Enron is obliged to return as part of the big man dance they're in.

"What the fuck that all about?" the kill squad leader, a dude named Busch, asks him as they make their way to dropdeck.

"I was standing guard at BigRig19," says Enron.

His fellow Groundsman raises his eyebrows and whistles. "No shit?"

The tradition in ArcGround is, if you're alive and able, you get a shot at taking out who tried to take you out. For revenge. From Ground, though, you can't tell dick about what's going on bigpic. All you wind up doing is going after somebody they *tell* you tried to term you. Big woof. If this revenge horseshit is some Terd's yanked-up idea of a morale booster, they must think CorpTroops are a lot dumber than they look. Enron got his medical clear just a few days ago. Only three or four CorpTroops even survived BigRig19, and he's the only one to make it back active. The last fucking thing he wants to do right off the bat is make a fucking fall, for revenge or not.

"Gear up and climb in, you miserable fucks," the ArcSpace deck Ensign instructs them. His sympathy is sincere. "When the red light starts to blink, exhale for all you're worth. Otherwise you'll bust a fucking lung on impact."

Each man's RHex climbs on, inserts its legs into the small slots running along the flanks of his armor, and hugs its master's chest. Their smell always reminds Enron of changing out the oil on his pickup, back before CorpTrooping, when he used to have a home. Each man then steps into his descend shell, lies down on his back, and hugs his RHex as if it's a small child.

"Gentlemen," smiles the Ensign sadly, "start your boxes."

Enron hates all of what follows. It's the purest shit he's ever had to put up with—and that's saying something. Descend shells are the size of coffins, stealth sleek at both ends with four biddy stub wings along the body for autoguide. The fuckers of course are windowless. Once that lid slides closed and sucks shut, all you can do is lie there and hope the hell it opens back up for you again someplace where you can roll out onto solid earth and draw clear breath. There's lots of stories about these things winding up at the bottoms of bays or accordioned into bluffs. Worse than any of that, for him, is the bounce gel. This one coming up will make Enron's seventh fall, and for the life of him he just can't get by his revulsion for the gooey shit. When the red light starts flashing he knows to exhale extra long and extra hard. Then the gel shoots into the shell, filling the tiny compartment along with Enron's nostrils, mouth, throat, stomach, and lungs. It's clear enough to see through and porous enough to breath in, but it smells and tastes like...well, Enron's never quite heard a description of exactly what bounce gel smells and tastes like. Vomit gets you vaguely in the ball park. Dead donkey ass zeros you in a touch more. Enron always imagines he's being forced to chew on an old cowpie, one that's sun-dried crusty on the outside but still a touch green-fiber mushy on the inside—only the gel tastes a touch worse. Add to that the hypersensation from your RHex. Makes you shudder big time when that gel swamps through you. The lone good thing is you're smeared for just the short, short spell while you fall like a brick toward earth. Being encased in gel any longer would drive a man plumb nuts.

Through his back, Enron feels his shell conveyor-belted then jettisoned. He experiences a woozy floating for a few seconds before the guidance kicks in. Soon after, he starts to feel an up and a down as more and more gravity takes hold. The shell spins and yaws in the upper atmosphere—another reason to take no vit—then levels downward to a serious plunge. Here's when the gel works its way up into your intestines, first the large then the small. Terds tell the Groundsmen they're just imagining it, but what the hell do Terds know anyway about real reality? Enron's the one falling head-first into who-knows-what. Impact is like one big full-body kick in the ass—and the one time you're damn happy for the gel. The shell lid is rigged to blow straight off after you hit. Enron rolls out, deploys his RHex for protection, then pushes his shell's autocrinkle, first thing, like he's trained to. The lander crumples itself down to the size of a boot, and Enron kicks it out of sight. Then he does what CorpTroops absolutely aren't supposed to do after a fall, but what they all the hell do anyway. He strips down naked. The gel mainly evaporates when it hits open air, but that doesn't take care of all the slime inside you. Enron takes a few minutes to spit, snort, and shit out all the muck he can. You're fine if you don't take too long at it. The RHex has your back. You just got to get right, though, before you head off down the road.

It's two hours predawn and he's in the narrow gorge. Check and check. So far things are plan. The night vision contacts on top of his all4s allow him to see, but most things are inverse from day vision. The lights are darks and the darks are lights. He'll get used to it. He runs a gear and bluetooth wireless check. Everything's doublego. RHex's online, and the other two members of the kill squad are in place and in one piece. *About time to move out*, figures Enron.

<Move out,> orders Busch. <Quiet to start.>

Enron doesn't know Busch. That makes him nervous. Working with a squad leader you've never met is not choice enough, but the presence of those two Netsmen makes him suspect Busch will turn out to be a goddamned company man—one of those stiff-spined yanks who'll jump up his own ass if he's told to. Enron doesn't want to be taken along for that ride.

Fuck that in no uncertain terms. The other squad member, though, is a Groundsman Enron's opsed with before. A fellow named Castroll. One solid fuckmother who keeps his shit wired tight. Best dude with the smackdown Enron's ever seen. *This guy can do major damage in a hurry*. Enron likes it that Castroll will be running disruption. That'll make his job easier.

<Where the fuck are we?> comes Castroll.

<That's need to know,> snaps Busch. End of discussion.

Enron thinks, *oh shit, it's starting already*.

<Fuck you, Busch,> snaps back Castroll. <I need to know where the fuck we are. I ain't never seen no place like this before.>

Enron's been thinking the same damn thing. Normal fall sets you down in some DollArcs-forsaken landscape, dry and flat and usually scruffy-ass as hell. That, or the odd deep jungle. Enron's only ever operated in two of them. Pure creeps. Give him desert ops any day. You wipe a shitload of brown scrawnies shouting whack lingo at you and wearing bedsheets or buttrags. Then you get the hell gone. Easy profit. But this place is all green and—damn pretty, well cared for. *Someone watching out for it*. Enron can tell. He's walking along an old and tended path on the north bank of a rushing stream. The forest around him is thick. The rocky walls of the gorge he's moving through are high and close. The sound of echoing water is like magic itself. When he comes to a small falls, the smell of mist in the air is something he's never smelled. His whole life. Enron has a terrible thought.

<We ain't in fucking EVe, are we?> he asks.

<Need to know,> repeats Busch, stressing some. <Still quiet to start.>

That can only mean fucking yes, they're in fucking EVe.

<Fuck me dry,> curses Castroll.

<Enough of the yak,> warns Busch.

<Fuck you,> both squad members say together.

The yub from the hub is that an insert recently fell someplace in EVe and got its ass wiped. Didn't even term a hundred ragheads, total, *and* it flat out missed two of its principles. That's piss poor kill squading. Normal mission for a CorpTroop is no sweat to term two or three hundred resisters by his lonesome. They must've run into some *shitstorm* friction.

<Castroll,> Enron bypasses the squad leader, something you're not supposed to do while quiet to start, <you and Rover be Dmega headsup, man. We ain't yanking sweetpuss here.>

<Back at you and Jowler,> replies Castroll.

<Okay,> cuts in Busch, <now that you two have had a fucking hug, do me a favor and shut the fuck up.>

Thing is, Enron doesn't buy that EVe terrorstruck BigRig19, it or the damn Space Elevator. Both targets sound choice, but neither strike amounted to nothing but fluff. Besides, sec is so tight on them two ops, only an inside job could pull off stunts like that. If EVe's cracked the Glassea and the Vator, Arc's in deep shit. *But them things can't be cracked. No yanking way.* And that's got him Dmega spooked. That and some other fruitcake yub sometimes feeding in over his all4s.

Ahead of him, Jowler's reached the first checkpoint. Now Enron's sure they're in EVe. On Enron's upleft, Jowler's looking up at an old fountain decorated with angels. On his upright, the digital map display of the skirmish site, Enron sees Jowler's in the little bridgehead square and that he's not too far behind, just starting to come into the city from the southeast on a road marked with the textsymbols Rue des Forgerons. Enron stops to orient himself. He looks to his left. Hugging the wall of the gorge is the tiny stone house marked Chapel de St Beat on the map. He turns around and looks up. Spanning the gorge mouth, some 60 meters up, is a graceful and arching vehic bridge—Pont de Gottéron—by the map. He swivels Jowler's head right. Up a narrow street he can make out the thick, block gatehouse mapmarked Porte de Berne. He steps Jowler to the left and swivels its head back straight to look beyond the fountain. There's the old, wooden covered bridge—Pont de Berne—massive and with red tile roofing. Only EVe could be this text heavy and intact. When they were briefing aboard the shuttle, Enron assumed the city map they were reviewing was of some tacnuked shithole like everyplace else he's fallen—Cairo, Bombay, Shanghai. This place looks like a goddamned fairy tale. No wonder Castroll got spooked.

<In poz,> he reports.

<In poz,> says Busch.

<Hold one,> says Castroll.

Enron takes this opportunity to check his down displays. Downleft is his suit signflash, downright the mission signflash. On those, cartoon hand signals tell him what's good to go and what's snafu. All are doublego at the moment—thumbs up down the list. He goes back upright to the digimap and sees how Busch is not far from him—due south. Except, he's about a hundred meters up, perched atop the curving cliff face that traces the river bend and overlooks the city. From there he's got clearshots up and down the length of the lower town, which juts out as a long and sloping peninsula in a deep curve of the river—the Sarine. Enron sees Castroll approaching poz at the head of a street marked Rue Pierre-Aeby—northwest over in the upper town, where Castroll fell and entered the city, having to make his way down a major route—Rue de Morat. Enron can imagine that's city proper, and that Castroll's had to come on a bit careful. His suit's camo is nowhere near as good as Enron's.

<In poz,> Castroll finally reports. <Had some movement up here.>

<Look,> says Enron to both squad members, <just let me and Jowler go in first and see if we can't tiptoe this fuckmother. I got choice coverfire from you up top, Busch. Castroll, you can come in and cut loose if I screw the pooch and need a bail out. What do you say? No use us tear-assing around if we don't have to.>

<Doubleneg on that,> comes back Busch without giving it consideration. <We go plan. That's that.>

<Anyway,> chips in Castroll, <why should you go and have all the fun, Enron? I bet the only thing that beats terming libbies is poking their puss. Besides, this town looks like it could use a good tear-assing. I bet it hasn't had one for a while.>

<Just a fucking thought,> says Enron.

<Don't go fucking thinking on me now,> says Busch. <We're a go. I say again, we're a go.>

Easy for Busch to say. His ass is high and dry, and he's got Fido up there with him to watch his back. But when the planman says they go, they yanking go. Rule one of CorpTrooping.

Kill squad is basic strategy. Squad leader gets some kind of perch to direct ops and snipe. He takes out inopportune unfriendlies and coordinates skirmish site. Leader's RHex is Fido, aligned to bring him his slippers and protect the poz at all costs. Fido's yank loyal. Try to go by it, and Fido will tear you a new asshole. The second squad role, running disruption, is the pure selfoblige spot on kill. His assign is to draw away and fuck up, so he's loaded for bear. Enron's seen CorpTroops running disrupt level city blocks. *No shit.* Disrupt's got Rover by his side, a recon RHex. It can get eyes and ears—and feel, smell, and taste—where you'd never expect they could be. That way disrupt knows where to hit hardest and how to evade. The finesse job on squad, role three and Enron's assign this time down, is the kill member himself. He's tasked pure and simple to term the targets—whoever and wherever the hell they might be. When the disrupt shit breaks loose nearby, that's killmem's cue to slip in to go for the throat. He's equipped with some special toys for the chore, but his best friend is Jowler, a stealth-term RHex. Most times targets don't even see what kills them.

Both Castroll and Enron move into poz two. Castroll stays tight to the storefronts and entryways as he heads southeast to the bottom of the street. He stops at the corner where he has clearsight over the central plaza of the upper Bourg.

<Poz two,> he reports.

Enron's move across the lower town—the Auge—is trickier. He sends Jowler across the covered bridge and maintains its heading straight on into the wide and open Place du Petit-St-Jean.

<I've got Jowler on my scope,> Busch informs Enron.

No shit, thinks Enron. *This buttwipe's getting on my nerves.*

<Check,> he replies, for procedure's sake.

Then Jowler smells something else Enron doesn't think he's ever smelled before—fresh baking bread. It takes him a while to identify the smell, but when he does it makes his stomach growl. Somewhere on the square, a baker's up and busy. Good intel to have. He continues sending Jowler southwest across the finger of the peninsula to the Pont du Milieu. Instead of crossing that bridge, though, Enron low-crawls Jowler into the river—the water strangely warm and slow-flowing—then dog-paddles it upstream for 200 meters to climb back out on the same shore, only now at the bottom of the cliffs running the southern edge of the Bourg—the upper town—as it slopes steeply down into the Auge.

<Eyeballing Jowler now,> reports Busch. Enron climbs it up the river-wall, among the thick trees, up the vertical rockface, then along the side and terraces of the six-story building until it finds the window Enron's looking for. <Jowler's go,> says Busch, which is useful newsbig to have.

With his RHex safely in place, Enron enters the city. He's shocked by how small it is. Nowhere near a meg. This tight cluster of buildings wouldn't even make up a ward back home. Standing by that angel fountain, he gazes up the rising spine of the peninsula. It's a jumble of red, tile roofs with half a dozen slender, tarnished-green spires jutting up here and there. At the crest of the hill is a weird, and kind of scary-looking, square stone tower with lots of angry spikes on top. What the fuck that's all about Enron can't imagine. Taking his time to be cautious, Enron walks across the covered bridge. He's never felt anything quite so solid underfoot. The eaves are low and the side barriers high, the guardrail topped with large pots of flowers. He has a hard time getting much of a look at the river. It seems deep green and lazy to him, medium wide as rivers go. It's damn full, that's for sure. That's a good thing you don't see much anymore. On the far side of the bridge Enron veers right up the narrow Rue D'Or. The cobbled streets, wrought-iron lamp standards, and ornate hanging signs make him feel as though he's stepped onto another planet. One where folks give a shit about where and how they live.

<Street's clear to your right,> says Busch.

Enron turns right and heads northwest up the tight Rue de Augustins. He comes alongside a building marked Église on the digimap. He finds a dark entryway opposite it, one with the textsymbol—10—beside it. He ducks in—a good enough go spot.

<Go,> he says.

<Go,> Busch tells Castroll.

Plain as damn day, Castroll strides diagonally across Place de Nova-Friburgo, through an archway in a gatehouse tower, to stop at the head of a long descent of stone stairs. These overlook the river basin below the south cliffs along the edge of the Bourg. Castroll sizes up Neuveville below him, then the stone Pont de St-Jean spanning the river. Just across that bridge is the Caserne he's looking for. Rover's already been down to scope it out. Rich target acquisition, as they say in Ground. Thirty or so tucked in their bunks. Castroll could even trace smell the alcohol on their breaths. These fucks must have it made. No more they don't.

<Eyeballing you now,> Busch says to Castroll.

<Yeah? Fucking eyeball this.>

Disrupt gets one laserguide to play with—a really yanking big one. Think of it as the wake-up call. Castroll shoulders, aims, and sends his rocket streaking into the northwest corner of the Caserne, which is one hell of a long shot coming off of high ground. The fireball rises well above cliff level and, even on the opposite side of the peninsula, Enron can feel the ground shake.

<Yeah, mommy!> Castroll hoots, pleased with his marksmanship. <Fuck me wet!>

<Move now! Move!> Busch barks at him.

<Uncross your legs, dude. I know what I'm fucking doing.> Castroll chucks the launcher down the steps and heads back up to the plaza. No one's had time to show up, but he knows they'll be coming from his left, busting ass down the Route des Alpes from the new city, and eventually from his right as well, coming up the Grand Rue from the old city. He wants to keep the old city faction full engaged so Enron can do his work. That means Castroll will have to mouse them around. Whatever comes his way from uptown, he'll just fucking wipe. Castroll pulls out his smackdown and stuffs his fist up to his forearm into its triggerhole. He smiles to himself as he adjusts the long sonic tube. <I think I'm in love.>

Two slick vehics with spinning blue lights on their tops and seesawing sirens howling like mad come zoomzoom down from the new city. Castroll lets them get almost into the plaza, right alongside some gnarled old tree fenced off on an island, then sends a pulse their way. It lifts both vehics off the ground and tosses them into some distant buildings. Then they blow up. Doublechoice!

<Smackdown!> he shouts.

Enron shakes his head and goes to work.

☆ ☆ ☆ ☆ ☆ ☆

At first Sinalco can't locate Mall. She's not in her room. Her initial fear is that Mall's out on one of her early runs. Then she thinks to check the workstation. There's Mall, where she is almost all the time, recently, leaning forward into her signscreen, padding intently at her console, listening to audioAMBIENT much too loudly over EVeWave.

"What the bloody hell's the matter with you?" Mall demands churlishly when she detects Sinalco lurking in the doorway, staring at her.

"Rien du tout."

"You look like you've seen a bleeding ghost."

"Pas des fantôme. Non."

"Well don't bloody creep up on me like that. You gave me a start." Mall turns back to her signscreen. "It's bad enough having to live underground most the sodding time. I'm beginning to feel like a troglodyte."

"Désolé," Sinalco apologizes. "It is for our own good." She glances about the room, especially looking into corners. "You stay here. Okay?"

Mall frowns. "What do you mean?"

"Do not leave. Stay in this room."

Mall turns again in her chair. "Has something happened?"

"Je ne sais pas encore. Reste ici. D'accord?"

"What time is it?"

"About five. Have you stayed up all night, or have you been up early?"

Mall's not understanding this conversation. "Been up early, but I was about ready to go out for a run over the bridge and up the gorge."

"*Non!*" Sinalco says vehemently. "Pas dehors. Not outside. No matter anything. You stay here, and I will be back soon. *Okay*?"

The last time Mall saw Sinalco become this serious they were soon sprinting the back alleyways of Oxford. "All right," she nods. "I'll stay put."

"Good." Sinalco turns to go. "What is that smell?"

"God, it's awful, isn't it? Smells like engine sludge and dead animal. I don't know what it is, but it just started a little while before you popped round. I imagine it's coming through ventilation."

Sinalco scans the room again. "Pas possible," she mummers to herself. She closes the door tightly behind her.

☆ ☆ ☆ ☆ ☆ ☆

On his upleft, Enron watches the jumbo woman leave the room. That had been close. She'd looked right at Jowler twice. For a second he thought he'd have to make a mess, then try to scramble it out. That's *not* what the Netsmen told him they want. They want pristine kills. Two of them, goddamnit. No evidence. No trace. Doublezilch. You can only accomplish that one at a time. He'll get back to terming this one, and wait for the giant one to come back. With his translator, he could understand what the jumbo one was saying. Enron was surprised, though, to discover he could understand the dark one without trans, even though she said her words funny. He'd always heard EVe was all outland. He nudges Jowler forward again. Even with the sound muffler you have to go slow. The woman turns around in her chair, again, like she hears something. She hasn't looked up at the ceiling yet, and she's given no obvious signs she suspects something, so Enron's not sure what she's up to. But he gets to looking at her again. *The satellite pics don't do her justice. Not near.* Enron's never seen a tits'n'ass like this—accept for a virho, and they don't really count. This one's skin isn't yellowed and she doesn't have that grotesque mix of skinny and droopy. This one could kick your ass. And her eyes. They look like they *want* to kick your ass. *Angry and smart.* She wouldn't put up with a smack from anyman. He's sure of that. *And that huge one. Holy hell. Never seen a giant tits'n'ass like her before. Plain yanking scary. What kind of sweetpuss do they grow here in EVe*?

<Where you at, Enron?> comes Busch, concerned with mission.

<Both targets acquired. First one under the gun.>

<Well hurry it the fuck up. That dumbfuck Castroll ain't doing so hot up top, and I've already got unfriendlies starting to snoop around my poz. *These* ragheads know what the fuck they're about.>

<No sweat. You got it.>

☆ ☆ ☆ ☆ ☆ ☆

Mall was convinced Sinalco's coming into the workstation would mean the end of them both, but the bizarre apparatus clinging to the ceiling hadn't moved. *Whatever it's up to, it apparently doesn't want to be discovered.* The thing looks like a cockroach, what with six mechanical legs on which to scuttle about, and is the size of a medium dog. She'd not heard it come in or mount to the ceiling. She'd first noticed it by its faint, noxious smell. Then, and this is the really curious part, she first saw it over her shoulder as a reflection in her signscreen. But whenever she turns around, it's just not there—not visible in the least. Mall has to keep reminding herself to be more frightened than amazed. She assumes the thing's not friendly. She assumes it's after her. How it got this deep into the complex is unfathomable. She's watched it start to millimeter closer again since Sinalco left the room. She's bought some time by turning around in her chair every now and again, which causes the thing to freeze. But she knows her time is fast running out. The big bug is quite uncomfortably close now. Mall pads in a final few instructions on her console and hopes for the best. She imagines these things are good at what they do.

☆ ☆ ☆ ☆ ☆ ☆

Enron's finally got Jowler situated in kill range. Targets never see it coming from above. Best kill spot is the back of the neck. *Here goes.* Just then a bright flash fills his upleft. It makes him flinch back deeper into the entryway. *What the yank?* He checks his downleft. Everything's still thumbs up on Jowler. His upleft screen is clearing. She's still sitting there like nothing happened. Maybe just a linkglitch because Jowler's so deep. Can't worry about it now. He goes for the kill. Jowler's right frontarm darts forward, spiking the target with a toxdart at the base of her skull.

☆ ☆ ☆ ☆ ☆ ☆

The instant Mall sees the hologram of herself disrupted she throws the small emp-grenade. It sticks—as though on nothing—and pulses. Everything in the workstation not fastened down is tossed as though by a sudden whirlwind, including Mall, now crouching by the far wall. The cockroach thing thuds to the floor, abruptly becomes visible, and lies inert. Mall grabs up a chair and starts beating any remaining life out of it.

☆ ☆ ☆ ☆ ☆ ☆

Enron convulses and falls to his knees. The violent disconnect of a RHex is akin to having a limb torn off—or worse. It takes quite a while for him to hear Busch screaming in the center of his head.

<Status, Enron! Enron! What's your fucking status!>

It takes another few minutes for him to get to his feet and respond. A RHex is a lowlevel, canine conplant. The kill squad CorpTrooper and dog train for months together to develop a loyal bond. Then, when they're ready, the CorpTrooper gets fitted with his special assault armor and the dog gets put down and its conscious streamed into a rudimentary nanoflock brain. Supposedly, the dog doesn't even realize it's dead. That makes the RHex unit not only superdevoted to its user, but capable of better, highlevel function than a regular mech. *Hell, there's no comparison.* Problem is, that bond runs both ways. Enron's had Jowler for near five years. They've run some asskick ops together as a kill pair. When the two of them are aligned in, Enron *is* Jowler and, he's always imagined, Jowler *is* Enron. What one feels and senses they both feel and sense. Now half of him's gone, just ripped away—but Enron's got to report. Friction could get shitstorm now without his RHex. He's got to depend on his squad, which is depending on him.

<Lost Jowler,> Enron finally manages to say. <I don't know how, but they took out Jowler.>

<Fuck Jowler,> says Busch. <The targets? Did you take out the targets?>

<Maybe one. I'm not sure. Something went wrong.>

<*Maybe* one?> Busch repeats, angrily. <You fucking shitubers,> he swears. <You yankers can't even pee straight.>

Fuck me dry, thinks Enron. *Busch is fucking Net, not Ground.* He should have fucking guessed.

<Fuck you, Busch. We're fucking out of here. This mission is bellyup. Call for lift.>

<Yeah, right. Like we ever planned pulling you back out. You or that other Parker piece of shit. Now get your ass down in there and term both those fucking targets yourself. Double*fucking*go!>

For the first time in his CorpTroop life, and he has no idea how such a notion even got in his head, Enron hesitates—then resists. <Or else what, asshole?> he answers so calmly he surprises himself. <You're already going to term my ass. Why should I do any more of your shitwork?>

<Simple, yankhead,> Busch tells him. <If you don't, we kill everybody you know. Any parents you got left, any aunts or uncles, any cousins, any buddies, any sweetpuss. The whole nine yards, smartass. That's fucking why.>

Yanking Net. Yanking Terds.

☆ ☆ ☆ ☆ ☆ ☆

Uphill in the Bourg, Castroll isn't having much fun. It started out amusing. After torching the Caserne and lofting two vehics, he'd run southeast through the Place de l'Hôtel de Ville to the mouth of the Grand-Rue. Rover had let him know a hefty force from the old city was moving fast up that street, which looks like a canyon with its tall, old buildings lining either side. He let them advance three lanes northwest before going apeshit with his smackdown. The sonic shotgun is a tube nearly three meters long with the bore of a small artillery piece manufactured as lightweight as possible, but you still got to be plenty buff to whip it out and swing it around. The double reverberators pulse out a sound wall of high amp but low frequency, somewhere down between five and ten Hz, below audible range. Even if you can't hear it coming, it can sure as hell be felt. The thing flips tanks and punches holes in concrete walls. Castroll had blocked off the Grand-Rue with an avalanche of parked vehics and building rubble. He's pretty sure he took out maybe ten ragheads along the way. Main thing is, he closed off that attack route, forcing them to skirt around to the north. So far, so plan. Feeling pretty good about himself, he ran north up the Rue des Épouses to head them off at the pass. That's when the shitstorm started.

☆ ☆ ☆ ☆ ☆ ☆

Capitaine de Corvette Cardinal of the Fortification Guards locked down tight the complex before she took out her response crew. The poor paysans in the Caserne, trainees only, were easy targets. Also the city police offered little threat to whoever had made this atrocity. She would be the one to make them pay, but when two of her team got sniped from behind on their run up Stalden, she knew this was a coordinated assault, and that they must have someone atop the high precipices cut by the Sarine. She transmitted for a second team to get up there, if for no other reason than to pin down the sniper. Later, after the Grand-Rue toppled onto them, and she heard the report from the cliffs that they had engaged some manner of bot, her worst fears were confirmed. TexArc. They have another Oxford on their hands. *Ggopäingj,* she'd transmitted to all under her command, *Bolze!*

If her one tactic was outflanking and her one advantage knowing the streets, Cardinal wasn't about to permit them translating her comm. And this son-of-a-bitch up in the Bourg must have a reconbot with him. A situation she would remedy first.

☆ ☆ ☆ ☆ ☆ ☆

Castroll had walked into a trap at the far end of the Rue des Épouses. When he turned the corner and looked right down the Rue du Pont-Suspendu, expecting to set a little ambush for the ragheads who should be coming up that way, he was hit by heavy-duty fire coming from his left. The fucks had skirted him, going faster than he thought they could on the Rue des Chanoines, behind the freaky, big fortress with the high, square tower. He pulsed the mouth of that street a couple times, and sprinted for the cover of the main portal under that tower. He'd never been hit with fire like that before. The pos-neg shield over his torso kept the killshots out, but his carbonfiber compos-armor got dented up bad. In a few spots the dicyclopentadiene healing agent hadn't even been enough to liquidfix the fissures. In those spots, mainly on his arms, he could feel himself bleeding. Then Rover went deadscreen and Castroll crumpled up and gelshit himself.

<Busch, you son of a bitch, I could use some fucking coverfire!>

<Tough shit! I got worries of my own up here!>

<Listen, fuckmother! I got a shitstorm blowing down here! Rover's out and I'm pinned! Where does goddamn Enron stand?>

<He's fucking around! You just keep making a lot of noise up there! You fucking hear me?>

<Blow me dead!>

Useless yank. Castroll decides *fuck this*, but he knows he can't make it back across the street and down the way he came. He checks his downleft. His suit signflash confirms he's got too many thumbs down to absorb another hail of fire. His trans is also giving him nothing but gibberish. What do these EVe fucks talk, anyway? Without trans and Rover, he's deaf and blind. Can't really tiptoe out, either. His camo is standard base reflective. Works best in the bush. Urban pacification is usually all about muscle. Shit, he just might be poochscrew. He's picking up more unfriendlies with infrared. He scans his digimap. Only way out is right in front of him, nipping northwest through the short Rue St-Nicolas. Only problem is, it'll put him in some open plazas on the far side. That could be the pure shit. While he's thinking it over, Castroll notices the elaborate carvings in the recessed doorway he's crouched in. Rows and rows of little carved dudes in funny pointed caps, and in the sweeping triangular space rising above the old, wooden, double doors there's some grimfuck scene with skeletons, and devils, and flames, and shit. *Fuck, what kind of sick fuck thinks up shit like that?*

One thing Castroll's still got going for him though is the smackdown, but he can't haul ass with that. He points the end of the tube around the corner down Rue du Pont-Suspendu and pulses seven or eight times, ripping hell out of things down that way. Then he drops the tube and runs. He's halfway across the Place de Notre-Dame and has the Rue de Morat and, he hopes, a clean exit in sight when they open up on him from a colonnade along the northeast side of the plaza. He tuck-and-rolls, coming up to one knee with his mister, and sends a cloud of sizzling metal their way. Three of the ragheads turn into purple haze. His shield takes a couple hits in the back, but holds. He turns and salvos in that direction. Castroll hears, then eyeballs, some kind of hard-ass armor vehic rumbling down the Rue de Morat. So much for a clean exit. He runs west, zigzagging through all the plazas and starting up the sharp incline of the Rue de Lausanne. The street's narrow and only takes him up into the new city, where he does *not* want to be, so he starts sprinting, as best he can, up a steep and covered stairway he spots on his right. The steps wind uphill, way out of line of sight. Castroll knows it's a choice place to get surprised, but he's got zero options. He leaps two or three of the stairs at a go for a while, but the grade starts to get to him—probably some loss of blood, too. His boots feel sloshy. He stops and slaps the adrenaline patch on his thigh, but nothing else. No painkill. He can't afford to go drowsy. Pain's his best friend at the moment. He hears the ragheads following him up the stairs, but they're keeping their distance. Doesn't take long to get educated about the mister. If he were a company man he'd think about turning it on himself right about now. *Fuck that in no uncertain terms.* He'll just take as many ragheads with him as he can.

Busch's voice is suddenly in his head. <Bye, bye, you shitube.>

Castroll's head seems to seize. He drops his mister and grabs his helmet with both hands. The top of his brain's on fire, like red-hot tongs are picking him up. Then something small hits and sticks to his chest. The world pulses blueflash—knocking Castroll on his ass—stunning him stiff. When he manages to open his eyes, the all4s are totoblank. Man, he hates the totoblank. He moans, but can't budge—like rigger mortis has set in. At least the vice-grip inside his skull has gone. Just then a tasty tit-s'n'ass in a dark gray unisuit swings down off of the roof right above him. She's like the nicest piece of live sweetpuss Castroll's ever laid eyes on. Lean and mean, baby, just like he likes them. Too bad he's in no condition to work up the hardnob. She steps over to him, leans down close to look in his eyes, and puts a boot on his throat. Then in strange and deliberate tones she talks mainly his lingo to him. "Hallo," she says, unsmiling. "I am ze Capitaine de Corvette Cardinal of Fortification Guards." She has cropped henna hair and a face full of pink freckles. "Willkommen to our EVe." Her front teeth aren't quite even and her eyes are a stinging turquoise. God, Castroll wishes he had the bone. "So you are knowing, you die here upon ze Escaliers du Collège."

While Castroll tries to grin and give her a wink, she places a cute little automatic to his temple and blows his head to paste.

☆ ☆ ☆ ☆ ☆ ☆

Enron leaves the safety of the entryway on Rue de Augustins and heads uphill. He turns left onto Rue de la Lenda, a narrow alley, then soon corners sharply right, putting him on Stalden, the main avenue climbing up out of the old town. This street is precipitous and not overly wide, with worn paving stones underfoot and thick, blockish buildings hemming him in on either hand.

<Hold one,> Busch instructs Enron. <Let me clear the path.>

<Don't do me any fucking favors.>

<I'm not.>

Busch goes 16x on his infrared scope: whir-click, whir-click. Two by the door. They both look jumpy. One's half hidden behind the wall, so Busch will have to do this quick. Take this one with a head shot, the other anywhere he can to the body. As he settles into the aim, Busch can see this guy didn't have time to shave this morning. Too bad about leaving a beautiful corpse. Just then a series of thundering smackdown impacts peals down from above. The dude behind the wall takes one step out into the street and looks anxiously up the hill.

<Sounds like Castroll's getting his rocks off anyway,> says Enron.

<Oh, yeah,> says Busch in a preoccupied tone. Paf! Paf! <You're clear. Now get your ass down in there.>

<Yank off.>

Enron hikes quickly up the street, sticking close to the shadows of the building fronts on the east side. When he comes opposite to Stalden 14 he holds to have a look around. The entrance appears harmless. Overhanging the door is a fancy iron sign, visible up and down the way, of some jumbo wildman clutching a humongous club. Curving underneath this figure are the textmarks—Die Höhle Grand Rababou. As Enron steps over a body, he's quite aware he's an infrared blur in Busch's scope. Inside looks innocent. There are old armchairs, sagging sofas, and a couple of walls lined with narrow shelves holding rows of thin rectangular objects Enron's never seen before. They got all sorts of textsymbols marked on them. By the bank of long windows looking out over the river valley, many small tables stand set with silverware, waiting for their morning bistro customers. Enron encounters no one as he makes his way down the first flight of stairs to the restaurant level below. Here's where he picks up Jowler's trail. He'd sent his RHex in through a tiny square bathroom window on the building's cliff side. From here on out, Enron knows just where to go without repeating all the slow, nosing around he had to do earlier when guiding Jowler. The techno-defenses are surprisingly lax. Jowler detected no motion or infrared sensors, so they had no disabling to do. Their locking mechs are straightforward, too, so Jowler had no major troubles moving around. EVe seems to rely most on do-it-yourself and conceal. Interesting. Enron starts to believe he can survive—this installation insert and target mission. He doesn't know how he'll survive Busch, though, if he gets back topside in one piece.

Following the downward-pointing arrow textmarked with Grotto, he descends a second, steeper flight of stairs into a large, windowless room. All tables are draped with white tablecloths and set with fine dishes and glasses. The walls are bare rock. At the far end of the room is a wide fireplace fit with cooking racks. It's around behind those where Enron needs to go. He expects guards but runs into none as he punches code and slips through the first security access. Disrupt just might be working. *Go, Castroll.* With Jowler juiced, either they'll be waiting for him or have their pants down. Enron's got no option but to go in—either way. He'll assume the worst and hope for the best. Hell, maybe he can even find Jowls and reboot.

The first hallway stretches out dark in front of him. He takes a step and it lights up so quick he retreats, thinking someone's coming. When no one does and the light goes out, he steps again, and again the light comes on. Problem. The floor must be ecotile, converting kinetic energy of footsteps into electric charge for lighting. Enron hadn't discovered it before because he always put Jowler on the ceiling. *This ain't a deal buster. It just jacks up the risk.* He won't be able to keep in the shadows where his OLED armor functions best. Enron's wearing a one-piece, totobody elastic deformation. Hooded and masked, gloved and bootied, supple but strong, it's covered with organic light-emitting diodes—P2 powered, piezoelectric and peltier effects regulating his body temp and running all the device taps on him. The suit computes any onlooker's viewangle, compares it to what's behind Enron, and projects that background image back out to the viewer, making Enron blend invisibly with the scenery. OLED isn't foolproof, of course. Jowler was coated in it and they got him. It works best in gloom and you got to steer clear of mirrors as much as you can. The suit just can't compute fast enough all those vizangles. But Enron's not too bad at the tiptoe. Otherwise fucking Net wouldn't have capitalized him for this ops. He's running on sound muffle, too, which helps a lot, and before it went deadfeed, Jowler ion sprayed the first target. Enron can track quick to her—or her carcass—if Jowler did manage to term her. Then it'll be just a matter of taking on that bizarre hulk puss he saw. *To be honest, I ain't looking forward to tangling with her.*

☆ ☆ ☆ ☆ ☆ ☆

If she *is* the principal target of these TexArc insertions, Mall's thinking, she doesn't see why Sinalco has put her sitting by herself, in near total darkness, in the central oval of the parley chamber. True, it is the deepest room in the complex, and would take quite an effort for anything or anyone to creep or fight its way down this far, but she is quite alone, and that invisible cockroach thing had all but stuck a venomous spike into the back of her neck, and TexArc has shown an uncanny ability to locate her. Understandably, Mall feels a pinch vulnerable while sitting isolated in the dark quiet for what seems an eternity. When she suddenly catches a weak whiff of the dead smell once more, she feels more than a little like bait. "Sinalco!" she shouts out, in anger more than fright. "There's something sodding in here!"

Mall figures there's no use pretending she's not in the room. If TexArc's here, they know bloody well she's here, too. Rather than sit, waiting to be assassinated, Mall gets up off her chair and gropes her way across the oval to the first circle of seats. She imagines someone or something must be watching her with a fancy device—and enjoying a right good old chuckle. *Sod them.* She hunts for an aisle and ascends half way up the amphitheater, unsure where she's going or what she's trying to accomplish, but knowing a moving target is harder to hit than a stationary one. She sidles her way about fifteen chairs into a narrow row of seats and crouches down. The ceiling is far overhead, and a burly cockroach would have to make some kind of a stir squeezing through, or coming over, all these seats. Slyly as she can, Mall removes from her thigh pocket the second emp-grenade Sinalco had supplied her with that morning. The one she'd used earlier shorted every console in her workstation, but its electromagnetic pulse, as Sinalco promised, stopped, in its tracks, the hostile contraption aiming for her. If it comes to that, now, Mall hopes she can get in another clear throw.

The holomaps come up. Hovering highest in the hall is the great globe, lit with brilliant reds, blues, greens, and yellows. Spread in a ring below it, individual maps of the continents hang just above the seats. In many places, if standing, one's head and shoulders would mingle with the razor-thin, suspended threads of light. The effect is to lace the amphitheater with a thousand different points of illumination. Mall has no idea how or why the holos came on, but standing practically over her in this altered backdrop is the indistinct form of a man. She can't be totally certain. He seems outlined partly by light and partly by shadow, erratic and sparkly along his edges but stark blank on the inside. Before she can be fully struck by how queer this specter is, the image springs forward to seize her. Mall struggles desperately in the headlock of this nonentity before her one hope, the emp-grenade, is wrested from her clutching fingers.

"I'll take that, honey," comes a flat and nasal voice in her ear. The breath accompanying the words is horrid. The dead smell is worse.

"Sod off you sodding bastard!"

Mall half twists around with an escape move and lands a glancing head blow with the back of her fist before the choke hold tightens to immobilize, almost as though she's dangling from a noose. Her attention turns to fighting for air, both her hands trying to pry the invisible forearm from around her neck.

"Just relax and enjoy it, sweetpuss," comes the voice again. "Not too sure what I'm going to do with you."

☆ ☆ ☆ ☆ ☆ ☆

Why Enron has broken kill protocol by grabbing the target instead of terming it, he doesn't know. He has no damn yanking idea. The holos coming up sudden like that spooked him, sure, but not goddamned enough to blank on years of protocol. What you're absolutely wired to do close range is put a toxdart into target's ass and *not* reveal yourself—no matter what. But before he knew it, he'd just jumped and fucking grabbed this one. *Yanking why?* He's toast for sure, if anybody's watching, and this fucking holoshow is compromising the shit out of his suit. Enron's thinking trap. It took him forever to track down this far in this fuckmother big installation, but he got down here way too easy, able to move about way too free, like they wanted him down this deep. Fuck, that's it! Is he too damn deep for bluetooth? Jesus fuck, he walked right into it. Enron needs to sig Castroll, warn him, but knows Busch, as leader, will bar that. *Doublefuck.* The flicker red starts to blink downright on his mission signflash. Thumbs down for Castroll. He's just bought the firm. Enron's never done a fall with a kill squad that took a kia before. He wonders if EVe got Castroll and Rover both, or if that yankwad Busch wiped them. Now that yankwad is in his head again.

<Term her, you asshole! Fucking term her!> The feed is faint and crackly, <What the fuck you holding for?>

How the fuck can Busch know his exact situ? <When I come up out of here, I'm going to fuck you up. See if I don't.>

<Think so, tubefuck?>

Enron's confused. So much don't wash. Net wants this target dead—but Net wants *him* dead, too. That don't figure. And now that he's got a hold of her, what else can he do but term her? He can't let her go, just tiptoe off like he was never there. And if he can make it back topside, and take out Busch, how's he ever going to get lift? Only squad leader can call down. *Nope. Pure simple yanked for true.*

"Sorry, darling," he finds himself saying to the woman as, reluctantly, he positions the toxdart at the jugular, the quickest and most merciful kill. Then, for the first time, he catches the smell of her hair, like something growing and sweet. He loosens his grip a notch and whispers again, "I am true sorry."

☆ ☆ ☆ ☆ ☆ ☆

Getting adequate air again, Mall is able to growl back, "Fuckall ta, mate." She tries to twist free again and the man's hold on her re-tightens. "I guess that's what I sodding get for trying to bring you sodding sorry lot the one big union."

The man lets her go.

"The greatest thing on earth?" he asks stepping back and pulling off a hood. A floating face appears. "Freedom from wage-slavery?" it asks.

Mall can't believe what she's seeing and especially hearing, but she has the presence of mind to answer back with an emphatic, "Yes!"

Peculiarly, the face responds, "Well fuck me dry," and smiles to itself. Then its hair gets scratched by a partially visible set of fingers, and it explains to her, "I just voted Wobbly myself."

Sinalco tackles the bodiless phantom. In the confusing lights, the two combatants roll painfully over the seat backs in front of them and down into the next row. Mall sees that Sinalco is trying to wrestle some kind of skullcap down onto the disembodied head. Her own head snaps back briskly two or three times as though she's getting hit, the punches sounding like a cricket bat beating on a cushiony sofa—but they seem to have no effect at all. Sinalco merely tugs harder at the figure's torso, ripping away enough camouflage clothing for a chest and the upper half of one arm to appear. The TexArc man is alarmingly large and muscular, with multiple scars dotting his breast and bicep. For all his brawn, though, he doesn't seem able to move Sinalco off him. They fight strenuously for almost a minute before he decides to reach for something alongside his thigh. Mall gives Sinalco a warning shout, “”Watch him!”

☆ ☆ ☆ ☆ ☆ ☆

The giant sweetpuss is totomindfuck. Enron's smacked her three good headshots that would drop a longhorn, but zilch. Not a twitch. What the fuck she made of? His toxdart got knocked away from him and in this tight space he can't push her off him. He makes a grab for his minimister. At close quarters that nasty little fuck might just kill. *One good scatter shot sure as shit will get this beast off*. The crazy puss keeps trying to pull something down over his head and that gives him his opening. Enron's fingers find the tiny pistol cached on his thigh and he maneuvers it point-blank into her face and pulls off a round. She's thrown backward, and Enron boosts her along with a two-footed kick in her chest. She hits the floor between the seats and stays the fuck down, both her hands covering her face. *That ought to yanking do it*. He has a tough time lurching up to his feet. When he does, he looks over at the other target cowering down in the row behind him. Her eyes are wide but not panicky. More like hate. They glue onto him. He realizes a lot of his camosuit is torn off. Enron throws down his minimister. He doesn't know what else to do. He's never felt the need before to apologize to a raghead for doing what he's been trained to do. He knows he's shitcreek now, though. No two ways about it. Tiptoe suit in shreds, not a heavy weapon to his name, Jowler gone, up to his neck in indian country, not a soul to get his back. Yep, time to buy the firm all right. *You had a pretty good run. A lot better than most for CorpTrooping*.

Just that moment, Enron's viewfield gets a sideways kick. *Good Christ almighty. Them fuckmothers are patching through*. And it hits him why: he's goddamned staring straight at target prime—this EVe bitch. Enron realizes Busch—that Net—is seeing exactly what the yank they want to see and what they want to kill. And they're using his all4s to see it and are about to use him, somehow, to kill her. *And here the fuck it comes*. Hair begins to stand at the nape of his neck. He can taste the surge order start to pass by. Busch must have him rigged to blow. Could be something they worked into his armor. Could be the bounce gel. Whatever they did, this will be the pure shit all right. A fierce twitch stabs its way up his spine. His arms and legs go strangely tingly and numb, like they're being drained. *Must be about three seconds to detonation.*

☆ ☆ ☆ ☆ ☆ ☆

Mall's rage becomes fascination. She watches the TexArc man's expression turn solemn, almost apologetic, when he drops the little gun. Then, just before he snaps rigidly to attention, like a man-sized puppet, she watches his face fall slack, as though all muscle tension were released. Once that happens, his curiously glittering eyes turn blank. He just stares at her, jaw dropped, eyes dead, unaware. Then he begins to tremor. Something compels Mall to leap over the seats and find the small metallictextile skullcap Sinalco had dropped. She hurriedly places it over the top of the man's head and tugs it down over his ears. Instantly, he collapses against her, his bulk almost knocking Mall off her feet. She steps aside and lets him slump down onto the floor. Then she's aware of Sinalco close behind her, her enormous face peeking over Mall's shoulder unmarked and unhurt—seeming just fine.

"Bien joué," she tells Mall. "You have saved us all."

"How the bloody hell–"

"We do much analysis now," Sinalco brusquely interrupts Mall's question, "then we will know better many things."

"Know better what?"

"Many, many things about the TexArc."

Sinalco is quite excited. Fortification Guard fighters are pouring into the amphitheater from every entranceway. Mall has to take this in. The holomaps vanish as the hall lights rise. Headminister Natwest has appeared, out of nowhere, down on the oval central floor. He's pointing eagerly up towards them, directing two armed stretcher bearers and two white-suited medics to hurry up into the seats.

"I was just the lure for the snare," she accuses Sinalco.

"Ma petite," Sinalco brushes hair off Mall's forehead and smiles, "how else can I get a man for you? Eh? And he is not so terrible looking. Regard his nice bulge. I am sure he is coming well equipped."

Sinalco's pleasantries fall very flat with Mall, but she does look down at the man's face. Beneath all the filth and the sweat, he might not be disagreeable looking. But he smells like a bloody goat, and he's a bloody fucking killer. Mall smacks away Sinalco's hand and squeezes her way out toward the aisle. Ascending stairs toward an exit, she speaks without turning around. "Sod off. You and Natwest—fuck-all both."

"I cannot blame you, my love," Sinalco calls after her. She lets Mall get almost to the exit. "Oh, and by the way, félicitations!"

Mall stops for this congratulatory afterthought, but will not turn to look at Sinalco. She shouts out her return, which reverberates in the grand auditorium. "For sodding *what*?"

Sinalco waits for the echo to fade. "You have been elected in what is called there by a landslide!" Sinalco smiles knowingly at Mall, who now has turned around to look at her. "Your Uncle Wobbly has won!"

PART TWO

TRUST THE MAN WHO WEARS THE STAR

Memos

COUNTERMEASURES PORTFOLIO #5476

* Urgency * / * Privy * / * Printext *

COMMUNIQUÉ TO CAUCUS

'The TexArc CorpTroop'

15.3.84

Prolegomena

So as to emit no electronic trace, this Communiqué to Caucus has been committed to printext. As is usual for these extraordinary cases, Communicants of Caucus need return Portfolio #5476 to Countermeasures once done with their reading. Of course, the current Administer of Caucus may retain her copy, but must keep it always with her person. Countermeasures appreciates greatly your cooperation in these precautionary matters.

Preliminary to anything, Countermeasures would like to ask pardon for the covert and perilous nature of its stratagem to capture a living TexArc CorpTroop. In order to confound a suspicious and powerful adversary, Countermeasures kept Caucus half in the dark about its operations, and certain EVe constituents were deceived and put at risk. Indeed, a good number of lives were lost during this dangerous endeavor. Countermeasures itself forfeited Underminister Harrods, the originator of the scheme. Countermeasures can only hope, in carrying out its charge as a ministry, the knowledge gained from this gambit will serve EVe well in her inevitable, upcoming, and, in all likelihood, definitive conflict with TexArc.

The captured CorpTroop revealed an abundance of information both passively via medexam and, surprisingly, actively via interrogation. In fact, the subject proved altogether cooperative during questioning. After an initial period of disorientation (the reasons for which will be described below) the CorpTroop behaved as though relieved by his capture and confinement. Increasingly, Countermeasures psychologists have become convinced of his sincerity. Nonetheless, Countermeasures retains a good degree of scepticism regarding all information supplied by the CorpTroop himself. For one thing, he could be disciplined, even without his knowledge, for responding to inquisition in this atypical and disarming manner. In such a way, he might more readily supply his captors with false intelligence by putting them off their guard. For another thing, to be frank, his level of basic education is appallingly low, especially when one takes into consideration the sophistication of the technology under his control. This particular CorpTroop is neither textliterate nor overly numerate. As a result, Countermeasures is not at all sure how clear he can be about his own circumstances in the world, let alone the collective structure and complexion of TexArcan society. In many respects, he seems a classic case of not being able to see the parkplaza for the electrautos. Therefore, although his native intelligence seems quite high, Countermeasures feels it prudent to question everything he tells us.

Finally, and needless to say, Countermeasures cannot determine if this man, who goes by the name of Enron, is a typical specimen for TexArc CorpTroops. Our cultural experts suspect his lack of formal education along any reasonable standards is an intended measure of control by TexArc authority over its soldiery. Likewise his physique, prodigious for a man in his late twenties or early thirties, obviously is the result of systematic and grueling training, and so should be regarded as normal for CorpTroops. Other than these two human traits, however, all crucial aspects of the CorpTroop that must be kept in mind are mechanic in nature.

The TexArc CorpTroop

First and foremost, the TexArc CorpTroop is a cyborg. Shockingly, TexArc would seem to be using cybernetic technology, widespread and as a matter of routine, well beyond the call of medical necessity (say, a synorgan or a synlimb) as we limit the practice here in EVe. At this point it is unclear whether all CorpTroops are cybernetically implanted, or just those five members (four dead, one living) of the Oxford and the Fribourg insert teams Countermeasures was able to medexam. (The third member of the Fribourg insert team somehow escaped capture or killing by Maneuvers fighters. Our search for this CorpTroop is ongoing.) According to interview testimony of the captured cyborg, all CorpTroops are so equipped. Indeed, he claims *all TexArcans are so implanted*. This claim strikes Countermeasures as wild and unreasonable, and perhaps is the result of his general misunderstanding or his subjection to prolonged indoctrination. However, Countermeasures knows the CorpTroops space-dropped into EVe to assassinate certain members of the Signification project were bioimplant with the following three devices.

1. *The motor-sensory cortex band* or *'Mot-sen/corband'*. This remarkable apparatus fits crossways over the top of the head, roughly from ear to ear, just underneath the scalp. The CorpTroop claims all TexArcans are implanted with the device at approximately the age of ten, when one comes of age for the workforce in that society. Physical evidence corroborates this disturbing assertion. The CorpTroops medexamined all showed the band long-since integrated to their skulls. The device itself is capable of expanding as the individual grows to adult size, and the microwire electrodes inserted shallowly into the brain (to a depth of only two millimeters)

are flexible and thus float so as not to dissect the neurons with which they are designed to interact. The BMI (Brain-Machine Interface) technology is straightforward and by no means revolutionary. For all its simplicity, however, what the *Mot-sen/corband* potentially can do is chilling.

The device fits along the motor and sensory cortexes. The motor cortex plans, controls, and executes movement involving delayed response, that is, conscious movement, with different areas along the motor cortex controlling different areas of the body. If one's motor cortex were to be electronically stimulated, one would react by moving a corresponding body part, depending on where the stimulation occurred. Similarly, the sensory cortex receives sensory information from the body about pressure, texture, temperature, and pain, with different areas along the sensory cortex receiving information from different parts of the body. If one's sensory cortex were to be electronically stimulated, one would report the sensation of being touched on a corresponding body part, depending on where the stimulation occurred. The reason for locating a BMI device along these cortexes thus should be apparent. These two cortexes work in close conjunction to control movement of the body. Given proper electronic stimulation, certain rudimentary movements of a person could be managed without that person's consent; equally, a person could manipulate a range of mechanic and robotic apparatuses through the *Mot-sen/corband*, such as the assaultbots accompanying the two insert teams. Interestingly, the captured CorpTroop displayed an unusual concern for the bot under his control. During questioning, he repeatedly asked after its functional status, seemingly hoping to be reunited with this versatile and lethal devise. [For a complete TexArc CorpTroop weapons report, please see Countermeasures Portfolio #5477.] Wireless signals transmitted to and from the brain are a simple matter of a small processor being part of the band. Signal functions include the ability to 'think' voice transmissions, rather like having a messager permanently situated in one's head.

Countermeasures can only speculate upon the degree of control the *Mot-sen/corband* allows. From the standpoint of the bioimplant individual interfacing with machines, such capacities are considerable, as was seen in Oxford and Fribourg. The TexArc CorpTroop is a formidable and self-contained fighting unit largely because of his cybernetic capabilities. From the standpoint of the bioimplant individual being manipulated by the device, however, it seems unlikely that any truly extensive command of a person's actions might be achieved. One cannot be reduced, for example, to the status of an abject puppet based on the rather simple neural-electrical principles by which this mechanism operates. At most, one might be arrested in one's voluntary actions or be made to carry out certain basic body movements or functions. The CorpTroop reported often being made to perform a variety of elementary operations. Such an invasion of one's corporeal autonomy, though, seems quite violent enough. Autopsies strongly suggest two of the CorpTroops who died in Oxford were not killed by our fighters, but rather by their *Motor-sensory cortex bands* overstimulating and, in effect, searing their brains. In short, they were terminated by their own military commanders.

2. *The ipatch.* This device wraps entirely around the sclera of the eye, that is, the external rubbery layer that holds in the gelatinous substance. The CorpTroop maintains, as with the *Mot-sen/corband*, that all TexArcans are fitted, on both eyes, with the *ipatch* at about age ten, again as a way to take part in the workforce. Implantation of the device requires the practical removal of the eyeball; moreover, the instrument cannot be taken off without doing irreparable damage to the eye. Hence, once installed, the *ipatch* is worn for life.

The function of the *ipatch* is basic telecommunication. Receiving transmissions through the small processor that is part of the *Mot-sen/corband*, the *ipatch* displays screen images directly onto the cornea, which is actually a specialized region of the sclera. In total, four such screens are superimposed upon the cornea, one in each quadrant of the field of vision. How these screens are held stable in the field of vision is quite remarkable. The *ipatch* is made of a rubber-glass, flex-plastic substance that is tri-layered. The middle layer suspends the telescreens in such a way that they float constantly in place over the cornea, each screen's innermost corner just infringing on the edge of the iris when looking straight ahead. In this way, the wearer can either look past the screens (and even, to an extent, through them; the CorpTroop described the screens as being semitransparent when not viewed directly) or expressly at one particular screen, similar to a HUD (Heads-Up Display) as the wearer chooses. What the wearer seems unable to decide, however, is whether the screens are active or not. As long as a vidfeed is being received, these telescreens will image. Even closing one's eyelids will do no good. Only signal block negates the functioning of the *ipatch*.

Transmissions received by this device is less clear to Countermeasures at this time. The CorpTroop tells of both a military use and a civilian use for the four quadrants. The military uses are combat related and so largely understandable. [Once again, Countermeasures Portfolio #5477.] The civilian uses, however, are more obscure; nor did the CorpTroop seem able to articulate their rationale to a substantial extent. Nonetheless, it seems the average TexArcan is constantly supplied with the following four vidfeeds. In the upper left quadrant of the *ipatch* is something called 'view world', possibly an information and bulletin feed. In the upper right quadrant is 'shop drop', apparently a consumer and advertisement feed of some sort. In the lower left quadrant is 'you choose', an amusement feed from the sounds of it. In the lower right quadrant is 'brand you', which seems to be a work-related feed. Countermeasures cultural experts were unable to ascertain any insight into these vidfeeds beyond their bare descriptions. Significantly more study in this area is required.

Finally, one consequence of wearing the *ipatch* that should be noted here is the phenomenon termed by the CorpTroop as 'the glassy'. That is, to the observer, the wearer of the *ipatch* would appear to have quite sparkly and ever-darting eyes, which, to the unaccustomed, might be disconcerting. In fact, before placing the sigblock skullcap on the CorpTroop in the Fribourg fortification, the signer witnessed this very phenomenon, as indeed did several of the fighters who survived their encounters with the Oxford and Fribourg insert teams.

3. *The ihear.* Supplying the audfeed for the *ipatch* vidfeed, as well as serving other one- and two-way communicative functions, is the device known as the *ihear*. Like the two instruments described above, the *ihear* is a bioimplant instated at age ten, evidently the moment when childhood ends and adulthood begins in TexArc society. Very simply, the *ihear* is a small wireless receiver grafted directly onto the acoustic or auditory nerve, thereby bypassing the ear completely. Thus the wearer has a normal range of hearing, plus access to any number of transmission signals used for, one can imagine, any variety of purposes. Unlike the *ipatch*, the *ihear* is surgically removable; however, as in the case of the *Mot-sen/corband* as well, the procedure is unadvisable due to the likelihood of neurological damage. Interestingly, there seems a redundancy in implanting two separate processors to receive wireless transmissions, one in the *Mot-sen/corband* and one in the *ihear*. From what Countermeasures teeks have been able to determine, the master signal would be taken in by the *Mot-sen/corband* initially, then routed to the *ihear*. However, the *ihear* itself easily could accommodate the master signal, even to the capacity of receiving vidfeed and routing that to the *ipatch*.

It should be noted in summary that the steady visual and audio cacophony supplied by the *ipatch* and the *ihear* would appear to take a toll on the bioimplantee. One can only imagine what it might be like to be engulfed in such a constant and invasive stream of clutter. The effect seems to be a negative habituation, that is, one grows dependent upon the intrusion. The CorpTroop reports it as being quite distressing to have one or more of his telescreens go clear, and that until the sigblock skullcap was placed on him, he'd never not had some manner of audfeed playing in his head (even if just background music while he slept) since he was fitted with these apparatuses as a child. Countermeasures cultural experts are quick to point out the potential for doctrinal inculcation that these devices afford. Indeed, so powerful was the effect of being suddenly cut off from his accustomed vid- and aud-feeds that the CorpTroop blacked out and, even once regaining consciousness, remained disoriented for several days while gradually surrendering to their absence. The process was not unlike narcotics detoxification. Once 'clean', though, of his 'feed dependence', as it were, the CorpTroop was enormously grateful for his re-found clarity of mind. He is quoted as having remarked: 'Like being a damn kid again'. Countermeasures psychologists propose that his gratitude plays a large role in his eagerness to cooperate with EVe now. It would seem in fact that he has come over to us mind and heart. Needless to say, Countermeasures counsels caution in believing his defection.

The TexArc Society

While TexArc geopolitical military methods and aims have been made altogether clear to EVe over the past half century, current TexArc society remains principally an enigma, impenetrable by real or by virtual means. Obviously, the capture of a living CorpTroop affords Countermeasures a rare window into that society, albeit one restricted in scope. Based on medexam and, more so, extensive interview of this CorpTroop (complete transcripts of both are available upon permission), certain keynote features of TexArc plausibly might be extrapolated. Countermeasures offers some few inferences below, but only those in which our cultural experts have a moderate-to-high level of confidence.

1. *TexArc society is rigidly hierarchical in nature*. From what can be gathered, there are four class divisions in TexArc, two being held upper and two being regarded as lower. The upper two categories are called 'Crat' and 'Terd' (also known as 'Gater'). As one would expect, they seem to hold the educational and technological, and thus the material, advantages in the society. The lower two categories are known as 'CorpTroop' and 'Serv' (also known as 'Parker'). They seem to perform the productive labor in the society.

2. *TexArc economic formation is based upon the initial determination of unequal capital stocks*. Such a phenomenon is, of course, concomitant with any social hierarchy. As always, the heart of the matter lies in property relations.

3. *TexArc society is dominated by four cardinal convictions*. These are: i) *anti-intellectualism*, as demonstrated by the common maxims 'Don't be too smart for your own good' and 'Don't go thinking on me now'; ii) *religiosity*, as seen in the widespread platitudes 'Let God take care of the big stuff' and 'God wants me to be rich'; iii) *machismo*, as demonstrated not only by the existence of a wholly warrior class but by an abundance of such belligerent quips as 'Make my day, bitch' and 'I say, bring it on'; iv) *jingoism*, which, somehow to the TexArcan, is epitomized by the curious dictum 'You can trust your car to the man who wears the star'.

4. *TexArc dominant ideology is subtly if not pleasurably inculcated as a mask to its otherwise brutal imposition*. Only this technique fashions such depths of ignorance and apathy.

5. *TexArc public education is selectively administered, miserably inadequate, or utterly absent*. Cultural experts were not able to determine precisely which.

6. *The marketplace is primum mobile to TexArc society*. Two of their more prominent official mottos are 'Wealth, Exploitation, Domination' and 'Market, God, Nation'.

Significantly more study in this cultural arena is required. It is the strongly held opinion of Countermeasures that the CorpTroop should remain indefinitely in our hands in order for this crucial analysis to be conducted further.

A Word on Caucus' Proposed Plan of Action

With respect, it is the considered view of Countermeasures that Caucus' proposed plan reciprocally to insert members of the Signification project into TexArc is little short of madness. Given our scant knowledge of that society, and given the vague nature of the so-called 'Uncle Wobbly' electoral victory within TexArc, such a mission has neither a high likelihood of success nor a clearly defined goal. Underminister Harrods himself never envisioned his counter-advocacy project to be carried to this extent; neither is the information regarding TexArc's interior provided us by the CorpTroop remotely reliable. To insert the signer and the teek, with the CorpTroop acting as their aboriginal guide, into such an unfamiliar and hostile environment can only prove reckless. No amount of Maneuvers protective guard sent along with them are likely to ensure bare team-member survival, let alone Caucus' indistinctly articulated mission success.

Underminister Harrods' quixotic scheme to slice ArcNet in hopes of discovering a way to disrupt the slander campaign now in motion there against EVe, while not thoroughly fanciful, was intended chiefly as a ruse to prompt TexArc concern, thereby fomenting contact with and capture of TexArc military personnel. With the main portion of Harrods' plan now splendidly achieved, it seems ludicrous to pursue its ancillary part. Waging a guerrilla culture war against what amount to cultureless thugs is truly folly. Placing alterity and KME before TexArcans are indeed pearls before swine. The signer and the teek are to be commended for their ingenuity and bravery during this operation, but their tasks now are at an end. It is time instead for us to amplify our success by delving more profoundly into the CorpTroop's active and passive knowledge of TexArc military operations. During early medexam and interrogation of the CorpTroop, Countermeasures used no tissue-disruptive or psyche-invasive investigative techniques. It is now time to probe deeper. Whether Caucus is willing to face facts or not, the only hope EVe has, currently, for commonwealth survival is to find ways to endure and then to repel the legions of TexArc that are surely headed our way. The captured CorpTroop likely holds those keys.

Once more, then, permit Countermeasures to declare that it is our fervently held belief that launching what amounts to a suicide mission into TexArc is not only fruitless to EVe's desperate enterprise, but wholly damaging to it.

This Portfolio respectfully submitted by:
Natwest, Headminister of Countermeasures

☆ ☆ ☆ ☆ ☆ ☆

21.3.84

Preliminary to anything, and with every deserved bit of respect, I say to you Natwest, Headminister of Countermeasures, sod off.

Secondarily over all else, save of course for the preliminary directly above, I submit to you Administer Movënpick, Chair-of-Caucus, that you and your fellow Communicants are quite the pack of cheeky little shits.

EVe constituents are generally not under the impression, Administer, that the job of Caucus is to conceal vital bits of information from them (us). A few such tidbits that leap currently to mind are, shall we say, our desperate vulnerability to overwhelming attack, this network of vacuum trains crisscrossing beneath us, these nuclear subterrenes you've developed that can worm their way through solid rock, and the alarming fact that it has begun to rain assassins from space. The boorish practice of state secrets lapsed with the bloody DDR, Administer Movënpick. I didn't ballot for you before for Chair-of-Caucus, and I very much doubt I will ballot for you in future. To the contrary, I'm contemplating standing my candidate, Uncle Wobbly, against you next electoral go around. You wouldn't have a prayer.

And as for you, Headminister, playing at secret agent man against a pack of psychopaths while using your compatriots as live bait? Really now. What is your ministry coming to? I've a mind to roll up your Countermeasures Portfolio #5476 and beat you about the head and shoulders with it. In fact, upon further consideration, if I should return from this expedition, I've determined to kick you squarely in the googlies.

These few things candidly off my chest, I will be all business from this point forward. I will have a great sodding eye for business. Headminister Natwest, you require progress reports from me, so I will bloody well give you progress reports, whether you approve of their nature or not. Administer Movënpick, you require cultural appraisal from me, so cultural appraisal you shall have. But I will not be restricting myself to the phenomenon of TexArc. I will appraise whatever bloody construct I please. As erstwhile decoy for official state skullduggery, I believe I am entitled. Hence follows my inaugural opinion paper.

Headminister Natwest, you are to be condemned for forming, and Administer Movënpick, you are to be commended for ignoring, the numbskullish recommendation by Countermeasures that EVe would be better served butchering to pieces the captured TexArc CorpTroop rather than enlisting his aid for a first-hand look into the astonishing electoral victory of Uncle Wobbly. The real value of Enron to EVe is not as laboratory specimen, but as chaperon into TexArc. Without his guidance, our venture would be unthinkable. (In fact, that you are *not* heeding the advice of an avowed liar, Administer, has me rethinking my position on your balloting.) Sinalco pulled off a remarkable bit of teeking to obscure her forward slice into

ArcNet. If they could not trail where we were going, the bastards will have no clue we are coming. The insert is worth our risk. Signification at least has the potential for lessening or even mending this conflict. Discovering more efficient ways to blow people to smithereens never has. (And fear not, dear Headminister. Should my counter-advocacy fail, your little plan for military carnage will remain not as an option, but as an inevitability.) Granted, Enron was ordered to 'term' me, as they quaintly put it in TexArc, and he quite nearly succeeded. But in that moment when he held his clearest opportunity, he chose not to kill me. Disobeying express orders and overthrowing decades of conditioning, he stopped himself. I admit, the coincidences surrounding my escape are extraordinary. That Enron hails from BoiCity, that his local electoral feeds found their way to him through ArcNet, even as a CorpTroop serving halfway around the globe, is nothing shy of waveamazing. The delusional among us, who possess the ability to discover design in happenstance, might clap their hands in praise and cry it providential. But Enron's response to Uncle Wobbly is no bloody piece of voodoo. It is not the consciousness of people that determines their existence, but their social existence that determines their consciousness. Enron's sympathetic reaction to Wobbly's message demonstrates how an advocacy project for alterity can have a positive effect in TexArc, how presenting even the sorely indoctrinated with the *possibility* of a different social foundation can excite their imaginations into embracing new views of the world. Caucus is justified to send us into TexArc over the shrill protests of Countermeasures, and I know Maneuvers is keen to take the fight to the away pitch. On now to my maiden report.

After spending a fortnight post-battle at the lowest levels of the Fribourg fortification, we boarded a vacuum train and tubed north, sucked along like supersonic glass-encased moles. The sensation of riding these trains still has me believing my insides are being steadily dragged out through my bum. Our first destination, we were told, was Moskva. But who can know? All undergrounds looks tediously alike. There, we boarded an even sleeker, more nausea-enducing train, to tube northward, toward the submariner base at Severødvinsk, near Arkhangel'sk on the Beloye More. There, we again resisted straying above one hundred meters of the surface, never mind catching a breath of sweet above-ground air. We were delayed at base two days onloading provisions and reconducting system checks. Tomorrow, at dawn, we board the deepsloop *Conscientização*. Then, I imagine, the 'mindfuck' ensues. Note: I will be working into my vocabulary as many TexArc idioms as I can master. Our friend Enron is brimming with them, all quite colorful.

For the record, our foray crew includes, besides myself as signer, darling randy Sinalco as my teek and the TexArcan CorpTroop Enron as our 'tonto' (his vernacular meaning, apparently, faithful sidekick and guide; this fellow is very perceptive and has been underestimated by Countermeasures). Our Maneuvers escort 'muscle' is led by the irrepressible Major Cardinal, who would refer to herself painstakingly as 'Capitaine de Corvette Cardinal of the Fortification Guards'. Ah, alte Schweiz Ordnung. I stress, Sinalco has been at pains to prevent dear Cardinal from 'terming' our poor CorpTroop as she hates him with a fury. Under Cardinal's command are six elite fighters you determined a fit number to protect our enterprise. Like Cardinal, they jabber their native Bolze incessantly, which luckily Sinalco can translate. By name they are: Forbetr, Renault, Pernod, Migros, Blaupunkt, and Toblerone. They keep to themselves, cleaning their ordnance again and again. At the moment, I have a difficult time sorting them out, one from another. Each strikes me as being as lethally inclined as the next. They really seem a murderous lot. I am sure that is why they were chosen to come along, and their talents will be beneficial where we are headed. (I must remark, though, I didn't know we, EVe, had such bloodthirst in us.) Thus we comprise a foray crew of ten. We few, we happy few. More will follow as things progress. If I manage to get my mind around the essential workings of TexArc culture, I shall send you a really full report. Until then expect dribs and drabs from me.

This Memo not particularly respectfully submitted by:
Mall, Signer of Signification Committee

☆ ☆ ☆ ☆ ☆ ☆

27.3.84

Cher Natwest. We continue our creep along the bottom, I am informed by le Capitaine Bovril. All moves very slow, and this deepsloop is very snug inside, like the sardines, and all days we must be exactly quiet. Mall has become un peu fou, saying all moments her eardrums must to bang. I am on the TexArc man close as you said for me to be. He is, I think, in love with our little Mall who, bien sûr, has not a clue. He asks many questions about her, but not I think in a dangerous way, if you see what I say. He wants to know *first* about Mall and second about EVe like he cannot believe his eyes and ears such things exist. I am in agreement with Mall. This TexArc man is not so dumb as you say. But he is not dangereux this way, I think. Not at this moment. I must keep Cardinal happy and busy aussi because as you know she wants to kill this TexArc man and any like him. I tell her patience. Soon we will have our chance probably. Capitaine Bovril takes me over our route. We cannot go in any predictable way, so we start and we stop. We go this way, we go that way. For a little time in one direction then turn right back and go another. Très lent. As TexArc do, their shadowboats waited for us just outside the mouth between the Kanin and the Kola peninsulas. On top of the continental shelf, they steam fast, but these TexArc boats cannot sloop so deep as us. We amuse ourselves with them a little around the Franz Josef Land. Then le Capitaine drops us onto the Barents Abyssal Plain where we move about crazy, then are deadstop for a long time. While we sit and sit, the TexArc man teaches us games at cards CorpTroops play. When Cardinal comes, she says no.

The one we play is not a CorpTroop game but ancien Maneuvers game she call 'Ach, Scheisse!' *That* starts the arguing. But this TexArc man talks her nice into playing, and I am sure lets her to win. You see? Not so dummy.

After sitting to make well sure the shadowboats are lost, we run many canyons through the Nansen Cordillera where this ocean is the most profound. Many runs and très vite. The fighters and me are excited by this ride. Mall and the TexArc man not so much. Capitaine Bovril tells me EVe deepsloops go either the east and south through Denmark or Davis Straits, or the west and south through Bering Strait. They go to TexArc east or west coast to hide deep and quiet en garde. The shadowboats try to find us again through those narrow places, but we will be safe and nous-mêmes seul, running south among the Palin Islands and down the long Gulf of Boothia, through the Fox Basin and Channel, and enfin more south into the au loin Nixon Bay. Shadowboats think no deepsloops ever are coming such a route. Capitaine Bovril says we will arrive in another two days, encore trois at the most. We still must go careful. Once insert in TexArc, we see if how we think things must go, *can* go. Toujours the mouse and cat, I think. Yes? But as this Enron man say, you never know.

Memosender: Sinalco

☆ ☆ ☆ ☆ ☆ ☆

1.4.84

Meine Damen Movënpick:

Of only the sehr important events you instruct me to inform you. Such event happens. One fighter is tot. He is Toblerone. Tobi we say him. So we are six Maneuvers fighters and no more seven. This TexArc land ist sehr fremd und unfreundlich. I need more fighters and see too late to have more. I am not glücklich for being here.

We are offload das Unterseeboot for two days. My fighters and me like to get offload it. Das U-boot always sehr kalt and air taste sehr bad. Marine man synrations taste auch more schlecht than marine air. You know from Fribourg, we like to eat only good things.

Herr Kapitän Bovril bring us well into the Nixon Bay. By the map we sink between the Eskimo Point and the Cape Churchill but more close to the Hubbart Point. To put out subterrene, we must get shallow aber nicht zuviel or we are being seen from above us by their satellite. I am surprise so big subterrene fit in our deepsloop. I know das *Conscientização* is EVe most gross und schnell and I know we are one special trip only. But big subterrene sehr good for us in this bad land. We can do one offload only. Two take zu long time and be too dangerous. Und so in subterrene we make the big hole Westen and Süden like the worm. Inside it overfull again like U-boot even more aber sehr heiss now also this time. Lithium pumps as the liquid from reactor core to outside hull to machen to glass all rock and dirt we pass in. Sehr sehr hot. Lucky we make no mark and TexArc do not know here we are. Wir zurücklassen nur that wide twelve meter glass tunnel far far under the ground.

As we plan, we come up Nordosten of Flin Flon burg where TexArc fighter say will not be zuviel Leute. I am ready not to trust but this fighter say true. No man there. Only field. Far, far, far in every way. Weizen. Nur wheat. Kilometer und kilometer und kilometer I can see no end to wheat and ist sehr unglaublich so much fields. Very beautiful. Very very beautiful. I am surprising myself liking this flat land so well. Not like our home mountains. Again like TexArc fighter say we can do, we walk to the Flin Flon town to buy the old autos for no problem here. Sinalco fabrizieren their DollArcs, but TexArc people want nur our weapon and so we trade some. I am not liking this but Sinalco say okay and TexArc fighter say we find many other weapon all ways in TexArc and this time I am believing him. Die TexArc Leute we are seeing up to now sehr unheimlich to us. They are bony and smell bad and their eyes are all the time flashing so they niemals can look right to you. Like all times they are seeing some things other. And the buildings and homes are dirty and falling down but autos are like the giants and all times sauber and shiny. Alles sind hier crazy and my fighters and me do not like this Ausländer things. But subterrene is gone now, and U-boot is gone now, and here we are. The two alten autos we get are as the TexArc fighter say them, the compact brand, but we are thinking them sehr gross like for the giant man. He names them Hummers and they oldest and littlest kind of autos here in TexArc. They petrol burn und so the weiss smoke smell bad and give you head hurt, and these auto roar like going to blow to parts. Mall say they perfectly beastly auto and I think so much, too. But we drive on the small Fahrbahn Süden and always South by nothing but wheat and wheat and auch between some much wide lakes. Then we come on big Autobahn #1 and drive Westen and always West by all fields and fields still. I can not believing my eyes that the fields more big als all of alte Schweiz, and the sky so big also like blau glass curving over uns.

And here is where bad things come. TexArc autobahn is like die Rennstrecke but where giant autos can push to side not so giant autos, but also where many autos have the turrets for gun on defense front and sides and back. Like war race. You drive 130 kmh and is too slow here. Most are driving 160-180 kmh and some even 200. All crazy types here. And stations where you buy the petrol like little fortress, too. DollArc only and DollArc first, and guards with the weapon, and dogs, and barricades, and big lights, and with die Kasse behind thick thick glass. All here is like the cowboys. Yahoo! I try but can not drive so fast on this autobahn. Sinalco have TexArc fighter drive. I do not leave him, so Tobi keeps to driving other auto following, but soon Tobi can not keep to us this fast and his auto is not seen any more by us. And this ist nicht wohl. Also Blaupunkt and Migros and Renault and Pernod are in this auto so they are five and we are five, and it is no good thing we get separate. When Sinalco say where is Tobi the TexArc fighter look backward in mirrors and say this is not well and drive as wildman across the middle part to opposite way of autobahn to go back find them. This Hummer auto like Panzer, or the bunker, on fat tires so I think you can not hurt it. When we see other Hummer finally is trying not be forced off autobahn by many, many Motorrad. Maybe thirty or maybe more. TexArc fighter say us later, these are gangs and sehr dangerous for the slow auto because they kill and rob you for the petrol, and the tire, and the parts, and for anything else. But these Motorrad also more crazy because coming out between legs of Reiter is the long männliche Glied thick like the salami pointing to the sky. Maybe out two meters and more and up curving like horn on bull. The TexArc fighter say these are penicycles and Mall say them satyrs on wheels. We are amaze. Tobi try to stay to road but not can do it. Penicycle peoples jump to top of Hummer and try to break glass of windows and then schiessen inside. They also cover over front window so Tobi can not be seeing where he is going. He swerve and swerve, and throw some these penicycle people off to ground but soon Hummer off road and almost turn over so Tobi must stop. My fighters jump out shooting and penicycle Motorrad ride in big circle around Hummer, shooting and doing hooting, and there is big big dust of cloud and big big roaring of Motorrad engine and we can not be there yet to help.

And TexArc fighter say, Sinalco if we leave them they are dead, and if we go to help we are dead too, and I say we go to help, and he say to Sinalco then give him a gun. I say no give TexArc man a gun and we are almost there to fight. Then Mall give this TexArc man her Pistole and he laugh and say well shit and fall back in it. So this TexArc fighter drive crazy to reach other Hummer and when we get to it he start to drive against the way of clock around the circle of penicycles, all the time honking his horn and shooting his Pistole into air until penicycles are stopping, and fighting is stopping too. Then TexArc man stop our Hummer and will be getting out and

Mall say him what the bloody hell he thinks he doing, and he say back to us, stay in Hummer no matter what happen and be ready to drive away macht schnell. And he walk out into middle of penicycle ring of Motorrad holding Pistole straight up over his head far as he can reach it and pointing Pistole up into sky and shouting over and again something we not understand sounding like high noon. So then penicycle man is getting off his Motorrad and walking into middle of ring with his Pistole holding up far high over his head. And this Mann is very tall and even look not so gaunt as others and wears a wide hat with many feathers stuck to it and auch a falsch dickle strapped on his crotch auch sticking up to sky. This man and TexArc fighter man stand to face at each other maybe fifteen meters separate and velcro to thighs their Pistoles, then all penicycle peoples count langsam ein zwei drei and these man pull off again their Pistole and shoot at einander. Pof! One time at same time. Only TexArc fighter man is left to standing. He shout some words and penicycle peoples drive off away and are gone like are never there.

We find Tobi is dead shot zweimal in chest, and Pernod and Migros also shot, but not sehr bad place. Sinalco take care of their woundings. We have to go far far off autobahn to make for Tobi a grave. It must be deep, deep so niemand will never be finding him. I let only me and my Maneuvers fighters do digging, and we can leave no mark. So that is where Tobi is now and for always, under the fields and fields of wheat and the sky that is so weit. This is all happening between the Stadt of Regina and Moose Jaw. Soon we be off these great plains und Westen mehr up to the continental divide and into the Reagan Mountains. I think we will be liking again to be in mountains land and feeling a little bit in our home.

And this TexArc fighter man Enron ist nicht so bad I think now. After the fighting he hand the Pistole back to Sinalco but I say him no, for him to keep. And Sinalco laugh to me. Few more days and we be to BoiCity place. I ask to Enron man how long since he being home and he say me many, many Jahren. I ask to him will be good to being home again. He say me, noway hozay. I am not knowing every words aber I know he mean nein. Er ist auch ein Soldat.

Memosender:

Capitaine de Corvette Cardinal of the Fortification Guards

☆ ☆ ☆ ☆ ☆ ☆

1.5.84

I've not reported to you very many times since my original memo because I know both Sinalco and Cardinal keep you, separately, informed. I've also not felt bloody much like reporting since Toblerone was killed and, weeks later, Renault died of the breakbone fever. Everyone else, except bloody Sinalco (who seems never to get sick) and Enron (being native to this god-awful place) has been fighting off malaria, west nile virus, or both. I've also not felt bloody much like reporting because I've had nothing good to report.

As I'm sure you've gathered by now, the barbarity of this sodding country is appalling. The majority of their population is tubed on to a gruel mixture that amounts to little more than puréed shit. Meanwhile their cars are spit-polished goliaths that down more petrol in a kilometer than Welsh coal miners used to drink stout on a Saturday night. They ride over glass-smooth, super motorways twelve lanes across in either direction whilst living in dilapidated wood shanties or flimsy tin caravans a pig would think twice before entering. In short, no civilization ever worshiped more the wheel or the bloody internal combustion engine. The hypocrisy is severe and everywhere palpable—if one cares to observe it. Every dozen kilometers or so along their freeways stand a cluster of three mammoth crosses towering a good hundred meters into the air, signifying how we are holy, holy, holy. (These crosses also serve as the bleeding transmitters for their unholy all4s signal.) But also every two dozen kilometers or so, along with the ubiquitous bloody McSlurrys, is a franchise Slop-Chute where they can purchase all manner of watery beers and distilled potato peelings to drink until their heads swim and their stomach linings are perforated. Or they can stop to browse a franchise AdultWorld where they can credspend for digital or virtual pornography of a violence and depravity that would make the sodding Marquis de Sade pale. Bugger-all. I've yet to run across anyone here even remotely text literate (though Enron is learning well enough). And the glassy—the sod-all glassy. You can't get by it. You can't break through. TexArcans are all locked into what they think is their own little world. But it isn't. It's someone else's little world made up for them to live in, walk in, eat and sleep, fuck and fart, and work in. All whilst severely unaware. The clutter is stupefying and, I believe, quite unimaginable to us. Sinalco and I have aligned in to its feed to watch the four channels singularly on palmbook. We can barely keep up with the stream of chatter on one of the screens. Only Enron has experienced the four-fold babel that must come through the Mot-sen/corband and then over the ihear and the ipatch. He has taken to wearing a chin strap attached to his sigblock skullcap for fear of ever being linked again to the feed. Once the feed has you, he warns me, you're gone to the glassy. Quite lost. He says he'd rather die than go back on feed. I believe him. I suspect, as does Sinalco, that if he ever were linked again, ArcNet would be alerted to our presence. TexArc likely thinks him dead along with us and Sinalco's original slice, all blown to pieces deep underground in the Fribourg fortification. Your pseudo-seismic tremor and false smoke release seems to have done the trick. That's why Sinalco and I have been hesitant to slice in again to ArcNet. If they recognize her signature, we've lost the advantage of being unknown inside TexArc. This does not mean we've been doing nothing. I've been up to a good deal of cultural and signification work, and Sinalco has taken her first cautious steps back into their stream, and finally we are making some headway. Hence my report to you now.

After the satyr motorcyclists, with their right jolly long cocks sticking straight up into the air, things didn't become really ludicrous again until after we left the old Trans-Canada Highway to drive southward along T-15. Traffic increased and became extra hostile. We drove in close tandem to avoid more trouble. We got past several minimegs—meg for megalopolis—and old ghostmegs (abandoned cities) such as Great Falls, Butte, and Idaho Falls without incident. At Pocatello we linked with T-86, and farther west with T-84, to cross a great desert to the supermeg of BoiCity. Kilometers distant, we spotted its Pyramid rise gold over the horizon, back-dropped by brown foothills. This Pyramid dominates the vast flats to the south and west of this city and is as inscrutable as any sphinx. Everyone constantly is aware of its being there, with no one seeming to understand why, or what is its function, or how it influences—or even determines—their lives. Thus far we've all made a point of simply keeping well away from it. The 'yub from the hub' (word to the wise) is that no good ever comes from wandering too close to the Pyramid or, for that matter, ever from crossing into the Gater district immediately encircling the Pyramid. So far, to maintain our anonymity, we've kept strictly to the parks—in other words, the great slums that apparently surround all TexArc megs.

Physically, the parks are just how Underminister Harrods described to me most of the rest of the world: the attrition zones of Africa and South America and most of Asia. Malnutrition verges on famine, epidemics are constant, social services and infrastructure are nonexistent. Whatever sewer system that once existed, for example, became overwhelmed long ago. Climate disasters are frequent and extreme: here, besides the heat, it's either drought or flood. The people describe intense windstorms and thunderstorms sweeping in from the west that, by the sounds of them, cannot quite be real. I'm told the season is coming soon. Like EVe, especially in our northern regions, the warming hasn't yet been devastating to TexArc. Northeast to us, the direction from which we came after our marine and terrene sub excursions, tundra has turned into boundless crop land, extending considerably the range of their great plains breadbasket. What TexArc lost to the south in arable land it more than made up for to the north. I see this phenomenal agricultural resource as one of the explanations for their world dominance, the others being brute military force and an internal régime of truth the likes of which I never before imagined possible. With irrigation, wheat and potatoes are grown in adequate abundance in the vicinity surrounding BoiCity, and a stringy breed of beef cattle seems to cope well enough—shabby, dead-eyed brutes that, like the Servs who tend them, seem perpetually in a daze. I wager their feed is drugged. Their headgear looks to weigh them down as well—dauntingly long, lethal-looking horns that make one thankful for the otherwise docility of the beasts. By all means, please grasp the allegory.

What distinguishes the parks from the attrition zone is that around the world such disaster stems from the abject want of resource and planning. In TexArc one sees the opposite. Here human misery is attentively coordinated so as to be commercially vigorous. Privation has been commodified into a full range of goods and services. One biz (enterprise), *Elements,* markets shoddy but sharp-looking personal protective wear, such as hats, masks, dark glasses, visors, goggles, hoods, capes, gloves, ponchos, boots, chaps, coveralls, escape aqualungs, hang-gliders and rafts, along with salves and ointments for all occasions: sunblock, windburn, mosquito repellant, tick kill, rat bite, ringworm, and the like. Another outfit, *Survival,* sells solar batteries and appliances, reflector stoves, water pure tanks, self-clean port-a-poopers, electra-gen bikes, waterless clothes washers, meat drying racks, small-animal filleters, and whole mobiles (small caravans most Servs live in) advertised as thermal balanced no matter the heat or cold outside. From what we have seen none of these items work well or for very long, and none are handily repairable once broken down. My favorite enterprise is enviroassurance. *Act of God* and *GoodHands* are two firms peddling schemes to protect you and yours from all the calamities of the bible: fire, flood, earthquake, pestilence, famine, drought, wind, heat, mormon cricket (locust), not to mention their low, low special rates for infant mortality. Many purchase these protection plans in an attempt to beat the awful odds, but no one we have come into contact with knows of a claim ever being recompensed. The crown jewel for environmental coping, of course, is the almighty air-cooling unit. Virtually every mobile has one chained in a window, with many being booby trapped. Virtually none of them work. The units break down easily and the price of parts is exorbitant, either on *Shopdrop* or in the flourishing black market. Even if one's air-cooler does function, few Servs can generate enough powerelectric to keep it running for long. Regardless, Parkers never fail to acquire this expensive item at first opportunity. Living in refrigerated air is the top status symbol in TexArc. All's a proper mammonist cockup here.

Ergo, what I am seeing here culturally is a degree of social cruelty and control unprecedented in a human history long congested with social cruelty and control. The Serv as the staple hireling in TexArc is socially reproduced at a level of efficiency unknown to me in the modern era—or in any bleeding other. It is the scientific management of Taylor reborn and spliced to the market populist fables of Gilder and Gingrich—in other words, the worst of the third mammonist century, early and late, rolled into one dominant ideology. With minimal cost, the Serv is born, grows, works, and dies glued to the lowest rung of the pecuniary ladder, specter and flesh kept barely enough together to perform necessary labor and consume necessary commodities. In point of fact, I believe I am close to clarifying precisely what is meant in TexArc by the term 'Corpfeud'. Unless I miss my guess, it looks to be a deliberate attempt to thwart historical materialism. Rather than permit technological developments to alter the economic base, and thereby eventually evolve the cultural superstructure, TexArc has imposed economic and especially ideological impediments to regulate technical and monetary advances so that they do not lead to social revolution. In other words, TexArc seems to want to grind history to a halt, to keep it in place right where it is. In point of fact, I am seeing increasing evidence, in order to accomplish this amazing feat, that TexArc, in effect, has nudged history backward a notch. Odd as it sounds, I think what I am witnessing in BoiCity is a neo-manorial system of some sort. Two overly advanced bits of vocabulary we routinely hear in the parks are 'demesne' and 'corvée' labor—can such words be used naturally by people who have never attended a school of any sodding kind or read static text? Perhaps this meg, perhaps all TexArc megs, are more or less self-sustaining economic units designed to be, paradoxically, both mammonistically acquisitive and socially stagnant. Indeed, that would be a deuce of a balancing act to bring about.

My theory is that 'Corpfeud' stands for 'corporate feudalism', a bizarre blending of mammonism and medievalism. This would certainly explain why EVe represents such a threat to TexArc. With our market socialism and knowledge of mass enablement, we are its antithesis—and one with which they desire no synthesis. Moreover, if TexArc has organized itself into self-contained super-municipalities managed by overlords (within the Pyramid?) and meant to stymie the productive forces, that presents them with an enormous dilemma. Without significant intermeg (not to mention international) trade, how does one sustain enough mass consumption of goods and services to survive? I've yet to work through this puzzle in their economic equation—perhaps so have they. We must never forget, however, that what TexArc seems to be going to such extraordinary lengths to preserve is smithprofitism in its most neanderthalian form. Such economic formation incessantly requires new consumer markets to survive. I alerted Harrods some time ago that market expansion was the basic motivation for TexArcan hostility toward us. We are at serious risk of suddenly being carted back to the dark ages—twice over. Whether he reported my warning to either of you, I haven't a clue. With TexArc's evident cybernetic abilities, ingraining populist sentiments in its population that cloud neoclassical economics is made all too simple. What I see before me in BoiCity is the disciplining of a vast underclass of consumers willing, no, eager to the point of patriotism, to credit-buy to the extreme of indenturing their very future labor for cheap merchandise now. All of this takes place, of course, with no consumer protection in place or governmental intervention to foil. Thus, on the one hand, TexArc is the mammonist's pipe dream. On the other hand, TexArc is probably also now entering its inescapable death throes. If one arrests history, by definition one has then no future. In the long run, corporate feudalism will be a self-destructive act. Once new markets are over, and I suspect EVe to be the last of those, Corpfeud must eventually implode. What will be left of human culture when that happens is awkward to predict. Social reformation bringing on a brighter day? Abject descent into hobbesian free-for-all? With earthly resources exhausted, and global statecraft ruined in the wake of the New TexArcan Century, I am inclined to predict the latter.

Bugger-all my ramblings. I've been without a decent cup of Sinalco's coffee for too long. I may be far off the mark here with my doomsday ruminations. They will remain at the level of hypothesis until I make contact with the lords of this manor. I view TexArc social structure exclusively from the bottom up. While this position allows me to feel acutely the consequences of their system, I cannot probably discern clearly all of the machinations that make it work. It could well turn out that 'Corpfeud' denotes something else entirely. There can be no doubt, however, that these Servs we live among are a bondclass, whether vassal or wageslave.

From this Serv existence comes the CorpTroop. For the Serv male, military service is the one avenue out of a life of meaningless and perpetually penurious day labor. Boys make their choice at age fifteen. If they last or live through the initial two-year training period, they become CorpTroops for life—which is not likely to be long. A ten-year service record is deemed a very good run indeed. Most buy the firm (are killed) in three to five years. There seems to be no advancing through the ranks for the CorpTroop. All are the same—equally expendable. An officer corps is all but faceless to them, just the Terds (for tech-nerds, strikingly like our idiom 'teek' for tech-geek) who more or less remote control them. From what I can piece together, urbpass (urban pacification) is the primary mission of the CorpTroop and as necessary domestically as it is in indian country (any hostile locale overseas). Managing urban masses, I surmise, is all that's left to the force that has subdued the globe. Interestingly, hoes (women) are not permitted to serve as CorpTroops, as neither is any non-Caucasian male. Mex, afro, and slope (Hispanic, African, Asian) needn't bother to apply. One can only imagine the kind of race-culture stress this places on TexArcan society—as well as, perhaps, a shortage of manpower in the CorpTroop ranks. I understand BoiCity, and the entire northern portion of the IMS (IntraMountain Spine, from Edmonton to Mexico City), is dominantly Caucasoid, a great supplier of TexArc's CorpTroops. Indeed, the IMS is the great backbone for TexArc jingofrenzy (family values, one supposes), that and the southern arc of the BHC (Boston-to-Houston Crescent) which also funnels many of its native sons into military service. In these two regions, the parks are kept segregated by perceived race-culture identity, causing much communal strain, and frequently the need for stringent urbpass. Apparently, in other TexArc corpents (corporate entities, meaning states or provinces) there's either a better tolerance of hereditary origin in practice or the inevitable uneasy mixture of peoples and customs is already underway—both occurrences of the utmost concern to the Crats of TexArc, judging by the apartheidist chatter coming over the all4s. In all, TexArc is divided into just five large corpents. Along with the IMS and the BHC, there is the GLR (Great Lakes Rim), the PTA (Plains-Tundra Argiworks), and the particularly troublesome PC (Pacific Coast). I gather all manner of perversion and subversion is likely to take place in this coastal devil's playground. By the sounds of it, I bloody well wish our slice had taken hold there. All the christers (the fervently religious) here in BoiCity give me the yanking squirms. What a pack of wankers. But onward to particulars.

We live in the Kuna Ward of the BoiCity parks. That's central to these sprawling ghettos, not quite twenty kilometers southwest of the Gater district and focal point of the Great Pyramid. We are on what is known locally as the sage plains between mountains running in a southeast-to-northwest diagonal north to us and a large river, The Cheney, running more or less along the same diagonal south to us. The river is unusual for its continuous flow of brackish water providing a kind of brown lifeblood to the parks. Sage refers to a hearty, pale-green groundcover that grows thick as bushes in this high plateau country, especially on its flat wastelands. In the parks, sage manages to sprout up through the many cracks in the asphalt and on the odd spots not trampled over by vehics (autos) or pedestrians, or taken up by rudimentary horticulture. Our anonymity as a foray crew is perfectly assured in this immense huddle of people. We inhabit a ramshackle lean-to behind three mobiles of some of Enron's 'people'—an extended family of sorts, one supposes. Their relationships are not quite clear. There are two older couples in our compound, probably in their forties, but looking to be in their sixties. Neither pair seems to be Enron's mother and father—just aunties and uncles, or perhaps great aunties and uncles. He is vague on the subject, nor has he been home to BoiCity for many years. Otherwise, everyone else in the cluster seems to be his cousin in some manner. No matter their family tree, these are salt-of-the-earth sorts of people, foolishly generous with the little they have and fiercely steadfast to their own. I would not wish to cross them if I were not included within their clan. We are careful to require nothing of them. We have our own provisions and means, of course, of manufacturing basic synrations. Because Enron dares not take formal employment, he spends his days helping us and his nights hunting. He has cooked for the compound many interesting stews with meats I dare not inquire too much about. Their vegetable garden, although rather sorry looking, is not inconsiderable, either. Needless to say, your Swiss Guard is not satisfied with these local culinary delights. Lack of herbal seasoning is their constant complaint. Water is our constant problem, both having enough of it and ensuring its potability. We are at altitude and in a very dry region. In the weeks since we arrived, there has been not the slightest threat of rain. I gather that north and east to us, in the high mountains, is quite an elaborate system of damns and reservoirs to capture and hold the precious liquid. Locals refer to this territory as the primitive area and seem almost religiously afraid of it.

Let me stress, amazingly, no one seems the least bit concerned that we, as obvious strangers, are here. Enron's people ask virtually no questions of us or about us. Near neighbors seem hardly to notice our presence. I attribute this firstly to their dismal preoccupation inside their own skulls with the all4s. Secondly, we are all Caucasian. I had worried as well that Enron, as a CorpTroop, would stand out problematically. He is much better fed and quite the physical specimen compared to your normal runty Serv. No one bats an eye in his direction, though, and on the streets I have spotted, on occasion, others who look to be truant CorpTroops. Perhaps deserters are not uncommon in TexArc. Perhaps a degree of solidarity exists among the Servs. Whatever the case, we are able to walk the parks and live openly without danger from higher authority. Not only do we cause no stir, but there's no evident higher authority in the parks. We have seen absolutely no police, no strong arm to keep the Parkers in check. By and large, due to their self-immersed ways, Servs carry out that function themselves. This is not to say there is no crime in the parks. There is an abundance of it, but it is Serv-to-Serv violence or petty property theft. Nothing threatening to the state. Enron assures us that if a serious resource riot were to erupt, especially near to the Gater sector, CorpTroops in number would descend from the sky. And he would know.

Troublingly abnormal about our group, however, is that we are predominantly women. With Tobi and Renault lost, only Forbetr and Blaupunkt remain as males in our foray crew. The rest of us are females manifestly not of Serv dimension or demeanor, and this has brought us decided hazard. Parker women and girls, by custom, receive less food and care than men and boys, growing fragile, and are conditioned to be pliant in every way. We women of EVe are amply nourished and not brainslow (mentally deficient by nuture). In the rape culture of TexArc we represent to Serv men objects of lust and objects of scorn. We are eminently more fucklicious (you gather this meaning for yourselves) than the gaunt Serv sweetpuss (sexual victim) they're accustomed to. Enron once told me, evidently mistaking it for sweet talk, that I am like a virho (digiprostitute) come to life. At the same time, because of our mental and physical strength, we contradict and offend all of their phallocentric beliefs. We are inherently uppity. To many Parker men, the only solution to our alluring affront is a good forced rogering. Cardinal has killed nine attackers to date, to include one night, while on sentinel, a rapegang of four—hand-to-hand—before any of us could arrive to her quite unnecessary aid. I've shot one man in the face and have simply outrun many more. Enron will permit me to go nowhere without his accompaniment. Sinalco, I believe, ventures out some nights for the very purpose of attracting and killing rapists. I shudder to think of, but also admire, her deadcount (body scorecard). During the day, she, like the rest of us, has taken to wearing a male disguise.

The other glaring victims of these parks are its children. With all parents at work at all hours, or constantly away from mobile in a desperate search to track down employment, the young, the alarmingly young, run more or less feral. Numberless clusters of them are ever aimlessly about, mucking about in the filth, dodging through traffic as a game, pinching items from the shops. As a consequence, children die in droves from malnutrition and disease. They get crushed beneath the giant tires of monstrous vehics. They are shot dead by self-righteous shopkeepers. They get abducted and sold into domestic and sexual slavery. Many run away, or simply wander off and are never heard from again. I would wager, perhaps one or two in ten make it to their tenth birthday. And the ceremony of taking one's child to the nearest *Implants* outlet to be fitted with the cortex band and the ihead gear becomes a matter of tremendous family pride and celebration, something like a holy communion combined with getting a youngster's first piercing. It's one more clan member who has survived to maturity and thereby made it into the workforce. Now, instead of just another troublesome mouth to feed, there is an additional provider in the mobilehold, and things will become easier. When things do not, no one seems to take particular notice.

The two greatest illusions TexArc Servs suffer under are God and Wealth. They believe there is one, and they believe they have some. Mindless evangelical religiosity is a talisman in TexArc used to justify all manner of stupidity and criminality. Insofar as I can tell, any number of Christ-based sects vie to out-zealot one another to garner more of the tithes market. The majority spiritual market share seems to have been won firmly, however, by an exceedingly reprehensible batch of hate-and-fear-mongers calling themselves Total Dominionists. Theirs is the vengeful warrior Christ from Revelations, founded upon the epistolary and televangelical frothing-at-the-mouth of St. Paul and St. Pat. God hates everyone, it seems, save for those who donate profusely to the TD collection plate. Likewise, every Serv is ardently convinced consuming is an act of creation and self-determination. They live to buy and seem only truly validated by their pathetic purchase of third-rate commodities. Meantime, I've run across no one here not in a deep, deep credhole (personal debt), which in the parks means the owing of workcreds (work credits). These work credits denote a practice of indentured service where one buys goods and services on the promise of repaying with one's future labor—future labor that will be performed, in essence, for no wages—necessitating even more credit spending simply to survive. The practice is sheer fiscal delirium, to be sure, yet such is the norm. It is truly astonishing to watch people fundamentally without money feverishly manipulating credit schemes and taking part in all manner of joint-stock ventures in the belief that their paltry—and more usually negative—sums can lead to personal financial security or that the equitable distribution of a society's collective assets can be achieved via a market system of stocks and bonds. The small investor—let alone the Parker who is in truth an inverse investor—simply hasn't the kind of funds required to get ahead in such a market arrangement. Yet somehow the Serv has been led to believe otherwise, trained in effect to behave as the monied class but without the money. At this point, we return to religiosity and ideology: a faith and belief in things one does not fully understand.

I am convinced that somewhere in ArcNet exists a great and perhaps brilliant puppet master, the überbuilder of TexArc culture if you will, who orchestrates the popular mind in order to propagate such extremes of delusion. Everywhere I look in this society I see the stamp of forestalled development, of arrested history. Specifically, the objective of keeping people obtuse and uninformed by all the methods of highmodern doctrine is being meticulously enacted. Life in TexArc is marked by 1) diversion—mostly in the seduction of trashy entertainment and hollow gratification, 2) the hatred of others—in native colorism and culturalism as well as their supreme bugbear of foreign terrorism, 3) isolation—extreme individualism and the complete disregard for communal well-being, and 4) everyone's seeming conviction that s/he is middle class—enabling further division brought on by pity-hate for the poorer and envy-hate of the richer. This puppet master, I propose, represents my counterpart and nemesis in TexArc. As of yet, I'm unable to put a face or name to it, or pinpoint its physical locale beyond that silent and sinister Pyramid. I anticipate, when we make contact with the Gater and the Crat classes, this puppet master will materialize. Without doubt, the conduit for the TexArcan regimen is the all4s. Its clutter, its constant pitch and yammer, cannot be random. While the cosmos is arbitrary, human culture never is. Culture deliberately gets forged, no matter how shabbily. I conclude my report by telling you what initial steps Sinalco and I have taken to disrupt this TexArcan sham.

As you've been alerted by Sinalco, the recall elections won by Uncle Wobbly have turned out to be a fraud, a feedhoax perpetrated on the BoiCity electorate. The contest is nothing more than a perpetual confidence game designed to convince Servs (and what of Gaters, I wonder?) that they have a say in local control, when in fact they have none. All of the candidates—not just ours—were virtual, mere digital politicians and phantoms of the feed. No elected assembly of any kind exists in BoiCity, only the mirage of representational government. I hazard the same is true TexArc-wide. Yet out of such a gaff by us comes learning. The limit situation is the quintessential educational opportunity—a gap power inevitably provides to the motivated mind. These weeks I've been out among the Parkers, speaking with them, asking them questions, listening to their concerns and gaining a feel for their actual lives. My interviews have not been easily carried out. TexArcan pupils jump ceaselessly with their artificial twinkle, making real eye contact impossible. Servs can never really look fully and directly at you. Nor can they concentrate entirely on what they or you are saying. They are ever in two (or three, four, or five) places at once. It's a piss-all bother to deal with them. In spite of such hindrances, I have developed a handful of generative themes for them to ponder. Armed with these, Sinalco and I have begun our next advocacy project. Several examples of my new feeds are attached. You will see I have continued to use Uncle Wobbly as a figure expressing genuine populist standpoints. And why not? His message as candidate Wobbly triggered enough dissident acts of cognition in Servs to gain him an overwhelming, albeit empty, victory at the polls.

What Sinalco has done once more is perform a peripheral embed slice, faux autocycle and maxevasive, but into the nonpriority, localized servcircuit of ArcNet only. Furthermore, this go around we have not patched into the streamwide autorecall loop, as before, but merely into its autoentrec (entertainment/recreation) loop. Arguably, this relatively minor circuit is among the most influential among Parkers. From what Sinalco can make out, to the Terds tending the BoiCity feed, the entrec loop is known as 'cocks and balls', that is, pornography and sports—the two great staples of TexArc popcult. Since the pedagogy of the oppressed can only take place within the habitus of the oppressed, I maintain there is no better site for Uncle Wobbly to make his reappearance. Such rote loops are little minded by their technicians. My second wave of Wobbly feeds are designed to pose previously unnoticed problems to viewers for the express purpose of unveiling Serv historical and political reality. These spots stage a critical intervention in the normal TexArc way of thinking. The intent is, in time, to dislodge cultural myths already ingrained in the popular mind. I believe two of my pieces accomplish this emergence of consciousness particularly well.

The first spot opens with Uncle Wobbly relaxing in his lollchair in his mobil's liveroom, several plasticans of Oly beer ready at his elbow. On his downleft he synchs into Total Youchoose idiversion, bypassing NASVEHIC and WFW (we have made other spots involving those popular pastimes) in favor of the MFL—the Me Football League. (MFL is TexArc digifootball, not real futbol. It's a static sort of bump-and-grind virsport where very large players don elaborate padding in order to visit grievous personal injury upon one another—quintessentially TexArcan. One wonders, why not just forego the sodding pads?) Rather than selecting as proxy, however, one of the glamor positions of Me Football—the comely chaps tossing, catching, or running about with the oblong thing—Uncle Wobbly winks at the viewer and, atypically, chooses instead to experience the game as one of its monstrous line-of-scrimmage players. These gigantic fellows with whopping overhangs for bellies and no necks to speak of between their thick shoulders and fat heads puff and grunt away against one another in 'the trenches' (a line of scrimmage). Invariably, their short but stubborn bursts of exertion go unnoticed, unless making a glaring error. They are certainly unappreciated by fans despite the fact that their efforts unequivocally permit those glamor chaps to perform crowd-pleasing stunts that garner credit for a win—a fact we begin to appreciate as we follow Uncle Wobbly's virexperience of the game.

I'm sure you've caught the drift of my lesson. This ad gives the lie to celebrity individuality, to the bootstraps, can-do, chimera brand of success. It demonstrates, instead, that social achievement comes only as a corporate effort, despite beguiling appearances otherwise. It points out how the exceptional (the comely chaps) stand on the shoulders of the ordinary (the portly grunters), taking credit when it is not due. The viewer sees as well how such beautiful people are self-serving wankers. Assuredly, there is much food for Serv thought as we leave Uncle Wobbly kicked back in his lounger, savoring his last Oly in the afterglow of a game well played for the good of the entire team.

A second spot, briefer and more grating, immediately puts a viewer in the perspective of a virbod on chan69, the most popular of the virsex feeds. The viewer cannot help but gaze down upon his own monster 'hardknob', that is, a virerection of such farcical size that it curves upward nearly to touch the tip of his nose. Suddenly, a virho is presenting on all fours before him, provocatively perched on the edge of a soft and feathery bed. She is a virho of color, as is plain to see by her nutbrown rump. The bedroom is shadowy and she is facing away from him. Wasting no time, our satyr-like viewer comes up quickly behind the virho and plunges his gigantic weapon whole into the backdoor—not the cunny—of the sweetpuss. Instead of emitting the usual compliant purrs standard during virsex, though, this virho begins frantically to wail and writhe in the shock and the agony and the terror of such a violation. She wildly reels her head around to get a look at her assailant. When she does, the viewer-rapist sees not the face of a digi-woman, as would be expected, but recognizes, in its place, the face of a stereotypical Serv man—one distorted in shrieking pain. We then cut abruptly to Uncle Wobbly, an obvious witness to these events, sitting across the boudoir in a frilly, pink cushioned chair. His legs are crossed. His chin rests in one hand. He looks quite troubled. His eyes move to meet ours and he asks us simply, 'How do you like it?' The stress falls on the word *do*.

Intrinsic motivation for political change stems from the oppressed making their oppression the object of reflection. Only in this way is the struggle for their own liberation born. We know these spots are yubbing flash (playing well) on the feed. Everyone speaks of them. Everyone refers to them. We can tell when they patch. Whole streets of Parkers stand still for their duration. Even traffic slows—or halts—an unheard of event in TexArc. Enron tells us, if we can slice in to simulcast on each of the ipatch all4s at once, that will be the most productive. Evidently, the chance to concentrate on just one thing at a time provides much relief to the Serv, and guarantees not only rapt attention by viewers, but will likely increase their sympathetic hearing of our messages. Frankly, the real problem facing us is how to take gnosis into praxis. It is not enough to kindle such awareness. Tangible action in the world must follow. I am shaping a series of spots featuring Uncle Wobbly explaining unionized shops and encouraging the formation of worker cooperatives to Servs. I have no idea if or how such notions will take in TexArc. Alterity tends to sell well to the mind and to the spirit, but is difficult to enact within the body politic. I intend to memo you again soon with the result of our more practical initiative.

To end with a personal note, I am happy I came to this fearful place. Though I doubt I will survive, I have discovered that my signification work is not a mere game of words, or a waste of my lifetime. We have found a society desperately in need of critical consciousness, not as an academic exercise, but as a pragmatic matter of life or death—that is, of either fashioning an equitable life or suffering a miserable death. I am glad, then, Headminister Natwest, that Caucus ignored your strong objections to insert into TexArc. We are here for good reasons, liable to perform good service to EVe, no matter the cost or what Countermeasures may have feared to the contrary.

In one final and more convivial observation, Administer Movënpick, I offer the opinion that certain members of your foray crew are possibly the randiest wankers on earth—and certainly the most tiresome when it comes to their uninvited carnal urges directed towards myself. It is tedious enough to have poor Enron doting on me, an impasse entertaining to Sinalco, but the extra burden of his ever acting the rival, militarily *and* sexually, with Cardinal is patently absurd. When not repelling assault or fending off disease here in the BoiCity parks, the four of us play out bad stage comedy in our tiny shanty, the denouement of our farce being Sinalco's opportunistic bedding of both my suitors. I have no doubt my teek is game for à trois were Enron and Cardinal ever to be persuaded. Shall I laugh at these libidinous antics, Administer? Or shall I bloody well cry? Shall I contemplate what such travesty might articulate about EVe? Are we an open and a generous folk, Frau Movënpick, with Sinalco's actions constituting a noble sacrifice to save the mission by keeping the erotic peace? Or are we a paltry and a dissolute bunch, for all our high-mindedness playing at a seduction culture little advanced over TexArc's penchant for violation? Or are Sinalco's merely egregious romps, epitomizing EVe's idle and ambiorgasmic ways? Alas, the riddle of sexpolitics. For my part, I'm left wondering why, oh why, did Harrods pair together an abstainant with a snogall?

Memosender: faithfully your most humble and obedient servant, Mall

The Simulacrum

Bleached Wheat stands alone in the Eye of the Waco Great Pyramid. The muzak playing is agreeable—not too loud and not too soft—and faintly militaristic. Bleached Wheat finds muzak makes the day go faster, it helps people relax so they can do their jobs well. That's what he believes. The floor he stands on is an enormous square of deep blue. At its center is the big white star, inside the thin red circle. Every time Bleached Wheat comes up into the Eye through the platform lift—every time—he puts a kiss on his fingertips and bends down to plant it at the center of that star—smack at the center. Every time. No one ever sees him do this. No one ever is in the Eye unless invited up to join him. The Eye is exclusively his. Bleached Wheat's. The big bossman's. The space is starkly empty save for the star on the floor. Necessarily, the Eye is pentahedron in shape, each of its four walls rising high up to the single point far overhead. Unity of purpose, loftiness of goal, simplicity of design, mystery of power. Bleached Wheat knows the symbol value of these structures. He conceived the meg pyramids himself, decades ago, making sure his Waco pyramid was built to be unsurpassable, overpoweringly massive, the biggest and the best. He stands at its apex on the two-hundredth story. Its base, far below him, occupies the equivalent of one hundred oldnewyork city shortblocks. The walls of its E are thick and control-tinted nanoglass—absolutely impact-proof. Bleached Wheat made sure all TexArc pyramids, besides being bureaucratic hubs and grand corpemblems, are by design impenetrable bomb shelters as well. Even a tacnuke will slide down their sides into containment areas constructed around their base, forcing the blast outward and away. Function and symbolism are critical, yes, but survivability. That's the real name of the game.

Bleached Wheat has situated himself as far as he can into the northwest corner of the Eye. The in-sloping angle of the walls prevents him from inching as near as he'd like to the edge of the floor, but where he stands still provides him with something of the highwire tingle he enjoys. He can peer far down a long ridge and two of the imposing golden facades of the pyramid. He can savor a commanding surroundview of CorpHQ spread out below him. He can see beyond the expansive complex to the low brown texas hills the full 360 all the way to the horizon. No parks have been allowed to sprawl up around CorpHQ. He wants only clear lines of sight, because you never know. That's Bleached Wheat's real motto, the one he repeats to himself. "You never know." Because you never do. A fat sun rises, rich red in the haze even through the tint of the nanoglass. The sol light causes Bleached Wheat to narrow his ice-blue eyes. This brings him to his executive decision. He thinksays: <Okay. Bring him up, Ponzi.> A moment later the floor panel slides aside for the platform lift. Ponzi and Busch appear heads first on the rise. Ponzi wears his usual regularjoe, exec outfit, all pleats and breezy. By contrast, Busch has on a Netsman unisuit, one of the natty oldnavy blue ones with a tilted beret. Ice and choice. Too bad. It's as though Busch has anticipated, correctly, the worst. *Oh, well. That's part of why he's Net*, Bleached Wheat thinks.

"The slice?" Bleached Wheat says to Ponzi.

"Still making zero sense. This time we can trail it forward but..."

"But what?"

"But not backward anymore."

"But it's the same slice as before, right?"

"Yes, almost certainly."

"And you're trailing it forward this time to BoiCity?"

"Yes. Somehow it's embedded itself in the local Serv autoloops there. Impossible to purge without screwing the whole system."

"Have you tried?"

"No, not yet."

"Why not?"

"The mayor's too jumpy. Says he can't have the servcircuit going void right now, especially not the cocks and balls."

"The pisswit. That's exactly what's being used against him."

"Quite honestly, the mayor seems less than netsavvy to me, sir."

"Quite honestly, the mayor is an IMS clodhopper, Ponzi."

"Yes sir."

Bleached Wheat turns back to his panorama. The hills are heating up fast for another scorcher. Waves of heat distort the sun. "Is the slice still localized? Have you managed to keep it confined as I requested?"

Ponzi hesitates. The news is not good. "No," he says. "As a matter of fact, it's starting to circulate."

"Oh, shit," Bleached Wheat says ironically. "Where to?"

"So far, to SaltCity, Denver, and somewhat down to Foenix. We've also had isolated reports of it as far north as Edmonton and as far south as Hermosillo."

"In other words, nearly the length of the Intra-Mountain Spine." Bleached Wheat clasps his hands behind his back and begins to rock on his heels. "Oh, if only the slice were isolated, and not the reports." He's quiet for a moment, then drops his sarcastic tone. "Fuck the mex down south," he tells Ponzi, "but I *don't* want it getting farther north. Do you hear me? And I *really don't* want it disseminating to the coast. That's imperative. It can't get into the Pacific Coast."

"So far we've confined it to the IMS."

"No, Ponzi. So far you haven't done jack. This slice does what it likes, when it likes. It always has. If it wants to get to the PC, I have no doubt it will get itself to the PC. You have no idea what you're dealing with."

Ponzi turns mean-faced. It's what he does when his tolerance as an underling runs out. "ArcNet's doing its very best, sir."

"Sure you are," Bleached Wheat replies with a deliberately unreadable voice. He brushes aside his blond forelock. "Net's not even aware it's still trailing this slice backward to source, just like before, and not forward to destination."

Ponzi looks to Busch, who knows his role is not in this conversation. Wisely, he wants no part in it. He maintains his silence, his rigid posture, and his Net stoneface. Finding no empathy from his fellow, Ponzi is forced to look back to Bleached Wheat, who is now staring at the subceo. "Sir," Ponzi puts things together, "that would mean..."

"That there is an insert *into* TexArc, Ponzi. Yes. That would certainly mean that."

"But...but, sir. That's impossible. That's...unprecedented."

"As far as *ArcNet* seems to know, it's impossible and unprecedented."

Bleached Wheat freezes in a shrug, his palms exposed. The Eye has gone crimson from the new sun. Ponzi's face, neck, and ears flush to match.

"You're seriously suggesting, sir, that we have EVe infiltrators, on the ground, right now, in BoiCity? Is that what you're saying?"

"So long for now, Ponzi." Bleached Wheat waves bye-bye to his subceo. "I'll let you know very soon what I need from you."

Ponzi's scowl disappears under the floor. The deep blue panel slides back over the lift aperture. Bleached Wheat turns to Busch, who has stepped forward, without being told, to stand at attention near the middle of the star. The Netsman's face remains deadpan. Pure issue. Bleached Wheat has to admire this dumb yank. He orders him to stand at ease.

"I won't bullshit you, Busch."

"I appreciate that, sir."

"That was an amazing job you pulled off in Fribourg. What you accomplished for me, there, was very important."

"Thank you, sir. Glad to do my job."

"Our people, here," Bleached Wheat nods to indicate Ponzi who has just descended, "believe that Groundsman you selected to run kill member for your squad blew the holy hell out of that Maneuvers instillation, killing their crack slicer. Their Countermeasures people, over there, believe we don't know our Groundsman was captured alive, giving them a guide into TexArc for an EVe foray crew we're also not supposed to know about." The ceo pauses to grin, mechanically. "That's some neat trick, Busch, fooling everybody."

The Netsman nods once to acknowledge the compliment. "We aim to please, sir."

"And how the hell did you ever escape their fighters and make lift, man? They had your ass pinned up on those cliffs."

Busch smiles, faintly. "We're Net, sir. We just do shit like that."

Bleached Wheat laughs, with a bit too much precision. "You guys just *do* shit like that, huh? Well it's just fucking amazing to me, I've got to tell you." The humor already has drained from the ceo's face, and Busch is quick to stiffen again. "But I have a big problem on my hands, Busch. A big, big problem. And this is where I'm not going to bullshit you."

"Sir."

"Servs are easy, Busch. Stupid. Gullible. You know what I mean?"

"Of course, sir."

"They'll buy anything, including shit, if it's packaged right. No problemo. Piece of cake. Am I correct?"

"Yes, sir."

"And they've bought into this recent EVe terror shit easily enough, Busch, as you might expect. The terrorattacks on the elevator and on the

Glassea. They've swallowed it hook, line, and sinker—as usual." Bleached Wheat wrinkles his nose and pauses for a few seconds, before carrying out his executive decision. "Those were staged, you know," he informs Busch. "Those were really *us*."

Busch shifts nervously. The cockiness seems to have left the tilt of his beret. "Sir?" he asks for clarification, hoping he can't have heard what he heard.

"Yes. Us," Bleached Wheat continues calmly, as though he's getting something off his chest. "Or rather, that was me." The ceo's manufactured chortle chills Busch. "My bad," Bleached Wheat confesses. "Now there are two people in the corp who know that, Busch. Both of them standing right here in this Eye. Just you and me."

There's an old saying in TexArc: the truth hurts. Busch knows his knowing topsecret information makes him deadcount, right where he stands. He knows it's useless to say anything. It would only make things worse. Bleached Wheat appreciates the Netsman's silence and obvious understanding in the matter. It speaks volumes for the service.

Busch simply snaps to attention and will wait for the swat, wondering how and how soon it will come. *Yanking bigpic. Sooner or later it gets us all.* Busch hopes he gets listed kia and not selfterm. The distinction brings the best buyout for next of kin.

"So here's my big problem, Busch. Or rather, here's my two big problems. You might as well hear this out." Bleached Wheat turns to face the hills again. "One problem is you Terds. While Parkers buy into the EVe roguestate feedhoax and are jacked as usual for a good preempt strike, you Gaters, and even some wipe-ass Crats, this time around, are being slow on the uptake. Polls indicate misgiving in TexArc, even reluctance over attacking EVe. Can you believe it, Busch? Doubt? In TexArc?" Bleached Wheat affects a whiny voice, "*What have they ever done to us? This is no push-over, third-rate power, you know. This time there's going to be a serious nuclear deterrent to deal with.*" He stops to sigh. "Libbies. Always the same story. Even after *all* this fucking time." He shakes his head. "You expect it on the coasts, you know. That's norm. But it's polling through the wheatland, Busch. Through the *wheatland*. That's especially not choice. TexArc must be getting soft. Too comfortable. Maybe that *is* inevitable with empire."

Bleached Wheat begins to pace clockwise along the slanting glass-walls of the Eye. He clasps his hands behind his back and words carefully his exposition. He seems to want to get it straight in his own mind. One great drop of sweat already falls off the end of Busch's nose.

"I can tell you one thing for sure, Busch. Getting soft sure as shit ain't gonna happen on my watch. No nobsucking way. I'll tell you *that* right yanking now." Busch thinks, *here it comes*. But it doesn't. "I'm in the process of giving these over-educated types some irrefutable fucking proof. EVe's treachery will be made manifest to those doubtom Terds and Crats. That's what you were doing for me in Fribourg, Busch, by helping enable their little foray crew. The EVens don't know it yet, but I will arrange for that crew to commit some horrendous act of terror on TexArc soil, something truly spectacular that will give us all our clarion call to justwar. United we stand, right Busch? Not to mention ends and means, means and ends." Bleached Wheat drifts away for a moment. "For half a century the noble lie has been the oldest trick in TexArc's book. It's never fucking failed. Sometimes the lie needs to be a bit more noble, the spin a bit more radical. Backward and upward. Right? Corpfeud marches in place."

Bleached Wheat pivots on his heels. His sudden turn startles Busch, who juicyfarts his joeboxers.

"Until quite recently all was going plan, Busch. All was going quite plan. Not even my subceos were aligned in on this one. Not even your ArcNet boss, Ponzi. Then big problem number two comes along, the one, sadly, that involves you."

Bleached Wheat stops in his tracks. Busch subtly shifts his weight. Bleached Wheat cocks his head to one side. Busch freezes in anticipation.

"Big problem number two is something unforeseen. Something outside my control. It's that fucking slice of theirs. I knew a slice would be coming, and I knew it would carry signification of some kind. That's all those EVe pixies ever fucking do. Talk. But I didn't know the slice would be so fucking maxevasive, and I sure didn't know it would feed signification so fucking revoevo. I tell you, Busch, this bitch they've got signing for them is one goddamn Dmega smackdown revoevo whiz. No shit about it."

Busch is confused by the term. He's never heard "revoevo" before. That's because it's strictly a Crat word, used only in Crat circles, such as on the turbolinks or in the nanosteam particle baths or when sauntering about the realtime geisha houses or over cocktails at the club or, especially, in the boardroom. It's short for revolution-evolution, what Crats suppress by all means necessary.

"EVe's playing our Servs better than we do. How yank is that? Just when I get the shitubers stoked for crusade so I can concentrate on the Terds, this slit ignores the Gaters completely and goes straight for the Parkers, getting them pumped for collective pissing bargaining. Fuck me. Who'd have guessed?" The ceo uncocks his head and begins to pace again, making Busch slightly more comfortable. "So you see, Busch, what's happened is, we've fallen into a classic case of crisis management. Exactly what I was hoping to avoid. I wanted the slice to cause a little stir in BoiCity, so I can seal my deal, but not too big a stir—and *only* in BoiCity. But now the slice has got out of hand. It's social upheaving *and* spreading, and is blipping on Net's radar. So now I have to pretend to be surprised and outraged over EVe's having the skill and audacity to insert TexArc. That means I have to pretend to be just as zealous as Ponzi, and everybody else, about quashing this heinous violation of our corpborders. See what I mean? That's why I just told Ponzi that there *is* an insert. At this point, it's just a matter of time before he finds out for himself. By chewing his ass over it, I look ice and guru, and I capture the high ground, which is the name of the game. Fox, huh?"

Busch tastes the vomit rising to his mouth but can't stop its splatting all over the star. Bleached Wheat takes no notice at all.

"So, as I'm sure you've figured out, I have to pretend to be quite upset by you and your evident fuckup in Fribourg. After all, if you'd done what Net sent you there to do, blown those bastards all to molecules, well, we wouldn't be in this slice and insert fix we're in, now would we, Busch?" Busch struggles to stand back at attention. "You screwed the pooch. So, regretfully, I'm forced to exercise my famous intolerance for fuckups. I'm afraid, Busch, I need you to be a deadcount of one." Bleached Wheat stops his pacing and finds Busch's eyes. "Regrets. Things like this are never personal. It's simply what's expected of me."

Busch braces himself. *This must be it.* He waits, shivering.

"I'm going to have to finesse the hell out of this fuckmother," Bleached Wheat muses to himself, unfocusing his eyes. "That's always the shit. I've got to allow a little rabble rousing, while looking like I'm trying to prevent any rabble rousing, while I'm really trying to stop too much rabble rousing. Hm. Kind of interesting."

"Sir," Busch murmurs. Bleached Wheat raises both eyebrows at having his thoughts disrupted. "Sir, it's been an honor doing my duty."

Bleached Wheat reacts with a sour face. "Oh, please, Busch, you're at the heart of the fucking shitstorm, for christsake. Just twirl around and die." He turns toward the glasswall facing east. "Duty's the bitch that one day chokes down your wad and the next day bites off your hardnob. Today it just sucks to be you." The sun is surprisingly high. Odd how it always nudges itself up there so fast without your really seeing it move. "Nice try, though," the ceo adds. "And thanks for hearing me out. I never get to share anymore."

Busch's eyes go wide, then wider. The smell of oiled gears and burnt rubber penetrates his sinuses. A throb fills his ears. Then he drops dead.

Bleached Wheat thinksays: <Jitney, get two of your removal dudes up here right away, and tell them to bring a mop. Ponzi, locate that assjack Dockers for me doublego. The mayor of BoiCity and I need to engage in some major facetime.>

☆ ☆ ☆ ☆ ☆ ☆

How dare they pull him, *him*, away from the MegMayor's Conference. He was in the middle of his personal growth seminar this morning, "Turbonegotiations on the Turbolinks," when some snotnose hovers up in a linkscart and insists he comes with him. *Insists*. Right there and then, in front of three of his fellow mayors. *Him*. Dockers—Mayor of BoiCity. The numerouno hydromeg of the IMS. *And* just when he's about to tee off on the fabled 57th hole—he only gets to play the fabulous CorpHQ domed course once a year at the convention. He was *so* looking forward to the afterdrinks session at the 72nd Hole Lounge. Power oozing out the ass there, baby, at that legendary arbitration watering hole. Well, he'll show them. Dockers is somebody with whom you do not want to fuck. He'll chew out some flunky. He'll kick the ass of some subsubceo or other. He'll make some little shit-bucket cry. Hey, but maybe this is part of the seminar. A test? He hadn't thought of that. Maybe he's up for promo and this is part of his being groomed. Yeah. That could be. It makes sense. He's been kicking ass and taking names for a few years as mayor. BoiCity Servs *and* Terds know who the hell is boss. That's damn straight. Wouldn't surprise him at all if they're looking to take him regional—or even bump him up to full corporate. Sure. Why not? Maybe *that's* what the hell this is all about. Better look good and company, then. *Get off your duff and take a goddamn look around.*

Dockers shoots up from the cushioned museum bench he's been moping on for the past half hour and walks, with a sudden display of interest, toward the nearest wall. He's never visited the TexArc CorpMuseum before, never bothered to go on one of the frequently scheduled mayor's tours they set up during the four days of the conference (though he does get rid of—he means, sends—the wife and kids on the tour every year). He's always too busy gladhanding and networking, the real work of a meg-mayor, to make time for it on his itinerary. It occurs to him now this might be a strategic mistake. This place could be very useful for kowtow and oneup. Just look at all this old stuff on the walls. Printads, vidads, holoads, old trademarks, historic corporate memorandums repieced together from shreddings, old profit readouts and Nasdaq numbers—the early Dow; *those* must have been the wild and wooly days—yellowed share certificates, figures on shareholder dividends, even a corporate prospectus from....what does that say? Can you believe it? 2024. Wow. Not bad shit. Riding the air on a loop is some old jingle playing: *You can trust you car to the man who wears the star!* Hey, catchy—and how true, Dockers starts thinking as he begins to hum along. Next it hits him—how prophetic the song is! As he listens more closely to the words he realizes the lyrics are spooky. Snappy damn tune, too. Maybe there's something to this history stuff. Maybe the right kind of history isn't bunk. Dockers starts wandering the exhibits. He particularly likes the detailed reconstruction of a turn-of-the-century "gas station," an old *SuperPower* from its signage, and the large, silent, wood-floor gallery filled with antique office art, especially all those soft-focus photographs with inspirational sayings, or sometimes even verse, superimposed on them. There's a misty, early-morning tropical waterfall with the ornate words printed in its lagoon: *Today is the first day of the rest of your business life*. Or the closeup of a darling, teardrop-eyed Doberman puppy reminding us: *There is no team in I*. He'll freebie a bunch of reproductions from the gift shop later. Hang them up in his Eye back home. Dockers never knew there was such a lot to learn from art.

In the room with all the gigantic old lapbooks on screenfreeze, Dockers starts to appreciate the majesty of corporate history. TexArcana, Inc. Based out of old Waco, Texas. The mother of all—what did they call them back then? Oil companies. Back when petroextortion matured as both a natural *and* a political science. The company had been at the fore, behind the scenes, in the struggle to liberate capital from all unnatural, regulatory fetters. Two scratchy "news" articles, each from July of 2029, reveal the definitive tale. Dockers finds them breathtaking. One, from *The New York Times*, is entitled, "When Lobbyists Get Elected to Congress." The other, from *The Washington Post*, is called, "The Ultimate Hostile Take-Over." *New York? Washington? Congress? Where the hell are they?* Dockers has never heard of those megs before. And "newspapers"? Hell, they're "new" to him, too. He knows it's sappy as hell, but the more he reads, the more he can feel his breast swelling with the pride of power—TexArc style. "Wealth, Exploitation, Domination." He begins to understand just what those words mean. Freeing capital from the "liberal aberration" of the previous century—he's reading the infoplacards by the lapbooks—had required conviction and guile. Legislative and judicial manipulation. Runaway military expenditure. Deficit spending. Censorship. Intolerance. Undereducation. Cultural misinformation. Faith-based initiatives. State-sponsored religion. Such traditional ideals had not been reinstated without a fight. Dismantling the pussy-whipped institutions of checks and balances that had marked the old, perverted US welfare state took neocorp guts and God. And that's exactly what the Founding Board of TexArcana, Inc. had provided in abundance for the corporate cause. That and shitloads of cash. Nothing defeats liberal mobgov—what used to be called Democracy—like good old-fashioned shitloads of cash. In fact, after educating himself thoroughly about the early corp struggle against the evils of biggov—and biggov's final, God-sent overthrow—the megmayor resolves earnestly never to take those corpconcepts for granted again. *Wealth, Exploitation, Domination*. From here on out he will be an even *better* company man.

After all, like he'd read back in the office art gallery, underneath one old black-and-white photo of some dictator named FDR, "If you don't heed the warnings of history, you'll be doomed to repeat its mistakes." *Holy fuck*, thinks Dockers, he's been in the CorpMuseum maybe twenty minutes and *already* he's getting cultured.

"Dockers?"

The megmayor turns quickly around from the displays, startled at hearing his own name spoken in the quiet. Standing close behind him is Yupcap, subceo for Market Enterprise. Subceo to the big cheese *himself*. Every year Yupcap presides over the MegMayor's Conference. Every year Dockers might pump his hand heartily in two or three reception lines, and exchange a few glib banalities with him, but that's always been the extent of their contact. Now here Yupcap is, come looking for *him*. *Holy shit. What's this all about? Promo? Could it be for real?*

Yupcap tires of waiting for a reply. "I didn't imagine to find you here. I've been looking for you for a good ten minutes."

Dockers can't read Yupcap's voice. *Is he pissed, or not*? The wayward megmayor chuckles nervously. "Oh...yes. *Here*." He looks around them. "Sorry. I just love to explore the exhibits. I get lost in them."

"Really?" Yupcap seems about to chuckle himself. *Calling his bluff? Busting his chops? Rattling his cage? Kicking his balls*? "I wouldn't have guessed that."

"Oh, *yeah*," Dockers insists, turning on the schmooze. "I visit every year. I could spend *hours* in here at a time."

"Is that so?" Yupcap's cold-steel eyes—what is it with these topexecs and their freaky peepers?—seem to come off automatic and kick into engage. "And just which display room do you enjoy most?"

"Um..." Dockers fights to remember any title. Any display room title will do. "'The Birth of Downsizing,'" he finally manages. "That one's just choice inspirational. Double choice."

"That's a good one," Yupcap concedes. "Don't you love how we reorganized the stupid fucks into those touchy-feely, euroloser work teams then brokeback their damn unions? Democratizing the workplace and guaranteed lifetime employment. Dude, how dumb do you have to be to swallow those bigmacs?"

"Yeah, boy," Dockers goes too far with a little chuck on Yupcap's shoulder, "that's culture change right up the old ass for ya, huh?"

"*Where* did we get those work team models from? *Hm*? I can't quite seem to recall."

Shit. Dockers has never been any good at remembering names. Or places. Or history. Or any stuff that's in the past. He's always been a consumer of the perpetual present. *Shit.*

"Finway?" he guesses. Then immediately, "*No*, Norland. Or maybe Scandihoovia...is it...maybe?"

"I see..."

"1984!" Dockers blurts out. "I do know it started bigtime in 1984. Hey, a century of rightsizing. Now *that's* a date to remember." He quotes the display infoplacard.

"A word to the bizwise, Mr. Mayor." Yupcap leans forward and lowers his voice. "For Dmega suckup these days, you can't go wrong with the pet projects. We needed secure access to global natural resources, so what we couldn't negotiate we took into protection. In the process we just so happened to void the fanatical raghead threat. Bombed them back to the pre-nano age. Collateral asset. Or now, play up the ingrate sons of bitches in EVe. We pulled their asses out of the fire, mil-spent out the wazoo for decades defending those gayboys. And how did they repay us? First with biz competition, then with policy betrayal. They're weasel sons of bitches, Mr. Mayor, and need to be reamed. Got that?"

Dockers really has no clue what the subceo's talking about.

"Oh. Okay. Thanks. I'll try to remember all that."

The subceo shakes his head. “Follow me.”

Yupcap turns and walks away, fast. Dockers has a difficult time catching up to him. He scurries behind the pastel Hawaiian shirt and loose-fit denims, thinking, *man, these subceo guys really are in ice shape*—and that he’d better start working out. He could stand to drop a few pounds around the middle. More than a few.

They stop, Dockers puffing, at a conference room door, where Yupcap steps to one side. “After you,” he invites.

The gesture doesn’t seem promising to Dockers. With no choice, he steps through the autoslide doubledoors. Inside he finds a variety of men already seated around an oblong table, all of them turning to stare at him. Experience tells him to meet the gaze, in deference, of whoever sits at the head of a conference table. Dockers finds himself looking into the unmistakable glacial fox eyes of Bleached Wheat. Not a touch of the glassy to their cores. *Holy fucking hell.* Dockers almost pisses himself. He bends at the knees a bit and has to lean forward just a touch. This can only be about Sawtooth Fluid and that doubleyank primitive area. He didn’t think word had got out yet—or so high.

“Nice of you to join us, Mr. Mayor,” Bleached Wheat smiles at him, bored. “I hope we’re not interrupting your busy and productive convention calendar.”

“Yes, sir,” says Dockers, then stammers right away, “uh...I mean, no sir, no sir. I’m glad to...um...drop by to...uh...”

“Shut up and sit fucking down.” Dockers does both instantly. Bleached Wheat yawns. “Ponzi, why don’t you go ahead and start us off.”

The room dims. A green and blue holomap appears hovering over the table. In the lower left corner is BoiCity, labeled and represented by its large, yellow patch. Spreading north and east of the meg is the wilderness area, represented by a huge, empty green. Lacing that space are myriad blue threads and blobs—the rivers and the reservoirs. Dockers knows for sure now he's shitcreek. *Promo*? He'll be lucky to live out the morning.

"To get us right to the point," Ponzi begins, "the IMS hydrobiz Sawtooth Fluid has suddenly turned co-op over the past few weeks. We believe it's due to—"

"We *know* it's due to," corrects Bleached Wheat.

Not bothering to hesitate, Ponzi soldiers on, "We know it's due to EVe insert and slice indoctrination. Let me repeat that. EVe *insert*," Ponzi pauses to glare into each face, save for the ceo's, around the table, "and *slice* indoctrination." He delays again to let these two key words take hold. He seems satisfied with the commotion they cause. "The situation now," he breaks back in over the murmurings, "to the best of Net knowledge, is this." Red dots with place-names pop up all over the holomap, mainly forming a distant crescent stretching due north to due east away from BoiCity. "The co-op firmly controls dams and hydrostations from Cascade, here to the north, to Mackay, here to the east." Those locations flash momentarily in the air. "But, as you can see, it's making inroads west. They've established a makeshift HQ on Redfish Lake, here, and recently captured Deadwood Reservoir, here, and even Magic and Mormon Reservoirs, out on the Cheney River Plain." These locations all flash. "Not only are they getting bolder, but they're getting dangerously closer to BoiCity and, more importantly, to Mountain Home ArcAir Base, here to the southeast." A companion yellow patch now appears along T-84. "I don't need to stress how necessary it is to keep that base launch."

Dockers, who so far has just been staring slack-jawed up at the holomap along with everybody else, begins to feel the accusing eyes on him. He fidgets, but keeps watching the floating image. Ponzi concludes his short briefing, "If the co-op should take Arrowrock Dam, here, and Anderson Ranch Dam, here, as we believe is their plan, both the meg and the base could conceivably be at risk."

"How," Bleached Wheat reminds Ponzi.

"Water withhold," Ponzi says dutifully, lowering his head.

Everyone in the conference room nods with extreme sobriety. When Ponzi sits down, the discussion conelights pop on, haloing each chair around the table so the holomap can still be read. Dockers knows it's open season on megmayors starting *now*. His new chum, Yupcap, takes the first shot. "Why the hell haven't you shock-and-awed these piss ants, Dockers?"

"That's wilderness area out there," Dockers counters legitimately. He squints in this harsher light. He's not about to just bend over and grab his ankles. "We chase them away, but they just disappear and regroup in the mountains. North of that red band there is nothing but nothing. Watershed area. The Lost River Range, the Salmon River Mountains, the Clearwater Mountains. That's all high, pine forest and scrubland, and deep river canyons and box ravines. Vehics can't operate in there. And aviation can't pin anything down with any kind of accuracy for very long." The country is unbelievably remote. Dockers himself had gone out, at first, for several fly-overs in his helihover, that is, until the co-opers started taking potshots at him. "*You* go out there and try to track the fuckmothers down. Be my *guest*. It can't be done with the milforce I have."

"Why not just yanking guard your dams and hydrostations better?" asks Jitney, the Security maestro, taking the obvious killshot.

Dockers is ready for it. "You don't understand," he explains. "They've gone *co-op*. Hydrowork is *Serv* intensive. Even most of our safeguard force is goddamn Parker, and those barneys mainly just take random shots with minimisters at the bears and cougars that come too close. We *have* no effective guard out there. The few Terds we need are pure tech dudes, and they've all been killed or turned."

"*What*?" demands Jitney. "You've had Terds who've *turned*?"

"Well, we don't know for sure." Dockers knows that overstatement might land him in even more trouble. "I don't know how else these shitubers are managing to run the pumps and controlgates by themselves. Hell, maybe they can. But I tell you what, if they ever start to figure out how to manipulate the whole hydrogrid, they could get up to some serious mischief."

"Come on," jeers Yupcap, "these are fucking shitubers, for christsake."

Both Ponzi and Jitney stiffen at the Lord's name being taken in vain, which, of course, was Yupcap's wicked intention.

"These aren't just your run-of-the-factory shitubers," warns Dockers. "These are high-mountain shitubers, rugged individualist IMS types. They're Blood-in-the-Face, you know, from that old survivalist stock. Believe me, they'll rip your head off and shit down your throat. Don't think they *won't*. These are Dmega steeldicked mothers."

"Is that why you're doing biz with them," asks Bleached Wheat—almost courteously, "because you're pooping-your-panties afraid of them?"

Shit a goddamn brick. Dockers has been banking on this bit of bignews not being out. From the looks of things, only Bleached Wheat knew. All the others around the conference table—the four subceos and their various flunkies—break out in a fevered whispering and tongue-tisking goddamn frenzy. If there's one thing Dockers has learned from his years at the top of the Pyramid, offense is defense. "No, sir," he returns calmly, considering who he's dealing with now, "as a matter of fact, I've been doing biz with the co-opers both strategically and out of sheer practicality. Not out of fear."

"Oh. Have you now?"

"Yes, sir. I figure that if we're negotiating with them, we're keeping contact open and an infoflow going. That can't be a bad thing for eventually tracking them down. And on the pragmatic side, if I *don't* biz with them, I've got a potential hydroshortage on my hands. That's never good for *anything*. You just hint at shortage and a panic tears-ass through both the inner and the outer meg." Dockers sees he's got them thinking, but, characteristically, he gets cocky and takes a step too far. "Them causing a shortage would also send the wrong message, don't you think? That they have some real power. I don't know about *you*, Mr. CEO, sir, but that's a message *I'm* not willing to let get around."

"Why you potbellied megjockey," Ponzi threatens, appearing ready to rip Dockers' head off and shit down *his* throat. "Don't you go thinking big-pic on us. You're only good for riding herd on your miserable parks. And by the looks of things you can't even keep your dick straight doing that."

Dockers doesn't get to jockey a meg because he fails to recognize when he's touched a nerve. "All I'm saying," he returns affably, "is that if you boys really wanted to nip this thing in the bud, either Net should have freaked that slice a long time ago, or Ground should have busted a fall into the wilderness area by now and termed these pricks *big* time. That's all I'm saying."

Ponzi leaps to his feet. "Why you fucking—"

"As it is," Dockers won't be interrupted, raising his voice and flirting with an angry tone, "I've been left to deal with this shitstorm on my own. So that's what the fucking *fuck* I've been doing."

Jitney comes in dogmatically, "Then why don't you use your infoflow and get your fatass security forces out into your stinking parks to locate these EVe terrorists? How fucking *fuck* hard can that be?"

Dockers smiles and shakes his head. "Subceo," he asks, "you ever been out in any parks?"

Jitney's not even sure about the relevance of such a question. "No," he says dismissively, "of course not."

"Neither have I," says Dockers, "and neither has any Crat with half a gram of brains in his head. The parks are like big cesspools, suceo, and because there's only shit in them, you can't find shit in them, if you get what I mean." Reluctantly, Jitney does. Everyone around the conference table gets what Dockers means. Parks are like domains unto themselves, volatile territories you handle, not truly control. It's one of the inevitable drawbacks of the system. "I've applied as much security pressure in my parks as I dare. ParkPol is out muscling around as best it can, but I'm not about to send any of my GaterPol out there and thin my defenses. Especially not now. At best I may be able to make these EVe bastards flush and run, but I'd have to get awful damn lucky to catch them cold."

"Interesting," Bleach Wheat observes. His voice lets everyone know to shut up and sit still. Ponzi plops back down into his chair, and Jitney drops the debate. "Quite interesting."

The elegant conference room, with its black, marble table top and sleek retronineties furnishings, goes silent while the ceo ponders matters. Bleached Wheat is beginning to regard Dockers in a slightly different light. The megmayor is a boorish dimwit, of course. The very heart and soul of the TexArc Crat. He's an asshole. But he's got a pair, Bleached Wheat nods to himself, especially when cornered. He certainly comes out swinging. He hadn't known this about Dockers, and it might be useful. Very useful. He calls for the breakfast service to be brought in and, refusing anything for himself, tells everyone to selfoblige, that it's the small, good things of life that bring the most pleasure. Latte, cappuccino, espresso, raspberry tarts, apple turnovers, gooey bearclaws, almond freedom crescents, whatever you like. Corp's plenty. Dive in.

While serving themselves, and even after returning to their seats, no one talks. Dockers simply brings the pot of latte with him, and fills to overflowing two small plates with pastries. It's at that point that Bleached Wheat makes his second executive decision of the morning. The bigboss clears his throat. Everyone freezes, mid sip or munch.

"Oddly enough," Bleached Wheat announces to the table, "the good mayor here has put his finger on it."

"What?" says Ponzi, almost spitting latte across the table.

"Let's face facts, gentlemen. Net should have disposed of that nasty slice by now." Ponzi bangs his wide-mouthed mug hard down onto the black marble of the table, nearly cracking the pale, bone china. "Instead,"

Bleached Wheat continues, ignoring Ponzi's display, "it's begun to distribute itself up and down the IMS."

Until this moment no one else has been aware of the hyperaggressive nature of the slice. *Now the conference room can buzz over Ponzi's poochscrew*, thinks Dockers, as he chews and beams.

Bleached Wheat adds, over the commotion, "And Ground really can't drop in to clean house quite yet."

"Why the hell not?" Jitney protests, vehemently.

Bleached Wheat lets Jitney's tone of voice slide. "Because," he explains, feigning patience, "as the mayor has so aptly pointed out, suppression at this point might encourage and spread the co-op movement, give it a credibility we don't want it to have."

To a man, except for Dockers, who's happily gulping latte, brows furrow around the table.

"Pardon me for asking, sir," ventures Yupcap, "but, um, how exactly is that going to happen?"

Good, Bleached Wheat thinks of his number three subceo. *Finally this puppy is starting to lift his leg to piss.*

"Ground crushes domestic disturbances frequently, and Vieworld attentively filters those events." Yupcap nods around the room to encourage the others to join him in nodding. All do, except for Ponzi and Jitney, and for Dockers, too, but only because he's preoccupied with choosing his next bakery item. "There, um, wouldn't be any credibility *to* be had. Would there, sir?"

"Under normal circumstances, no, Yupcap, you're quite right of course." Bleached Wheat's almost fatherly tone chills the backbone of every sub and subsub listener. "But we're not working under normal circumstances at the moment, are we?" Yupcap shakes his head no, as do quite a few others around the conference table, none of them knowing really why. "We have EVe infiltrators on the ground, now, who've shown themselves to be elusive and sophisticated. Frankly, Yupcap, that's got me worried. So Mayor Dockers' notion of maintaining infoflow is, I think, a sound one." Dockers flashes a shit-eating grin ear to ear. He tries to court as much cheap eye-contact glory as he can around the room. "It's best if we capture and interrogate these insurgents rather than just misting them to atoms. Don't you agree? We need to know how they got into TexArc and how they're streaming this troublesome feed." Bleached Wheat pauses perfectly, masking the theatricality of his pause. "Who knows?" he asks, not quite dramatically. "Their activities might just be the start of some kind of drastic EVe offensive."

Furrowed brows deepen around the table, with some cautious glances added, particularly between Ponzi and Jitney. No offensive can touch TexArc, not in any drastic way. And TexArc infoflow is based solely on how better to obliterate resistance. Nothing else. Nothing mindfuck. Counterintelligence hasn't had to be a corp concern for some three or four decades.

"I'm sorry, sir," speaks up Ponzi, aware he's likely taking his life in his hands, "I just don't see what you're zooming at." He shifts in his chair and swallows. "Nothing of what you've just said to us, sir, is, well, plan. It just isn't plan at all, sir." The conference room seems to take a surreal tilt out of normal time and space. Everyone starts calculating his one-notch bump upward now that Ponzi has begun the grisly process of subceo selfterm. "EVens are beyond the flock, sir. Outside Christ's fold. Dominion demands their slaughter, sir. Nothing short of that is gospel."

"Amen," says Jitney.

"Amen," repeats every subsuber on Jitney's and Ponzi's staffs.

They're uniformly TDers. Bleached Wheat had needed the frenzy-christers, especially during the China subdue and the building of the Space Elevator. Total Dominionists love to erect monuments to God almost as much as they love to slaughter deviants beyond the flock. But

Bleached Wheat knows dealing with EVe will need a different tact—one not so holyroller. Ponzi, Jitney, and all the rest of them have taken up their usual prayer gesture. TDers wear small medallions around their necks, solid gold disks at the end of solid gold chains, stamped with a fist clutching a cross held at a right angle, like a weapon. All of them now hold these medallions between their thumbs and forefingers, reverently rubbing. It will be a bother to reboot Ponzi's and Jitney's topspots. It takes a long time to precondition a subceo, but he must have a more secular touch. That's why Yupcap's in the pipeline. Yupcap sees these Soldiers of Christ for what they are: yanking lunatics, indispensably useful for some things, but enormous asspains for others. *Shit a brick*, muses the ceo, this is turning out to be quite a morning for executive decisions.

"You're quite correct to question me on this, Ponzi." Bleached Wheat's already got everyone off pitch. Now he'll tweak their yaw a bit. "And I commend your sense of loyal opposition for saying so. If only all my subs were so committed to the teachings of our Lord and Savior." Bleached Wheat scans pointedly around the table, but winks at Yupcap in a way no one else can see. All the subs are stunned. "But unusual circumstances call for unusual measures. We've never had a foreign threat so deep within our borders. I believe a bit of finesse is in order. We've got to permit this insert and slice indoctrination to run its course a little longer so we can draw out and hammer their foray crew. Otherwise, we may never get them."

"If I may be so bold, sir," pipes up Jitney, anxious to bonanza on these apparently new kudos for candor, "finesse is quick to backfire. Muscle's the prime guide for corpland security. No one should know that better than you."

"I said committed to the teachings, you sanctimonious son of a bitch, not braindead because of them." Bleached Wheat can't stomach the humble arrogance of christers, their crux hypocrisy. Hiding their greed behind the Book. Nor can he permit things to get too far off kilter with this touchy-feely shit. "Java," he calls toward the end of the table, "are you ready?"

Java nods and stands. "Of course, sir."

The holomap and conelights vanish while the ceiling border illuminations return. Java touches a pad and the double doors open. In walks a scrawny amerslope no one recognizes. Not a Crat, that's obvious. A Terd. A dykebitch. She's tall for a slope, but looks to weigh in at about twenty kilos. In fact her piercings, about nine encrusting each ear, two bolted through the outer walls of her nostrils, plus the current fashion, a bullring dangling from her septum, look to be heavier than she is. She's got a shock of powder blue hair spiked up all around her skull, as if she's perpetually electrostimulated, and she clogs in on amazingly tall, high-heeled thigh boots—skin-tight and vermilion on her twin twigs for legs. Hip bones protrude through her ivory thong, and shoulder blades jut out above her ebony microhalter. She has no hooters to speak of, but her nipples are enormous and ringpierced as well, poking through the halter cutholes.

"Now that's one skinny-ass puss-and-boots." Dockers chucks the subsubceo sitting next to him in the ribs. They laugh under their breaths, both starting to sprout hardnobs.

Once the woman has taken a seat next to him, Java pads again and a blank holozone appears over the middle of the table.

"Watch this," says Java.

Mall's "How *do* you like it?" spot runs, except one thing has been added. After Uncle Wobbly asks his pointed question, we cut back to get a look at the unidentified viewer-rapist. He turns out to be the cute little Monopoly Man. Just like in the game, he's dressed for the opera with his tails, cane, spats, and top hat. He turns out to be the one, an insanely toothy grin beneath his handlebar mustache, nailing the screaming Serv. As the Monopoly Man continues feverishly to pump the rump, he leers right at us with lust-crazed eyes and a string of drool dangling out one corner of his mouth.

Afterwards the conference room is dead silent until someone finally mutters, “Fuck me dry.”

“You can say that again,” says Java.

Java is subceo for Culture. He’s got a shade of something uncomfortable in him, mex or afro—or damn both. Not slope. His eyes are right. Java’s pigmentation is pure concession to the two coasts, particularly to the PC. Hell, even the southern rim of the BHC is getting a little fruity any more. Bleached Wheat had no choice but to let one mongrel in. Everyone admits, though, that Java cuts a fine upleft-op. He’s doublego rangy, with a close-cropped goatee that wings out in points along his jawline and a fade cut with different logos sides and back. Pretty smack for a nearnig. Not brainslow like them, either.

“This is from the slice?” asks Jitney, noticeably alarmed.

“Yes,” says Ponzi before Java can answer.

“My lord.”

“Oh, wait,” says Java, “there’s lots more.”

Java is enjoying this, Bleached Wheat notes with interest.

The subceo for Culture shows them a whole series of ads, all of them featuring the Monopoly Man and most of them involving Uncle Wobbly. Each is targeted at the downright, at yanking up the notion of Brand You. Pure anti-plan. Here’s the bare-bummed Monopoly Man perched above a Serv who’s hunched busily at a cubicle in a Downright DayTrade, obviously working markstrat on his parkport. The Monopoly Man is obviously working his own cratport and laughing gleefully while taking a dump down onto the Serv’s head. The Monopoly Man’s screen reads, “Sell!” while the Serv’s screen reads, “Buy!” Another ad depicts a long row of hopeful Servs lined up at a jobs window handing over their immaculate pictograph résumés to a smiling Terd behind the counter. The Terd, in turn, is passing them over her shoulder to the Monopoly Man who, without even giving them a glance, uses one after another either to blow his nose or wipe his ass before tossing them aside. Standing close by, Uncle Wobbly, shaking his head, asks, "Free agent in a dynamic, job-rich environment? Or fuck-all wage slave?" A brief, static, and powerful spot simply recreates the GET OUT OF JAIL FREE card. In this version, however, the smirking Monopoly Man is getting booted out of the parks and over the walls into the Gater district, his trajectory clearly lifting him toward the Pyramid. Ad after ad like these pop onto the holozone. Each time, nothing TexArcan is sacred. The culture change of workplace teams is turned on its head as surveillance and degradation. Perky efficiency suggestions from management become speedups and layoffs for labor. Job opportunity transforms into caste captivity. The marketplace as purveyor of freedom and democracy mutates into bonanza cratprofit for bigtime shareholders, flattening then lowering wages for those who do the work, causing sourceout, sizedown, coercion, cartel, guns and muscle, bustunion, disenfranchisement, enforced consensus, fiscal, physical, and psychological exploitation. After fifteen minutes, the Crats around the conference table begin to fidget and growl that they've seen enough of this heresy, of this unadulterated libby jackshit. Bleached Wheat waves an impatient hand, signaling for them to shut the fuck up and watch every goddamn second. They do.

The very last spot is longer than the rest, more involved, more intellectually complex. It ends with Uncle Wobbly, wearing a coonskin hat, sitting on top of the Monopoly Man who he's just shot through the forehead with an old-timey flintlock. The Monopoly Man has x's where his eyes used to be. With the gun barrel still smoking, Uncle Wobbly pushes back his furry cap with one finger, spits a long stream of brown tobacco juice off to one side, then delivers a small homily. Nothing tedious, but deliberately not simple, either. In it he points out that economic freedom and democracy means a reasonable standard of living for everybody, not just for the bigwig few. That biz, by its very nature, doesn't get us anywhere near there. Biz feeds off of poverty and helplessness. Biz can't rid us of those things. That what we really need is job security and a safety net, not this tear-you-a-new-asshole stock market always tilted towards the money-bags. That what will get us to where we need to go are co-ops and gov-regs and farewel—everything we ain't got now. No union means no democracy, says Uncle Wobbly in a slightly worn-out voice. Only with a union can the wage-maker ever have a say in the industry, so's it doesn't get out of hand, out of the real people's control, and end up doing no damn good—like biz does now. Uncle Wobbly then chuckles to himself and pats the Monopoly Man on his dead ass. He looks square at us. "Now who the hell else is going to do this for you? No one else. That's who. There's just certain things in this world we got to do for ourselves."

If possible, the conference room is even more silent than after the first ad played. No one squirms or let's out a long whistle or tries to wise-crack. It's just heavy quiet for a long time. Finally Java comments, "I've shown you these in the order the splice steamed them onto ArcNet. There are others since these. New ones appear almost every day. And there's an older set as well, the original ones that came out as part of a local recall campaign some time ago. They certainly started all the trouble, but they're not as Dmega revoevo as these. These I've shown you are the real ball busters."

Java pads off the holozone.

"And who the fuck's getting fed these?" Jitney demands.

"All the Servs in BoiCity and its immediate vicinity, and now more Servs up and down the IMS."

"Only Servs?" inquires Yupcap, to show he's ice.

"Exactly," acknowledges Java, happy to team with the other junior sub-ceo.

A few soft, prolonged whistles follow. That's a lot of parks.

"What are these co-ops calling themselves again?" asks Jitney. As Security boss he should have been up to zoom on this from getgo. He's pissed that he's been outlooped until now.

"Wobblies," answers Java.

"Yeah?" Jitney is staring at Ponzi, "and who exactly is this Uncle Wobbly, anyway? Where'd *he* come from?"

"We're not sure," Ponzi answers, taking the opportunity to slap down the mongrel pup. He adds menacingly, "No one in Culture has ever heard of him before. Culture has no previous vid or aud or even printext record of him. Zero." Ponzi looks to Bleached Wheat, who nods approval for him to continue. "He's versatile, though. Depending on the feedsite, he'll show up as afro, mex, or slope speaking ebon, hispan, chink or viet—whatever in hell he needs to be speaking. These are no amateur productions."

Dockers can't stand any more. "What the fuck does that matter?" he breaks in. "So what if the whole rainbow of yanking shitubers are down-righting this shit?"

"All4ing," Java corrects him.

"Okay, yanking all4ing this shit? So what? Servs are morons, just poor crusty sludgesuckers with no more brains than sheep, or family values than goats. Fuck 'em. They can't do anything to us. They can't touch us in our Gater districts, let alone the Pyramid."

Yes, Bleached Wheat thinks, *this crass and craven fellow will do nicely.*

"You were singing a different tune a minute ago," snaps Ponzi, "whining about these Wobblies being too clever for you to get your hands on."

"Out in the fucking boondocks, yeah, you can't pin them down. So what? Let them run around the goddamn primitive area all they want. These glassy clowns aren't going to organize themselves into anything that amounts to a damn. This Uncle Wobbly guy is just farting smoke. What kind of revoevo strategy is that, to tell a bunch of smelly apes they've got to take things into their own hands?"

"It's a classic strategy, actually." No one noticed the subtle nod from Bleached Wheat to the woman sitting next to Java, a nod granting the Terd permission to take part in the Crat exchange. "Only the oppressed can free themselves," she explains.

A dykebitch is any ho trying to butt her way too far up into the mancrat corpworld. The only classic strategy going on here, as far as the Crats sitting around the conference table are concerned, is your typical dykebitch talking out her ass. Dockers rolls his eyes and scoffs out loud at the goofy contribution she's made to their Crat conversation. In spirit, so do Ponzi, Jitney, and Yupcap. So do all the subsub staffers in the conference room. Their reactions don't faze the woman in the least.

"If these Wobblies can establish solidarity with members of the educated class," she continues, "in this case, I'm assuming that will be with the EVe insert, their movement could obtain and grow. Such cultural and technical knowhow, combined with mass unrest, makes for a powerful conjunction—potentially a dangerous one. They might organize themselves into a formidable popular insurgence. They already seem to be well on their way."

"Honey," Dockers begins patronizingly, "I don't know where you come from or what you're used to, but here in the Big House it's best for puss just to keep its yap shut and look gorgeous. Why don't you go get your skinny self four or five doughnuts over there and just do what I'm sure you do best— which is being a nice piece of dickwear."

Only Java refrains from laughing. Even Bleached Wheat smiles, but not necessarily out of amused derision. Apparently used to this sort of thing, the woman returns to her explanation as though Dockers had never spoken.

"The name Wobblies refers back to a popular labor movement during the first half of the twentieth century, the 'IWW' or 'International Workers of the World.'"

"Ooo, unions," mocks Dockers, still playing to the table. "I'm crapping my pants."

"As our ceo pointed out," she finally acknowledges the megmayor, "I believe you have been when trying to deal with this co-op."

The taunting clamor of “you’ve been bitchslapped” rises in the room at Dockers’ expense. “And for good reason,” the woman adds loudly to shut every Crat up. “Like all labor movements, the Wobblies advocated and actively agitated for collective bargaining and governmental supervision of production—both concepts anathema to Corpfeud. Their efforts were by no means inconsiderable. The Wobblies had to be crushed by brute force and the good fortune of a world war coming along, but labor unionionism as a viable entity endured into the seventh decade of that century. And only then privilege shrewdly marketed as jingofrenzy did it in. The concept of hirelings being compensated suitably for their time spent in travail, as primitive as that idea might sound to us now, always can be packaged as an appealing one to the demotic mind.”

“To the *what*?” Dockers tries to make fun of her inflated vocabulary. “The *demented* mind?” At this point, few bite at his joke.

“Presented well, the notion of a living wage has the potential to stir up trouble, and this series of pitches,” she gestures to where the holozone had appeared at the center of the table, “I must concede, is absolutely brilliant. Vintage Freire with Foucaultian underpinnings. Remarkable. I didn’t think anyone was working retro any more. This Uncle Wobbly figure we’re seeing is a deft invention of the EVe fabricateur.” She turns to Java sitting beside her. “That’s why Culture couldn’t locate him. He’s innovation. He incarnates an entire range of ideo-economic contentions from the past, say, three or even four centuries. Surplus wealth, pareto optimality, dialogical intersubjectivity, disciplinarity mechanics refutatio, power tectonics. It’s quite a mix.” She turns back to face many pairs of wary mancrat eyes. *Where’d a ho learn to talk like this?* “Left unchecked to spread,” she tells them, “I believe this splice and a resultant worker crusade will cause TexArc tangible inconvenience, perhaps even actual peril to municipal stability.” She recognizes the need to downgrade her bottomline for the bizdumb. “That is to say, you could get your nuts caught in a wringer.

Sitting on your hands is not an option."

Several silent moments of bizdumb follow.

"All the more reason for Ground to fall and mop," Jitney declares.

Ponzi does him one better. "Or send in Net directly. If this thing is really that dangerous, why fuck around?"

"Gentlemen," Bleached Wheat announces, wanting no more debate, "meet my finesse." With a sweeping gesture he motions down the long table towards the woman at its opposite end. "Meet Doctor Brand. Board Chair of Culture Construct at the Yale School of Reconstruction." Murmurs now, even some curses under the breath. "For all you yokums who've never set foot outside the wheatland, that's one of TexArc's finest TerdTechs, located in the extreme southern reaches of the Boston supermeg." A brief frown from the ceo checks any remaining bellyaching. "Fellas," Bleached Wheat then assumes a brotherly grin, "believe me. Brand knows her shit when it comes to revoevo. She's going to put the kibosh on this thing pronto."

Jitney, who increasingly chooses to ignore clear signals from the bossman, protests, "Sir. Bringing in a pedanterd, and from the northeast?"

"Yes, Jitney, I know." Bleached Wheat will play along—a bit. "They wear their butts for hats and are worse snobs than paralibbies from the westcoast. But in this case, Jitney, that's just what I'm looking for. Gentlemen, this time we're going to fight fire with fire."

"*Sir*," urges Ponzi, suddenly speaking through clenched molars, "for fuck's sake just *exterminate* all the brutes. We don't fight fire with fire. We don't fuck around. TexArc kills what*ever's* in its way."

True. That is Pax TexArcana. Bleached Wheat's been fortunate to have a plodder like Ponzi as ArcNet boss for these many years. It will be a shame to cycle him through. But time marches on.

"We've been over that, Ponzi," the ceo reassures him. "I know plan. This time, I think it's important to deviate, to improvise, to show them that if someone wants to insert and yank with our heads, we can yank right back with theirs."

"*Sir*," Ponzi pushes his luck, "that makes absolutely no sense. This Wobbly shit is corpheresy worse than the obamanation, and you *know* it."

Hmm, perhaps he'll need to cycle a little sooner than expected. Too bad. Such trouble. "I'll wager I'm seeing a larger agenda here than you are, Ponzi." Bleached Wheat rises from his chair and moseys to the refreshments. He takes his time selecting an immense bearclaw and preparing a wide-mouthed coffee cup of cappuccino. He carries these items carefully back with him to the conference table. After setting them down and reseating himself, he occupies a minute sampling each before speaking. "No, Ponzi, we're going to counterpitch this EVe slice. We're going to put them right out of the revoevo biz. We'll put a stop to this little Wobbly uprising *and*, in the process, we'll get our hands on EVe's foray crew. Brand will be account planner for the project." No further challenge comes. The bearclaw is far too sweet—making your teeth hurt—just as Bleached Wheat likes them. "In fact, I've asked her to prepare a brief presentation for all of you."

Brand stands up decisively, moving with a strength and confidence her gaunt frame does not suggest. She begins to walk a slow circle around the conference table, forcing her audience continually to turn in order to track her. "Gentlemen," she begins in the clear tone of a seasoned TerdTech conference presenter, "at Yale we specialize in the Simulacrum. That's what Terds go there to learn. That's what we teach them to master."

"Mastur*bate* is more like it," Dockers quips.

"Mayor Dockers," Brand stops and addresses him aggressively, as she might a student, "I'm well aware of the Crat disdain for hire education, but I can assure you, without TerdTechs, our corporation couldn't function." Dockers makes sure to show his surprise at being addressed directly. "Crats may devise the bigpic, but Terds turn that bigpic into go. We execute, as well as make *plausible*, the reality you invent. I suggest you listen carefully to what I have to say. After all, Mayor, it's your meg and, if I may say so, your fat cratass that's on the line in this particular situation."

No Crat in the room is prepared to hear a Terd talk like this, not to one of their own—no matter how much of an assjack Dockers is.

Bleached Wheat doesn't so much as twitch during Brand's dressing down of the megmayor. In fact, once she's through, the ceo takes a long slurp of his cappuccino and smacks his lips contentedly. Brand resumes her circling.

"The totality of the all4s—the ipatch, the ihear, and the motor-sensory cortex band combined, is what we refer to as the Simulacrum. Not the gizmos themselves, but rather the cultural experience we, through them, produce in persons embedded with these devices. The Simulacrum, in other words, is that little vid-aud-sensory multiplex built directly into every Serv head that can play, twentyfourseven, whatever cinematic experience TexArc thinks best, for the sake of productivity. We construct a total description of the world, gentlemen, and that's a huge undertaking and responsibility."

Java sits nodding. Culture is considered soft, bottom of the ladder, as far as subceo duties are concerned. He can see Ponzi and Jitney aligning out already. Even Yupcap, no doubt to suck up to the big bossman, interrupts by asking, "What's the big yanking bowwow anyway? Market Enterprise supplies the bread," he points out. "Culture just supplies the games. Big transaction."

"It's one hell of a lot more than that, Yupcap," Java defends, trying his best to sound country-club casual. "Culture's like riding a bucking redhead virho or driving that par-23 out there on 57 when they got the crosswind turbines blasting. It's tricky shit and pure finesse."

"Finesse is what *makes* Culture shit," opines Jitney, disinterested.

"Subceo Jitney," Brand risks addressing him, "with respect, we're talking more than virsport, virporn, and Shopdrop here. We're talking about exercising the overall effect of TexArc's strategic positions, an effect made not simply as an obligation or prohibition on those who do not get to decide what TexArc's strategic positions are. Such muscle is your purview in Security, sir. In Culture, we're talking about instead investing TexArcans with plan so that Corpfeud is not only forcibly transmitted to them, but, in time, is voluntarily embraced *by* them and passed along *through* them, even when it is not in their best interests to do so. We're talking about nothing less than the formation of the individual subject, Subceo, and that's never as simple or as straightforward a matter of control as you might like to think."

"Uppity dykebitch," Jitney tosses to no one in particular to demonstrate that he has not acknowledged her address. He roughly pushes back his chair to go pour another small cup of espresso.

"Whoever's designing that EVe slice certainly grasps these concepts," Brand hazards. "I can assure you all of that. Look, if you stop to think about it, having a boot on someone's throat is actually a sign of a weak state, of one verging on collapse. Otherwise, why would such overt means of domination be necessary? What Subceo Java and I are talking about is a subtle, shifting, ever-contended, ever-in-flux network of control that produces citizens who police themselves without their knowledge. That's because all they have is *our* knowledge, the knowledge produced by TexArc plan and delivered by the technology of the Simulacrum."

A testy silence follows her tenable points.

"Still," Ponzi finally counters, "no one ever mistakes the function of a good boot on the throat. That's pretty much foolproof."

"I grant your point, Subceo Ponzi," says Brand, happy to have coaxed out discussion, "but consider this: Mere physical command leaves free the mind and the spirit to resist. The Simulacrum captures those things first so the body readily follows, and the only realy productive body is the subjected body."

"And a mister burst to the temple or tacnuke to the downtown produces only *dead* bodies," points out Jitney, refilling a third shot of caffeine concentrate, "which never resist a *damn* thing."

"I grant your point as well, Subceo Jitney," nods Brand, "*if* the objective is only to eliminate. If the objective, however, is productivity, then the Simulacrum obtains a far better result than deadly force. Within the world of the all4s, plan and control are veiled as pleasure and profit. Corpfeud is experienced as a positive force in life, not as subjugation and tyranny." Brand hopes for more objections to field, but none come. She moves to her main point, "After all, I believe plan is to render EVe friendly to freemarket, is it not? Not to wipe it off the face of the planet."

"Yep," admits Yupcap, after a while, "that's true enough." Ponzi and Jitney appear not to be so sure.

"Then we'll need the Simulacrum to insinuate and to inculcate consumerism into EVe. Successfully counterpitching their slice could be the first step. Who knows? Maybe we can find a way to inverse and ride their own slice *back* into EVeWave. We could initiate a clandestine corpitch to them, just as they've secretly pitched revocvo to us. Culture Construct works both ways, you know."

Brand has stopped her circling, standing lost now in her own account planning. She'd love to get her hands on a virgin audience of ultralibbies—*and* face the communication challenge of actually having to break through stream clutter rather than, as is now the case with the implant of the all4s, merely design and maintain stream clutter. *That* would be real Reconstruction. Not just babysitting industrial zombies.

She looks up and realizes she's lost her classroom of Crats. They sit staring bizdumbly at her. Brand shifts her slight weight from one elevated bootheel to the other, also shifting her narrow hips and her pouting thongcrotch. *That's what they're all probably staring at anyway*, she imagines. Even for a Terd dykebitch, Brand's bodyart is extraordinary—aggressive and outrageous. Besides the wide, Egyptian eye tatooed on the inner curve of each upper thigh, a diamondback rattler coils down her spinal column to end with its spade-shaped head darting out a forked tongue to lick at the top of her butt cleavage, and full-color, ink-graph hands—one male, one female—grasp at her neck in a choke hold. She also wears the newest Terd craze in mood makeup. *Moment by Moment*, a foundation cream that bodychems a vivid color glow, a kind of sheen or aura, to the facial features depending on the wearer's humor. Now, Brand's face is glistening solar yellow. With nonpermanent texter, as a finishing touch, she also has a message for the day graffitied between her navel and pubic region: "*fuck you instead*."

Jitney sits back down with his fourth steaming cup of espresso. Bleached Wheat lingers over his gargantuan cappuccino. Sensing the initial skirmish over, Java invites Brand, in as few big words as possible, to delineate the crux principles of the Simulacrum. She returns to her seat and runs through them quickly. Believing is seeing. Matter over mind. She points out as well its ingenious instrument. The Simulacrum does not watch you. You watch it. Perforce. Crude, high-modern, benthamian architectonics are no longer required for factories, schools, barracks, hospitals, prisons. Instead, all of their inculcatory functions are now wholly interiorized, naturalizing plan from inside out, not the less reliable outside in. Thus, visibility is no longer the trap. Visioning is. The mind's eye. You panopt. You are not panopted. In this way Corpfeud achieves optimum illusion of its inevitability, its providential certainty. Whatever is, is right, because it's right in your head. Ignorance and docility are cultivated ne plus ultra within the inescapable confines of the glassy.

"So tell us something, then, bony buns." Dockers has been waiting for his opening. "Why is it this goddamn slice is fucking with my Servs' heads so bad? If this Simulacrum of yours is so surefire, how are these stinkass Parkers managing to think for themselves all of a sudden?"

"Because your local feed has been disrupted somehow, Mr. Mayor, and the ArcNet Terds can't figure out how to make the reconnect."

"Wait a minute. You're telling us that a mere slice is now managing an entire feed?"

"This is no ordinary slice," Ponzi affirms. "It has principles and features that just can't be explained. I've never seen anything like it."

"Nor have I," adds Brand, anxious to stake Ponzi as an ally rather than an adversary.

"So what the hell are you going to do different," Dockers challenges Brand, "that ArcNet can't do?"

"I'm going to slice the slice. Fight fire with fire."

"How?"

"My staff and I will figure that out. At Yale, as Reconstructors of the Simulacrum, we work hands-on even deeper in than ArcNet. We'll find a way."

"But with yanking what? What the fuck you going to slice into their slice?"

"Glad you've asked that question, Mr. Mayor. Questions are perhaps the most important form of classroom participation."

Smiling and irradi-blending into a deep conifer green, Brand pads four or five times on the console down by her right hand. The ceiling lights dim and the holozone reappears. An ad plays:

Sunrise over a prairie. Voiceover [deep, male, inspired]: "One DollArc, one vote." Solemn solo horn music begins. Cut-scene to a small boy's face, freckled, wonder-eyed, gazing upward. The boy speaks: "Golly, what's that, Pa?" Expand scene to an adult hand resting on the boy's shoulder, then to father and son standing together gazing upward. The father wears dirty overalls and scuffed workboots. A blue and red bandanna is knotted around his neck. He's sweating and a bit breathless. He pushes back his cap and replies: "Why, Son, that there's success, just waiting for you to grab hold and start pulling yourself up it." Cut-scene to low-angle shot now behind the father and son. They're standing on the prairie. The father's other hand is resting on the handle of a plow. To their right, the red ball of sun is just above the low dark hills on the distant horizon. Directly in front of them, stretching up into the sky, mysteriously luminous, is a golden ladder. Boy speaks: "Who put it there, Pa?" Father replies: "The Invisible Hand, Son." Boy speaks: "Whose hand is that, Pa?" Father replies: "Don't rightly know, Son. Some folks say God's. Some folks say Freemarket's." Boy speaks: "What do you say, Pa?" Father thinks it over a moment, then replies: "For my money, Son," he looks down at the boy, who returns upward his gaze, "I say both." Solo horn soars. Cut-scene to wide-angle shot pulling rapidly back and up from the father and son. As the two figures grow smaller and smaller in the expanding landscape, and as we see the mule hitched to the plow and the squat homestead nearby with a lone spiral of smoke curling out its crooked stone chimney, the miraculous ladder just keeps rising and rising, higher and higher, into the early morning sky. The reverent voiceover returns: "Backward and Upward. Climbing right where you are."

The holozone blanks. Sudden staccato applause vibrates the conference room. Brand's face deepens into a gratified night blue.

"Now that's what the fuck *I'm* talking about!" vaunts Java, pounding a fist on his chest.

"Dude!" extols Yupcap, happy to see Market getting some arch feedtime for a change over CorpTroops and terrorops. "That kicks EVe right where it doubleyanking hurts!"

Jitney and Ponzi applaud along unenthusiastically, not looking overly displeased. Bleached Wheat remains motionless, holding his cup to his lips, watching attentively the reaction to the ad. Brand had told him it would be a winner, even without her usual days of market research.

"Gentlemen!" he shouts over the clamor. Everyone quickly grows quiet. "As a specialist in new management culture change and its corporate implementation, Dr. Brand is fully aware of where the distortions lie in Corpfeud. After all, if she's to do her job right, she has to know what to sweep under the rug. Don't we all, gentlemen?" Crats nod all around. "That's why she's the very best at pitching for TexArc. That's why, as I hope you've just seen, in this time of crisis she'll be the very best one to counterpitch those who would seek to destroy us. Fucking people over, masked as the will of the people, is the supreme accomplishment of Corpfeud, and of the Simulacrum that promotes it. The EVe slicer knows this. That's why these Wobbly ads are targeted to rip out the very heart and soul of TexArc—the deeply-forged, popular conviction that freemarket is inborn, sacred, representational, and the friend of the little guy. Without these well-constructed truths, our corporation couldn't stand."

At the ceo's prompt, Java reaches out and depresses a pad. Low in the background the TexArc corpanthem, "Privatization, Deregulation, Globalization," begins to play. A subsub staffer speaks the common Crat benediction, "Jesus, CEO," and others respond softly, "Amen."

"Dr. Brand's job will be to reconstruct TexArc credo in the all4s of these poor, infected, IMS Servs. Her planners are already at hardwork on the account. The ad you've just previewed is a prototype for an entire series of plugs to be put up against Uncle Wobbly. We'll get on top of him and stay on top of him." Brand is glowing saffron once more. "Gentlemen, have no doubt, we will recapture the vox populi. The Simulacrum is a medium of the populace. What has gone wrong within the Simulacrum can be put right within the Simulacrum. There's no call for deadcount."

"We'll see," mutters Ponzi.

"By God, we *will* see!" bellows Bleached Wheat. "We will not surrender our faith in people's ability to make sound economic decisions within our freemarket!" He lays an index finger alongside his nose. "Selfoblige, gentlemen! Selfoblige! Huh? Am I right?" A scattering of the subsubceos eagerly nod their agreement. "The crowning achievement of Corpfeud is making people eat shit and enjoy it! Hell, to be indebted to us for it! *That* is the name of the game, gentlemen!" He then shouts the following phrase at the top of his lungs: "'Just make mine a *shitbritches*!'" Out of the blue, Bleached Wheat tosses his empty cappuccino cup high in the air over his shoulder. He waits for its heavy, thudding shattering on the floor. The eyes of each of his four subceos then get assessed—in detail. "As of this moment," he says perfectly calmly to them, "we're go with Java's counter-pitch scheme." No one says a word. Bleached Wheat next looks down the table at Dockers. "As for you, my good megmayor," he says, "Brand and her account planners are your responsibility from here on out. They'll conduct their work out of your Pyramid. Take damn good care of them." The middle finger gets pointed Dockers' way. "Whatever they want. Whatever they need. Got that?"

Dockers can only stammer that Bleached Wheat needn't worry about a thing.

"Whatever the hell you do, Mr. Mayor, don't screw *this* pooch. You got me? That's the real name of this game for you."

Bleached Wheat enjoys nothing so much as manning his ship of fools.

It's the Water

Oak dangles his filthy feet in the amazingly cold and clear waters of Redfish Lake. He really can't remember the last time he had his boots off. The past few months have been all shoot and scoot. Plain butt-ugly. It must be getting near to mid June by now. The heavy spring surge is over and all the snow is gone off the Grand Mogul and Mount Heyburn, off to his right, peeking up over the tops of the pines along the lakeshore. No snow means low flow. From here past late summer and into early fall the word is *conserve*. Even the giant thunderboomers don't add much to the aggregate. Only this year Oak's going to have a new word for them. *Reserve*. He ain't giving a drop of it up less they kiss *his* ass. Turnabout's the damn best payback.

Oak cups his palm and reaches down to bring water up to wash the blood off his forehead. Just a nip, but it feels big enough to scar. That sure don't make a damn. He's been getting plenty worse, lately. He's sitting at the end of what's left of the old tourist docks, where he comes to sit when he's in a particularly foul frame of mind. He understands now to sulk on things a while before making the profit decisions. Don't rush into anything. Commonsense joe. This time they snuck up along Fishook Creek and got way the hell down, almost to the lake, before his boys finally noticed and opened fire. Suck-yank Terds. They're clever damn bastards, he'll give them that. *Hell, this bunch might even be Net themself.* It's that mindfuck this time. Oak's not sure what to make of it, but he knows he needs to be thinking clear. After three handfuls of icy water the sting starts to numb up. Watery blood falls back into the lake to drift. Like everybody else, Oak's heard the stories of there used to be honest-to-god red fish, about the size of trout, in this lake. *Regular trout used to be in all the rivers and reservoirs out here, not like now, just in the narrow canyon streams. But these fellas in here was fire red and so lazy or smart you could dangle bait in front of their mouths and they wouldn't move a muscle to hit. Not a twitch. Now that's contentment—or maybe control.* Oak ponders if maybe he ought to be exercising some control about now.

Oak's sulked enough. He pulls his boots back on and stands up, deciding the red fish are likely a crock of shit, just like all the stories from back when. He walks fast back in to the Lodge. It's a two-story, built out of logs, the only building in the whole compound that's still got its full roof. He goes inside and checks with Hap at the situation desk. "Where the fuck we holding them?"

"Honeymoon Cabin."

Oak has to chuckle at that. "How many dead of ours?"

"Fucking twelve, most by that purple-headed bitch."

Both men shake their heads. "And theirs?"

"Just the one. A cock."

"At least that leaves more sweetpuss to go around."

"At least."

"There any more?"

"Don't know yet. I got men out looking."

"In our vehics?"

"Hell, yes."

"Okay then. I'll be over there."

"Your head okay?" Hap points. "That there's a bit too close for comfort."

Oak touches the graze. The bleeding's stopped. "Don't mean nothin'."

He walks past the crumbling gazebo on his way to the Honeymoon

Cabin. Underfoot is soft, the mix of sand, loam, and brown pine needles. Not a speck of cloud is anywhere in the bigsky. Sun blazing down to beat hell and the air smelling bone dry. High summer is setting on. Can fry a man to death.

Inside the dim and sultry cabin, Jiplap and six other Wobblies hold automatics aimed at the Terds. There's five of them, one yank and the rest puss. Should have been nobrainer to take them out, but the gals fought like hell. Oak pulls out his minimister and kneels in front of the purple-headed bitch. She's been beat on worse than the others. He pokes the snub nozzle up her one nostril, deep and irritating. Lately Oak's been calling his minimister his Terd-persuader. If he doesn't get what he wants out of one, the spray of plastic pellets isn't enough to break through the skull. They just scramble the brains in a hopeless way without making a big mess.

"So why'd you tell your people to stop fighting?" Oak asks her, leaning in close.

"Pigdog," the woman sneers back because of the gun up her nose, "you can suck on my ass pucker."

The Wobblies laugh, impressed mainly. Oak looks over his shoulder to his brothers and nods, grinning. "Well, let's not get ahead of ourselves, sister," he says, more to them than to her. "Biz before selfoblige."

"I told her to."

This is the tall, black-haired sweetpuss talking, the one with the dark eyes that are all the time telling you she'd like to kick you in the kernels. She looks a runner or some kind of ball player. The sleeveless skinshirt she's got on is sweated gray, and there's all kinds of fancy pockets on her soldier's pants. She looks Net to Oak, but he had no idea they let puss in. Oak pulls the minimister out of the purple-headed bitch's nose, squat-waddles, duck-like, over to this other Terdbitch, and sticks it up *her* nose.

"That why you never shot back?"

"Yes."

She hadn't, either. Oak had distinctly seen that during the firefight. In fact she'd tried to stop the whole thing from the start. That's the main reason, afterwards, Oak went out onto the docks to sulk on things a little. That and the funny way all these Terds talked. None of the Wobblies had ever heard anything like it.

"So, what, you telling me you're way the hell out here for a social visit?"

"More like solidarity."

At the mention of this Wobbly word, Oak withdraws the minimister from the woman's nose. He looks harder at all the features of her face. "Now what the hell you mean by that?"

"You know perfectly well what I mean. The one big union. The greatest thing on earth."

"Now how'd she know that?" says Jiplap. "That's some spooky shit, Oak."

"The fuck it is. Net would be monitoring all the feeds. She just stole that."

The Terd woman asks, "But where did Uncle Wobbly come from in the first place? Who's feed is that? It's sod-all not coming from ArcNet and the Pyramid, is it now, brother?"

What turf has to do with anything at the moment, Oak don't know. He jabs the minimister back up her nostril. "Your Terdbitch sisters, there, killed twelve of my men. That ain't solidarity, so don't you be calling me brother."

"Self defense," the woman manages to point out. "Your men opened up, Oak. What else could we do until we knew you were Wobblies?"

Oak doesn't like it she now knows his name. He glares over to Jiplap, who looks guiltily down at the floor. And Oak really doesn't like it that she's talking sense—weird sense, but commonsense joe. Come to think of it, he didn't know where in the hell the Uncle Wobbly feed came from. It had to be coming from someone someplace. He'd just never thought to wonder about that before. This is what yanking Terds always do. They make you feel brainslow and all bad about yourself, like they're just aligned in a lot better than you and know all sorts of shit you can never know. It just ain't fair. Well, fuck that in no uncertain terms. Oak's had his goddamn fill of that feeling. He pulls the gun back out of her nose and speaks with his face close up to hers, so she can smell his rotten Serv breath and eyeball his brown Serv teeth.

"Listen, pussbitch," he says low and calm, "I don't give a good shit what all you can spout off about Wobbly. It won't save you. You're Terd for certain, and probably worse, you're fuckmother Net come to wipe us for good. Now I ain't made it this long taking bonehead chances, and I sure as shit ain't about to start now with you." Oak stands up and backs to the doorway. "Jip," he orders, "have two boys take that one dude there outside and shoot him." Two of the Wobblies jump at the chance and drag outside the only Terd man of the bunch. "Meantime, you can get things started off on this one. On little Miss Wobbly, here."

Jiplap hands off his automatic and signals to a buddy to flip her on her belly and sit on her head. Meantime he moves around behind her and begins jerking down on her pants. "Sorry to muss up your fancy britches, darling," he apologizes with a grin. The purple-headed bitch lets out a war-whoop and struggles up to claw at Jiplap's back. Another Wobbly applies the butt of his rifle sharp to the side of this puss' head to knock her tame.

"Now wait your turn," Jiplap jokes. She's lying on the floor, dazed and bleeding from the ear. "It won't be too much longer now before I get to you."

He smiles and winks at the other Wobblies around the room. He resumes working down the pants on the first Terdbitch and finally tugs them down around her ankles. He climbs in between her long legs and begins forcing them apart with his knees. With the other guy sitting on her neck, she fights for air while screaming and kicking at Jiplap.

"Now, now, darling," Jiplap coos, petting her bare butt cheek while unzipping loose his hardnob. "You best just get used to this. There's lots of us Wobblies up here in the primitive area these days."

Totoglassy snaps onto Jiplap's face, freezing a blank and bewildered expression. It's as though, in that second, he's been transported off someplace to find himself gawking at something else altogether. He falls onto his back and starts pumping the air violently with his pelvis and stiffyanker, humping upwards at nothing like a man bewitched. A few seconds more and he's gurgling and drooling with the exertion, like he's about to have a damn heart attack. Before the Wobblies know what's hit Jiplap, it hits all of them. Without warning, every nobber in the room is sprung tall and every guy is pitching, jerking, and rolling around on the floor in the same sick sexfrenzy as Jiplap.

It's then that a CorpTroop comes sailing in through the open window. After a shoulder roll and gunsweeping the room, he pulls up the Terdbitch's pants. Then he stands over Jiplap and begins to kick the holy hell out of him, even though Jiplap can't stop his glassy and slobbering yanking.

"Enron, stop it!" shouts the Terdbitch while rolling over and fastening her pants. The CorpTroop draws his hunting knife.

"I'm going to cleave off his little dick and stuff it down his fucking throat!"

"No!"

The woman places a calming hand on the CorpTroop's arm. He gives her a hard look, but she shakes her head no. The CorpTroop holds the toe of his boot down on Jiplap's windpipe, telling him that if he ever so much as touches her again, he'll jam the knife right up his ass. He has no idea if the man can hear him or not. He kicks the asshole loose to continue his rolling around on the floor. All the Wobblies continue their disturbing gyrations.

"Whatever's wrong with them?" Mall asks.

"Got me," shrugs Enron. "Ask Sinalco. Like usual, she's got them wired up doing some damn thing."

Sinalco has stepped through the doorway. Oak, humping hard at nothing like every other brother in the Honeymoon Cabin, stares up at this giant puss, his eyes wide with disbelief.

"I have them on the autofuck," smiles Sinalco, "and they do sheep." She offers to pad something new onto her palmbook. "I can make them be fucking something else. Maybe themselves?"

"No, no, that's all right," says Mall. "Just leave them at it for now. Where's Blaupunkt? They drug him outside a moment ago. Is he hurt?"

"He's good," Enron answers. "Sinalco got them all dry humping before they could shoot old Blau."

"Thank god for that."

"Et alors, où est Forbetr?" asks Sinalco, surveying the floor of the cabin. Oak opens his eyes a little wider at her odd talk.

"Dead," says Mall. "Killed in the skirmish back at the creek."

Enron, who's now bent over others of the foray crew checking to see how bad they've been beaten, shoots a look at Sinalco. "I told damn Cardinal not to try to sneak up on these boys."

Cardinal has found her way to her feet. She's bleeding and seeing double. She stumbles over to the Wobbly who clubbed her and spits blood down on him. "Very soon you I kill one night as you sleeping." Then she tries to focus on Enron's blurry face. "Fuck all you fucking cowboys," she says to him, laboring to get the words out. Enron goes to her and helps her settle comfortably in one corner. The others tend to her. Pernod and Migros have fewer injuries.

"So what we do now?" Sinalco asks Mall.

"Well, we could let them all fuck themselves to death. That does seem to be what they're best at." Mall notices Oak managing to watch her carefully past his all4s, which must be feeding him some fairly harrowing images at the moment. She finds such focused tenacity unnerving from this sallow-skinned, rat-like, little man. "But I suppose we'd better release them. We've got a lot of explaining to do."

"Let me collect up these guns, first," says Enron, policing around the cabin. "I already took the ones from all the fellas outside."

"They will be very angry after this, tu sais," Sinalco points out.

"Better let them have it off," decides Mall. "That will calm them."

With fingertip élan, Sinalco pads in a series. A few moments later every Wobbly in the Redfish valley is creaming his coveralls at the very same time. "I make it a big one, too," she smiles. They can hear the wails coming through the pines.

Oak's the first Wobbly back on his feet. He stares down at his dark-soaked crotch and trembles like he wants to kill something. "You crazy bitches!" he shouts at Mall and Sinalco. "How the fuck you do that to us?"

Enron steps forward, shouldering many automatics and pointing one at Oak's nose. "Why, Oak Wat," he nods in wonder, "you sorry son of a bitch. I always did take you for a muttonfucker."

"That really you, Uncle En?" asks Oak, jolted now into acting mortified. "What the fuck you doing mixed up with fucking Net? Or..." he slowly frowns, then looks distrustfully at the strange-talking big blond with the flashy panelboard, "these fucking slits ain't *ragheads*," he juts an accusatory thumb out at them, "are they?"

"You *know* this chap?"

"Yeah, Mall," answers Enron, "I know him. This little prick's my nephew. About the only man I ever heard of who washed out of CorpTroop training for noncompliance and lived to tell the tale."

"You don't ever wash out, Uncle En. You know that. I fucking skipped out."

"Really?" says Mall. She steps closer and studies the flashing, ever-darting eyes of the wretched Serv. "You know, Oak," she says to him, "we can get rid of that glassy problem for you."

Oak looks to Enron and notices for the first time that his uncle's eyes aren't blazing away with the all4s. He also notices—how did he miss it —the dopey-looking cap Enron's got pulled down tight over his head. He looks back to Mall and answers hopefully, "No shittin'?"

Mall laughs kindly. "No, absolutely not. No shitting." She pronounces the word deliberately. Then she strikes the back of her fist across his mouth, leaving it bleeding from the corner. "My name's Mall, Oak. I'm not a Terd. I'm not a slit. I'm not Net. I'm not a raghead. Are you following me so far?" Startled and holding his mouth, Oak nods. "Good, because there's so much more to tell you. So very much more. Oak, you and I are going to be fast friends, but I must warn you about one thing. If you ever tell one of your men again to touch me, or if you ever try to yourself, I will kill you before even your Uncle En can. Understand?"

☆ ☆ ☆ ☆ ☆ ☆

Brand sits shaded in the small grove of palm trees. Her atoll is a coral crescent sheltering a jade lagoon, and surrounded by a wide, turquoise sea. A gull cries. A breeze stirs the long, massive leaves drooping overhead. She's suspended, quasi reclined, in her relaxer just above the white sand, running her fingers through its warmth whenever she likes, something Brand does often, absently, as she studies the thinscreen cradled by her knees. A high-necked tumbler of herbal tea, sending up steam, sits at her elbow. An island jingle starts to play on the air.

"Yes?" Brand says aloud.

"More shit," says a perturbed voice.

"Please come," replies Brand.

Dockers steps onto Brand's island, dressed in his everyday Crat wear, including a collarless shirt showing a western flair—decidedly cowboy—and embroidered about the shoulders. He looks his normal self. No bodyenhance. This guy just doesn't care for the imagination.

"What's the problem now?" she says.

For her part, Brand sits topless, showing massive boobs with no tan lines. A shapely nine or ten more kilos fleshes out her frame. Her thong is the newest ultranarrow, colored shockneon pink. Silky blond hair is gathered high in an exceedingly long ponytail that flows down over one shoulder and curls coyly around one of her huge hooters. She keeps the atmospherics set on musk—anything at all to gain the advantage.

"Jesus," complains Dockers, unable to stop himself from staring at her tits, "when are you going to stop fucking around in here?"

Brand has always noticed how Crats tend not to like being in digiland. Something about Terdfantasy upsets them, even seems to scare them a bit. She really has to undertake a formal study of it some day. She just smiles and removes her darkglasses, revealing luxurious sapphire eyes, a perfect match to the endless ocean stretching out around them. "I'm sorry if my work environment upsets you, Mayor. Personally, I find it relaxing. I'm much better able to concentrate in here."

"Well start concentrating on this." Dockers puts a fist on either hip. His power posture comes off asinine beneath the swaying palms. "Subceo Ponzi is breathing down my neck like an Arc-horned bull in rut. These nob-sucking co-opers seem to have figured out how to link all the hydrofacilities out there into network. I mean, hell, they're doing it better now than our own damn Terds could before all this shit started to happen." Annoyed, Dockers kicks one foot out sideways to keep the sand from sifting into his shoe. "Lucky for us, the bigboss doesn't seem too all-fired concerned about it at the moment, but who the hell knows how long that will last?"

"What's different now? How are they able to do that?"

To Dockers, her questions are irrelevant. "Hell if I know. To me they're just dumb shitsuckers that can't even stick their thumbs up their own butts right. You'd think there'd be no way for them to figure out something so maze as the hydroworks."

"I've found in my work over the years, Mayor, that all the Serv really wants is opportunity, the chance to make a better life."

Dockers makes a heartburny face. "Oh, fuck. Spare me the libby bullshit, honey, if you please. It doesn't matter a fuck what the goddamn Serv wants. We give him what *we* need. So save that crock for the drone you feed them over that Sim-u-whatzit thing of yours. Parkers get ridden for their own damn good. Hell, if it wasn't for us forcing them to work, they'd drink and yank away their day, and then those constant litters of little parkrats they squeeze out would starve to death. We're doing them a damn favor."

Brand sits up straight, wishing maybe she didn't have jiggling mammaries attached to her chest. "Mayor Dockers, I beg to differ. I've discovered—"

"Aw, what the hell have you ever discovered, *Doctor* Brand? The 'noble savage' hid deep inside the TexArc Parker? The goddamn 'natural man' in the Serv?" Carried on the balmy sea breezes, the cry of one distant gull is answered, eventually, by that of another. "No offense, Doc, but what you do is horseshit, just like what I do. But at least mine is good old-fashioned, honest-to-god horseshit. I don't play pretend I ain't screwing somebody over or riding on their backs. I am. Hell, that's all I do all day long, every damn day up here in this goddamn Pyramid. What about you in your Yale School?"

Normally Crats aren't blunt *and* insightful, though often one, and sometimes the other. Rarely in combination. Brand thinks to turn off the musk, and clears her throat. "Mayor Dockers, there must be a middle way—"

"Oh, Jesus," he interrupts her again. Dockers drops his fists off his hips, shakes his head down at the sand, then looks up at her under his brow. "You ever really *talked* to any Parkers, Doc? You ever really been out among them?"

"I conduct a lot of focus groups, yes," Brand vindicates herself, "to test the accuracy and the effectiveness of my pitches."

Dockers snorts. "Yeah, safe behind a bulletproof viewmirror, I bet, so you don't have to be in the same room with them and smell their stench."

Quite true. She always sends her gradstus in, wearing the outbreak bug breathing masks and sanogloves, to do the actual personal contact work. Brand tells them it's good realworld experience for them. Hands-on. Service-learning. That kind of thing. There's always security standing by in case of any trouble.

"Yeah," Dockers nods, "I thought so." He takes a good long look around her digiland. *Damn nice stuff. Extremely detailed, with all the senses brought into play. She took a hell of a lot of time on this construct.* "Now look, sweetmeat," he goes on in a reasonable tone, "I don't know what you've been doing up to now, all safe in your little pocket of paradise here. As I made clear back at CorpHQ, I really don't give a shit. I think what you do is useless squatdoodle." As he speaks, the megmayor approaches her relaxer and squeezes out a small seat for himself at its bottom, Brand having to retract her feet to make enough room. Dockers stares at each colossus tit up close, for several seconds, before looking the account planner in the face once more. "All I do know, Doc, is that while you've been playing with your mumbo-jumbo pitch campaigns in here, your ads ain't been doing shit out there. Not in the parks. Not in the wilderness area. Not anywhere it matters. These fucking Wobblies have just got smarter, and now we know they're getting stronger, too."

Surprised, Brand asks, "In numbers, you mean?"

"In numbers. In tactics. In damn firepower. You name it, and they're getting better at it. I just received word they overran Arrowrock and Anderson Ranch—in a yanking late-afternoon, coordinated attack—like my damguard wasn't even there. Shit, I got rumors coming in that they have goddamn deserter CorpTroops joining them. *CorpTroops*, Doc, fighting right alongside goddamn *Servs*. Shit Almighty, what's this yank world coming to?" Dockers stands back up. Before he turns to leave, he points a finger at Brand's bosom. "So please, honeypot, if you got it in you, you stop yanking around with bodacious ta-tas and get some serious-ass propaganda shit out there that will do us some kind of good for a change. Just because the big ceo wants to go all artsy-fartsy on this one, I don't want to end up with *my* butt in a sling."

As soon as the mayor leaves, Brand vanishes her atoll. She looks out the thick, sloping Pyramid window of her workquarters to see the awful sun has finally disappeared below the horizon. Quickly, she changes into her unispandex and laces up her Nike Ultaletes. Time, at last, to train. She's been quite frustrated with BoiCity as a meg. Not only is it small and, culturally speaking, lacking—not a top bistro to be found and less than zero in the way of live theater—but it's only a demicircle because of the mountains. The half-moon shape of its Gater district seriously curtails her ultrarunning. When you're on a fifty-to-sixty-k trainer, you don't want to be backtracking all the time, seeing the same scenery. Brand dares not run in the parks. Fortunately, what's called the Brown Belt runs through the district, following the river. Pleasant enough as a repetitious running route, athough recently, for reasons she doesn't understand, the water's gone inexplicably low and the newly exposed mud is horribly smelly, even after the sun bakes it dry. Brand uses these ultraruns to clear her head and think over her conceptions. This evening, though, even with the first ten k's under her belt, nothing starts to conceive. Not a thing. She keeps rewinding her past few weeks of evident failures, thinking she can pinpoint where she's blundered. Brand has found the ads she's attempting to counterpitch to be every bit as maxevasive as the slice that feeds them.

She began the account with what she imagined would be a knockout punch—biggov. A standard, sure, but it always brings serious hangtime. Her pitch revived the antique hobbyhorse—tax freedom day: "You remember, folks, in the bad old days when you worked one-third, one-half, two-thirds of the year just to pay off your bigtaxes, leaving you and yours a pittance of your hard-earned DollArcs?" A solid retro pitch. The visuals were choice, the music both heart-breaking and heart-warming. The voiceover a touch folksy, but not syrupy. Lots of flags—well-made material. Everyone on staff thought so. So they focus-grouped it, and got the nod. They fed it. They hoped. They looked for tangible impact. None.

Within hours Uncle Wobbly countered with an ad—exploitation freedom hour: "You know, folks, that point in your current workday, coming surprisingly early in the shift, as a matter of fact, when you've earned enough money to support you and yours, and how the rest of your day's labor is spent in 'surplus labor' creating 'surplus profit' for your loafer, fat-ass bossman?" The parody was palpable. And focus groups *loved* that last part showing the Monopoly Man, round as an elephant, puffing on a cigar with his feet up on his desk while below him on the shopfloor, Servs scrambled, working away like so many ants.

Next, Brand went for another standard, but the ass-kicker, one celebrated in account-planner circles as—bootstraps. Can't miss. TexArc rugged individualism. Don't tread on me. "We're a corporation of proud individuals." Servs eat it up as fast as Crats. Her angle was the parkport and savtrade. Her hero, the investor-pioneer—the freemarket mountain man, rugged individual unshaken by sizedowns and negtrends who knows it's all part of the bigpic. "Our freemarket needs room to roam—and *I* ain't afraid to roam with it. Give me *my* bottomline in stockopts only. Wages is for libbywimps and whiners. I'll quad *my* profit in no time flat with savvy markstrat. Don't fence *me* in with employment!"

Brand's team produced an entire series of fast-paced, cut-scene pitches depicting the exciting world of daytrade and the insane bonanza of reward awaiting the nimble and the ballsy. They capped it by producing several lengthy infopitches featuring rags-to-riches Servs who hit it big-time in the daytrade, not only zeroing out their credspending but enjoying their well-gotten gains: an especially lengthy penicycle, indoor plumbing, a bungalow propped up on cinder blocks. "Go, daytrader nation!" These

Servs of course were actually talented Terd actors in heavy makedown, but everyone's heard stories of successful daytraders and the magic of their hardwork. That's commonsense joe!

Wobbly countered, again, with just the one pitch. It showed Monopoly Men raining out of tall buildings and splattering hard on the sidewalks. As they lay in crumpled heaps, with x's for their eyes, a scruffy dog wearing a hobo bandana tied around its neck walked calmly about lifting its leg, on a mission, it seemed, to pee a fine stream on every last one of them. Meanwhile, a series of numbers ran across the bottom of the frame: 29, 87, 00, 06, 08-11, 17, 26, 37, 42, 48, 54, 61, 72, 78—the really big crashes. Uncle Wobbly's wistful face comes into view. "Ah," he smiles, "now them were the days."

In desperation, Brand pursues her least favorite stratagem—jingofrenzy. "When clever invention exits your pate, it's never too late to turn up the hate," is an old saying in the account-planner biz. With nothing else taking hold and CorpHQ increasingly impatient for results, Brand found her hand forced to it. Of course, some members of her staff wanted to run with jingo from the start, so they're feeling vindicated now. Brand, though, never likes to feed the standard schlock, not even with jingo. You know, those junkpitches with swarthy and greasy ragheads raping small, blond girls and the like. No, no matter what the genre, she prefers to tug at the TexArcan soul, not wrench the TexArcan gut. So she devised some innovative jingo. By tapping into the corporate meat and potatoes, so to speak, Brand pitched to elicit, from the breasts of Servs, their deep love of corp. Such an angle was risky from the start. Very peculiar for jingo, and many of her staffers let Brand know it. Don't blow things, they warned her, any worse than you already have. But Brand dug in her heels. She concepted a fifteen-minute piece on the Founding Principles.

PA.

With softfocus lens and uplifting background strings, Servs in the street bow their heads and speak reverently, “PA!” In epigrammatic, dialogue-free visual stories, four different scenarios of trap and trace, sneak and peek are played out where the wise heads at FISA issue timely security letters enabling intrepid corpagents to ensnare enemy combatants just in the nick of time, before they terrorstrike, then incarcerate them, without pointless trials, and throw away the key. In between each minidrama, Servs in the street bow their heads and speak reverently, “PA!” By the grateful looks on their faces, we see they feel secure inside knowing such evildoers exist now in the perpetual humiliation, interrogation, and torture—where they belong—of corpdetention. A long closing sequence symbolizes Total Information Awareness as the faithful watchdog of personal safety, keeping packs of hungry, badlands wolves away from a small paddock where the fluffy, white lambs of liberty bleat nervously while the hard-working and honest homesteaders sleep at night. Again, Servs in the street bow their heads and repeat reverently, “PA!”

The pitch won several top academic awards. It was lauded as elevating the genre of servfeed to new emotional and intellectual heights. With gratifying recognition from her peers, Brand started to hope this ad, finally, was having its desired effect out in the parks. Beeper studies, fixed camera analysis, and shadowing were all quite positive. Parkers were buying it. Then Wobbly’s counter lashed out. A long and self-conscious burlesque of Brand’s ad, filled with slapstick and scatological humor, with Servs in the street bent over exposing their bare bottoms to the sky, farting, “PHHHHA!”

After that, Brand’s pitch never had a chance. It zeroed out in post-counter focus groups. Absolutely zeroed out. And that’s where Brand finds herself now—out on an ultrarun trying to pick up the pieces. The Wobblies are getting stronger, bolder, smarter, and she’s trying to start the account all over—yet again. But it seems pointless. If corpatriotism won’t hunt, what in the hell will?

Brand takes an extra long warmdown. The path along the riverside is paved and well-lit. The air is still quite warm from the day. She's dripping with sweat and smelling like ammonia. She sucks on the last bottle of Ultaide off her carrier belt. The heavy district traffic on T-184 provides a dull, steady roar, seeming farther off than it is. She powerwalks southeast towards Julia Davis Park. There, she'll turn northeast on Pyramid Boulevard and follow that to Pyramid Park. She'll stretch in her rooms, get something to eat, call her staff together, and get back to work. On what, she still can't conceive. She's blank. Totoblank. At the bottom of 14th Street, well off the path and down by the river in that awful-smelling mud, Brand sees a stooped-over maintenance Serv clearing away debris from the mouth of what looks like an ample discharge pipe. The pipe is almost gigantic, plenty wide enough to crawl up, almost to walk up, bent double. Brand decides to walk down toward the Serv. To her relief, she soon notices he's quite frail with age, probably in his late forties, and thus harmless. They don't often let the young bucks demesne work in the district, just on big projects, and never at night.

"Hello, there!" Brand calls out.

The Serv stops his work and turns to look up at her. He's holding a thick piece of driftwood in one hand and some kind of furry drowned animal in the other. He tosses these items down into the flow of the river before answering, "Howdy!" Brand approaches as near as she can without getting her trainers in the mud. It's near enough to see the Serv's hollow cheeks and gray stubble, and to watch the glisteny dance of the glassy on his ipatch.

"Can I ask you something?" she says, not having to shout now.

The Serv doesn't answer or move. Brand's not sure he heard her. She's not sure he even knows she's there anymore. He's looking right at her, right at her eyes, but, behind the glitterings and the glowings, she can't be certain he's still registering her. Servs get easily distracted like that. She's seen it often in her focus groups. The old man's breathing comes heavy and irregular, maybe from his task, maybe from disease. Brand can't help thinking the new, bad odor she's smelling is probably his servstink added to the reek of the mud. After a while she decides to ask, "I'm trying to figure something out, and I was wondering if you could help me?" No response. She presses on, "I want to ask you a question—a big question. Is that okay?" Nothing. "Okay. Well, here goes anyway. If you could have anything you wanted, anything at all, no matter what and no matter how unlikely, what would that be?" Brand pauses hopefully. "I'm talking outrageous now. *Any*thing," she clarifies. "What, out of anything at all in the whole wide world, would you *want*? The sky's the limit."

Brand wonders, if the man's even listening to her, will he ask for freedom, for opportunity, for a better education, for a trillion DollArcs? The Serv seems to be thinking over her question, but she can't be sure. He hasn't moved since returning her greeting. He's still stooped in front of the broad-mouthed pipe, his boots and coveralls filthy with the caked mud, his mouth gaping with what might be surprise. Brand is about ready to give up and return to the path when suddenly the Serv grins at her, showing a tooth or two left in his hollow skull. He shouts out abruptly in a phlegmy voice, "A cold Oly and a hot sweetpuss!"

His gurgly cackle dogs her all the way back to the path, and all the way along the path as she walks slowly back toward center district. Beer and babes. Brand is shaking her head. What did she expect? Oldest law of the pitch—you get out what you simulate in.

Then it hits her. Absolutely hits her. *Audience*, you dumb bitch. *Audience*. He's the wrong damn one.

☆ ☆ ☆ ☆ ☆ ☆

It's past ten and Jjill's still cleaning up. Tonight makes eight late nights in a row. In a row. Gradstus always get the shitwork. Most of the rest of the staff got to leave an hour ago, maybe two. She knows her advisor is bigtime—as bigtime as they come—and this account assignment is choice—doublechoice—but the slopebitch has lost it this time. This meg has turned out to be a hole.

Definitely lost it. Definitely a hole.

How many focus groups can you run productively in one day? Her advisor suddenly seems to think that number's seven. Seven in one fucking day, and for—gee, let's count—eight days straight. Fifty-six yanked-up foci in a row. And why alternate groups of Terds with groups of Servs? Why focus Terds at all? You already know how they're going to sample. Preaching to the converted, there. What's the damn point of that? And why waste realfood on these stinkass Servs, anyway? Does anyone really think a yanking Serv is going to appreciate calzone? Be better off pureeing the pies and pouring the glug down their crusty shitubes. Jesus, they all give Jjill the shivers. Fucking glassy zombies with over the top b.o. and those nasty corpbands fused right to their scalps. Yuk.

Definitely lost it.

"When you're finished over there," Doctor Eb calls to her from across the session room, "we've still got some exit numbers to crunch."

"Aw, E-B, come on," she whines. "Can't the numbers wait until morning to be crunched?"

"In the morning you'll have an appalling hangover."

"Exactly my point, Doc."

Assistprofs are ice, fresh out of TerdTech. They're young and still know the drudge. Jjill watches Doc E-B, a little bit against his will, crack a hint of Terdy cute smile. She knows she's got him. He is kind of cute, in his own Terdy prof way.

"What's on tap for tonight?" he asks, continuing his reading, trying to mask amusement.

"Consent Tent Night at ClubSpud on West Bannock and North 16th.

Check your inhibitions at the flap, slip into their complimentary bodycondom, and shank the night away." When he looks up at this, Jjill flashes him her flirtiest grin. "Care to join me?" She'll let him conclude whether she's serious or not.

"As appealing as drunken frenzy and victimless sex always is," he smiles back, "thank you, no. We really do have a lot of data tonight, but I'll sift it out. You go ahead."

Jjill drops what she's doing and hurries across the room to gather her things. Before she goes, out of a fraction of guilt, she takes a peek over Doc E-B's shoulder at the figures.

"Mm, lots of numbers, but I bet you don't know yet what it is we're looking for."

Eb sighs and lowers his thinscreen. "So you've noticed?" he says.

"E-B," she raises her thin shoulders and her thin eyebrows at once, "*everyone's* noticed. She's getting her ass kicked."

"Well..." Eb hesitates to negspeak about a tenured, and especially not to a randy gradstu who's more or less propositioned him.

Jjill sweeps the lanky green hair off her face and presses the issue. "She doesn't know what we're doing anymore, *does* she? How else do you explain all these spank focus groups we're doing?" She leans closer and speaks lower. "This is *ass*lick, Doc, and we both know it. For one thing, these cowpoke Crats out here never did give two shits about what we're doing. To them, we're all some kind of gayboy joke. For another thing, why suddenly start treating these sorry-fuck IntraMountain Servs so human? She's serving them *real*food, and holding our sessions *out*side the Pyramid, and not having *any* security around. *N*ow, she's mingling with them, sitting right the fuck down with them and asking them questions and rubbing elbows with these crusty fucks. That's all *quasi*."

Eb clears his throat. "It seems...out of character," he concedes. "I'll grant that."

"And for a last thing," Jjill's saved the worst for last, "why the hell are we sampling Terds? What the fuck do we need to know about them we don't already know ten times over?"

Eb can only shrug. "Jjill, to be completely honest with you, I've no idea. Nobody on staff does. She won't tell us a thing about this new strat of hers. We're all equally in the dark here."

"These new pitches are way too long and funk. Their message is pure, but they're way too busy. Too entailed. All the intercuts, all the filmictech going on. Fuck, Doc, they *over*simulate. You know? They start to make you *think*."

"I *know*, I *know*," he admits the fatal flaw, "but what the fuck can we *do*? She's the BoardChair."

"Yeah, but she's fucking *lost* it, E-B. All this 'whatever is, is right' shit. I mean, Christ, what the fuck kind of pitch is that? Servs don't have a prayer with it, and it's over the heads of most the damn Terds we focus. They don't know what that means. So why are we still fucking around with it? Is she trying to *teach* them or something?"

Eb agrees the situation is outrageous. "I *know*," he says. "It's fringe. Then, again, she's always had a rep for cutedge stuff and maybe..."

Brand bustles in from the adjacent screening room, searching for something. "Oh," she startles, her face turning quickly firengine red, "are you two still here?"

"Just checking over the last showing numbers, Doctor Brand," Eb explains in an overly normal voice.

His Chair takes no notice of his odd tone. "Yes, exactly what I was looking for. Give them here and you two take off. Escape. Go!" She walks over to be handed the thinscreen. "Dr. Eb, I'm sure you've got an article you should be polishing. And Jjill, well, I bet you're quite a ways behind on your vodkashots and shanking for tonight."

"You got that right, Doc B."

"Well, go forth and don't multiply. You have my blessings."

Once they're gone, Brand sits in the session room staring at the day's results. She doesn't know what to make of them. For the first time in her career, she's not looking for something. She's looking for something to look for. That's quite different, though she's not at all certain she could articulate what that difference is to anyone—including herself. All she knows is that the reconstruction work she's always done won't do. It just won't. It impresses, but it doesn't stick. Not in the deepdown. It brings no longterm takepower. For that—so her innovative theory runs—she needs to touch something deep inside an audience. Something that is all their own, that is already there. Something, in other words, that hasn't been previously feed-mastered into them. Something inborn. But just what in the hell can *that* be? Brand doesn't even bother to scan the numbers from the Serv foci. They're meaningless. They started out as a familiar baseline for comparison, but Serv responses have no relevance to these new pitches. None whatever. Wrong audience. She maintains the Serv focus groups mainly as a ruse, as a cover for this fringe shit she's trying. Until she knows she's onto something real, Brand wants to keep her staff off balance, and Dockers way off balance—maybe even the Wobblies off balance, though, living as she has been exclusively within the greenzone of the Pyramid and the Gater district, she has yet to think of Wobblies as anything but abstractions. Servs, on the other hand, surprisingly have become a lot more real to her. Interacting with them has proved interesting, even informative in a rudimentary way. That's another reason she keeps their focus groups going. That, and also to give the poor bastards some realfood for a change, a chance to sit down and do nothing for an hour or so, and the opportunity to talk to someone real for once. Brand finds she enjoys the not-so-simple, not-so-innocent attitude of these people.

The pressure changes in the room. Someone's come back in. Probably Eb. He's a worrier. That's why he'll go far as a pedanterd. Brand calls out without looking up from the thinscreen. "I thought I told you to escape! To go home!"

There's no answer for a long time. Then she hears a strange woman's voice, with a more than strange accent—one that Brand has never heard, never even imagined. "Would that I could."

Brand looks to the entranceway. Two figures have entered the session room. Both wear tattered servponchos, but neither moves like a Serv, postures like a Serv. They're too steady on their feet, too sure of themselves. The foremost figure lowers its hood. The no-nonsense face of a young, dark-haired woman emerges. Her eyes are opal in the muted ceiling lighting. Brand sets aside her thinscreen, knowing she's not going to need these numbers anymore.

"Can I help you?"

"Is there anybody else here?" The lilt of the woman's voice is positively charming. There's something captivating about it, magisterial. Brand immediately wishes she could use it on feed.

"No," Brand answers. The still-hooded figure promptly walks into the screening room to see for itself. "Are you looking for someone in particular?"

"No. We've found her right enough."

Right enough, thinks Brand. *What a phrase!* The other one returns, shaking its hood.

"Are you Wobblies?" asks Brand.

"After a fashion."

Once Brand deciphers what she thinks that means, she asks, "Are you two from EVe, then?"

The woman doesn't answer for a while. Instead she takes a good look up and down at Brand: her sextoy costume, the nervy body painting, all of her jewelry adornments, the hued sprout of hair. She's so long at it that Brand is forced to look down critically at herself, her bodychem face cream starting to glow slightly rose.

"At your bloody service," the woman confirms at last, with considerable contempt in her voice.

"So it's true," Brand muses.

After a long, uncomfortable moment. "What's sodding true?"

"You're *not* ragheads. You're blood-in-the-face. Like us."

"Like 'us'?" the woman repeats. "Oh, you great wanker," she screws up her face in annoyance, "don't be bloody stupid."

Sodding, wanker, bloody. Just amazing. Brand could listen to her talk all day, but she'd better get as much cultural information out of her quick as she can. GaterPol will be here any moment to drag these two away. Once Dockers gets hold of them, Brand knows she'll never see either one alive again. Too bad. She's going to have to learn to pitch EVe, and soon.

"My name's Brand," she offers. "And you are?"

The woman hesitates and looks to her partner. The partner shakes its hood no, but the woman shrugs. "Mall," she says.

"Mall, it's my pleasure."

"To be sure."

Ironic or polite? Or both? This one's very interesting. "What do you do in EVe, Mall? What's your job?"

"My *job*?" Mall laughs at the absurdity of the inquiry. "My *avocation* is with the Signification Committee, if you must know. Old England."

"Really? Signification as in semiotics? As in signifier/signified?"

Mall nods.

"Is that an academic position over there?"

"It is and it isn't. Academics and realworld don't find themselves separated and at odds in EVe."

"How very interesting," responds Brand, not really appreciating what's being said. "What's your degree in? Your work?"

"CultRhet."

Brand ventures, "Cultural Rhetoric?"

"Very good."

"At?"

Mall doesn't understand her question until she realizes the woman is sniffing for pedigree. "Oxford," she tells her, not without a trace of pride. "You've heard of it, perhaps?"

"My god, *yes*." Brand's admiration for the name of the ancient university is honest. "I didn't know if it still existed, or if it was just a myth."

"No, we are quite real, and doing very nicely, thanks."

Brand has to rethink this EVe woman. She's tall and nicely muscled, thin, but not quite gaunt enough for the ideal of an ultrathlete. Brand imagines she's grown slightly more wild looking than usual—sunburned and windblown, generally worn rough around the edges from all her time spent in the parks and out there in that primitive area. Then it occurs to Brand that she might be talking, not just to some feedflunky smuggled over to *distribute* the Wobbly slice, but to the *originator* of Uncle Wobbly. Could that be? It would certainly explain the maddening flexibility of the Wobbly pitches. Their unnerving ability to instantly respond and counterpitch. Do EVe academics conduct field studies *that* deep? If so, she's got to find out everything she can from this Mall person.

"Well, I have to tell you, Mall, or should I address you as Doctor Mall?" Mall ignores the question. "Your man Wobbly has us stumped. I can't seem to get around him to break back through to my audience."

"Surely you must mean to your drooling pawns?"

Brand uses her gradstus laugh, reserved for her seminars—the one of cavalier superior intellect. "Come on now, Mall, anyone can see that freemarket is a medium of pure consent. Supply and demand treats us all as free and equal. That's what makes it, as a system, natural, democratic, and, some would say, even divine." She inserts a practiced pause. "Commercial production only reflects popular desire, and popular consumption only endorses the freemarket way. Bizmen are public servants, the ones out there taking all the risks and creating all the jobs in a constant venture to better serve the customer."

Mall looks to her hooded companion, who tilts its head impishly to one side and giggles. It's a bizarre moment. "See there," Mall chides the hood, "didn't I tell you? I think I win that particular wager spot on." The hood nods then, apparently from chagrin, shakes itself from side to side.

Brand's not accustomed to having her pearls ignored, let alone the butt of frolic. "I'm sure the same holds true in EVe," she won't relinquish the lectern, in spite of having no knowledge about what she's claiming. "Otherwise, how would anyone ever earn a living?"

"You call what these Servs earn a living?" Mall offers Brand ample delay for a response, but none comes. "No?" she says at last. "I didn't think so. I'm sorry, Doctor Brand, but mammonism is the last and best formation of primitivism. You are just too up-to-your-ears in it to see that."

Attack the terms, Brand tells herself. She can guess easily what mammonism is, but the other sounds vague. She shoots back, with the triumph of the leading question in her tone, "And, in this case, 'primitivism' *means*?"

"Exploited classes," Mall answers, with no hesitation, as though surely every schoolchild knows this answer.

"Oh...okay then." Brand must scramble. "But...you're relying on the rationalism of biggov if...if you, um...want to prevent all competitive advantage," Brand points out, recovering. "Yes. To benefit from the boons of choice and service, you have to maintain faith in the unhindered marketplace carrying out its task of natural selection."

Mall turns again to the hood and jokes: "La-de-da, by its *invisible* hand." A restrained laugh emerges from the hood. "No, Doctor Brand," Mall returns to the account planner, "I'm afraid those of you who can only believe will have to forgive those of us who can only think. If you actually fancy that your sodding freemarket offers choice and service to people, rather than coercion and monopoly, particularly to the Servs, but to a nearly equal extent to Terds like yourself, well then, I'm afraid you are an ass." In all her professional life, Brand has never before been called an ass—at least not to her face. The simplicity of the suggestion renders it potentially devastating. "You Terds provide the coercion, what with your ArcNet and your all4s and your Simulacrum and the like. The fatcrats meantime contrive the monopoly."

Where are those yanking GaterPol when you need them? "So how do things work in EVe? Have you achieved a libby shangri-la over there?"

"Sod liberal, Doctor. In EVe we're not afraid really to compete. We take care of everyone. We educate everyone. Of course that's an enormous nuisance, but the alternative is frankly too shameful to contemplate. Don't you think? Letting the birth lottery and bleeding inherited privilege run its course seems the far more irresponsible way of doing things."

"In Nice Land, perhaps," counters Brand in a sugary tone, "but in the real world, chicita, that's just not how things work."

"No, that's just the way TexArc forces things to work."

Brand shifts in her chair. "It certainly seems to be the way to *make* things work. Last time I checked, our way dominates the globe."

"Ah, I didn't say your way is not puissant, Doctor. I said it's not conscionable."

"Come now, Mall," Brand continues to condescend, convinced she's finally turned the argumentative tide, "all you're describing to me is that tired, century-old, failed, bleeding-heart pipe dream of the subsidy state. Freeloaders riding the biggov gravy train. The indolent and the obtuse leeching off the enterprising and the entrepreneurial."

"Really? Tell me, dear Doctor, have you ever performed a day's worth of Serv work?"

"That's an old dodge, Mall. I put in extremely long hours at what I do, and I'm not about to accept–"

"*Bloody have you?*" Mall shouts. The session room is left quite silent after her demand. For the first time it occurs to Brand to be scared.

"No, Mall. Of course I haven't. Who has?"

"Besides daily millions of your buggered Servs, recently I have, Doctor. Days and weeks of them. And I've been living their bloody awful Serv life for sod-all longer than that, and I'm telling you straight out, anyone saying a 'subsidy state,' as you call it, is just the lazy and the stupid living off the brisk and the clever hasn't a bloody fucking clue in hell what she's talking about. And anyone claiming that seeing to the well-being of every citizen is just too far-fetched a whimsy to realize is, in fact, nothing more than a pompous tosser with too great a stake in preventing it."

"Auch nicht menschlich," adds the hood. Brand physically flinches at such abnormal sounds coming from beneath the cowl.

"Also not human is right," Mall agrees. "Your unchecked markets stunt people, Doctor Brand, not bloody enhance them. You're a proper pack of dehumanized buggers here in TexArc, every kind of you. At the top because of greed, down at the bottom because of poverty, and you lot in the middle because of your astonishing bourgie blindness, living in this fool's paradise of a Gater district the way you do. You're self-serving and self-defeating at once, Doctor. Without doubt, you TexArcan Terds have to be the stupidest educated mob in human history."

Brand has become exceedingly concerned that patrol hasn't burst through the door. *They have to know what's going on in here*. Maybe Brand has become some kind of bait. She wouldn't put that past that fucker Dockers. Maybe she needs to keep just playing along.

"So you risked coming all this way to critique our social-economic formation?" asks Brand. "Is that why you're here?"

Mall starts to stroll among the sampling stations in the session room, looking down at their picture-questionnaires and smiling to herself. "No," she says. "But one reason I am here is to tell you that you needn't bother with any of this any longer. In fact, you needn't to have bothered with it for some time now."

"Oh? Why is that?"

"They're not even on your nasty feed any longer."

"What do you mean?" Brand cannot suppress her shock. "That's not possible."

"Not only possible, but factual. You see, we're manufacturing masses of little caps that obstruct your signal. Even more smashing is that we can now overwhelm your wave with one of our own. At the moment it's a touch limited in field, but we're steadily expanding. For the past several weeks every Serv in the wilderness area, and most in the BoiCity parks, have been aligned in to WobblyNet, not to ArcNet."

"WobblyNet?"

"Quite."

"So my pitches haven't been imagesensing to the Parkers? They haven't felt a single one of them?"

"Not for quite some time now. No, I'm afraid not." Mall offers her a broad smile. "Sorry about that."

Brand is furious, her faceglow turning a variegated orange. "So why the hell have you been *counter*pitching me all this time?"

Mall smiles even wider, "I'm afraid it's been just jolly good fun. As Signification, your spots are rubbish. Easy as pie to neutralize, you know."

"My pitches obtain tangible results," Brand defends her work—irate.

"No," replies Mall, realizing her mistake, "not rubbish in that sense. Sorry. I'm confident, under these circumstances, tangible results are quite readily obtained by your spots, Doctor. No, what I'm referring to as rubbish is the fact that you trendologists impoverish and make cretins out of a large portion of your populus. Then, in pseudo-anthropological studies, you figure out ways to make them buy more and more of the goods they make with their own hands, but with labor for which they are not compensated sufficiently to be able to afford without dipping drastically into debt."

She frowns at Brand. “If one really stops to think about it, that’s quite a barbaric way to maintain your property relations.”

It takes Brand a moment to untangle this long string of thoughts. Once she does, she answers, she believes, pithily, “We ‘trendologists’ just sell. It’s up to the consumer to buy or not buy.”

“Isn’t it pretty to think so?” Mall walks near Brand and picks up her thinscreen. She smells like outdoors to the account planner. Woodsmoke, pines, a touch of sweat. “You won’t be needing these numbers any longer, either,” Mall informs her. “Even if you did know at this point what it is you are searching for.”

Brand’s anger becomes alarm. She hides it poorly. “I’ve no idea what you mean.”

“This past week or so, since you’ve moved your sessions outside their Pyramid, I’ve been able to sneak into a few of your screenings, just to see what you were up to.” Mall sets down the thinscreen, and looks into Brand’s expressive and alert asian eyes, trying to ignore the show of colors passing across her face. “I know what it is you’re up to, Doctor, even if your staff and the local thick-skulled Crats do not.”

“I, ah...”

“Your newest advocacy project—your counter-counterpitch—‘The Best of All Possible Worlds,’ I’ve seen it. I see through it. And I must say, in all sincerity, it’s quite simply bloody brilliant. I wasn’t sure you had it in you. The intercutting, the constantly interesting energy and mix of technique with action. It’s Clucusian at heart, isn’t it? But clearly not realized for the Serv viewer audience, eh? Servs haven’t a chance at keeping up with these spots, have they? Far too rich and textured and layered for them.”

While Brand enjoys the professional compliments, she must deflect their implications. “Clucusian?” she asks. “You recognized that? You know his work?”

“He happens to be, as a matter of fact, my maternal grandfather.”

Such a revelation floors Brand. “No possible way! Yeoman Clucus is my all-time favorite filmaker.”

“Mine as well.”

“I didn’t think anyone still viewed his work.”

“Give me a decent bottle of beaujolais, and I’ll view him all the night through.”

Brand has no idea what “beaujolais” is, but she can’t help feeling that she’s met her filmate. “Your favorite?” she tests.

“*Imperfect Enjoyoment*, unavoidably.”

Brand smiles. “Holy shit!”

Seeing Brand’s enthusiasm is genuine, Mall cocks her head and smiles in return. “Holy shit, indeed,” she concurs.

“Die Zeit,” speaks the hood.

“Quite right,” Mall nods. “Could you please check the street?” The hooded figure exits the room. “So, my dear, are you quite through attempting to delay us long enough for GaterPol to arrive on the scene?”

Brand’s mounting sense of panic now floods her stomach. She manages to reply calmly, “They should have been here by now.”

“Functionaries.” Mall shakes her head. “Always late when you need them.”

“So you’re here to kill me?”

“Oh please, Doctor,” Mall reassures her, “don’t be absurd. We’ll leave that sort of thing to your bunch. My associate and I are only here to escort you out of the intellectually and socially restrictive confines of your Gater district. We believe it’s time for you to come breathe the fresh mountain air, both literally and figuratively, along with us Wobblies.”

“You mean leave the meg? Go out into that wilderness area?” Brand’s legs actually begin to tremble. “You can’t be serious.”

“Nonsense. It’s lovely.”

“You...you’ll never get me out of the district. Security’s doubletight now and... and I'm an important person in BoiCity. They won't let me go. In fact, they're watching me right now. They're watching all of us." Brand points vaguely to one corner of the ceiling. "GaterPol's always watching, everywhere in the district. They've probably captured your friend right outside. You'd better surrender, too."

"No need to concern yourself with any of that," says Mall. "We've got our own way in and out of the district, and we disabled surveillance well before we even stepped through your door. Isn't that right, Cardinal?"

The other Wobbly has returned, with her hood pushed back. Horrible healing bruises are evident on her face, one otherwise full of freckles. Half of her hair, from her roots out, is chocolate brown. The rest hangs to her shoulders an eccentric copper-purple color.

"Ja, einfach so," this creature answers, revealing strange mouth movements and oddly aligned front teeth, while all the time staring at Brand with intense distrust.

"Look," Brand pleads, "please just leave me here. I'm worth more to you in the district than out of it. In here, I can do whatever you need me to do, pitch whatever you want me to pitch."

"Sorry," Mall apologizes. "We've really got other plans. You've suddenly become valuable to us."

"No, listen to me," Brand becomes desperate. "I am a secret libby, you know. There's lots of us Terds who are. Lots and lots. More than you know. Especially in the TerdTechs." Brand touches Mall's arm, but removes her hand at once when Cardinal takes a quick step toward her. "I just said all those things before because I thought I had to, because I thought they were watching me." Brand again indicates the corner of the ceiling. "I thought the *vid* was streaming. I *had* to look companyman. You don't *understand*."

Brand's right. Mall and Cardinal don't. "Right," shrugs Mall. "Come along, anyway. Secret libbies are especially welcome in the wilderness area."

Brand jumps up and, on uncertain legs, runs to the back of the session room, as far from the entranceway as she can get. "You don't *understand*!" she screams. "I've never *been* outside a Gater district! *Never*! Not in my whole *life*!"

When she encounters the far wall she slumps to the floor a fragile twist of legs and arms. Mall signals Cardinal to stay where she is and slowly approaches Brand, who's trying not to sob out loud.

"I'm afraid I need your help now, Doctor Brand. That's simply the situation we're in, and the only way for you to help me is for you to come outside the district to see things for yourself. You must experience things for yourself out there. There's simply no other way to go about this."

"I can't help you. I can't. You're just taking hostages," pleads Brand.

"Oh, but you can help us, Brand. In point of fact, I believe no one *but* you can help us at the moment. If you don't come with us, I believe our situation will become quite impossible."

"Bullshit," Brand murmurs, sounding more and more like an unconvinced child.

Mall takes a deep breath. She's standing over the TexArcan Terd. How much to reveal? It may as well be all. Without this eccentric stick-woman, the Wobbly cause may spread wider amongst the Servs, but will never attain the cultural and technical clout it needs to survive. Mall speaks calmly, "Brand, you're trying to slice *my* slice. Remember? Counter *my* counterpitch. Right? I know that you've given up on the Servs as your target audience and are now pitching uniquely to the Terds." Brand seems to stop breathing and shrink. Mall continues, "I am well aware of what you're trying to do, Brand, because it's exactly what I would be doing were I in your place. I'd be advocating like mad to keep the educated class separate from the laboring class. Solidarity between Terd and Serv is the only serious threat to the Crat regime. You know that because, evidently, you study your history."

Brand stares up at Mall now, afraid. Her tears have streaked her face paint. "Well, I cannot allow you to do that, Brand, because bringing those two groups together is precisely what I intend to do. What I *must* do for the Wobblies to be viable."

"So you *are* here to kill me," Brand accuses. "Or take me hostage to torture me and decapitate me over the Net to make an example of me."

"No. No one's here to harm you in any way. I am here to stop any more of your ads from feeding out." Brand looks quickly to the floor. "You don't think we *haven't* been monitoring the sample adverts you've been streaming selectively into this Gater district and down to Mountain Home ArcAir Base, do you, Brand? Surely you can't take me to be *that* naive."

"You can't tap into our Terd stream. That's impossible."

"Doctor, think who it is you're talking to. We're very much able to tap into your Terd stream. We just can't seem to find a way to feed into it ourselves. That's one of the areas where I'm counting on your help. That's why we're here for you, Brand."

"What do you mean?"

"Collaboration, Brand. I'm hoping we can work together. Isn't that an old TexArc saying: 'If you can't beat them, make them join you'?"

"ArcNet would kill me if I show you how to slice into the Terd stream."

"In so many ways you're dead already, Brand. But you're going to have to dare to set foot outside of your precious Gater district to be able to see that." Mall pauses a moment before adding, "On a less abstract note, if you don't show us, Brand, you continue to condemn millions of Servs to their miserable lives and deaths, not to mention the miserable billions around the world suffering under TexArc domination. I'm afraid matters are that brutally straightforward, Brand."

Brand pulls her knobby knees up to her bony chest and wraps her slender arms around them. "What if I won't collaborate with you? What if I refuse? You'll have to kill me then."

"I'm wagering that you will collaborate, Brand, once you realize what's taking place outside the district. That's why you must come. There's no other way."

"What if I refuse even after I go out?"

"That can't happen, Brand. I most sincerely assure you, that can't happen."

Lies, Brand tells herself and buries her face. "You're telling me lies."

Mall looks over her shoulder at Cardinal. Mall drops to her knees before Brand. "Brand, dear, perhaps you're not fully understanding me. This is really all your own doing. If you had kept up with your silly ads to the Servs I wouldn't be here now. I would still be counterpitching you for a lark. But you broke through to the crux of the matter with your 'Best of All Possible Worlds' campaign. You anticipated me, so well in fact, that you *pre*counterpitched me, if you see what I mean. In plain terms, your new adverts are too damn good, Brand. I had to get them off stream."

"Die Zeit," Cardinal says, as a reminder, not as an imperative.

"Your adverts are so good, in fact, I realized you and I must work together if the Wobblies are to have any chance in hell against the Crats. That's the other area, I'm afraid, where I'm utterly counting on your help. Together, you and I, Doctor Brand, could pitch the Terds over to the Wobbly cause. I'm probably incapable of doing that on my own. I need your insight. I need your sophistication. I need your passion as an insider. You will know instinctively which nerves to touch. All I can do is retune the social theory."

Mall hopes she's getting through. If not, she's uncertain what her next move must be. She may well have to shoot this woman right here where she cowers.

"Go on," comes Brand's small voice.

"Your new adverts are inspired, but they have a few fundamental faults in their assumptions and appeals. You're not yet pitching to Terds how they *need* to be pitched. How they *deserve* to be pitched."

Brand is unresponsive for some time. Then, reluctantly, she asks, "What faults?"

"Shareholders are not the same thing as citizens, Brand. Biz serving customers is not the same thing as providing for basic human needs. The popular will is not an innocent and naturally arising phenomenon. Good lord, who better to know that than you? Popular desires, therefore, are not always good, necessary, and socially responsible things. In fact, they seldom are. No, Brand, I'm sorry, but left to itself, the Market is *not* a beneficent entity. It just is not."

"Says *who*?"

"Come step outside the district and see for yourself." Brand doesn't respond to Mall's challenge, and she won't meet Mall's gaze. "The heroic bizman you've created as the centerpiece of your ads, Brand, is brilliant. Kindly and grandfatherly and wise. But not only do you have him advocating unsound macroprinciples, you also have him appealing to basically the wrong gut response in your viewer."

Brand turns and angles her head slightly toward Mall, attentive.

"You have him appealing only to self-preservation and fear, the manic scramble to care for only you and yours. Those impulses are too base, too narrow, and in the end, too limiting. They bring about only isolation, and eventually willful self-destruction." Brand shifts uncomfortably. "Working in collaboration, Brand, you and I can amend and broaden your pitch. As a matter of fact, I'm thinking we could create a new series of spots that continue and play off of your current ones—a kind of advocacy trap cleverly sprung on the viewer. You're leading them nicely down the self-interest garden path right now. If we were to follow these up with a truly sensational reversal, a right jolly part two kicker, we might just be able to smash through all the clutter. We might just be able to pitch, effectively, something that has an actual chance at preserving and freeing Terds—at restoring their essential humanity."

It doesn't take Brand long to bite. "Like *what*?"

"Like their essential humanity. We pitch solidarity, Brand. We pitch we're all in this together. That's the gut response to which we appeal."

"Bullshit."

"Come outside and *see*."

Brand's hooded eyes well up. Great, fat tears roll over the ridges of her cheekbones. She begins to quiver as though she's deathly cold. Mall puts a hand on her lean shoulder. Brand flinches back. "Brand, my dear," soothes Mall, "calm yourself. Calm yourself." Brand makes an effort. "Listen to me. Right now, there are only two points you must take in. Are you listening to me, Brand? Are you ready to be calm and take in these two points?" Brand nods, convincingly enough. "Good," Mall says. "Listen to me. Point one is this: No one is going to hurt you. Do you hear me? No one is going to hurt you. I promise, and more to the point, Cardinal here is going to make certain of that." Brand looks nervously over Mall's shoulder and across the room at the Wobbly, who nods back without affectation. "And I can assure you," continues Mall, "out there you want no one else looking after your well-being than dear Cardinal. No one. Believe me. She rips bloody people's throats out, if it comes to that. I've seen her do it."

"You can stop, now, with point one," Brand says. "You've passed the part that's supposed to make me feel better." Her tears have nearly stopped. "What's point two?"

"Point two is this." Mall is grinning, and uses her sweetest voice, "Liberal is *part* of conservative—of the Crat rightwing, deary. Just get that through your sodding head right now."

Oak, Pharaoh

All of July is dedicated to first procedure: amass. This has two prongs: waters and mindfree. Both make commonsense joe to Oak and his top consultants, so they partner up easy enough with the EVe bitches. Even with their milplanner, the purple-haired hellcat that always looks like she'd like to claw off your ballsack. She's got some grand tactic or other in mind against the meg. Some fancy-ass milstrat. Hell, Oak and the boys just want to kill all them Crat sons-of-bitches and take what's theirs—simple as that. But Oak can see these EVens know what they're about. They got the knowhow to fiddle with the mac shit and to get all the fancy stuff done. They're a lot like Terds in that regard. So they're useful—for the time being. They talk the Wobbly talk good. Long as they keep walking the Wobbly walk, Oak figures he'll stick with them, but he won't trust them whole—not even Uncle Enron. That boy's got himself pussified somehow. He's still CorpTroop tougher than hell and can reach down your throat to pull out your lungs any time he pleases, but he's bangboning that big bitch and puppydogging around after the smart one, and that's got him good and whipt. Damn shame, too, in Oak's point of view, but he can see how it might happen. Being off feed now like they are, well, there's too damn *much* time to think. Like the opposite of the glassy. Lots of times there's nothing to do *but* think. That can drive a man nuts. Seems clear to Oak that's Enron's problem. He's thinking way too much about things. You can't be too careful about that.

The Wobblies spend the high summer channeling or diverting all hydrosystem waters they can lay their hands on into one of the three forks of the Boise River. The big bitch does the hydroengineering. The purple-headed bitch just keeps telling them more and more. Find more waters. The South Fork of the Boise descends from the high mountains of the Sawtooth Forest into Anderson Ranch Reservoir, then, below the Anderson Ranch Dam, continues northwest into the long, winding Arrowrock Reservoir—their staging reservoir. This southern watercourse is an isolated branch of the systems, but it brings heavy flow down from the Sawtooth snowpack every spring. In a good year, that makes for a steady tumble even into midsummer. Lucky for the Wobblies, this has been a crest year. To the north, the Middle and North Forks, besides cascading hard down all the canyons with their own melt, can be patched in with pumpstations to the Redfish Lake shed and the South Fork of the Payette. That's complicated hydronomy and depends on no airstrikes. Strange, none occur after the EVens arrive. Not a one. Early in the tussle, ArcAir flying out of Mountain Home harassed the hell out of the Wobblies. Since the middle of June, though, skies over the wilderness area have been nothing but empty, crystal blue. Oak just finds that damn queer, and won't believe it's permanent luck. But, like the bitch the other bitches call Cardinal, he's all for taking full advantage of the situation. They construct, like hell, culvert and pipeline to redirect key flow-works through the high summit passes. As a result, the fattened North Fork of the Boise joins the fattened Middle Fork several klicks below Black Rock at a spot that's become a lake in its own right. All of the flow then sweeps broad down the river, southwest, emptying into Arrowrock Reservoir at a point about halfway round its long, steep-sided dogleg. At the source end of the staging reservoir, waters back farther and farther up the South Fork, flooding thousands of new acres. At the downflow end to the west, Arrowrock Dam looks about ready to bust. That Cardinal has ordered the spillways shut tight to everything but the topmost overflow. Cracks have come in the dam face, some of them gushing, and the earthworks around the structure are getting saturated. The dam just wasn't built to hold back all this subregional hydro-accumulation. None of that bothers old Cardinal a jot. She's a hard bitch, that's for sure. She's looking to lower the level of Lucky Peak Reservoir, the next holding reservoir below Arrowrock, so any other milplanner watching her ops would think she means to withhold waters from BoiCity—which makes good sense. Why not squeeze down the flow of the Boise River through the Gater district Brown Belt to a stinking, muddy trickle? Why not parch the bastards out? That's siege mentality, needing a force outside the walls equal or bigger to what's behind the gates, and the besiegers have to have all the time in the world on their hands. That ain't the Wobblies, and that ain't Cardinal's milplan, either. She's got some other strat in mind. One she's trying to hide from the Crats and Net. What she calls an Old Soviet strat of overwhelming forces. She's always saying she knows damn well how to hold a fort, so she should have a pretty good idea how to take one, too. All through July, she tells that big mac-savvy Sinalco gal to pour more and more hydro into the upper BoiCity flowworks. Meantime, that other prong of the first procedure comes along just right. Mindfree.

Soon after coming into the parks, months back, Sinalco and the brainy bitch Mall set up little manushops for making those sigblock skullcap doohickeys. Lord knows enough jobless guys were around to work them. To skip detection, they'd spread the shops out over the parks. One in Kuna, one in Tiegs Corner, two kind of close to one another in Blacks Creek and Owyhee, with easy access to T-84, and a bigger, remote shop way out in Melba. All these shops kept producing even after the EVe crew left the parks to find the Wobblies out in the primitive area. They had brought rucksacks filled with the caps. Back in the parks, Enron's kin kept the shops busy, assembling and distributing, and dodging the damn ParkPol. Week after week, more and more Serv eyes started to clear of the glassy, of the hub's damned mindfuck. Once joined up with Oak's bunch, the EVens began launching manushop startups in the wilderness, in the remote spots of the Redfish Lake region. These were sprawling and well-camouflaged shopworks. One in Stanley, one in Sunbeam, another in Obsidian. Soon, so many wilderness caps were being produced that regular smuggle routes were established, through Emmett and Star from the northwest and Mayfield and Regina from the southeast. SigCaps, as they came to be called by Wobblies, flooded the parks. But they were *never* for sale. *Never*. SigCaps *never* changed hands by trade or transaction of any kind. Commerce was the only way the Pyramid would ever know they were there, because commerce is the only thing the Pyramid gives a shit about in the parks—DollArcs changing hands. If Servs didn't buy or sell the SigCaps, the Terds and the Crats would never catch wind of them. Pure solidarity, Uncle Wobbly style—something for the good of everybody, not just a few—just give the damn caps away. Sometimes they get called Solidarity Caps, or SolCaps for short. Whatever Parkers call them, they have come to be standard Wobbly kit. These glinty, metal-textile sons-of-bitches make Servs look fresh from the loonybin: their ears doubled over, splaying their hair down and out by the tight rolldowns—but the *whole* motsen/corband has to be covered over. Wobblies don't give a shit if they look like walking rootboots. Looks don't mean a thing to them. To Servs, SigCaps get worn with fellowshipride. Fellowshipride and the mindfree.

Toward the end of June, Sinalco saw a way to improvise on her WobblyNet slice. Deep in the hyrdoworks systems, sorting out how to network waters, she recognized some masterfeed sigcast for the whole of ArcNet. Something hidden deep in the align. Suddenly, there it was, fat and pulsing. Sinalco found a simple way to roguefeed and knapsack on the mastercast. ArcNet would now *carry* WobblyNet, and SigCaps, designed first just to block ArcNet, would co-instantaneously transceive and feed WobblyNet.

"Sodding genius," Mall described it. "Breakthrough. Inconceivable that anybody could meddle with their ArcNet, let alone see the mastercast." Right away Mall set hard to work setting up a roguefeed for Sinalco to knapsack. Mall knew, if SigCaps cut off the mindfuck of the all4s for Servs, she couldn't re-establish anything like that with WobblyNet. It had to be something different. It couldn't be something forced on you. It had to serve you. Detox from the Simulacrum was known to take Servs up to two weeks, sometimes longer. Even then, Parkers frequently relapsed because they missed their virshopping, virsports, and virsex. Hell, idiversion was hardwired tight to *be* habit forming. Once rid of it, though, most Servs, like Enron back in EVe, say they'd rather die than backslide to ArcNet feed. *Much* rather die—Oak included. Understanding, Mall makes WobblyNet transcept as minimal and freewill as she can, to be under totocontrol of the SigCapper. *Of the SigCapper. Now that's Dmega doublefuck choice.* Over one screen at a time, wearer's choosing, Servs pick from a stream of realinformation, realtraining, realeducation. No compulsion, no bullshit. Things to use, not used by. On a second screen, an instruct stream is for various job-ops or fight-ops. If a Serv wants both screens feeding at once, so be it. That's servchoice. Only one screen streaming, fine. That's servchoice. No screens at all going, the all-to-yourself, superb. Servchoice ace. With WobblyNet, your eyes, ears, and mind are your damn own. That's how Servs suddenly find themselves on a level feed with Terds—even with Crats. The skinny, Terd bitch they kidnaped said only the lowstatus in TexArc are implanted with the motor-sensory cortex bands. There isn't even an equivalent detachdevise for the upstatus. And with Terds and Crats, the ipatch and ihear are removable, cornea lenses and audcanal-mics. Everything's detachable and optional for the upstatus, but the dumb sons-of-bitches use them, anyway.

Oak did complain to Mall that her new WobblyNet was boring, that

Servs can't live on realinformation alone. So Mall and the slope-bitch Brand teamed up to select and stream some kind of entertain over WobblyNet—something edifying. Mall decides on a vintage film feed, pre-realignment and preCorpfeud. Really old shit. Although Mall has thousands of EVe and Old Euro titles at the ready, Brand convinces her to stream only the bygone Lower North American films as a way to help restore what she, Brand, worked so hard to erase through the Simulacrum: any sense of history, personal identity, group struggle. To hear Brand describe it—any emergence of consciousness by a critical intervention in reality. Mall agreed, but found only former LAN films with an edge of alterity would do. She didn't mind how weird the upshots or their endings. Mall wasn't looking to put on more propaganda. She figures Servs would see through that. Mall wants only stuff that makes you think. So she and Brand locate and stream hundreds of old, old films: *Modern Times*, *The Grapes of Wrath*, *Blade Runner* (director's cut), *Brazil*, *Bamboozled*, *Roger and Me*, *Fight Club*, *The Great and Powerful Dub-Ya*, *Ripped in MacLand*, *Monkey See*. Lots and lots more. Both are nuts in particular over some Yeoman Clucus dude—one strangeass filmaker—but he ain't half bad.

So there it is. Waters and mindfree. Massive subregional hydroaccumulation, SigCaps, and WobblyNet. Once these conditions were put right, Wobblies were ready to move on to Cardinal's second procedure—the really big one: disrupt and overrun. Years from now, they would come to call it The Pyramid Scheme.

☆ ☆ ☆ ☆ ☆ ☆

Blaupunkt belly-crawls slowly, wearing a full camomat on his back, the final demi-klick to within clearshot of the dam. Lucky Peak. His motherforce, AC Wobbly, two days before, had gone ahead of him, west towards the monster city. That's fine with Blau. He's high-mountain born and accustomed to being and working alone. In fact, he prefers the quiet and responsibility. He hated to come down out of what TexArcans call the wilderness area and back onto the flats. As far as Blaupunkt is concerned, only bad things happen on the flatlands. For the past week his Attack Crew, a small unit of fast-move lightfighters, about one thousand, has been swinging wide below the upper BoiCity flowworks, south of the South Fork of the Boise River, skirting along the mountains' edge to avoid detection. As they moved, the spillways of the Anderson Ranch Dam, behind them, had been opened wide, sending the full waters of the uppermost reservoir down the South Fork to add to the already glutted Arrowrock Reservoir—the staging reservoir. Now, as Blaupunkt crawls, careful to remain noncontour and to make no sound whatever, he hears the demolition command go by for Arrowrock Dam, above his location. Simply opening its spillways will not do. The surge must be devastating. He hopes, once his job is done, he'll be able to get away from the waters' path. Lucky Peak Reservoir, the lower-most reservoir in this southern watercourse, is soon to go from ebb, to flow, to ebb again—in a tremendous rush.

It's just past dusk, the ideal time to camomat crawl. Blaupunkt is their best at it. Another reason he drew this job. He freezes when an unbelievably bright flash of lightning, or series of flashes, Blaupunkt can't distinguish, silhouettes the western horizon for five or six seconds. Terrifying, but key to the second procedure. Fifteen seconds afterwards, he hears distant thunder sounds, far-off and muffled. It sends a shiver through him. Blaupunkt has never heard or felt such power in the air as these TexArc storms bring. Immediately after the thunder, Cardinal's voice is in his ear. "*Jetzt*."

He hopes he'll have time to get off several shots. As he rises to one knee, he swings the smackdown from his side. Two pulses at base and one more mid, run a huge fissure up the face of the dam. Before Blaupunkt can fist out one more pulse, he's misted by Dam Guard, on doublego alert for weeks. How the fighter got this far past perimeter is inexplicable to them. Less than fifteen minutes later, a wall of waters sweeps through and washes away Lucky Peak Dam.

☆ ☆ ☆ ☆ ☆ ☆

While among the Wobblies, the EVens had heard stories about thunderboomers. Twice during July, high in the wilderness area, smaller storms had appeared that the outlanders at first mistook for boomers. These were frightening thunderstorms, but Wobblies just shook their heads and told them, "Just you wait. You ain't seen nothin' yet. Believe you me." The Wobblies had been right. At dusk, when the towering thunderheads glide toward BoiCity from the west, serene and majestic, rising jet black into the upper reaches of the sky, all the EVens, Sinalco included, aren't able to believe their eyes. These clouds are airborne tidal waves, dwarfing the hundreds of hightowers of the meg, eventually eclipsing the golden burnish even of the Pyramid, leaving that ugly spike a dull, leaden, blueish blush. As they approach, these thunderheads, like an airborn tsunami undertow, suck the atmosphere toward them, producing a warm and deadly calm that contradicts the violence drawing closer. Watching this spectacle, Cardinal regrets her decision to assault under stormcover. She had no idea a storm, a thunderboomer, could be anything like this, but she'd had no choice. Wobblies cannot strike the meg while vulnerable to ArcAir attack. Their motherforces are stretched thin enough as it is, and Mountain Home fighterwings must be weathergrounded if the second procedure is to render. Plus, the timing of the disruption has to be perfect. Storms from the west and waters from the east must converge. In the twilight after sunset, while AC Wobbly huddles near Hillcrest, just east of T-84 and just outside the tall Gater district walls, Cardinal gets her first wish. A burst of cold wind rattles the flimsy buildings hiding their forces, declaring, at last, the arrival of the storm. The freshest air any of the EVens ever have smelled comes next with the first titanic raindrops plopping on the thick, western dust. Over WobblyNet, for all SigCap Wobblies to hear, Cardinal orders the double dam blow above them: Wobblies blowing the dam they control at Arrowrock and Blau taking out Lucky Peak with a smackdown. If those execute, there will be no turning back. The storm is here. The waters will be on their way.

A genuine force-one thunderboomer hasn't ripped into BoiCity for a few seasons. When this one hits, it's biz as usual. Parkers, in their flimsy mobiles, get the shit kicked out of them. Gaters in the district batten down the hatches. Both good reasons for the Wobblies to come under stormcover—GaterPol and ParkPol will have their heads down. You'd have to be an idiot to be out in this. Long, arching, sheet-lightning lights up the clouds continuously. Thick and prolonged bolts of ground-lightning relentlessly strike, coming seven or eight to a barrage. You almost feel your hair standing on end from the electricity hovering over the meg. The thunder is more like an earthquake—shaking the ground. In spite of the torrential, horizontal rain, storehouse fires spring up around the parks. Tin roofs sail off buildings. Soon mobiles are riding mud rivers—what used to be streets and roads—downstream, careening into each other and off of whatever happens to be in the path of these giant gullywashers. On top of all this, the winds are random and treacherous—always shifting. One gust can lift you off the ground or knock you down. Cardinal's Attack Crew lose seventeen Wobblies to the elements while waiting for the river to arrive. That doesn't take long. Half an hour after Cardinal directs the dams brought down, the inlet at Barber—the southeast start of the Gater district walls—is walloped and submerged under so much churning waters the grated archway, hundreds of meters high and curving over the monumental floodgates, collapses inward under the mass of the lead swell. The swirling river then eddies against the district walls on either side of the breach, held back a minute, at most, before pushing open an even wider gap to flood. After that, as Cardinal planned, the waters knife the meg in two.

Tens of thousands of Gaters die in the initial washout along the Brown Belt. Stately condos and trendy studios are swamped and, tumultuously, voided of their contents. Deluxe armored SUVehics—GrandCanyons, Tetons, MileHighs, Exploiters—bob and spin like twigs down the wild current. TurboGolf links are swallowed whole. Shopvillage showindows implode. Foundations beneath hundreds of hightowers start to slip, then start to fail. Collapsing like dominoes, smogscraper after smogscraper, each eighty to ninety stories high, tilt, topple, then are sucked under the waters and are gone. The waters gain ferocity as they're pitched and directed through the Belt, accumulating more and more debris. Meanwhile, giant waves boil up all sidestreets, compressed by the narrow canyons of the downtown. Every thing and every Gater within their reach is crushed and sucked away.

Deluge underfoot. Thunderboomer overhead. Disrupt achieved. Now comes overrun.

AC Wobbly divides. Pernod leads one group west to the airport. For some reason, it's underguarded, as though no onc anticipated its ever being a target. After the briefest of skirmishes, Wobblies secure it, easily. Cardinal rushes a second group to the main Terd depot of Parker Motors, not far from the airport on West Gowen Road. There, Hap hacks in some securecodes he knows, and soon the thousands of vehics on the lots are theirs for the choosing. Hap picks the latest Viper32—that being its cylinder count. With Cardinal nervously riding shotgun and with a long caravan of oversized and overpriced petroguzzlers following his lead, Hap highspeeds through the storm directly to the Broadway Avenue Gate, the southernmost of three major portals into the Gater district. If the Wobblies can't open at least two of these, Cardinal calculates, they might as well all go home. As anticipated, the gate is lockout, understandable considering what's going on inside the wall. As hoped, the gate guard is scarecrow, also understandable. GaterPol is urgently needed throughout the district. Driving up in a stolen vehic, and punching in a false idcode and dated entercode, Hap certainly gets the attention of the desksergeant left behind to watch the shop. After swearing at him in a series of colorful expressions over the vidscreen and claiming entry a matter of life or death, Hap finally coaxes the gatekeeper to step out to speak with him in person. The GaterPolman is dead before he's opened the access door wide enough to step through. Wobblies own the first gatehouse! Dodging pile-ups, Hap next careens up T-84 to the double-mega T-184 Gate further to the northwest. This primary district portal intersects T-84 at the apex of its long, western bend towards the Napa and Caldwell wards. Hap pulls the same stunt, this time driving up with monstrously big GaterPol patrolvehics on either side of him flashing their bluelights and maxvoling their sirens. The desksergeant is so perplexed he steps outside, unbidden, scratching his head. Wobblies take the final portal, the northernmost Chinden Boulevard Gate, from inside the wall. Staying behind at the central T-184 Gate to command the western overrun, Cardinal sends up Hap and some boys. No one knows they're coming. In the chaos of the night, GaterPol isn't communicating particularly well.

Not so with the Wobblies over WobblyNet. For the past hour, every SigCapped Serv in the greater BoiCity vicinity has been watching the progress of AC Wobbly—the Attack Crew designated to knock the Gators for a loop. Now that district gates are secured, Cardinal signals their allmobile. Doublego! Using the central gridworks, she swings open the three great thresholds at once. Like a second flood blast, a hundred thousand Parkers or more, poised at the ready under the cover of the storm, race forward and push through these gates. Their roaring joins with the din of the shrieking winds and the hammering thunderclaps.

☆ ☆ ☆ ☆ ☆ ☆

Attack Crew Uncle—the motherforce designated to make Gaters cry uncle—had gathered days earlier due north of the meg at Bogus Basin.

Because of all the waters, they'd needed to skirt north and west of the upper BoiCity flowworks and then, undetected, come south through the mountains, finally infiltrating down into the foothills above the Gater district. Their bigpic job is to wait for the waters to hit and the allmobile from Cardinal to sig, then blitz and take control of eastern BoiCity, that smaller ribbon of meg running between the Brown Belt and the hills. This elite sector, where the Crats live in manors thickly walled and heavily defended, require AC Uncle numbers far into the thousands. Within this main motherforce is also a Sneak Crew, one having the go/nogo job of getting inside the Pyramid to flush the topCrats. Only their livecapture will give the Wobblies leverage enough for clout—not to mention survivability. Seizing the meg may be a cakewalk compared to keeping and living in it afterward. In a political concession, Oak is to command AC Uncle. Cardinal has placed Mall by his side, however, to keep an eye on the little shit. No telling what he and his boys are liable to do let loose in the district. Sinalco directs the Sneak Crew, assisted by Migros. They'll have the toughest time of it. No one's ever penetrated a Pyramid before. As a general precaution, all the EVens stay in constant closedcomm with one another on a safeline.

When the allmobile doublego sigs, AC Uncle punches holes in the perimeter concertina and rpgs the key guardtowers. Well-armed Wobblies pour down out of the black hills. As a line, one thrust led by Jiplap quickly advances past Hill Road to the northwest of downtown, where everything bogs down in bitter street fighting from Collister down to West Irene Street. The strat had been to sweep rapidly south to West Main Street, about where the waters would be at that time, and push toward the Pyramid. Jiplap can see such a speedstrike isn't going to happen. The Crat manors are like small fortresses surrounding central bunker units. While their landscaping is decorative and immaculate, their autoshields are also deadly, and the Crats inside are armed to the teeth. Wobbly after Wobbly is picked off just trying to get over adobe hacienda ramparts trimmed in pastels and festooned with climbing roses. The deadcount grows alarming. It doesn't help when the first few Terd private security guards, who try to defect, are beaten to death. Word gets out, and from then on, guards either flee toward the river or are forced to fight to the death alongside their Crat employers. When these manors do, at last, start to fall to the Wobblies, painfully and one-by-one, no livecaptures at all are taken—man, woman, or child. Cardinal screams over WobblyNet for team guides to stop the butchery, for Jiplap to do something, but to no effect. Jiplap comms back that he's found a damned elephant gun in a damned rec-room, and he's going damned elephant hunting. It's then Cardinal gets her first inkling that along with the storm and the flood, she's tapped into powers that cannot be controlled.

To the southeast, Oak drives the other thrust of his motherforce straight for the downtown, hoping to form a pincer movement with Jiplap's thrust coming in from the northwest. Oak moves without resistance through the Old Fort Boise Military Reserve, but suddenly encounters high barricades thrown up by GaterPol along West Fort Street, only blocks from the Pyramid. These defenses seem to be springloaded to pop up out of the road pavement, and the Wobblies can't bust through or outflank them, especially not to the south where the flood waters roil. Even with all the disrupt, GaterPol has managed to set a protective umbrella around the Pyramid. The GaterPolmen behind it are armed with misters and vaporize, right and left, the Wobblies Oak sends against them. Without misters, AC Uncle isn't likely to make it past this barrier and into the heart of the meg. Cardinal anticipated such fortification. All Oak has to do is thrust up to West Fort Street. That advance will give Sinalco's Sneak Crew the chance to work.

Sinalco had been slicing deep the BoiCity megnet for weeks, looking for doorways into meg infrastructure. Among the tens-of-thousands of items she scanned, a plot date of 20.4.04 appeared for an ancient geothermal system that used to run under the old city: thousands of meters of pipelines, primarily under the downtown sector, had carried hotsprings waters to public buildings for inexpensive heating—the type of ecologically sound ideas long since abandoned in TexArc as fringe, libby soft-think. Enlisting the help of Parker demesnes performing levee work along the Brown Belt mudflats, Sinalco eventually confirmed which of those pipelines remained intact and passable. She discovered one line open all the way from a river discharge location at the bottom of South 14th up to a source well in the old Military Reserve—passing directly under the Pyramid. One eccentric oldtimer had been up and down its length plenty of times, talking and cackling to himself as he reverse-cast over WobblyNet ipatch sigimages of every meter of the pipeline for Sinalco to study and simlocate aboveground. There was no mistake. The Pyramid had been built on top of the line, and the line was still open. To Sinalco, the pipe cylinder looked wide enough to crawl through, almost big enough to walk in, bent double. The only questions would be how far the flood waters make it into the geothermal systems, and would Sinalco be able to find a way to get from the pipeline up into the Pyramid itself.

As the firefights intensify along West Fort Street, her Sneak Crew hurries to locate and uncover, on the Military Reserve, the hatchhead of BGL Well No.2, one of the headsources for the geothermal pipeline. Sinalco, Migros, and five good underground Wobblies descend into the black hole to begin their long crawl-squat toward the Pyramid and toward the answers to those questions.

☆ ☆ ☆ ☆ ☆ ☆

South of the Boise, a river now swollen beyond the girth of the Brown Belt and teeming swift with black and lethal waters, the Parker army spreads inward from three great gates. Cardinal's milplan calls for overrun and secure of all GaterPol stations and other key points: vital intersections, solarworks, major greeneries, and the like. Once inside the district walls, though, the

Parkers overrun everything they encounter in TerdTowne, anywhere they go, anything they see, enraging them more. The lawns sprayed green, the homeunits fixed in solid ground, the streets paved smooth, the shoplazas stocked full, the vehics bought new, the realfood in every home and restaurant kitchen—all are red capes flapping before the noses of stampeding Arcbulls. Parkers have never imagined such a prosperzone, never dreamed of so tonic a safespace. All they can think, as they rampage on, despite Cardinal's constant urging for them to stay within milplan, is that all they see is something they, as Servs, can never, ever *earn*. Not them, not their kids—ever. No matter how much they hardwork. So the looting is thorough. The destruction of property monumental. The killing becomes orgiastic, bacchanalian. Terds not run headlong into the rush of the flood to be washed screaming away are hacked to death with sharp weapons carried by the Parkers, beaten to pulp with the dull ones, or simply torn, limb-from-limb, by hand. Some of the very Terd young are spared, but not many. Towering fires blaze up at Ustick, Perkins, Boise Junction, all along Broadway Avenue, gobbling up furniture, appliances, compgenart, palmbooks, fat family pets, glossy family digialbums, fine collectibles, hotwaxed SUVehics. The owners of all these Terd items get pushed, hurled, rolled, or lofted—kicking—into the same flames. Parkers smash their way into shopvillage boutiques to stand transfixed, taking in the unimaginable: buffed wooden floors devoted to the housing, of rack after rack, display case after display case, of dresses, jackets, pumps, sandals, blouses, skirts, jeans, coats, rings, watchwrists, necklaces, colognes, perfumes, light scents, coitusrubs, bath oils, solarblocks, body washes, teddies, thongs, pushup bras, satin sheets, sexpillows, scarfs, berets, panamas, sombreros, sunshorts, outback boots, blazers, powersuits, deflectvests, sungoggles, windwear...on and on. In the cafés, Parkers hunch over the curious items shelved on dessert carts, shaking their heads. In the lavish church sanctuaries, Parkers pick up the collection plates to hear the beatific automessage speak to them: *Please, brethren and sistren, no con-*

tributions smaller than one thousand DollArc bills. Praise the Lord. Inside the long, anesthetic hallways of the hospitals—the Parkers don't even know what it is they're gawking at.

Cardinal is powerless to stop the southdistrict riots.

☆ ☆ ☆ ☆ ☆ ☆

The Sneak Crew crawls southwest, veers southeast, then due south, then finally ninety degrees due west for hundreds of meters in the dank pipeline. Its diameter is tighter than it looked over reversecast. The silence they move in is that of a tomb. Suddenly, ahead of them in the circle-light of Sinalco's handlamp, is what they feared. Flood waters rising too far up into the geothermal system, and they have a considerable straightaway still to cover before a sharp right north will bring them under the Pyramid. Without looking over her shoulder, Sinalco tells Migros to keep the others where they are and wait for the opportunity to move ahead. Then she wades on all fours into the brackish water until she submerges into the halo of her own handlamp and disappears, frogkicking, downpipe. The trace glow of her light takes time to fade completely. Eventually, Migros turns to face the five Wobblies. The shock on their faces matches hers. Seven minutes and thirty-seven seconds later—Migros always times such ops events—the waters suck away from their hands-and-knees, draining the pipe in front of them. The crew follows quickly to the sharp right where they find Sinalco, crouching and dripping. The pipeline south has been sealed off somehow. Before anyone can speak, their crew director signals them to follow her through the pipeline heading north, away from the direction of the waters. Soon they come under a narrow perforation burrowed up through meters and meters of concrete and titanium plate. Sinalco holds up her hand to prevent any questions from Migros, who can't credit what she's seeing as being physically possible, then wriggles her way up into the lowest level of the Pyramid. Migros and the Wobblies follow, bewildered, yet preferring the unknown dangers of the Pyramid to the probable grave of the pipeline. Migros and her team must locate the armory and begin smuggling out misters. Sinalco's job is to go topCrat hunting.

☆ ☆ ☆ ☆ ☆ ☆

Dockers had begun his evening by admiring the fury of the approaching thunderboomer from the safety of his Pyramid Eye. Then, without warning, the tidal wall of water played through his meg. In disbelief, he watched his financial belt tumble, eddied downstream. Reports came in of the gate-breaches along the district wall, but it was too stormy and dark in that direction to spot anything specific. Behind him to the north, however, the flash of explosives and small-arms fire were frequent and clear, descending in a long, arching line out of the foothills. Dockers anxiously tracked their progress, hundreds of strikes along violent and fast-moving battle lines as the fighting drove into the northmeg, street-to-street. With relief, he saw the pincer advance gradually falter, then freeze as GaterPol finally managed to establish a defensive perimeter, though too close for comfort. Unable to be too careful, Dockers orders a Pyramid lockout and scrambles the Pyramid Guard, also siging Mountain Home ArcAir Base every fifteen minutes begging for help. Each time, he's siged back: "grounded by weather." After an uneasy period, he thinks the worst is over, when the impossible happens. Somehow—some *fucking how*—Wobblies are inside the Pyramid. Dockers *has* to give in and siglink Waco. If *this* didn't call for CorpTroops, what the yank did? Thunderboomer or no fucking thunderboomer, fucking Ground has to make the fucking fall. Hell, fuck that! Send in Net! Shitubers are running berserk inside his goddamned Pyramid.

CorpHQ is the kind of place you can only siglink *once* for help, so it better be damned good. Dockers is confident this situation more than qualifies. After waiting on hold twenty minutes, enough time for 300 GaterPol outside, and 37 Pyramid Guard inside, to go kia, the brief, automated reply is, "We regret that the ceo and all his subceos are unavailable at the moment. But your call is important to us. Have a nice day."

Jesus Hellfire Fucking Christ. Dockers is *not* having a nice day. He regrets not reporting to the bigboss how the skinny dykebitch had gone missing—probably shanghaied by fucking Wobblies. If he had, maybe Bleached Wheat would be more inclined to believe now that BoiCity is undergoing a shitstorm of biblical proportions, that the meg needs rescuing—pronto, that these are no ordinary shitubers they're facing—that these fucks are troops.

☆ ☆ ☆ ☆ ☆ ☆

Enron hates missing the fighting north of his poz, but Mall's orders are crucial. If he fails, Wobbly fails—short and simple. For two nights he'd moved carefully south from Long Tom Reservoir, where he split off from Cardinal's bunch, and toward Mountain Home. He's surprised how lax the ArcAir base security seems to be—unlike having to tiptoe into some raghead installation. ArcAir seems more concerned with big ground assaults, not one-man infiltration, but Enron didn't try to beat the approach defenses by climbing over the fencing around Perimeter Road. Right after sundown, he'd just strolled in through the main gates mingled with a long convoy of supply vehics—easy as pie. He'd bet on ArcAir not expecting some guy in a camosuit walking in off the sage flats. He'd bet right. The EVe Terds—or he best call them teeks—had done an A1 job of patching back together Enron's OLED armor. *Kind of nice being back in,* he thought, *except I miss Jowler.* The teeks couldn't put him back together.

ArcAir bases look a lot like ArcGround bases, and Enron soon has his bearings. He'll avoid the low, long building bound to be base ops. Sec will be heaviest, there. He's looking for quarters, and officers quarters aren't hard to tell apart from enlisted quarters. Enron keeps to the shadows on one side of Gunfighter Avenue, Bomber Road, and Silver Sage until he sees nicer, bigger housing. It's just a matter of finding the nicest place among them. That will be the Wing Commander's quarters. Turns out to be a whole one-story houseunit to itself—real grass, real shrubs, painted clean white, with lots of windows to watch the big sky. Enron's anxious to meet this Terd, this AirColonel. He's heard tell of him. Hell, every CorpTroop has. Some years back, when this Terd was a flyboy Captain, he refused to take his squadron down to wipe a jungle villpod full of sweetpuss and kid ragheads. Flat refused the order. Said there was no good reason for it. *Shit, that right there's corptreason.* Somehow stratwise, though, it came out to be a good thing not to wipe the villpod—either that, or this Terd was so good at flyboying, Air couldn't afford to tank him. Some damn thing like that. *Who the hell really knows with rumors?* Anyway, instead of getting stood up against a wall and shot, this flyboy Captain got commended and promoted for his independent initiative—*which you know is big bullshit*—and become a yub legend for CorpTroopers. The Terd who told them to shove it—and lived through it. *Every guy's dream.*

Enron's respectful once he's inside this Terd's house. He looks things over carefully and inspects some photos on the shelves, but he touches nothing. He'll wait for the Wing Commander to come back home. *Sure as shit*, Enron thinks, *he's in the base ops about right now, worried by the big thunderboomer coming in from the west, and sure as shit Crats in BoiCity will be on his ass soon, to scramble up help*. Enron hopes he can get to the AirColonel in time. If he still had Jowler with him, he could send him into the base ops to sneak after the Terd. Without Jowler, all Enron can do is sit tight and count on some luck.

☆ ☆ ☆ ☆ ☆ ☆

Jiplap's been having the luck with his elephant hunt. The front of his coveralls are speckled near solid red—nope it ain't blue—from Crat blood. Little white blobs of Crat brains cling to his legs and boots. He's cut Crats and their flunky Terd security guys in half with the big rifle. To save shot, when he gets in close, Jip applies its butt to the side of Crat heads or swings it around, wild, like a long club. The more Cratmanor recrooms the Wobblies manage to bust into, the more vintage ordnance they find: Uzi, M16, AK47—oiled and in mint condition. Shit Jip had only heard tell of or studied on the old all4s war channels. Damn, Jip sure missed his old shows. These guns ain't misters, but they take his boys from single-shot to automatic, and that starts to make all the damn difference in the world. Wobblies also come onto frag grenades and Stinger shoulder mounts. With these, they start blowing through the prettified cratwalls and lifting the light-armored GaterPol vehics up off the street. Jip's bunch really starts to go to town until Cardinal gets them back on task over comm.

Stupid fucker Jiplap! Are you where?

Dumb bossy bitch can't talk for shit.

<I'm doing my job killing shit! That's where I am! Where the fuck are _you_?>

Where my job is already finish! What your poz is? Tell your poz!

Jip's got no damn idea what his poz is. He asks his lieutenant, who he told to keep track of shit like that. <Almost to the junction of West State and VetMem Parkway, you fucking nosey bitch! That's my damned _poz_!>

Arschloch! Oak is almost to Pyramid! Sinalco gets inside! You must come from the west! You must come schnell!

<Don't be creaming your panties, sweetheart! I know my goddamned job! We ain't dicking around with Terds up here like you are down there! These fucking Crats knew somebody was coming after them someday, and they was fucking ready for us!>

Frog leap, stupid fucker! Do not take every castle! Und fuck West Main! Just get West State Street and go southeast! Hurry!

Leapfrog? Oh. Jip hadn't thought of that. <Okay you dykebitch! Hold onto your pie! We're on our way!>

Faster! At 9th Street you find high blocks up from roads! Get your fighters over them!

Jiplap's not sure exactly what she means by high blocks, but he's got some idea. It doesn't sound good. <If Oak's boys ain't getting over them, how the hell do you expect me to?>

*Migros bringing misters out from Pyramid! *Misters*, stupid fucker! These make your tiny dickie hard, *yes*?*

<*Misters*! Why the fuck didn't you say so in the first place, you goddamn slitlicker? For misters I'd be happy to fuck you!>

For no reason you are happy to fuck hole in ground! Now move your asses!

Old Cardinal's right. Just the mention of the name "mister" gets Jiplap about half stiff.

☆ ☆ ☆ ☆ ☆ ☆

The last thing Dockers has time to watch, safe from his perch up in the Eye, is the GaterPol perimeter breaking down along West Fort to the northeast and 9th Street to the northwest. The gun flashes coming from the Wobbly side are suddenly longer, brighter, more wrathful, more excruciating, and more effective. The flashes begin to advance closer and closer to the base of the Pyramid. Then, without even asking permission, the Captain of the Pyramid Guard ascends into Dockers' Eye to inform the megmayor the Wobblies now have misters. How the hell they got their hands on them, he doesn't know, but they're punching through. It's time for Dockers and his megcouncilors to get to the hardroom before it's too late. The Captain covers his left ear with his palm to ihear better. He then looks up to report that Wobblies are on the lower tiers of the Pyramid. How the hell they got in, he can't imagine. The Captain can't guarantee megcouncil safety any more outside the hardroom. They must go, now.

Alarm Status One sounds as the passageways leading to the hardroom seal tight, only opening before and closing after the party of 30 or so megcouncilors as they rush for their hardened sanctuary situated at the very heart of the Pyramid. Nothing can get through this fluid corridor seal as they move. They make it to the hardroom tier, but there are rocked off their feet by several explosions somewhere on their level. The Captain covers his ear to ihear better, then, in disbelief, looks to Dockers. "The hardroom's been demolished," he tells the megmayor. "Blasted from the inside. Engulfed in flames. There's nowhere safe to go."

All the megcouncilors look at one another in panic. Where the fuck can they run? Before any of them can conjure up a suggestion, the corridor seal in front of them melts away and a gigantic woman opens up with a small handgun, single-shoting three of the escort Guards through the foreheads before any other Guards can raise their misters against her. One spray in her direction seems to vaporize the intruder, except there's no bloodcloud left hanging in the air. What the yank? Before the Crats can puzzle long over this newest mystery, Alarm Status Two sounds signaling totofail of passageway security. All the hardseals vanish around the megcouncil, leaving their party helplessly exposed. Alarm Status Three follows, an alert never heard before in a TexArc Pyramid. "Encroach verified. Evac advised," is repeated over and over in an objective, male voice. The Captain of the Guard covers his ear one last time. The West Bannock threshold has been thrown open. Inconceivable, but verified. Hundreds of Wobblies are storming in.

The thunderboomer over BoiCity is lessening. The gusts and the windsheers have steadied to a constant howl. The rain descends more vertical than horizontal. Lightning flashes merely two or three strikes to a cluster. Still, it will be hours before anything from Mountain Home can get airborne.

The Brown Belt severing megnorth from megsouth has settled into a wide torrent choked with flotsam and bodies. The southdistrict, TerdTowne, is lost to mayhem. In the northdistrict, CratVillage, cratmanor after cratmanor gradually succumbs to the new Wobbly misters.

☆ ☆ ☆ ☆ ☆ ☆

AirColonel Bacardi throws his flightcap across the bedroom and tosses his keycards onto the bureau top. *Fuck this shit*, he's thinking, *I'm at least going to get a couple hours of powersleep. Maybe by morning the Crats will have their heads out of their ass for a change.*

Not too likely.

It's two or three in the morning. Bacardi's lost track. He's been up and on duty since four the previous morning. Between the Crats from CorpHQ badgering him for weeks to keep his Wing on constant highalert and, just tonight, that fathead megmayor siging base ops every two minutes soprano about BoiCity being simultaneously washed downstream *and* overrun by the barbarian hordes, this Wing Commander is pretty fed up with command. The megCrats want his entire Wing scrambled airborne *yesterday*. The CorpHQCrats, hell, subceo Ponzi himself, tell him to exercise extreme caution in this developing situation, to protect the AirBase at all costs, commit only one squadron, at most, to the defense of BoiCity. Then, not a minute later, none other than old blueyes, CorpKing of the world, securelines in to inform Bacardi, in pleasantly threatening tones, that the bigpic requires ArcAir to drag its feet on this one, to let the megmayor stew in his own juices for a while before taking any action. The ceo will be back in touch with the AirColonel to let him know exactly when, or if, it's time to scramble any fighters. Meanwhile, just sit tight. There, there. That's a good Wing Commander.

Crats. They're born with theirs heads up their asses.

It's all academic, anyway, because of the storm. This is one of the biggest, most violent weather events Bacardi's ever experienced. He wouldn't risk a single one of his pilots no matter what anyone tells him to do. He'd ordered all craft stowed underground as soon as he saw the storm massing on satelliteimage. There won't be anything flying until it passes, daybreak at the earliest. Then the Crats can resume stabbing one another in the back all they like. This AirColonel's stopped caring. Right now it's time for some shuteye.

In the bureau mirror, Bacardi sees over his shoulder the glinting outline of the man standing in the shadows on the opposite side of the bedroom. He decides to talk before turning around, "Well, you're not here to kill me, anyway not right away, because I'd be dead already and never know it. Right?"

"Yes, sir."

CorpTroop, by accent and tone. Interesting—and potentially good for Bacardi. But it's damn odd.

"So you're not Net."

"Fuck no, sir."

"Good. I hate those assholes."

"Doublecheck that, sir."

"Can I ask who you are?"

Indecision. Then: "CorpTrooper Enron, sir. Up from BoiCity way."

"CorpTrooper?" There's no ArcGround presence in this part of IMS.

"Used to be, sir. I'm sort of with a different outfit now."

"That being?" There's a long silence. Bacardi rephrases it. "Who are you with now, Enron?"

"The Wobblies, sir."

"Really?" Well maybe subceo Ponzi's not just a paranoid dickhead after all. "Have *they* sent you here to kill me?"

"That's the one thing I was asked particular not to do, sir."

"Is that right? Are you here to spread socialistic peace and harmony instead, then?"

"I don't know what that means, sir."

Bacardi rubs his eyes and turns around. "Sorry, Enron," he apologizes. Realizing it's too disconcerting, talking to a void, he turns back around so he can at least see the man's outline in the mirror. "I've been up all night, and I'm very tired."

Enron removes his camo hood and mask. "Ain't we all, sir?" he says.

Bacardi turns back around to study the rugged face suspended without body in the darkness. He judges Enron to be about fifteen or twenty years his junior, and by what he can make out of the eyes, to be one of those Groundsmen who see through the yub. *That means this man's survived a lot of action and been neck-deep in the shit many times. The only pathway for such CorpTrooper enlightenment. He's also free of the glassy. Now how in the hell did the Wobblies swing that? Very interesting.* His visitor is not one to fuck around with.

"Doublecheck that, trooper." Bacardi tries out a smile, which is returned. "May I ask, without being a smartass about it, why *are* you here?"

"They want you to watch this, sir."

Camo gloves get removed. A hand apparently reaches into a thigh-pocket to produce and hold out a simudisc, no bigger than a thumbnail.

"What is it?"

"Don't know, sir. I ain't watched it. Told me it was for Terds to watch."

"Who told you?"

Enron tells Bacardi, in some detail, about Mall and Brand. The AirColonel pays attention to his words like Enron's never seen a Terd heed a Parker before. Never. Enron likes this AirColonel. He hoped he would—and now he's glad he can. When Enron's through explaining, Barcardi walks slowly across the room to allow the CorpTrooper to place the tiny simudisc on the tip of the AirColonel's upturned index finger.

"It's not going to melt my brain or anything, is it, Enron?" Bacardi jokes, inspecting it.

"No, sir," Enron laughs. "Not in any gloopy way. Mall and Brand did mention it might change your mind about a few things."

"They did, did they?"

"Yes, sir," nods Enron. "They did."

"And if I refuse to watch it?"

"Then I'm shit-ass out of luck, sir. I'd be on my own to try like hell to get off your base."

Bacardi shakes his head. The unsophisticated courage of some of these CorpTroopers is humbling. These men don't even realize to demand in return for their service.

"Well, we can't have that. I better get to watching it then. How long will it take? Do you know?"

"Maybe fifteen, twenty minutes."

The AirColonel looks to be considering things. Enron hopes he's not *re*considering them.

"Look, Enron, that's a long time for me to be out of the loop right now. You know what I mean. I have to thinksay something to my base ops. I'm also going to say it out loud so you can hear what I'm telling them. Okay?"

"Sure thing, sir," Enron shrugs. "I get you."

Bacardi's been wondering what the strange cap rolled down over the CorpTrooper's head is for. *Surely not fashion.*

He thinksays out loud to ops: "Anything any different from that candyass Dockers?" He looks at Enron and the two share a grin about Crats. "Just the sameold? Good. Listen, I'm out of it for about forty-five for some powersleep. Say nothing—and I mean nothing—to me unless the storm is clearing or the sky is falling. Got that, chief? Yeah, thanks. Out."

The AirColonel sits down on the edge of the bed. He reaches up to slot the simudisc just behind his right ear. "Here goes," he says.

☆ ☆ ☆ ☆ ☆ ☆

Full digiland. No, wait. More than that. Taste quality. Emostim overlaying the fivesensestim. Whoa. Vivid, too. Feeling good and starting off—is it?—familiar. Simuimages I've recently been? Are they? Yeah. Right. The best of all possible worlds. Sure. I've been this on the TerdChannel before.

Nice goodfeel stuff. Warmfuzzy with optimism. Here's that one with the sweat running off my brow and the heat and the noise I'm a factoryhand hardworking along simple life but dignified life honest and sure and true. Yeah, now I'm going from shopfloor arms lifting heavy things and my young back like tungsten steel to teamleader then straight up to foreman where I'm seeing and making happen the factoryplan. The joy of ladderclimbing. The pride of distinction. The gratification of material reward. Now I'm all the way to plant manager with the corner office and hot realcoffee and cream-cheese bagel the bigpic firmly in hand and big DollArcs finally coming my way. For me and mine, pursuing happiness. What I deserve. God, isn't it good to be me? Oh, yeah, and now here's moving day. So exciting. My family and me leaving our snug little mobile behind in the birdchirping greenfields of the sunny simplelife parks movingup to a new and spacious TerdTowne condo with the walk-in closets and my bare feet cooled by ceramictile on kitchen and bathroom floors where the wife is close to the shopping and the kids to the good schools. I've made it haven't I? My God, only in TexArc. We've made it and all it takes, all it takes is some sweat and brass, some nose to the grindstone. All me. I've made it all on my own and I'm free and happy, free and happy, happy and free. Hey what the? Okay then. Hey, yeah, okay. Now it's that one I'm a CorpTrooper. Being all I can be in the CorpTroop of One. Miltraining's no easy business. My lungs burn, my palms blister. Get over that wall! Crawl under that barbed wire! We're under live fire! Just like jobtraining for Honor Duty Corporation. Honor Duty Corporation. Chest swelling with the Pride of Power. For my corp, for my future. My parents so proud of me. The old neighborhood so proud of me. The smart uniform, the new cock in my walk, I'm a new man. If only every Parker would just knuckle down like I'm knuckling down. Just try. There'd be no poor, there'd be no misery. Just knuckle down and give it a try. Everything's all there for the taking if they'd just knuckle down and try like I'm knuckling down and trying. I'm doing the airborne shuffle, klick after klick, with the sun on my face, klick after klick. My legs ache, but I'm proud to be insync with my unit. Now I've a chest full of medals, and my mama's so proud at the ceremony, proud of me defending my Corp, proud of me. Disadvantaged, my ass. The opportunities are there. A little elbowgrease. Rags can go to riches. A little elbowgrease. And them corpflags waving. Lone Star. Them corpflags waving. Yes I can. Hey, big switch now. Whoa. Okay. What am I? Who? Oh, all right. I'm that bizman now. That CorpCrat extraordinaire capitalserving for the good of the common shareholder. The Corp heart and soul. The wheel. The deal. I'm the well-deserved on top of the world. It's no free ride up here among the limos, the boardrooms, the sushibars. There may be plush carpet underfoot but there's highfinance hectic 24/7/365. Serve the client. Serve the client. My sacred trust. I provide the basics everyone wants, everyone needs. The social benefits the public demands and deserves. Foodfast. Goodscheap. Zoomzoom. I work the One Market, Under God. Long hours keeping a million details in mind. My sacred trust. Your corporate servant. Backward and Upward. The best of all possible worlds. Wait. What? That's not how...So I'm skimming a little off the top here. Playing my advantage a little sharp there. What's the harm? What's the big deal? Who's to know? What will it hurt? Why the hell not? What, are you naïve? I'd be a damn fool not to. For me and mine. For me and mine. You wouldn't do the same? Huh? No? Hey, yeah, I'm buying this election, stealing it, fixing it, manipulating it. Easy enough to do and no one wants to believe it's being done. The candidate's got the right stuff, the right mind. It's for the greater good, my greater good. Who's to know? Sure, I rig the taxcode. Cash flows to the top—and pools. It's for the commongood. The commongood. Incentive. Investment. Job creation. Trickledown. It's all natural selection, you know. Survival of me—the fittest. Hey, you wouldn't do the same? Human nature's not to watch out for number one? What's the real harm if nobody knows? I feel fine about it. I apologize for shit. I'm entitled. I hardwork for every penny of it. Let everybody else bootstrap their own way to the top. God wants me to be rich. Get your fucking mitts off my inheritance, off my trustfund, survival of me first! Hey! Why the fucking CorpTrooper again? I don't want to be the fucking CorpTrooper again! Why's the fucking drillsergeant kicking me in the fucking ribs? Why the food deprivation training, why the gangrape training on the little raghead girl, why the execution proficiency—the singleshot technique to the base of the skull on the long line of kneeling raghead detainees? I'm burning out a villpod, I'm smackdowning a cityblock, I'm gunning down ragheads in the streets—piles and piles of the bodies—kill the fucking ragheads or else Net kills me and mine, or else my mama's hauled in for a bayonet dummy, or else they stick a mister up my ass and fire! Once a CorpTroop, die a CorpTroop, you stupid fuckmother, stupid son of a Parker bitch! What the fuck else did you expect? Hey! Why now the factoryhand again? That's not how it's supposed to be, the boss screaming in my face day in and day out, no fucking ladder to climb, my feet sore, my back sore, my eyes dead, a stinger at the base of my neck, my shoulders drooping, me getting nowhere, but older—more tired, more worn out. Fucking sizedowned. You've got to be kidding. For this shitpay? No work at all, and the stench of my shitube, my stomach always growling, my kids always howling, my wife yellow scrawny, and always bitching. My kids run wild in the garbage heaps of the parks with the wild dogs scrapping and humping with the rats, big as cats, snuffing underfoot with the coyotes, lean and loony-eyed as night ghouls, prowling around in deep mud and around the tin-can mobiles, and the outbreak bugs. I die where I was born, and my kids die where they were born. Here and ever only here. I live it out fuckedup, fuckedover, then I fucking die miserable—start to finish. Hey! Okay! Wow! That's better! I'm a kid now, and there's a baseball and a field. Well, a ball of string, rags, rubber bands, and duct tape wrapped over, and over, and over—tight—and a vacant lot, not too full of junk, scrap, and dogshit. And the sun's on my young, freckled face—hot and strong. I whack the hell out of that rag ball with a sawed-off broomstick handle and I got that good stinging-numb feeling in the palms of my hands of a solid base hit to left-center and, hell, I'm flying for extra bases, trying to stretch it into a double. My feet are barely touching the ground, but every time they do, every time my foot touches the ground, I kick up a little puff of powdery dust. Man, I'm flying! Yep, I bet I make it. I'm going to lay out headfirst and slide. I'm going to try it. I don't care what I might hit, I've got to be safe—got to be safe. Hey, my father, all stern-faced, is holding me down, holding down my shoulders, and I'm laid out on a long chair and my mother, all teary-eyed, is resting a quiet hand on one of my pants legs, like there's nothing else to do. Why am I laid out in a long chair? Hey, I'm strapped down and some leering asshole labcoat don't-give-a-shit guy is talking bullshit to me. Just relax. This won't hurt a bit. This will be over before you know it, in a jiffy, and hey my head's shaved bare and then that son-of-a-bitch labcoat guy is leaning over me, close, breath smells like distilled potato and my father's hands go hard and I'm screaming bloody murder, screaming bloody murder, and I'm getting a Mot-sen/corband welded across the top of my skull! O god. O god. O god. O god. Why now the image, the image, tight-shot, the image of one red rose—one rose growing up out from a steaming pile of manure—a pile steaming and huge, steaming the stench, the vapors intoxicating and deliberatly wrapping sick fingers around and among, coiling wispy into a sick stranglehold among and around, the tender young blush of the petals? Why?

☆ ☆ ☆ ☆ ☆ ☆

Wing Commander Bacardi wakes in a sweat—an awful one. He's flat on his back on the bed. Tears, running straight down from the corners of his eyes, have pooled in his ears. He sits up, startled to be released from the digiland taste. "Holy fucking hell," he says. Then he asks into the darkness, "Enron?"

Across the room, a pair of hands hover in the corner, like they've been keeping a respectful distance. They now start to float toward the AirColonel. "Sir?" says a voice.

"What are you doing?"

One of the hands glides up to remove the camo mask, exposing Enron's face. "In case anyone came by I wanted to be ready, sir," he explains. "But I didn't want to be totosneak, either, so's you wouldn't know where I was when you came to."

Bacardi considers this answer, nods, then shakes his head. "How long have I been out?" he asks.

"Seventeen and a half minutes, sir."

"Holy shit." Bacardi swings his feet down onto the floor, having to clench his teeth with the effort. He realizes how quivery he feels all over. "And you say you *haven't* seen this? You've got no idea what's on it?"

"No, sir. They told me I could watch it if I really wanted, but there'd be no real point to it. Said I already know better than anybody what's there. Something about habitus, I think Mall called it. Some damn EVe bigword like that. You know what I mean."

Bacardi imagines the CorpTrooper means habitat—the lived environment. What in the end generates what you become, who you are. And here comes the rush of guilt: the usual vaguely feeling bad about it. What Terds always feel when they come into close contact with Servs. When you get up close enough to see the whites—really the yellows—of their eyes. Then, to Bacardi's great surprise, the ensuing indifference, resignation, fear, disgust, dread, distortion, exasperation, resentment, affront, hostility, or the outright hatred that normally follows an episode of Terd guilt over Serv life does *not* come. It simply does *not*. Nor, to Bacardi's greater surprise, come any of the pathetic self-justifications or self-exaltations that so easily pop into mind. In fact, nothing comes of that customary, comforting, ignorant bullshit. Instead he's left with only the shame.

Not the old kind that only paralyzes you, the passive shame that lets Terds turn their backs and walk away. Somehow, that comfort shame, that extraordinary degree of privilege and luxury, is no longer available to Bacardi. It's gone. It's absent. It's left him. Bacardi knows that's because he's *tasted* Parker reality—really tasted it. He really knows what it feels like, what it thinks like, and he's glad it's not him living it. *That's* what's killing him—as it should. This means at last he's got to do something about it.

"Enron," Bacardi has trouble locating the other man's eyes in the dim, "I know this won't mean shit or do shit about anything right now, but I need to tell you something."

"Sir?" Enron asks, breaking the AirColonel's long pause.

"I need to tell you, well, that I'm sorry. I know that doesn't half do it, but I honestly don't know how else to put it. I want to apologize for what's been done to you all your life, for what's happened to you." Bacardi drops his head. "Shit, for what I've let happen to you. No, check that. For what *I've* done to you."

Enron's not one to let emotion linger long in the air. "They told me you might say something like that, sir, on account of this taste being so hard. They left it up to me, of course, but recommended I say something back, like I appreciate,sincerely,the thought but, for the time being, can we just get on with the doing shit about it part?"

AirColonel Bacardi smiles and ejects the simudisc from behind his ear. He then makes a decision. "Absolutely we can, trooper." He holds the disc on the tip of his finger. "Here's what I can do. I can priority slice this simu into every Terdnet on base. I can guarantee every Terd will watch it through, from beginning to end, at least one time. *That* I can guarantee." Enron's face brightens at the plan. "What I *can't* guarantee, though, is how any of my people will react to it. That, I just don't know. I hope most of my pilots will react to it as I have. I think most of them will, but I can't be sure.

All I can do is give it a try."

Enron stops his nodding. "Hell, sir," he says, "you giving a shit enough to give it a try is sure as hell something new to me. I do thank you for it. I say let's fucking give it a whirl and see what comes of it."

"Okay, that's a firm, but I can tell you right now, Enron, there will be a few Terds on base, about eight Netsmen to be exact, who will *not* go for it. No matter what. No matter if their own mothers' lives were at stake. You know what I'm saying?"

"Yes, sir. Toto, sir."

"If that turns out to be the case, if my ArcAir people go for it but the Netsmen don't, which they won't, can I ask a favor of you, Enron?"

"You know you can, sir."

"Can you take care of my Net problem for me?"

Enron replaces his mask and pulls back on his gloves. Bacardi faces an empty room. "Just point me in the right direction, sir."

☆ ☆ ☆ ☆ ☆ ☆

Dawn very gradually reddens the edge of the eastern foothills. In the new-day twilight the air's been ripped clean by last night's storm. The weather invert is gone, leaving visibility infinite. From the rooftop of the 120-story Bank of TexArc, one of the few hightowers along the financial belt situated far enough back from the river to have been spared the flood, Dockers surveys what's left of his meg. Below him, in all directions, is smoldering ruin or washed-out tangle. The megmayor knows the dead-count will be Dmega. Unimaginable and inexcusable. Dockers and his megcouncilors know they're insanely lucky to be alive. The Captain of the Pyramid Guard had raced them out the North 8th Street threshold of the Pyramid, away from the invading Wobblies, as the stronghold fell. The topCrats had run south to the edge of the floodwaters where they turned right to hightail it down West Main and finally into the safety of the Bank tower at 1200 Main. None of them had ever run so fast in their lives, not by half. None of them had ever had to. Dockers was dripping sweat like a pig after one block, and two council members keeled over, apparently from cardiac arrest. First one, then a minute later the other, clutched his chest and went down like a sack of gravel. No one bothered to stop. Once at the bank, the megcouncil rode all the way to the top on the elevators and scurried out onto the roof, thinking ArcAir might be able to airevac, but the Crats wound up huddling together against the wind, the rain, and the lightning all night while, on the top two floors below them, what was left of the Pyramid Guard set up their last-ditch blockade. In all the confusion of the night, their group hadn't been discovered for several hours. Since that time, the Guard has been successful in fending off sporadic Wobbly attempts at coming up the stairwells. Now the topCrats—unaccustomedly tired, hungry, wet, and cold—anxiously scan the morning sky, hoping to spot air support from Mountain Home. The storm is long passed. Where the yank are they? If Air arrives, the Crats have a chance. Damn it, if Air arrives, Dockers might even be able to get his meg back.

From the sounds below, the Wobblies have been reenforced. They're making their final push. Suddenly several ragged men pop over the low wall rimming the roof. Somehow they clambered upward out of top-story windows. These men are frantic, scarecrow looking creatures. Like rodents. All twitchy with sunken eyes and scooped out cheeks. They level misters at the nest of Crats and gape, as if they've never seen anything like them before. The shitubers all wear glossy, rolldown covering over their heads. They look like deranged blowpops. The firefighting stops on the floors below. Long moments later the roofport slides open. An assembly of Wobblies steps through, but what immediately catches Dockers' attention are the obviously nonParker women among them. Taller, straighter, healthier, brighter-looking. In fact he looks for Brand, fearing many Terds have defected. That's when engine vibrations begin to agitate the air, followed by an all-but-inaudible whisper. Both Crats and Parkers lift their chins to the sky, which still appears empty. Some Crats point at the displacement, excited to be saved. FotoFighters. Dockers hopes for an entire damn wing of them. What he's been siging for all night. These attackcraft are coated with organic light-emitting diodes that compuproject background image to fly invisible, perfect for recon-and-raid. Dozens of them could be hovering over the meg and no one would be able to tell.

"Hah!" Dockers taunts the newly arrived group of Wobblies. "Now you parktrash are fucking deadmeat!"

☆ ☆ ☆ ☆ ☆ ☆

For some reason, whatever's flying ain't attacking. Oak feels a pressure on his chest he knows comes from sonic waves, but he doesn't see a damn thing hanging in the air over the roof. Maybe it's because he's about bug-eyed tired. They'd tracked these damned topCrats all over hell trying to find them, Mall all the time saying it's "imperative" that they do. First they'd gone through the whole damned Pyramid looking for them, then traipsed all around the downtown. Now they've got them cornered, Oak knows what *he'd* like to do.

Something big is landing on the roof, hovering, then touching down. Oak can feel the big weight settling in. Crats and Parkers back away. Splatter from the rain puddles geysers up from the engines no one can see. Then there's silence—shutdown. Oak doesn't know what to make of this, but he knows it beats getting damn strafed like they were out in the wilds. There's a long moment of nothing, then a head pokes up out of thin air, then a torso, then an entire man climbs down out of the fightercraft. Even to Oak he's obviously no ArcAir flyboy. Too tall. Too burly. Looks more like a groundsman. Hell, Oak grins to himself, finally recognizing the walk, the profile. *It's Uncle En. Jesus fuckmother Christ.* Enron heads straight for the EVe bitches, where they all fall into shaking hands and clapping shoulders. Mall even gives him an awkward-assed little hug. Well, Oak will just see about that. He walks right over to the fat topCrat who'd called out the shit about them being parktrash and gets up uncomfortable close in his face. He says plain and slow to the fat asshole: "Looks like you the cocksucking deadmeat this pretty morning fella."

With his nose wrinkled up, Dockers looks down at Oak, unable to conceal a sneer. "Congratulations, my little friend," he replies. "You'll get plenty of ransom for us, no doubt, but I'm afraid, in the long run, you'll never get away with all this." The Crat sweeps a grand arm to indicate the demolished BoiCity around them.

"*I* may be little," says Oak, "but," he makes a grand sweep of his own to indicate the armed Wobblies standing behind him, "*we* ain't." He pushes the Crat hard in the chest. "I ain't your friend neither, to none of you cock-sure sons-of-bitches." He half turns to look for a moment at Uncle Enron and the EVe bitches still happy about themselves. Mall catches his eye and takes a few worried steps toward him. Oak shakes his head at her, warning Mall to keep her distance, then adds, "And we Wobblies sure as hell know you bastards ain't ours." He faces the topCrat again. "Name's Oak," he tells him. "Oak Wat. I lead these boys." His tooth-baring grin reveals browned and pointed front teeth. "And I *shit* on your damned money." Nimbly Oak sticks the nozzle of his minimister up one of Dockers' nostrils and easy squeezes the trigger. He squeezes off another before the lard-ass hits the roof, just for good measure. Behind Oak, Mall's wails, "*No*!" and Enron jumps in to hold her back.

☆ ☆ ☆ ☆ ☆ ☆

Hundreds of thousands of Parkers continue to watch Oak over WobblyNet. They hurrah each time he has a megcouncilor, one by one, pitched over the side of the hightower. After that spectacle, Oak rises for the first time into the Eye of his new megPyramid. He takes his time looking around. Finally he plops down in Dockers' poshleather, ergonomic rollaround chair, nodding to himself how his ass never felt so at home. He leans back and bangs his muddy boots up on the desktop, knocking on the floor a massive black lapbook and two or three framed digifotos. Even better, he brings his boots back down, pulls them off, then swings his calloused and stinking feet back up to the desktop. Ah, goddamned heaven. He swivels around to gaze out the tall, triangular windows surrounding him. A sunny day is on the far side of all four. *Naught but big sky out there*, he thinks. *Naught but big sky*. "Now this is more like it," Oak declares out loud, to himself.

The night of 7 August 2084, the Siege of BoiCity. Planning and execution will be credited to Capitaine de Corvette Cardinal of the Fortification Guard, EVe Maneuvers. Her battleplan will come to be regarded as textbook megassault, the first and arguably the best—the much-studied Pyramid Scheme. Her victory will engender a military aphorism: "It takes a guard to beat a guard." No one will know whatever became of her.

The morning is 8 August 2084, the onset of the Great Crat Massacre. Oak Wat is not content tossing a handful off a smogscraper. Terds who come to Wobbly are spared, but Crats, the way Oak sees it, have naught to do but die. No two ways about it.

PART THREE

HOW *DO* YOU LIKE IT?

Lord of Misrule

8.8.84

Poursuivre?

countermeasures instant privy reply memorandum, secid #16471680-WAGS: By all means.

☆ ☆ ☆ ☆ ☆ ☆

12.8.84

Madam Administer and Sir Headminister:

Salutations.

I memo you now, quite officially you understand, from the newly christened meg of 'OakCity' which, as all the world should know, is the designated seat of government, this minute constituted and proclaimed, of the sovereign state of 'Wobbly'. Ours is virtually a diplomatic correspondence.

I tease you not.

The ticker tape—in truth, thousands upon thousands of unraveled spools of Crat loo tissue, a luxury item not imagined, experienced, nor, I suspect, comprehended by Servs for its actual use—yet clogs 'Grand Oak Boulevard', formerly West State Street, as a result of the magnificent inauguration procession just concluded. The Parker millions lined the way to cheer their Great Man as he glided by, waving and draped in dignified vestments, perched alone some seven or eight meters high atop one of the elephantine and warlike TexArc motortransports. Behind him, atop their own monster trucks, came his immediate cortège, a gang of hearty renegades from the rugged hills. All of them dressed the part of the guerrilla darlings, dashing yet dangerous. After them was column after column of the freshly commissioned 'Oak Guards' on the march, their misters prominent and held high. One poor Guardsman, caught up in the ebullience of the celebration, discharged his weapon into the air. The thousands of flesh wounds resulting from the minuscule lead shot falling back down to earth cost the entire Guard Corps the embarrassment of having to set their safeties on lock.

So much for martial display.

Once at the northeast steps of the Pyramid—renamed 'The Gold Butte'—again, not kidding—the Great Man delivered, over WobblyNet, a gad-about oration a full hour in duration in which he promised his 'fellow Parkers' the moon and the stars. He then had himself crowned 'Grand Pooh-Bah of Wobbly'.

I wish I were joking.

I feel, for my part in these occurrences, a perfect Victor Frankenstein, only I have not abandoned my plebeian creation. I fear he has abandoned me. What I describe above might pass for amusing were it not following four days of horrific slaughter inaugurating what promises to be one of the most disastrous regimes in human history. A mere tens of thousands of Terds survived that first night in the southdistrict. Cardinal and our new ArcAir allies now have them under protection. As for Crats, I doubt a single one of any age has emerged alive, and we were powerless to prevent any of this carnage. To my surprise, both Enron and the Terd commander of Mountain Home were philosophical about the killing frenzy perpetrated by the Parkers, commenting only: 'I can't say as I blame them'. The cruelty has been quite unimaginable. Random, wayard Crat killings marked the night of and morning after the siege. For the day or two after that, choreographed executions of topCrats fed continually over WobblyNet. Most of these were done by the now infamous minimister nose trick. When these individual spectacles grew tiresome, whole Crat clusters were bound, weighted, and catapulted into the middle of the still inundated Boise River. Very popular 'Crat shoots' were organized and held. The more ancient customs of lynching, tarring-and-feathering, riding-the-rail, dunking, and stoning were reinstated as well as jamboree centerpieces to massive revels. It has all been appalling. I am relieved to report, however, that while the rapegangs held their sway for a short time after the battle, some mysterious and well-streamed vigilante action by our crew quickly made it apparent that a few moments of vicious lust visited upon women of any class are not worth the risk of the violent amputation of one's 'bangbone'. A compelling visual statement. We unhappy few refuse to be entirely powerless.

When Crats became scarce and hangovers perennial, our Grand Pooh-Bah wisely turned public attention to the foundation of the new Parker state. Efforts in this project exemplify form over function. Appointed as 'Wrangle Minister', for example, is Jiplap Ball, my erstwhile attempted ravager. He is possibly the most gun-loving and dim-witted thug among this race of mainly gun-loving and dim-witted thugs. 'Minister Jip', as he's now known, spends most of his day careening about the ruined streets of OakCity in a large-wheeled, insect-like military vehicle, enjoying explaining his activities to the WobblyNet digicameras as 'circling the wagons'. He sports a pair of vintage, pearl-handled 'six-shooters' on his hips, and seems to be anticipating some manner of dragoon attack.

The position of 'Grub Minister'—logistics, I suppose, and possibly transportation—has been bestowed upon Happymeal Straw, a cunning former preowned motorvehic salesrep. One does have to hand it to 'Minister Hap'—he's got a knack for organization and a keen eye for the good deal. With lightning speed he has consolidated all foodstuffs and commodity items within the former Gater district and is doling them out, shall I say, advantageously. He has headquartered himself in the largest and most opulent of the former Cratmanors in the northdistrict. Minister Hap has taken up, among other habits perhaps intended to help him better understand his new duties, the sipping of old France cognac and the puffing of fine, hand-rolled Israeli cigars. It seems safe to surmise, that not only does our Grand Pooh-Bah appreciate the manipulation of pageantry, but the utility of nepotism does not escape him, either. Behold the Crat within.

The practical view tells us this nascent Wobbly state is doomed. Frankly, we're baffled by TexArc's lack of response to our little coup d'état. What on earth can they be waiting for? True, the finessing away of Terds to our cause at Mountain Home ArcAir Base certainly must give them pause, one hopes even considerable fright. ArcAir cover not only allowed Cardinal's siege plan to execute but protects, at least somewhat, our vulnerable meg, now. Separating the plutocracy from its technocracy is without doubt a paxrevolutionary step. Yet all of us know TexArc cannot and will not, for very much longer, hold off, and that its eventual response will be decimating. How can they allow anything else?

Nonetheless, we will continue to prod.

My Signification partnership with the TexArc Terd, Doctor Brand, has proven to be invaluable. Aside from her eccentricities of personal style, we are like blood sisters—doppelgängers. We share likes, approaches, ways of reasoning, and feelings about the world. Once Brand saw the true material and cultural plight of the Servs, she embraced alterity without reserve. Based on her own experience of conversion, we two devised the digiland taste that was so effective at Mountain Home. It is a deliberate reversal of her previous proCorpfeud spots within the TexArc Simulacrum. Its impact is predicated on the theory that an average TexArcan Terd is so sheltered from the dirty facts of the Corpfeudian economic matrix, the shock of the simustim exerience of actual life at the bottom of the heap—what that *feels* like, what that *smells* and *tastes* like—will knock all absurd cultural myths out of her/him. As we saw with ArcAir Terds, the success rate of our taste is little short of phenomenal. All but a handful of those Terds came over to the Wobbly cause. The same success rate was repeated two days ago when we managed to slice our spot into the local meg Terdnet. The vast majority of BoiCity—pardon me, of OakCity Terds elected to remain, in spite of the recent southdistrict riots. The insane success of our spot is due in large part to the supercharged delivery of its signification. A 'taste' in TexArc stimulates well beyond normal feed. Receptors among TexArcans, whether implants or pullons, routinely trigger actual physical sensation. In the case of a taste, intense emotion can be targeted and excited as well. Brand tells me tastes are reserved for quite special announcements in TexArc, usually spots of a political purpose. Servs receive the great majority of them, being hardwired, as it were, for such a feed. Our using the technique on Terds, I take it, is slightly against convention and not entirely cricket. Brand warns me that tiptop Crats will not be pleased to have one of their favorite tricks turned against them. She has taken an awful personal risk in divulging to Sinalco and me how to induce taste over ArcNet. So be it. Our message needs this medium. Terd clutter is otherwise too dense, too self-gratifying, too complacent to crack. By the way, those few Terds in the former BoiCity who did not embrace Wobbly were escorted, at the ArcAir base commander's insistence, to safety under military protection and allowed to leave the meg. This, Cardinal, Pernod, and Migros accomplished, with air support. We managed to convince his Grand Pooh-Bahness that live Terd word-of-mouth of his glorious Wobbly victory will make the Crats think twice about a counterstrike. Truthfully, it's likely to have the opposite effect.

Nonetheless, we will continue to prod.

We are in the process of attempting to slice our digiland spot into the Terdnets of other IMS megs. We may even manage to disseminate the spot more widely, that is, outside of our immediate Corpent. Brand tells us the Pacific Coast is an especially rich target audience for our communiqué.

She and Sinalco have worked hard on the tech side of such sophisticated slicing. Given that Brand represents the nearest thing to the great puppet master of the Simulacrum, she and Sinalco together stand the best chance of negotiating successfully the onion maze temperal flow of ArcNet. Already, Sinalco is confident she has captured full control of the local grid, converting it wholly to WobblyNet. Along with Brand's added knowledge of the ArcNet deepsystem, those two have spawned freaks, as I understand it, capable of freaking the network freaks, to use teek jargon. That means that we have sliced our simustim taste into several IMS megs and we believe, into some random and partial Terdnets on the western coast as well. I anticipate these to be Pyrrhic victories, however. As Sinalco puts it, this latest slice of ours is rather like poking a stick up the bum of a frothing bull. It's sure to turn around and charge. As I see it, our unlikely series of successes here in TexArc have landed us betwixt a hard place and a rock. The Crats will retaliate, and we haven't the adequate military means to protect ourselves. Oak Wat controls the mob, and I cannot guarantee he will be persuaded in any way to follow the most alteritive course of action.

Nonetheless, we will continue to prod.

Administer Movënpick and Headminister Natwest, I appreciate your kind words of encouragement, that our insurrectionist endeavors within TexArc are having, from your vantage point in EVe, a palpably positive result. It's good to know their immediate forces have drawn back. I must say, though, from our vantage point in OakCity, we cannot help but feel something terrible and ugly has been released by our actions, something we never foresaw nor intended to set loose. I read apprehension and futility in the face of Cardinal, two emotions I never expected to see there. Even Sinalco strikes me as atypically sad. I don't know where this will end, but I predict with confidence that it will end unhappily.

Sorry to have become such a perfect misery guts. I feel like poor Harrods. To make amends, I close with a few lighter observations.

I have become, once again, addicted to real coffee. Sinalco informs me that in the many galleys of the Gold Butte she has stumbled upon a vast quantity of the real item. She insists on brewing, just for me, several cups of it a day. Evidently, like the bourgeois Victor, I am most at peace when I have been restored to my creature comforts and the peasants are dancing. Shame on me, but the coffee does help me stay focused on preventing my Wobbly monster from getting farther out of hand. With reference to the sexual circus taking place around me, Enron has become convinced that Sinalco is some manner of devil-woman and has ceased his carnal exchanges with her—perhaps a contributor to her sadness. Cardinal, of course, is encouraged by this development, although the addition of Brand, whose appetites seem omnivorous, to the erogenous landscape is of new concern to everyone. To everyone save me, that is to say. I carry on as a committed abstainant. My months in TexArc confirm me in my prior beliefs that coitus is delirium and procreation is dementia.

On that bright note, my fellow EVens, adieu.

☆ ☆ ☆ ☆ ☆ ☆

Naked she lay, clasped in Oak's longing arms.

Wait...what...how?

Oak filled with love, and she all over charms.

O god.

Both equally inspired with eager fire, melting through kindness, flaming in desire.

Where?

A gossamer breeze stirs the wind chimes outside the rococo french windows, their narrow, double doors slightly ajar. Somewhere out in the garden a nightingale chirrs, doleful, sensuous. One plush, velvety pillow bolsters her trim fundament and narrow hips, occasioning her fur patch to ride high. Hovering over her, half-seen in the moonlit darkness, is Oak—her lover.

Perfect white teeth glisten in his boyish grin. Under an open sark, his powerful chest and midriff ripple with taut muscle. Oak. Her secret passion. Oak. Her paramour denied too long. Oak. Her savior swain.

Hold on now.

Kisses no longer sate their want. She wills him farther, with keen, liquid eyes beseeching him to be bold. Coarse but gentle hands come beneath her flimsy chemise. Cunning fingertips tease skyward the twin nipples crowning her pert hooters. Within her panting bosom, her heart beats madly, fiercely, like that of a fearful hummingbird. Oak's knees insinuate themselves between her own, asking, yet also insisting, beginning faintly to pry. Her body now reveals her soul! Her token resistance masks so feebly the primal hunger. Her desire drenches her as an aboriginal force more potent and briny than ocean current. Have me, speak her eyes, her yielding thighs. My darling, have me! Have me deep! Have me hard! Have me again and again! O have me, have me!

O crikey...this is bloody rubbish.

The rigid tip of his mammoth mantool tarries at her balmy brinks of bliss. Just whetted! Just moistened! Her legs discern his question before her head or her heart, and, without forethought, they swing open! Her heels dig into the small of Oak's sturdy back—and then they pull! For all they are worth—they pull! Tremor racks the two entwining forms. Yang and yin. Rapture uncoiled. Ecstasy unfurled. Mighty Oak is throwing the all-dissolving thunderbolt below!

☆ ☆ ☆ ☆ ☆ ☆

Mall jolts stark upright on her cot. She's mucky with tepid sweat. Queasy in her lower region. Feeling impaled. Her temples ache dreadfully.

Her temples.

She reaches up to find the apparatus stretched across the top of her head. She pulls it off and brings it before her eyes, having to twist first to switch on a light. She recognizes a mot-sen/corband. She knew one would be there, slipped atop her head while she slept. Bloody fucking hell.

Bloody fucking Oak.

Mall switches off the light. Outside her window wall, the perfectly black sky reappears, crowded with stars. The meg is exercising blackout, as a precaution. It can't hurt. She hurries out of her southface flat and, still barefoot, pads down the long Pyramid—Gold bloody Butte—corridors towards the core. She barks at the locator to pinpoint the Grand bleeding Pooh-Bah. He's not in his Eye, she's informed. Then where the bloody hell is he? His Greatness currently is at rest in his Personal Penthouse and doesn't wish to be disturbed. Mall tells the locator to piss off.

The EVens understand the interior workings of the Pyramid far better than do the Parkers. Mall monkeys with idcode to access several small offpassages, making her way around the ridiculous Oak Guard. She enters the former executive suite from a side door. The space is mid core, expansive, palatial in decor—and saturated now with the shit smell of Oak. Mall finds him seemingly asleep, naked and dwarfed on the huge triangular bed. His eyeballs are rolled back into his head and twitching under lightly closed eyelids. His little wanker, gnarly and slender, reminding Mall of an organically grown carrot, is as stiff as it gets. Having it off, are we? She prods the pointed tip of the serrated killknife she's clutched in her hand the whole way there against his taut scrotum. Now Oak is the one jolted awake, his feedtube, though topped, emitting one of those foul, involuntary bellyfarts.

"Fancy some exceedingly fresh Reagan Mountain oysters, darling?" she asks him, positioning the knife to slice.

Oak's up on his elbows trying to back his nutsack away from the jagged edge, but Mall won't let him.

"Ah, hell," he tries to muster the tone of a man having given his sweetheart a box of chocolates, "I knew you wouldn't like it."

Mall escalates the edge's pressure. "Rape, vir or otherwise, isn't my cup of tea."

"It ain't rape," Oak defends himself. "I let you do all the imagesensing, didn't I? That was your depict. I just tossed in a notion of my own now and again."

"Like a viryank the size of pine timber?"

She uses the flat of her knife now to spatula up for inspection his limp little mantool, all its meager glory long since fled. The dab of flesh lolls about pathetically, like a kipper.

"I should of known you was off feed," he leers at her. "All the gayboy frills all of a sudden was gone and you was a real wildcat."

The killknife is at Oak's throat. Mall begins to draw its ragged edge across the knob of the Adam's apple, initiating a small cut, but with her other hand, holds up the motor-sensory cortex band instead. "This is the real rape," she jeers at him, shouting and shaking the pullon in his face. "Fuck your virsex and your virbods and your virslits, you little shit of a man! This is the real fucking rape!"

Oak has yet to flinch at the slash to his throat. A glob of blood trickles down across the blade of her knife. Free of the glassy, his eyes stare back as hard as hers.

"Don't I know it," he hiss-whispers.

Mall's up and walking fast toward the far wall, well away from the absurd triangle bed. She stops and throws back her head in frustration. Over her is the suite's skyceiling, domed concave. The visual it projects feeds live from the semispherical 360 horizon lens fixed at the apex of the Pyramid. From her time in the wilderness area, Mall's become quite accustomed to the constellation patterns of this hemisphere. She spots her favorite: Orion. What she's never got used to are the gigantic space billboards constantly orbiting by. No less than five of them glide overhead at the moment. The one that finagles her momentary attention is, of all things, for penis enlargement. *ICBC®. InterContinental Ballistic Cock*, quite an image to behold sailing through the firmament.

“You never do ask about the early days.” Oak’s trying to sound the hurt lover. “Out against Sawtooth Fluid.”

Mall won’t play along.

“They gutted us, Mall. Hung us up by the feet and split us clean wide. Then left the carcass for the bears. Hydrobiz is one of them free to do whatever it takes. Just keep the water coming no matter what.”

Mall should start her solidarity lecture, but can’t bring herself to it again. It seems hopeless.

“And that trick with a minimister up the schnoz? Hell, you think I come up with that, Mall? Yank, no. I saw that done near every damn afternoon over Sawtooth’s bizalign. During their lunch twohour the topexecs liked to pop off five, six known Wobblies at a go. They’d leave them to bleed out the nose on the pumpstation floor, you know what I mean, as warnings for nobody more to go union. You got no idea what went on in them early days, Mall. No idea in hell.”

“No,” Mall finally has to admit, sighing, “I suppose I don’t.”

Oak hops off the bed and throws on a thick blue terrycloth bathrobe with a circlestar insignia over the breast pocket. The robe is three times too big for him. Not bothering to tie it closed, Oak stalks to the wetbar opposite the room from Mall and grabs the first bottle of something brown. He pulls a long swig or two.

“Look, Mall, I just come to lead the Wobblies ’cause I was too ornery for Sawtooth to catch or kill,” Oak confesses. “For some reason, I answered Uncle’s call early and wasn’t scared to do unto them bastards just what the hell they was doing unto us. That and more. Simple as that.” Oak switches to a bottle of something clear. “Did Uncle Enron tell you I washed out of CorpTroop basic way back before all this Wobbly biz got started? Normal washout means you get killed training to do their shitwork.

But me, well, I stuck a knife—and one a damn sight bigger than that little toadsticker you was fixing to use on me tonight—in the belly of a Netsman Terd son-of-a-bitch because I got simple sick and tired of him hollering and kicking at me. Do you know what *that's* like? No? I didn't think you did. I stuck him when we was on the ground, out remote on maneuvers. Somewhere so's I could skip away. You see, Mall, I ain't smart, but I ain't stupid. Took me five weeks to track back home, but I did it and I hid myself good in the parks ever since. Not many Parkers alive that can claim all that." Oak settles on a smoky indigo bottle with the sweet liquid. His favorite fluid, even if it hasn't got quite the punch of the others. "That's all the reasons I can think of that I come to be head man. I'll do the shit every other guy wants to do but's too afraid to do. That's why I'm Grand Pooh-Bah. I don't fool myself thinking I'm the smartest guy or the best guy. Hell, all them boys got themselves killed a long way back. I'm just the meanest son-of-a-bitch guy, Mall. That's all I got on offer. And for richer or for poorer, that just seems to be working out for me so far."

Mall collapses into a round and downy womb chair, puts one of its plump cushions on her stomach, and curls herself around it. They've begun the conversation she's not wanted to have. "Your being an ornery son-of-a-bitch, no question, has served you extraordinarily well up to this point, Oak. To be perfectly truthful with you, you've survived what I can't even imagine. The parks themselves are an awful place. From what I can gather, the TexArc jobsite is a hundredfold more cruel. But..." she's come to that aspect of the conversation that strikes her as preposterous, yet Mall knows no way around it, "perhaps you should consider changing your tack. What brought you to the Pyramid might not be the best thing for carrying you farther. Can you see what I'm suggesting?"

"Yep," Oak says and, to her surprise, Mall believes him. "Like I said, I ain't stupid. But I don't know as I'm smart enough, either, to know how or what I ought to swap to. You get *my* meaning?" Mall nods. "You got to understand how Dmega mindfuck all this shit is for Parkers. Uncle Wobbly's in our heads saying all he was saying was yub whack plenty for us. Then you pack of dykebitch ragheads show up claiming Uncle ain't real and you been making him up and feeding him to us from outland. That right there will mess with your head." Mall scowls at Oak, he knows for his use of the word *dykebitch*. *What's she want?* He reminds her how she's got him not saying *slit* no more. "Now on top, we got CorpTroops and Terds coming over to our side. That just ain't natural."

"What can possibly be upsetting about CorpTroops turning Wobbly? They're Parkers, too, after all."

"Like hell they are. Mil-ed makes them toto companyman, and snooty to go along with it. Eating real vit gets them damn big. The drill they do is nothing but gungho twentyfourseven. Shit, you get that damn buff and jingofrenzy about things and you ain't real Parker no more. Not for a fact. Yanking CorpTroops even get their feedtube hid good and sealed off tight. No more bellyfarts for them or glops of flying McSlurry. Nothing like *that* for making you feel better than everybody else."

Mall hadn't taken into account how brutal military indoctrination might even be seen as an educational advantage, a mark dividing Servs from a common brutal origin. Oak is telling her that CorpTroops forget where they come from. They commit the cardinal sin of class pride. But for those imagining they're climbing the ladder, wouldn't the parks be the first thing you'd want to forget? "CorpTroops are being horribly manipulated, Oak. You've seen that firsthand for yourself. I'm sure they mean no slight to their fellow Parkers."

"Oh no?" Oak looks at Mall pointedly. "That why they get all the damn gals?"

Mall holds up the killknife. "If you're trying to paint yourself the spurned lover in this scenario, you shit, you can forget it."

Oak changes the tune of his complaint.

"And now we got Terds telling us they're all for us, now, and on our side. That's ten kinds of horseshit. That goddamned TerdTech galpal of yours throws out words even bigger than you, and smears on all that dark-glo bodypaint. What the yank we supposed to make of that other than she's useless? Her hogwash ain't for shit, and you know it. And these Terd flyboys overhead now is damn nice, no mistake, but they'll cut and run first sign of real trouble. Terds always do."

"Those ArcAirmen have given up everything for the Wobbly cause—absolutely everything. As has Brand. As has every Terd in BoiCity who decided to stay on. Can't you appreciate the enormity of their sacrifice? Their new commitment to solidarity?"

"Don't you be painting sweet pictures for me, Mall. Them Terds have come over Wobbly because you pulled your mindfuck on them, just like you did on us with your fancy feeds. That's the only reason them Terds turned. You think they give a rat's ass about us? About Parkers? You think they're all itching to embrace their Serv brothers? That's slogan shit, Mall. That shit ain't for real."

"Well, in any event, Oak, we'll see, won't we? No matter what else happens, we know their dedication to the Wobbly cause soon will be put to the test." She speaks pointedly, now. "*Everyone's* dedication to the Wobbly cause soon will be. *Won't* it?"

Oak shakes his head.

"Mall, Terds and Servs jobbing together is as crazy as Crats starting to pitch in with us, to boot. They live *inside*, Mall. We live *outside*. What more you got to know?"

"Is that why you can feel justified in slaughtering tens of thousands of them?"

"*After* I don't know how many hundreds of years of them killing us every fucking whichway they can think of, Mall? Is that part of your question you're leaving out? Starving, outbreak bug, CorpTrooping, heat, storm, thirst, workcred, crewterm? You name it, Mall, and they been killing us with it. Or they sit by on their fat asses and let it damn happen. Terds and Crats don't give two shits about Servs, and they never will because they never have. How do you expect me to cred any of this solidarity talk, Mall? Huh? How you expect me to buy into uppers holding out a helping hand to the downers?"

"All right. Sod it," Mall says angrily. She'll step up to her lectern, but not before adequate preparations. "You got any bleeding coffee around here?"

Oak pokes at the wetbar panelboard a half dozen times. Finally he gets some of Sinalco's special brew sent up to the suite. He carries the steaming, potbellied mug of it across the room to Mall, bringing his indigo bottle with him. Mindful of the killknife Mall has, Oak stretches to hand her the coffee. The drizzle of blood tracking down his throat is nearly dried.

"You drink too much of that shit," Oak offers an impression.

"And what's that to you?"

"Nothing. Except it smells like old motoroil, is all."

"You are an unsophisticated lout, remember? You have no refined tastes."

"Oh, yeah. That's damn doublego for me." He takes a gulp from his bottle then doubles his chin against his chest, getting a look down at the end of his feedtube. "I don't suppose I even got that much taste in my mouth." Without irony, Oak pours some of the purplish fluid into the opening of his tube, spilling a good bit of it that runs down over his belly, leaving a stain.

Mall guesses it's a bottle of Pacific Coast burgundy Oak's got his hands on, probably a very expensive one from a very good year. But she's not about to start feeling any pity for this wee bastard. Oak's thoroughly capable of putting on the charm when need be. In a voice indicating she's not falling for it, Mall begins, "Look here, Oak..."

Oak holds up his hand. "No need to teach. I got the bigpic pretty good.

Before you come along, I paid close mind to Uncle Wobbly, believe it or not. That means I already paid close mind to you." Mall remains skeptical. "I loved that old fart, Mall. Only guy I seen ever talked straight and not for his own good. It pissed me off when you come along and told me he's you, that Uncle's just vir. That was like somebody in clan died." He tosses the wine bottle far across the suite. "So I got a good idea of what you want to say. I know what Uncle would school me on right now."

"Do you? And what would that be?"

"He'd tell me that alterity comes from historical people before us hunting after fraternity, then back before that, after equality. Then before that, liberty. Then back way off they was looking for eternity. Now, I don't give a shit for the eternity part, because it sounds like bullshit, but them other things is right and good. People just hunting after a way to live that's fair and that don't eat up the world. Uncle would tell me too how it's the love of *stuff* that twists us up so bad, that we got to let go of the need for greed biz."

"Oh, really now? Uncle Wobbly would tell you all that?" Mall's impressed. Oak *has* been listening. "Is that all?"

"Hell, you know good and well that ain't near half of it, Mall. Uncle Wobbly could talk your ear off about all that framework and foundation shit. Most tangled damn fix I ever run across. But for our mess right this minute, I know he'd be warning me to watch out for property privilege, hiding the fact how us working Parkers get all the time fucked over. Bad enough the Gaters own every scrap of what it takes to make shit, but them owning our work, too, breaks the mule's back. Ain't no Parker not up to his eyeballs in the credhole—and credgrades is always climbing sky-higher. Most the time a guy's working off what he owes and not working on what *he's* owed. Then they corvée our butts whenever and wherever in hell they please, mainly for us to get ourselves CorpTroop kia fighting over shit we don't even understand. Killing poor ragheads even worse off than us. Uncle would ask me why should I give a shit if some country's getting uppity with the Crats when I can't even raise my own kids decent? Last he'd kick at demesne. Ask me if I'd noticed how, when Gaters shit in their own nest and need it cleaned up, they get a Parker to shovel shit for free. How's a man ever to earn a damn ArcDime around here? Yes sir, I can hear old Uncle Wobbly barking it out right now. 'Boys!' he'd be hollering. 'Watch them tricky sons-of-bitches! Watch 'em like a damn hawk! They'll skin you alive without you ever knowing it!' His cheeks'd be redder than damn beets, too."

Mall's never heard Oak hold forth like this. She had no idea he could. "So what are you really saying, Oak? What is it, exactly, that we're talking about here?"

"About damn cocksucking Corpfeud, of course. What the hell else is there to talk about, Mall? Them yankers is pushing us backwards, stopping our march. It's got so bad we got to fight our way back forwards a good chunk just so's we can start moving ahead again."

Bloody unbelievable. And bloody brilliant. "How do you know this, Oak? How do you know about Corpfeud?"

"I been listening to the shit on all the megmayor's talkboxes. I heared the word. Heared it being talked about. I put one and one together."

"I'm...stunned, Oak." Mall adds, she hopes quickly enough, "And I'm sorry I'm stunned."

"What you think I'm doing all day up in the Eye? Whacking it?"

"Well..."

"All right, all right. I know Parkers is all supposed to be miserable dumbshits and for the most part we are. But we been feeling this shit direct on our backs our whole lives, Mall. And that right there, I figure, makes for some kind of smart. It ain't your kind of study smart. I know that. But I figure it's some kind of smart."

Mall's intrigued. In EVe they never carried out the extensive kind of market research Brand conducts in TexArc. Signification is considered a craft and an art. The pseudo-science of focus groups only nullifies that.

Mall would conceptualize and create an advocacy project, then put it out there for real to see how it fared in the culture. She never hedged her bets with audience testing. Authentic and terrifying trial and error, when something really is at stake, is the way to hone your advocation and to grow your vision. Not shrink it. But the opportunity to put Oak to the test, to discover precisely what and how much vital information from her Wobbly project actually had managed to slip through the clutter proves too tempting for her to resist. Mall begins asking him a series of alterity questions. How is it that the Crats are stopping our march? How are they grinding historical materialism to a halt? By keeping Parkers brainslow and by keeping Parkers apart is Oak's reply. Smart folks working together get shit done. Stop that, and you stop the march. How do Crats keep Parkers brainslow? Oak shoots back: how in hell Crats *don't*? No ed but mil-ed and job-ed. No readrite. No rithmetic. No nothing. When Parkers ain't jobbing or beerbent—or both—they're glassy with the all4s or jacking it to a virho. People can't get much more brainslow than that. Mall admits these are all fine points, but asks how do Crats keep Parkers apart? There are millions of them packed together into every meg. What can he possibly mean by Parkers being kept apart?

Oak shakes his head as if *she's* brainslow. "First off, Parkers are all the time inside their own heads, glued to the damned all4s. The damned glassy, don't you know. Next up, Parkers get fed pure shit over them all4s, just like they get slurried pure shit at the Arcs. Nothing but. They end up abiding by the what-is of the yub, the pure shit TexArc way. Parkers buy into the me-first. They trust their car to the man who wears the star—even if they can't afford to own a yanksucking car. They won't trust one another. But Parkers can't know no better because they're brought up knowing nothing else. And last thing, Crats got things set out so that Parkers never do get half a chance to put their heads together. They're too busy with the whole mad-ass scramble just to stay alive. Hell, the whole way a meg works fucks a Parker up."

"How do you mean that, Oak? *Specifically*. About the meg." Mall's certainly hard pressed to believe what she's hearing. Is this Parker *aware* that TexArc maneuvers and foils technological development so it won't lead to social revolution? Is Oak claiming he's actually *seeing* this manipulation?

"Well, if you think on it, the whole meg is a closed biz." Oak's taken up some of the mannerisms of pontification: stroking his chin, wagging his finger. He's enjoying being listened to. "Everything you really need going on is already going on. What food there is. The shit to credspend on. All the basics is done right here. You know what I mean. So we don't need no other meg to get along. Not at least that I ever seen." A thought dawns on him. "Hell, I ain't even ever *been* to no other meg, don't know no one else who ever has, and, come to think of it, I ain't never seen a Parker from no other meg walking the streets around here. That just don't happen."

"Why not do you suppose?"

"To stop the moveon—make things stay just the way they is—forever. Meantime Gaters can do whatever they like to Parkers. Jump the rents, cramp the pay, fake up fees, pinch in or dish out more labor. And where the hell else Parkers gonna go? What the hell else Parkers gonna do? Nowhere and nothing, that's what."

"It's the development of underdevelopment," Mall contextualizes the theory. "Kill the productive forces, and you thwart social development."

"Whatever you say, Mall. You're sounding all dykebitchy now."

Mall tells him to sod off. She could go on and on. Indentured servitude blunts productive forces. Labor market competition is nonexistant. Innovation due to competition is rendered unnecessary. Subsistence arrangement heightens dependence on the neofeudal status quo. Backward and upward.

"Of course," Oak concludes, "I guess if a man really wants to break free of his work being swallowed up by credspending, he can always ply his one piece of Corpfeud leeway. He can lie down and go deadcount."

"Parkers certainly are free to die within a meg," Mall allows, "any time you like."

"Damn straight we are. But now we aim to be free to live. And I do thank you for that, Mall. Until Uncle come along I never had a way to think or talk about any of this. All I could do was act up. Throw rocks at GaterPol as a kid. Right from the start, tell the bossman to shove it. Get bent on Oly and beat the ass of some guy bad in a saloon. Lame-ass shit that just got my own ass in dutch. But hell, I didn't know what in the hell else to do."

Mall sets down her coffee mug on the lush, trueblue carpeting. She leans forward to speak to Oak, feeling quite satisfied with herself. "So slaughtering half the population of the Gater district represents the ultimate in lame-ass acting up, right? Tossing people off of buildings and lodging tiny pellet guns up their noses are the actions of an obtuse thug, correct? Not that of a true Wobbly? You are prepared, now, to follow a more knowing political strategy that you've adopted as a result of the schooling you've received from Uncle Wobbly? Yes, Oak? That *is* what you're telling me. Yes?"

It takes a moment for Oak to make his way through all the hopeful rhetorical questions Mall has posed to him. When he does, he answers simply. "Nope."

"What?"

"I already am following a more knowing political strategy. One you and Uncle showed me."

"Oak, when have Uncle Wobbly or I *ever* said anything about going out and killing masses of people?"

"'Only the oppressed can free themselves,'" Oak quotes back to her.

"What?" Mall feels her panic as sudden tingling in her fingertips and toes. "*Not* by killing innocent people."

"Ain't a Gater on earth that's innocent."

Oh bugger.

"Look, the Crats are shit, yeah, but the Terds, more or less, are just following along. They don't really formulate the workings of Corpfeud. Most of them don't even understand exactly how TexArc functions. Believe it or not, for all their techwhiz, and maybe a little because of it, Terds live sheltered and ignorant lives. That's just how they're raised. That's just what they've been fed by the ArcNet drone. You've got to believe me, Oak. Terds are little different from Parkers. They have little more choice in the matter than you do."

"That's Terdtalk, Mall. And horseshit. And you know better. We all got a choice in the matter. That's the whole damn Wobbly point. We all just got to wake up to it and step up to it. And that's just what in the hell I'm trying to do. Fact of the matter is, Mall, Terds ride on Parker backs same as Crats do. Terds live a fine life off of us, just like Crats do. So what's the goddamn difference between them, Mall? What? They're all just damned Gaters."

Oak's spot on, of course. He's marked his Uncle well. But for paxrevolution to evolve, bringing with it, eventually, true alterity, Mall must forge a Terd-Parker alliance in TexArc. That's vital for paxrevolution to work. She tries to explain the transition to Oak. Mind workers and body workers must unite in their majority to overthrow the tyranny of the minority—the rich money panderers. Without the greater solidarity between educated and labor, one gets only bloodbath, such as witnessed in BoiCity. And history shows that bloodbath results in chaos, and that chaos, counterproductively, favors the standing orthodoxy—that is, the *plutocratic* state. Chaos colors the mammonistic status quo as the safe, sane, familiar way to preserve "order." But *Crat* order—the TexArcan bottomline, jingofrenzy, the corpatriotic mindfuck, the sacred so-called freemarket—is just what Oak battles against. It's exactly that from which Parkers are struggling to break loose. Therefore, Parkers have no choice but to ally with Terds, to try to occasion paxrevolution. Without such a union of interests, Wobbly will lead nowhere.

In her heart, Mall always has suspected TexArc to be too far gone, too class-divided, to be capable of maturing into alterity. Old Europe had managed it because people there never slippery-sloped irretrievably into the selfoblige. Not so with Old Lower North America. People there likely doomed themselves a century ago. Rescuing themselves, now, is far, far too late. Because Mall never imagined she could bring matters this far in TexArc, to the point of paxrevolution, she never bothered to lay the proper groundwork for it, particularly not in her Wobbly advocacy to Parkers. She'd viewed her purpose as primarily agitation—not deep education. Now she sees she must do her best, and instantly, to correct her miscalculation. However, just as she'd had no faith in TexArc's redeemability, she holds little hope for changing Oak's mind about Terds. But she will try.

"Oak," Mall pleads, "don't reject the Terds. Don't reject Brand. They and she can be of tremendous help to you in what you're trying to do. They could make all the difference in the world when opposing the Crats."

"I'll keep that beast in view, Mall. I know Uncle would be preaching fellowshipride at me about now too—that being the Wobbly way."

"That's right, Oak. I would. I am now. We're all in this together."

"The way I see it is, though, here's where the rubber of your fancy notions hits the hard of the road. If only us oppressed can free ourselves, well, I don't see that leaving a lot of room for Terds to come along."

"But Terds *are* oppressed in a way, Oak, just like Parkers are. They may not be beaten down and starved, but they're bamboozled and misled. They're mindfucked into becoming companyman. Just like you said Parkers are when they get turned into CorpTroops. But look how Enron came out of that. And look at how all the Mountain Home Terds came right over to us. Good god, that's fellowshipride at work right there, Oak. I promise you, Terds feel awful about what's been going on, about what's been happening to you Parkers. *They* want paxrevolution, I can assure you."

"Terds want it because you zapped them with your mindfuck to want it and because they need us to whomp the Crats. That's all."

"You need *each other* to whomp the Crats, Oak. That's the whole Wobbly *point*. And, yes, the Terds required a bit of 'zapping' to be brought out of their familiar habits. But no more than you Parkers required some zapping, *too*."

Oak looks up at the stars across the ceiling, then back down at Mall. "All that may be, I admit. But to be right honest with you, Mall, from where I sit, I just can't cred that. There ain't any collateral to it. And Mall, don't take this wrong, but me and the boys have agreed we don't see much room for you and yours in this fight any more. Not any more. We're all grateful as hell for what you done for us and for how you brought us along Wobbly. But from here on out we got to do for ourselves—even if that means fucking up some. Seems to me that's the biggest Wobbly way there is."

From where he sits? Cred? Collateral? What language is Oak speaking? "Oak, you cannot be serious about this."

"As a heart attack, Mall. I can."

"But you need our support. Our military savvy."

"If you don't want to give us them no more, I understand. We'll just have to make do. Hell, maybe Brand and ArcAir can help us out some. But me and my boys will be calling the shots from here on in. That's plain bottomline nonnegotiable."

Bottomline nonnegotiable? Bugger all. The words chill Mall. Where did Oak pick up such nonsense, listening to the megmayor's talkboxes? This is potentially disastrous, but she can't overreact. "We'll be allowed to help out then?"

"Sure. Long as you don't get in our way."

Mall nods her false appreciation.

"So, you and your boys have developed a plan, have you?"

Oak smiles like he doesn't mean it. "The way I see it, Mall, no matter how long we been stuck in megs spinning our tires, it's been for too long.

We got to get history back moving again quick as possible. That means two jolts—that we got to wake Parkers up to two facts. One, that megs ain't standalone. Two, that Parkers ain't standalone either. Parkers can't just keep scrambling about every day hoping to hold body and soul together. We got to open our eyes and start working together."

"Minus the benefit of Terds, yeah?" Oak won't be provoked. "Fancy notions, Mister Grand Pooh-Bah. Where's the rubber hitting the hard of this road? Tell me that."

"Water withhold will tell quite a tale that megs can't do it all on their own. On top of that, keep spreading the good word of the One Big Union to show Parkers how to join into one labor force that can't be pushed around. Far as I can see, Mall, them's the only two clubs I got to swing with. Waters and mindfree. That's how we took BoiCity."

While Oak's plan is undeniably reasonable, beyond the Wobblies' present scope it is plainly unworkable, too, without widespread Terd defection to the cause. Mall and the others will just have to maintain their slice efforts on their own, more or less in secret now. "The Crats will come back at you hard, Oak, and eventually with everything they have. You know that, don't you? It's a small miracle they haven't annihilated us already."

"Yeah, it's damned strange, all right," Oak acknowledges. "I know if I was them, that's what in the hell I'd be doing."

Mall gets up from her overstuffed chair. She steps to Oak to stand over him. "All right, I suppose there's nothing for it, then. I'll inform my colleagues of our new status as helpmates." She inspects, for a moment, the curved and bevel-toothed, slightly blood-spotted blade still in her possession. "We'll do our best at staying out of your manly way." Mall inverts the killknife and lets it drop. Its point ploks and sticks with a most dramatic punctuation squarely between Oak's lackadaisically spread thighs. Mall does not look over her shoulder as she walks across the enormous suite towards the hidden door. "Oh, and Oak, let me tell you that should there be another interlude of this kind, I'll be sending Cardinal along to chat it out with you in my stead. Are you catching my drift?" Mall allows her question ample time to take hold. "She'll be far more inclined to serve you up those fresh oysters I mentioned earlier. With relish, I'm sure."

Still staring at the killknife, Oak nods his understanding of the truce and swallows hard. His response doesn't find Mall, who's already through the door and gone. "I know for a damn fact she will."

☆ ☆ ☆ ☆ ☆ ☆

This streams on the totoupleft, corpwide, panfeed, and allnets:

<<Wherever you go, there we are!>>

<<More youdecide breaknews!>>

<<See the world, be the world!>>

<<The newsbig of the day: live exclusive coverage of Our Bossman's big climb to the top! We align you now to our topcorp correspondent, Cabbage Patch, direct on the scene in [loud and forced guffaw]—golly, is that a hoverer I see you're in, Cabbage?!>>

<<[loud and forced guffaw] You bet it is, Trend! I'm hovering high above majestic Yosemite Corporate Park, where The Man himself is undertaking an historic powerclimb up the rugged and vertical rockface known as El Capital, one of the world's largest monoliths and one of our grandest corporate treasures! [livevid of a lanky man in spandex halfsuit gaining hand- and footholds up a sheer cliff at an amazing pace, majestic Sierra Nevada Mountains background this speedclimb] Let's see if we can get a Vieworld exclusive interview! Mr. Ceo! Oh, Mr. Ceo!>>

<<Yes, hello, Cabbage! [huge sweat-beaded face of Bleached Wheat abruptly fills the feed, the blueice hue of his irises are without a touch of the glassy, their cores approaching the hyperreal, he does not stop his climb] How are you!?>>

<<Well, from safe inside my Vieworld hoverer here, sir, I'd say I'm

sure doing a heck of a lot better than you are right about now! [interviewer and interviewee share a loud and forced guffaw] But tell us, Mr. Ceo, why is it you're putting yourself on the line like this, pitting yourself against well over 2000 meters of unforgiving stone?! Why are you attempting an unassisted, sub-ten-hour powerclimb of El Capital, one of the planet's most notoriously challenging and, dare I point it out, dangerous ascents!>>

<<Great question, Cabbage! You Vieworld guys always cut right to the chase! To be perfectly frank with you, Cabbage, today I'm sending a message! A very important message that I want everyone in TexArc to hear! Everyone highup and lowdown, Cabbage! Everyone who can hear and see me right now! Everyone! [Bleached Wheat stops his climb, fastening his gaze on the viewer] You see, Cabbage, for me, this grand old mountain is a symbol! A symbol of our great corporate character as risktakers who watch out for number one! You know, this big old chunk of unforgiving rock is just like our freemarket, there for the taking for the guy that's got the rocks big enough to take it on! And let me tell you, Cabbage, we sure got some big-rocked guys in this grand old corp of ours! Guys who know what it takes to get to the top of the heap! You know what I mean, Cabbage?! [cut shot to Cabbage nodding thoughtfully] My goodness, Cabbage, I mean, what could be more fair?! Here's this mountain, just like our freemarket, big and impartial, exactly the same to all comers! And here's me, a regular commonsense joe looking to get ahead! What could be more simple and natural?! You just put the two together—the mountain and the guy—and bam: you got yourself the greatest corporation on earth! That just makes me tingle, Cabbage!>>

<<[vidcut to a grinning Cabbage] I know it makes me proud to be a TexArcan, too, sir!>>

<<[vidcut back to a grinning Bleached Wheat] You bet it does, Cabbage!>>

<<But why you, Mr. Ceo, and why now?! Gosh, you've already made it to the top, sir! Why should you risk yourself by taking on this hair-raising climb?!>>

<<Gosh, that's the whole symbolism of it, Cabbage! We've all got to climb, all the time! Even me, the big boss! Otherwise, everything grinds to a halt! Heck, that's what competition in the freemarket is all about, Cab! Everybody's got the same chance to get ahead, and everybody's got the same chance to fall behind! [pause for an almost glaring, white-toothed smile] But I will tell you one thing, Cabbage! There's no room up here for whiners! That's for sure! [prolonged background guffaw from Cabbage] If you've got the doublego to make it this far, you might as well go all the way to the top! And I'll tell you one other thing, Cabbage! [trombone shot zeros in tight, centering a closeup of cold and level eyes] Any guy out there thinks he's already made it to the top, gone as far as he can go, is just fooling himself! There's always more to have! Always more to take! Always higher to climb! You just gotta have the rocks to keep going! [offvid Cabbage's sanctioning guffaw swells to the point where it sounds as though he might chuckle himself right out of his Vieworld hoverer] A guy's just gotta understand that the right time to stop is never! [extreme eyes frame for a silence of fivecount, then a slow pullback to full face: crux, razor, keeping his lean] We all know the old saying, Cabbage: nobody watches out for number one like number one!>>

<<[vidcut back to Cabbage safe in his hoverer] Truer words, Mr. Ceo! Truer words! Thank you for your time, sir! Good luck, and good climbing!>>

<<[vidcut to livevid of Bleached Wheat continuing his climb] Thank you, Cabbage! And God bless TexArc!>>

<<[vidcut return to Cabbage for wrap] No, thank you, Mr. Ceo! And God speed! Well, there you have it, Trend! Our Dmega doublego bossman always on the gain, always on the job! He's truly an inspiration to us all! Now

back to you for more breaking news on those continuing EVe terrorattacks on our doorstep! This has been Cabbage Patch, reporting live from the beautiful—no, the breath-taking PC!>>

"That's a cut! We're out!" Java shouts on set.

Bleached Wheat lets go his finger-and-toe-holds to drop the meter down onto the thick padmats spread out on the floor of the bluescreen studio. He's cautiously approached by Java. "That was ice, sir," the subceo praises his superior. "That hit both culture messages doublechoice."

"*If* there's some fucker out there to catch the deeper one," Bleached Wheat kicks Java's enthusiasm in the balls. Impatiently, he towels off the mist sprayed over his face just prior to the shoot. "We don't even know what the fuck we're dealing with yet."

"No, sir. We don't. You're quite right."

Java's sad little half-darky deadpan touches Bleached Wheat's sardonic heart. "Don't fucking mope," he instructs his underling. "You did good. Now go think up some more of this culture bullshit. We might need a whole lot more of it."

As Java hurries off, Ponzi and Jitney come into studio, looking frenzychrister grim as ever. Whenever these two sunbeams tandem up, Bleached Wheat knows he's bound for shitstorm. He decides to get in the first shot. "We got any God damn confirm yet?"

"Afraid we do, sir," answers Jitney, trying to overlook the taking-in-vain.

"Fucking *and*?" asks Bleached Wheat, after a wait.

Jitney and Ponzi turn to look at one another, like they'd yanking rehearsed it. "Gone," reports Ponzi—not unhappily enough.

"One or both?" the ceo asks.

"Both."

"Jesus fucking shit!" Bleached Wheat swears as he kicks over a heavy digi steadycam. Sparks fly along the floor where it crashes down. "A meg *and* a cocksucking ArcAir base?"

"Yes," nods Jitney, a touch smug. "That's confirm."

"Holy fuck," Bleached Wheat says to himself. "This is *too* big."

Ponzi interjects in a lowered voice, "This is feasible revoevo, sir."

"Yeah, yeah. You two holyjoes told me so. You both fucking did. Dockers is a yank. What else could I fucking expect? Okay, fine. Enjoy your moment of TD sanctimony. It fucking suits you two saints."

"There's more, sir." Jitney smiles.

Bleached Wheat has to refrain from smacking it off his subceo's face.

"We've just received confirm of water withhold in the IMS," Ponzi elaborates. "It's bad."

Bleached Wheat's tone does not signal a question. "How bad? Where?"

"As of right now, SaltCity is bone dry." Jitney continues to smile while Ponzi continues to elaborate. "Denver is on low reserves. Foenix already is into emergency rationing procedures."

"*Shit.*"

"Just a day or two more and the entire southern Spine will be parch. And, where this withhold is located, the mid PC will be threatened as well. Portland's already registering a mild shortage."

"*Piss.*"

"And," Jitney is happy to add, "they're extending their slice range, too." Bleached Wheat clenches his jaw and both his fists. "For the first time they've managed to chink outwall the IMS."

"*Fuck. To where?*"

"To the PC, sir. Where else?"

"*Fuck.*"

"Oh, it gets worse, sir," tops Ponzi. "Something that still idcodes itself as ArcNet is not just knapsacking our Servfeed anymore. It's completely replacing it. And it's not ArcNet. It's something called WobblyNet. And it's spreading. Only Simulacrum basstech would let them do that."

"That fucking *dykebitch*?"

"Has to be her, sir," nods Jitney.

"The one fucking thing I tell that fuckwad Dockers not to poochscrew. The *one* fucking thing."

"Sir," adds Ponzi, no longer having to rub things in, "I'm afraid ArcNet will have one hell of a time trying to freak their slice now. And there's no telling what they'll be able to do with it. I have unconfirmed reports of their streaming some kind of taste."

"Some kind of *taste*?"

"Yes, sir."

Well, Bleached Wheat had wanted a legitimate threat. He'd worked hard to engineer it, and now here the fuck it was. Luckily, in mid August, lots of Gaters and Terds are off farnorth on beachresort vacation.

"Start with a Stryker probe," he orders his subceos. "I want to go in on ground only."

"Manned or unmanned?" asks Jitney.

"Fucking unmanned, of course. We can't let shit get out about this. Not goddamned shit. You hear me? Why the fuck do you think I've had that mexcoon Java working doubleshift these past few days on culture decoy? I don't want to end up with a whole shitload of giddy minds to distract."

"Should I have ArcGround on alert for a fall, just in case?" Jitney's trying to anticipate plan.

"No. And leave ArcAir out of it, too. We can't trust the Terds or the CorpTroops in either branch now. This Wobbly shit seems like it can get anywhere."

"What then?" asks Ponzi. "What if the Strykers can't do the job?"

"Then ArcNet and ArcSpace only. Pull out all the stops. I only want companyman Terds taking this one on. Terds that dykebitch can't get her hands on."

Great Salt Lake Desert Storm

"I hereby call this meeting of my Wrangle Ministry to goddamn fucking order."

"Jip, sit down and shut up, you miserable, tubed son-of-a-bitch."

"Now see that, Oak? That's what I been saying. I know he's your clan and all, but goddamn fuck it, he can't go round hard talking me like that. And specially not in front of my own fucking Ministry fellas."

Oak says nothing. Jiplap sits down at his place around the conference table. He shoots a mean glare at the CorpTrooper, one meant for his own ministry fellas to see, not so much for the CorpTrooper to notice. Fact is, Enron scares hell out of Jip.

"Take a look out the south window, boys," Enron tells the room after leaning back comfortable in his chair. "If any you tubers still think this ain't dead-ass serious shit we're dealing with now, study that a minute."

Out the south-facing window of the Eye of the Gold Butte, running in panoramic, three-dimension across the entire horizon, plays a silent spectacle of ancient assault helicopters rocket-attacking some slope village in some slope jungle, someplace. The way the clouds or the sunlight, or, at night, the way the stars intermingle through the images—there but not there, inflecting the tableau, but not interrupting it or really altering its 3D—make the apparitions seem more real than the environment they're projected onto.

"How many days and nights that been running now, Chevy?"

Chevy's one of Jiplap's top Wrangle Ministers, so he isn't sure he should answer the CorpTrooper. Seems like it might be a slap to Jip. But Oak nods at him. "Four," he admits, his face sunburned almost to leather.

"Is it scaring shit out of folks in the meg?"

"Enron," Chevy answers, "you know damn well it is."

The images started one sunset, just as twilight faded. In fact it looked as if when the sun faded down, the picture show faded up, big and bright, full-color and alive all along the flat of the southern vista. At first it was just damn curious. Monster-size 3Ds walking along the skyline. Then people got to watching them. Bombs going off. Buildings collapsing. Troopers charging while they yelled, and screamed, and rapid-fired. Hypersonic attackcraft diving from the sky with noseguns blazing. House-to-house combat. Bound men, women, children kneeling, sometimes blindfolded and sometimes not, being shot one-by-one close-range in the back of the head. Heavyarmor tanks rolling over mounds of rubble and corpses. A glorious march of Christer Soldiers on their way, millions and millions of them, banners flying high and flapping crisp in the strong wind—the big white star inside a thin red circle against the deep blue background—and Gold Cross, after Gold Cross, after Gold Cross held aloft and paraded proud, profiled day and night against the bigsky. TDers on the march. What could be worse? The specters changed constantly and, in four days, never seemed to repeat. Some were almost comically melodramatic anime—but violent, always very violent. Some were staged and too perfectly framed, like filmclip. Others, the most tormenting, had the unmistakably raw and random feel of newsreel, like breakingnews footage, so casually fed and watched over Vieworld each and every day. Only now, the newsbig would be BoiCity. Though he told no one, Enron recognized more than one bombed-out city he'd helped raze on ArcGround falls. In these panoramas, no matter what filmic style the sequence came in, the targets were always ragheads of various sorts: slope, mex, afro, and all shades of brown in between. And always these ragheads were getting flat-out trounced. Always. They were getting helplessly hauled out of their houses—the ones that weren't already smoldering heaps—and shot down cold in the street. No exceptions. The only break in routine was when the women were gangraped first in front of their men or when the children in front of their parents were tossed up high in the air to come down on pikes.

"Holocasts, boys," Enron tells the Wobbly ministers. "Airborne source. Likely coming off of a dozen or so of them Superheavy Airlifters flying damn round the clock." The image suddenly changes to a scene involving vintage CorpTroops from over a century ago. A platoon of them are holding down young slopeslits and taking turns on top of them. Behind them a jungle village burns. "Boys," Enron continues, "mind you, these are just their damn *toys* meant to spook us. I seen it before on falls. Softening up the target's what they call it." He stops to watch the show. "You can't even imagine the real shit they'll be bringing against us. No offense, fellas. You fought hard taking this meg. There ain't a wimp sitting at this table—that's certain—but you for true can't even think what Arc might have in mind for us. I can."

The surly silence of outmatched men. Enron looks in the face of each and every Wobbly around the triangle table, a dozen or so in all, before he speaks again. "Don't you see it, boys? *We're* the damn ragheads now. *We're* the ones they gonna be marching over all holy and wiping off the face of the earth. *We're* enemy and outcrop."

"I ain't gonna go back to shittubing," Jiplap declares. "*That's* for fucking certain. Their fucking picture shows ain't gonna make us give up and give in. Right boys?"

Most of the ministers around the table nod, swear, and agree there's no giving in. Another ritual for outmatched men.

"Surrendering ain't an option at this point, boys," Enron raises his voice over their display. "Even if we damn want to." He has their attention again. “We crossed ’em. That means we’re term. End of feed. That’s it. All that shit out there on the horizon is just to make us shit ourselves before they come at us hard. Arc don’t take no surrenders, fellas. That ain’t plan.”

“So what the fuck you telling us, Enron?” says Skol, a pinch-face and notoriously virhorny little bastard. “That we bone up the ass?”

“Yep,” Enron nods. “Pretty much we are, Skol.”

The Wrangle Ministry looks to one another, trying to read in each other’s faces how much they should panic over this bad news coming from a CorpTrooper. Everybody knows Enron’s not really one of them any more. Not a true Parker. Not by a long shot. Hell, he’s been gone CorpTrooping for near ten years. Who’s ever heard of some guy making it alive for *that* long? Then them damn EVers got hold of him for that outland spell. Who knows what the hell *that* bunch did to him? Those make him double-not Parker. So can he really be a Wobbly, now? One of their true own? He’s sure talking a lot of deep-corp, mil-ed now. And he’s been going around talking way too much libby EVe moveon these past days. Can they really take his word on anything?

“So we sit here and jack our dicks doing nothing waiting for the CorpTroops to fall? Is that the map, Mr. Enron, sir?”

“Now, you see, Jip,” says Enron, calm and leaning forward in the fancy exechair to plant his elbows on the table, “here’s where your tit-in-a-wrench stupid catches up to your butt-naked ugly.” He pauses for those insults to take. “Arc ain’t coming with CorpTroops. No way in hell. Ground’s out the picture, now. Probably so’s Air.”

“Yeah?” grunts Jiplap, no brighter comeback occurring to him. “And why the fuck’s that?”

“Terds and CorpTroops crossed ’em at Mountain Home. Or don’t you recall?” Every man in the room knows he’d likely be dead right now if it weren’t for what Enron did turning the ArcAir base Wobbly. “And if Wobbly can get to Terds and CorpTroops once, Jip, Arc will damn well figure what's to stop Wobbly from getting to Terds and CorpTroops again? So they can't take that chance. Arc won't be trusting conventional Terds and CorpTroops with this particular job, boys."

To be mulish, Jiplap pops the question no one truly wants answered, "Well what the fuck will Arc be coming with instead?"

"Net." The lone word kicks at every Minister's guts. "They'll be coming at us with strak-hooya Terds and nobody else. That means ArcNet for sure, and who in hell knows what all besides." Enron's not even trying to be dramatic. "Whatever they come with, it'll be more than doublego nasty, boys. They'll be out to shock-and-awe. But you don't need me to tell you that."

"But we do need you to tell us about Net, Uncle Enron."

To Enron, his nephew sounds a touch more snively than mean of late. Not enough where the Ministers would hear it, but enough to bother Enron. It ain't usual. Oak's normal just cocksure ornery.

"Oak," he replies, "I wish to hell I could, but I don't know shit about ArcNet. No CorpTroop does. We're the shit end of the stick, remember? Netsmen Terds do all the wagging, and they're plumb sons-of-bitches, no two ways about it. You been there. You know."

Oak nods and grows quiet. He seems jittery.

"Well, anyways, we fight 'em, no matter what, eh boys?" Jiplap rallies the Ministers sufficiently to raise some faint nods and gestures. "No two ways about *that*, neither." But the man dance is slow to get going. Net's something you just don't want to think about. "We got one hell of a big Wobbly army and it looks like we got no goddamned choice in the matter, so I say piss on their holocasts, and piss on whatever in the goddamn, fucking hell else they want to throw our way. Bring the fuckmothers on is what I say!" Jiplap, at least, is not faking. "Net ain't just strolling into *our* meg without us kicking at his balls for all the fuck we Wobblies is worth! We kicked ass *taking* this meg! We can damn well kick ass *keeping* it!"

Enron's laugh is rich and good-natured, not at all intended to mock the

Wrangle Minister, who, after all, is doing his job. "No insult, Jip, but yanking GaterPol just ain't nothing like Net. Not by a long shot. Son, you're talking postmod battlespace now, not chasing down a few fat cops with misters. You got no damn idea on earth what that's like."

"What's the 'postmod battlespace'?" Jiplap derides the bigwords. "Enron, you been slipping it too much to them damn EVe sluts. They's making more than just your billyanker soft. You startin' even to talk like a goddamned dykebitch."

The Ministers enjoy these jabs. EVe bitches are considered sluts because they *won't* have anything to do with the top Parkers.

"Jip," Enron chuckles along with the rest, "your nuts is too numb to feel when somebody's kicking at 'em, you know that? Battlespace nowadays eat you up and spit you out quick. Doublequick. Before you can blink a goddamned eye. I ain't exaggerating. This isn't your fucking Oak Guard marching up and down proud as you please with your lame-ass chain of command running down through it. This is postmod, Jip. That means decentral. That means dealing with chaos the best you can, Jip. And that boils down to meaning the killchain's short as shit out there, brother. *Real* damn short and *real* damn quick. And you know it, too, when your butt's out there flapping in the breeze playing hide-n-find. If you get spotted, you get identified, fired on, and blown away all while you draw the same breath. *No shit*. Ain't no bot clearing it with no damn hume whether or not it's okay to wax your ass. It's over and done in a heartbeat and already on to the next. Hell, they've already termed the next damn dozen of you. Bam, bam, bam. Happens just like that. So I don't give a good fart in hell how many of your damn Wobbly army you put out there, Jip old boy. In open battlespace they gonna be deadcount in minutes. In *fucking* minutes, Mr. Wrangle Minister, your Honor, Sir."

"I thought you didn't know what Net has," Chevy breaks in like he's clever.

"I don't," says Enron. "All I'm talking now is what I seen and done myself being a CorpTrooper. I been the one out setting the killzone, Chev. Any raghead I ever did a fall on got termed lickety split, like he wasn't even fucking there. All except when I falled on EVe. Now them folks can hold their damn own. Only ragheads I ever saw who could. But I know Net's got shit I never even seen, never even caught wind of. That's how them strak Terds operate. They keep the best shit to themselves. So I'm just figuring a regular guy out in Net harmsway don't got prayer one to survive it. That's because, to be straight with you, Chev, I doubt I could."

"A CorpTrooper can't survive a Net attack? Is that what you're telling us, Uncle En?"

Enron had been thinking Oak wasn't listening. His nephew had that away look to his eyes.

"All I'm telling you boys is that Netsmen ain't your normal prissy Terds who like a soft time of it. I know you had to see that in basic, Oak, no matter how short it was you stuck." Oak looks down at the table. "Fellas, it ain't my meaning to jolt ya. It really ain't. But a good career Netsman will suck your eyeballs out for breakfast and then shit 'em out to reheat for lunch. No spoof." Enron looks across the triangle table at Oak. "And your bossman there damn well knows it."

Every Serv at the table looks to Oak. The Grand Pooh-Bah continues staring at the table top.

"Well," bawls out Jiplap, "I guess we just pop a cold Oly and wait to buy the firm then, fellas! Who's got their stiffyanker up for some good virhos, huh? Is that it, Enron? Is that what you're telling us to do?" This outburst feels like diversion to Enron. "We just supposed to give up the ghost right now and be done with it? Be done with our meg? With Wobbly?"

"Fuck no, Jip. That ain't it and you know it. All I'm telling you is, don't go about it stupid. And you'd be just the one to go about it stupid, Jip.

You'd get everybody killed for nothing."

"Instead of getting us all killed for *some*thing?" asks Oak, still gazing hard at the nanowood. "Is that what this all boils down to, Uncle?"

Enron's not about to hedge. "Yep," he says. "That about sums matters up as they stand right now."

Oak draws an angry breath and looks up at his kinsman accusingly. "Uncle En, I believe you *have* been listening to them dykebitches far too close these days."

"They got us this far, Oak."

"Sounds like to me," says Jiplap, "they brung us to the end of the god-damn line is all."

Enron stands so he can see better what everyone's hands are doing. "Listen to me, you two brainfarts. Them women didn't take us nowhere Arc didn't let us go. If you two wasn't so busy pimping up all mighty and high this summer, you'd be seeing what I'm seeing, too. We're being played with. Any damn time Arc wanted, it could've ground our Wobbly asses into the dirt. But it didn't. Not so far, anyway. Why they waited so damn long I goddamned don't know but wish to hell I did. Something's up with them to let things slip bad like this. We can only guess at what. But if we can just get things to slip a nudge more, just a little damn touch, mind you, we might actual have something here. Something important on our hands."

Jiplap stands up himself. "Something like fucking what?"

"Something like a real chance for Wobbly to spread."

The Ministry strikes Enron as being lukewarm toward this good news.

"Not a chance for us to spread with it? To live past this shitstorm coming our way?"

Enron shakes his head and shrugs honestly. "Probably not, Jip. Sorry."

"So what the fuck we talking about exactly?" says Oak, making a wild gesture at the whole world around them. "Just what the fuck we supposed to be up to then?"

"Buying Wobbly some time. That's about all we can do."

"Time for fucking what?"

"Time for our water withhold to tip another meg or two. Time for WobblyNet to slice to more Servs and Terds. Time for things to get a bit too far gone for Arc to handle."

The plan makes unfortunate commonsense joe, and Oak knows it. That don't mean he has to like it. "And then we get to be dead heroes?" he asks. "Is that the plan, Uncle En?"

"Dead heroes for a damn good cause," Enron adds to the sentiment. "Yep, Oak. That's it pretty specific."

The Ministers go to grousing down low. Oak turns his face away to scowl out the south window. It gets dead hush in the Eye. Then, across the table from Enron, Jiplap whips out his new pearl-handled minimister, whoops out the Wobbly warcry, and fires a fine spray toward the pointed ceiling. The pellets by their thousands come raining back down on everybody. "Way I see it, boys," Jip hollers, "dead heroes is better than dead cowards! So I say fuck Net! Let 'em come! You just tell us what the fuck you want us to do in this 'postmod battlespace' of yours, Enron, and we'll fucking just do it!" Jip pulls off another shot. "So long as I get to term some Terds, it's all the fucking same to me!"

This is bullshit show, too, and Enron's not buying it. What do these Ministers got going on, anyhow? "Yeah, Jip," Enron plays along, for now, "you the fuckmother Man all right. Now put up your damn peasprayer before you poke somebody's eye out. Let me tell you what needs doing." Jiplap fancy spins the gun before holstering it and sitting back down. His clowning breaks the heavy mood. "Jip," Enron starts, "only thing you and your crack Oak Guard got to do is stay put here in the meg. Hear me? No matter what you see or hear, *don't* come out into the open. *Hear* me? The open is where you get cut down. Just get everybody inside the Gaterwalls and damn-well keep them there. It'll be crowded for sure, but you got plenty of water and vits, so you'll be fine."

"Wait now," says Oak turning back to the table. "Where the hell you taking off to?"

"I'm going forward, towards 'em."

"Towards 'em where? How the fuck you even know where Net is?"

"Net's southeast of here a few hundred klicks. Out in the salt desert where the big lake used to be. They been dropping in steady for days, massing."

"Now how the hell do you know that?"

Enron snorts. "The dykebitches. How the hell else we ever know shit around here? Them and the Terds at Mountain Home been keeping tabs on the counterstrike."

"Look here." Oak's hot. "I can't and I ain't gonna trust those she-brutes no more. And I ain't gonna start trusting Terds. All that's just gonna bring us nothing but more goddamned trouble."

"No, Grand Pooh-Bah." Enron's hot right back. "All you're about to do is shit and fall back in it. It's way too fucking late not to trust those women and the Terds. You best just be man enough to face what's coming our way." Enron looks to Jiplap. "We're dead no matter what. Unless we're in this together with them, all the freedom we've beat out of Arc so far drops dead on top of us."

Oak's ears are burn red. "Enron, I swear to shit, you ever talk to me like that again and I'll fuck you up good. I run this meg."

"Little nephew, fuck you. You run shit and you ain't man enough to fuck up a goat. You're a mean and sneak son-of-a-bitch that never has run nothing since Mall got here. You just been the clown in the circus." With such inordinately thick nanoglass encasing it, the Eye of the Gold Butte can become a very quiet place, given a few moments. "Now I'm taking south with me all the used-to-be CorpTroops I can gather up. Some I'm leaving to help guard Mountain Home. That'll be a buffer for the meg against Net getting north. Others are coming all the way south with me to attack the fuckers. You boys just arm every damn Wobbly you can and hunker down for the long haul. Whatever comes at you, you give it holy hell—but you do it from inside the damn district. Hear me? I'll be back to help with whatever I got left."

Oak's voice is struggling, "I can't...and I ain't gonna...let you do any of that."

"Too late, little nephew. It's already done. The EVe fighters that's left are coming with me, too. Mall and Sinalco are already down at Mountain Home slicing and counterslicing ArcNet. You just mind the store here." Enron starts to back his way toward the platform lift. His tone turns to mollifying. "Look here now, Oak. Best we can tell, SaltCity is that close to going Wobbly. That close. That's another reason for Arc to be massing down near there." Oak doesn't look to be listening. He just keeps running the palm of his hand over the stubble on his cheeks. "And Arc's still taking us casual, Oak. Real casual. They don't seem to care two shakes if we know they's coming. All they're fretting about is word getting out to the rest of the corp that there's a meg gone over to Servs." Enron stops backing up. "Don't you see it, Oak? Arc's scared to death of *Wobbly*, of his ideas getting loose and free in the corp. They ain't scared of shitbritches like us. They been terming our kind too long and too easy ever to worry about us doing anything big. But Wobbly now, well, he *is* big. They got to keep him under wraps. That's why they're trying to scare us back into companyline with that shit there out the window. That's why they don't want nobody else knowing about what's going on out here in the IMS. It's the *knowing* that spooks 'em, Oak. It's the *Terds* knowing Wobbly that really spooks 'em bad. I seen it, Oak. I watched what Mall's taste did to that AirColonel Terd. It turned him around hard, Oak. Hard. It fucking put him inside out. No shit. He came out of that sweating and ashamed of himself and all for us Parkers. All for us. That's something Terds never are and never have been, Oak. And that's after just one dose of Mall's taste. Just one damn dose. So we got to keep the knowing passing along, Oak. And this time right now likely will be our last chance to strike 'em in a way that can make some difference. That can give Mall more time to slice. So we got to take it."

Oak won't reply. None of the Ministers speak. Enron backs onto the lift and triggers it. Once his head descends past floor level, he calls, "Hey, Oak! I sure do like your view from up there, though! It's a whole new way to look at the world, ain't it?"

That it is.

☆ ☆ ☆ ☆ ☆ ☆

The desert floor is almost completely white. In some directions it runs level for over one hundred and fifty kilometers, making visible at the horizon the curvature of the earth. Jagged salt crystals cover the ground. Daytime temperatures exceed 60^{C}. The glare sears retinas. The air is so thin that where the land and the sky meet appears white and washed dry and indistinguishable. As that same sky mounts overhead the blue intensifies rapidly, finally to the hue of a robin's egg. Nighttimes are silent and cold, no atmosphere at all seeming to intervene between the planet and interstellar space. The last waters evaporated from these basins decades and decades ago. Mountains rising spiny in the distance look to be the sailfins of behemoths dropped dead in their march a million years since.

<Everybody in poz?>

Enron's display lights allgo. Forces set. He'd never wanted to be corpsuited up again, especially not aligned in again to a RHex, but he knew they'd be needing them. They'd be needing everything they could get. Luckily, Air had everything they needed stockpiled at Mountain Home—the whole shooting match. It might just give them a fighting chance.

<Listen, fellas. When your RHex goes it's gonna smart like hell. Don't worry about shitting yourselves. Just recover quick as you can and keep firing. Just keep fucking firing.>

Enron hates playing pop-up. He'd much sooner go house-to-house. Least then you have some control. Hide-n-find is pure crap shoot. You don't know what shit you're going to pop-up into. Just got to depend on the filter overload.

<On their way,> comes report from point.

<How many?> says Enron.

<Too damn many.>

Figures. Whenever Arc does something on the cheap they do it by the many, to make up for lost quality. What the hell else is massprod for?

<ETA?>

<Don't step out to lunch.>

Their excursion into the wastelands has been marked by nothing but nasty surprises. The biggest one they got was discovering an ArcSpace base nobody knew about just west of the old Lakeside Mountains. Wasn't until they got a scout and his RHex up on top of Desert Peak they found that out. Airborne recon couldn't pick through the masking. A guy had to eyeball it for himself. They decided to go through with the bushwhack anyway. They were all set up well to the northwest of the base, far into the Newfoundland Evaporation Bowl. Enron has no idea what an ArcSpace base can do, and he's damn sure he doesn't want to find out, but turning tail made less sense. So here they lie, buried in salt, waiting for what's just coming into view.

<Fuck me dry,> somebody forward says.

Twelve hundred Strykers roll almost soundlessly across the basin. They've formed into their individual battlediamonds, a layer of eight around a core of four. The armada of one hundred such diamonds moves in the aggregate shape of a giant spearhead.

<Shit,> somebody else chatters over comm, <not these fuckmothers.>

<Wait for it, boys,> Enron tries to reassure everybody. <Let 'em get on top of us.>

Mec can scare hell out of you. Enron himself doesn't like even being around them, never mind having to face them. You never really know what the hell they're going to do. Strykers are fat and highriding 8-wheelers, about 16 metric tons and armed to the gills. They're mainly used for no-mans-land probe, and they're damn good at that gruntwork. Enron's seen these killbots wipe whole raghead battalions, dug in nice, at a go so CorpTroops didn't have to go in and do it. He was damn happy enough for the mecs then. Now he's got to take down an entire spearhead of them with nothing but Ground and a little Air. Lucky for him, Stryker isn't too smart. Its ladar scan emits and snaps only about 200 pics-per-sec—more than enough to overload, but not enough to deal well *with* the overload. Its brain is also tucked inside someplace well armored from the front, but you can get to it from underneath or behind—if you're good and know what you're looking at. CorpTroops are and CorpTroops do. Located so far away from their objective, not expecting anything to happen out here, these Strykers might also be running in half-mind transit mode to conserve circuitry and drybattery. That would give the Wobblies a crucial advantage firstsecond.

The mecs have rolled over them. Enron tries to moisten his lips but gets only salt. He thinksays: <Go.>

Roughly three thousand RHexs pop up from nowhere off the salt. The luck of the firstsecond is with them. Only half are blown to particles instantly. After the thirdsecond, only half of those are in-op disabled. That gives about seven-hundred-and-fifty RHexs time during the fourth through the seventhsecond to orient and glom on. Of those, before getting shot, half again scramble-crawl to targetpoint and self-detonate. Before the engagement is ten seconds old, three-hundred-and-seventy-five Strykers split apart in orange fireballs. Collateral damage flips and grinds into the desert floor twenty-five more. Four hundred down and eight hundred more to go. A promising start.

The screaming over comm from all the RHex disconnects comes thick. Enron has no choice but to wait it out. They're CorpTroops. They'll take the pain. They'll be back up to doublego in another tick or two.

<Now,> he instructs by the fifteenthsecond.

Wave after randomized wave of tiny decoys the CorpTroops call bottlerockets fly up into the air.

<And go!>

CorpTrooper after CorpTrooper pops up from his camo-poz to sight-in and fire on what he can fire on, pop back down, wait a twocount, and do it the hell again. Kia, after one pop-up, is three hundred. After two pop-ups, another two. Good sign. Killrate's going down. The air aboveground is literally thick with exploding lead coming off the Strykers. As a collective, the more their numbers go down, the more firepower those remaining try to spray out. The bottlerockets are confusing them. The killbots seem to be trying to match the decoys with their own timed fire. CorpTroopers, meanwhile, have extra instants to find the mec sweetspot with their lasar-guide Stingers. That does mean, though, you got to stay popped up longer to sight-in and squeeze-off. Killshots to a guy's head and torso, if there's not too many rounds at once, that is, are being kept off pretty well by the pos-neg shielding. But off shield, the carbonfiber compos-armor just can't keep up with the bullet traffic. CorpTroopers are losing hands, arms, legs, and feet fast from the lag in liquid-fix repair. Enron's bleeding from both arms but has personally waxed four mecs. Next pop-down he checks his mission signflash downright. This shit seems to be working. CorpTroops down to two thousand—only a third of his force deadcount. Strykers down to five hundred—more than half of theirs. So far, this is turning into a postmod battlespace success. Enron decides it's time to jack the volume.

<Roll-and-go!> he tells everybody. <Shoot-and-scoot!>

Enron pops up and rolls several meters to his left where he stops, sights, squeezes, and rolls again. Spread across the wide salt basin, two thousand—now eighteen hundred—CorpTroops are doing the same.

<You're up, Cardinal!>

Ja, she confirms Enron's request. Then, to Pernod and Migros, she gives the order: *Doppelgänger.*

All among the Strykers, crews of EVe fighters materialize in the shimmering heat off the salt. They're running, they're leaping, they're lowcrawling, they're firing. Unsupported by adequate surround sensors, killbots take vital time distinguishing these holospoofs. Mecs might fire on a single image three or fours times before processing the zero effect. During this interval of misdirect, dozens of Strykers voom up into blacksmoke and smithereens. Cardinal pops up from her poz to find herself in a shadow. She flips over to stare directly at an undercarriage. After reaching up to attach the emp on an axle, she quickly rolls back over and hunkers down, knowing she'll only get a little singed. Everything pulses blue. Above her the Stryker frizzes out like a cheap toy. She pops up again, using the wreck for cover while gauging their status. Cardinal had wanted to be brought into the skirmish much sooner, right from the start, but Enron wouldn't allow it. For one, he'd said, EVe bodyarmor isn't as resilient as CorpTroop. For two, the Wobblies had to hack the numbers down considerable before throwing in spoof and morph. Otherwise the number of killbots remaining, that learn to ignore the misdirects, would have been too many to handle. Cardinal sees that Enron was right. The few hundred Strykers that are still ops are no longer targeting the holos. But there are only a few hundred of the mecs left. Cardinal also sees the price the CorpTroopers have paid in hacking down the numbers so her fighters could jump in for the kill. Thousands of mangled Wobblies lie scattered across the salt, many almost completely shredded. Great swashes of splattered blood fleck out in all directions over the white canvas of the desert floor. Cardinal puts down her head and sprints for the nearest active Stryker. Two bullets graze her before she can dive and roll and come up throwing. The emp sticks and pulses the same instant. She freezes three more mecs before giving her next order, *Die Gemeinschaft. Pernod. Migros. Jetzt machen wir. Die Gemeinschaft.*

No replies come. Off to her right, a Stryker first implodes then explodes, throwing Cardinal to the rugged surface. Even protected by earmutes, she struggles back up onto her hands and knees with her head ringing fiercely.

Migros! Pernod! she tries again. *Nächst! Jetzt gerade! Wo bis du?*

Pernod comes back, but thinksounding exhausted, *Migros.* There's hesitation, as though gathering the thought. *Sie ist tot.*

Nein. Scheisse! They must stay mission. *Wie geht es dir?*

Pernod takes time to answer. *Geht nicht so gut.*

Geht's noch? Pernod! Geht's noch?"

Pernod takes a longer time to answer. She's alone now somewhere out there, and probably bleeding out. *Jawohl.*

Cardinal encourages her. *Sehr gut, sehr gut. Langsam, ja? Pernod? Langsam.*

Ja. Langsam.

Zusammen, Pernod. Ja? Wir machen diese zusammen. Pernod?

Cardinal thinks she's lost her. That they're all lost. Then Pernod finally responds. *Ja. Jetzt.*

Cardinal can do nothing but repeat in confirm, *Ja. Jetzt.*

Cardinal pulls off her slim rucksack. She removes from it the slender cylindrical tube. She pads in a series along its side then twists open the top. The Community emerges, hundreds of thousands of them. Nanomorphs. They flock upward, quickly disappearing into the harsh blue of the sky. She can only hope that somewhere on the battlespace Pernod has accomplished the same—and maybe been able to release Migros' as well. Two wounded CorpTroops dart by her, one helping the other to run.

A Stryker smashes between burning mecs, firing, and makes the leg fly off one trooper and the arm off the other. Cardinal emps the killbot and scurries to change poz herself. Surviving the next couple of minutes of deconflict will be tricky. Two Strykers are rolling toward her, but stop to train their guns upward. Diving from the sky are a pair of stream-curved Strike UAVs. The Strykers open on them while the turbojets go evasive.

<Hop to it, boys!> Enron's voice comes over allcomm. <Got to take out as many as we can now while we got the clearshots!>

One hundred or so more Strykers get obliterated while the killbots focus on the more dangerous UAVs. Those two aircraft dive and bob, weaving over the battlespace but, strangely, never fire a shot and never get hit by the concentrated fire rising up off the basin. This interact lasts scarecly a minute. Then the Strykers, as a unit, simply stop firing at the aircraft and return their attention to the ground assault. At that second, the two UAVs vanish from the sky. Seconds later, six Panzer tanks appear among the closest concentration of Stryker battlediamonds. Once more, the killbots cease fire on the CorpTroops to concentrate on the new, more significant threat. With more clearshots available to the CorpTroopers, more Strykers go up in a blaze.

<What ya think, Cardinal?>

Ja. Yes. Do it.

After just thirty seconds, the Strykers ignore the Panzers to return to the CorpTroops. The Panzers dematerialize and several hundred more CorpTroopers augment the force already dotting the plain. These figures draw and take fire with no ill effects for only a very short time.

<Hit the deck, fellas!> Enron warns. <Here the fuck they come!>

Falling perpendicular from the highskies are twelve real Strike UAVs out of Mountain Home. These are low-observable, Uninhabited AirVehics that can loiter subsonically over a region for days, waiting to be told what to do. Mainly, they're used for recon or for ground attack, since they're not too hot air-to-air. If Cardinal's nanomorphs have done the job, these fly-mecs should just about do the trick. The series of EVe misdirects should have soaked inside the Stryker master OODA loop by now, fucking up their Observe, Orient, Decide, and Act process. Enough information saturation can backlog the filters that establish priorities and eliminate marginal data. Today, thank fucking goodness, it works like a goddamned charm. The remaining Strykers, maybe two hundred of them, ignore the incoming aircraft completely to maintain fire on the hostile ground forces. Even after the initial UVA attack spread takes out nearly a third of the mecs, the kill-bots continue to ignore the aircraft threat. Two more unopposed passes wipe out the spearhead. Then the UVAs are bolting skyward like they never were there. Left on ground are about five hundred CorpTroops A-and-A—Alive and Ambulatory.

<Sorry, boys,> Enron tells all survivors, <if you can't walk, better slap 'em. No use baking out here in the sun.>

On his downleft he checks his own suit signflash for medstat. BP thumbs up. Blood loss thumbs sideways. Selfpatch thumbs up. All more than acceptable. Enron slaps the adrenaline patch on the outside of his right thigh, just above the knee, but nothing else. No poppy. He can't afford to get drowsy now. Gain through pain, the old training saying pops into his head. Gain through pain.

<Everybody still mobile come towards my poz. I figure we got a few minutes before we need to skedaddle.> On his upright digimap he watches those green blips start to move toward him. Not a bad count from the looks of it. It's sure good to see all them yanking red blips are gone. <Help out your brothers,> he reminds the CorpTroops. <Kick 'em as you come.>

Enron steps to the nearest downed CorpTrooper whose hand isn't already resting by his right knee and gives that spot a kick, injecting the overdose for him, just in case he's still alive. All the CorpTroopers moving toward him are performing the same rite on as many of the fallen as they can. Cardinal finds him. She's holding in her hand three slender cylindrical tubes. Enron points to them. The two go off comm.

"The fuckers couldn't deconflict *their* input quick enough," he says.

Cardinal shakes her head, agreeing. "Na."

"Pretty fucking neat trick."

Cardinal studies the tubes in her hands. Flitter nanobots. Flockform into whatever you program them to. Nonlethal, of course. Just for morphing. All the same, KMD. Highly precarious GNR. Not things to play around with lightly. She took a risk releasing them into this unfamiliar and bizarre environment, but fortunately all of them had returned. Enron hadn't wanted to commit his airpower to the battlespace until he was certain it could finish off the Strykers. He's quite paranoid about not tipping off any of Wobbly's hand to Net. For filter overload, then, Cardinal had suggested they use not only EVe holospoofs, which are better than any decoys TexArc can deploy, but the nanomorphs as well, a device Enron had never heard of. She'd recognized in his worried demeanor how anxious an Attack Crew chief can get before going into a battlespace where she knows the odds are bad.

"You not for telling Mall. Yes?" Knowing she needs to augment her poor verbal communication, Cardinal looks Enron in the eyes very seriously. "She will piss herself with angry."

"Understood," Enron nods to give her a visual sign that he does. He scans over the Capitaine de Corvette's shoulder. He also quickly checks his display timekeeper. "You by yourself now?"

Cardinal appreciates what he's asking. "Jawohl," she says. Cardinal attentively packs the three tubes into her rucksack. Then she slings it, ready to go. Enron watches her.

"You EVe fighters stealth the best I ever seen. The hands-down best."

Cardinal watches the battered CorpTroops gathering toward them from all directions, all of them limping or dragging one leg. She looks at the mangled corpses and at the smoldering remains of the massive Strykers scattered over the hellish salt flats. “You CorpTroop sehr brave,” she says back. “Nicht sehr smart. But sehr, sehr brave.”

Enron cracks a smile. “Aw, hell’s bells, ma’am. We equip the man. Damn Terds just man the equipment.”

Cardinal eyes the skies. “Und where now to?”

“Northwest just fast as we can.” Enron looks first in that direction, then back to the southeast, half expecting something to be coming after them this soon. <Leaving in one,> he announces over comm. “You and me’s heading all the way back to Mountain Home. I’m leaving a first line of defense just north of this desert along the south Sawtooth Forest. Between Cache Peak and Jackpot there’s good mountains. Good overlooks and good hiding. I figure three thousand of us there and another three at the ArcAir base ought to keep Net off BoiCity for a time.”

Cardinal is pleased not to hear it called OakCity. She will never trust that little Scheissekopf. As they wait for final regroup, she notices how the CorpTroopers, as they approach, kick at the knees of their comrades prone and coiled on the ground. They kick even if someone just before them has kicked. She looks to Enron, who’s been watching the same thing. “I was thinking always you leave motheryanking Niemand behind.”

Cardinal’s picked up some of his lingo. Enron’s picked up some of hers. “We don’t leave nobody behind *alive*,” he clarifies. “That’s the one promise CorpTroops know’ll be kept because we’s the only ones making it.”

☆ ☆ ☆ ☆ ☆ ☆

ArCommander Abercrombie had just returned to prime console in Situation-Ops from the break room, ready to enjoy his steaming cup of latte. He was thinking how this Hill ArcSpace Base is quite a place. All the comforts of biz but out in the middle of godforsaken nowhere. Jesus, he’d never imagined so desolate a terrain could exist. And that IMS meg, SaltCity. That place was a pit. Bone dry for some reason, and with roving packs of Parkers getting into its Gater district at night, making it dangerous to go out clubbing. Damn hicks. What's this corp coming to, anyway? He's interrupted in the middle of his first experimental sip of latte with some absurd infoflow, and two big bloops of his drink wind up on the front of his brand-new uniform shirt. He hopes to hell it doesn't stain. "You're telling me *what*?" he snaps at the Sit-Ops duty officer while quickly reaching for his napkin. He presses his tongue against the corner of his mouth. He's sure he's burned himself.

"Just *gone*, sir," the duty officer repeats. "The whole damn spearhead. At first we thought it was just glitch. With the heat out there, that's pretty normal. They were off align for maybe fifteen minutes max. That can happen out in the flats. But when align came back up none of their sigs were there. Not *one*."

Abercrombie has only a vague idea of what the officer is actually telling him. Bottomline sounds to be shit happened. "Well, get something flying out there to take a look. Big dumb hunks of shit like that don't just disappear."

"No need to scramble, sir," the officer explains, politely. "Space is already eyeballing the scene."

Abercrombie has done the best he can cleaning himself off. Two big damp spots remain. He can only hope they dry clean. "Well," he says impatiently, "show it to me."

"Um, on the mainscreen, sir?"

"Fuck, yeah. Put it up there. I don't give a shit."

The duty officer pads his console reluctantly. On the huge mainscreen, for everyone in Sit-Ops to see, the satellite image appears: basically, twelve hundred roaring bonfires spotting an otherwise pristine desert floor.

"Not disappeared, sir," says the duty officer. "Destroyed."

"Holy fuck," Abercrombie says strictly to himself, even setting down his cup of latte. "What the fuck could have done that?"

"Look at the bodies, you ass wipe."

Everyone in Sit-Ops snaps to. ArCommander Subprime on deck. ArCommander Abercrombie is unfazed by his sudden appearance or by his rude interjection.

"Oh, yeah," he answers smart-ass, squinting to see all the prostrate forms distributed around the fires, "will you look at that. Now who the fuck do you suppose they are?"

"They're CorpTroops, you idiot. Who else in the world do you think could take out a spearhead of Strykers?"

"Ground?" says Abercrombie, serious now. "They can't be Ground. These Wobbly jokers are just a bunch of stupid, smelly Servs, too lazy to scratch their own butts. They can't do shit like that."

"CorpTroops *are* among the Wobblies now, Abercrombie. Quite a lot of them. They also own Mountain Home ArcAir Base, where they'd have access to lots of sophisticated equipment. Or haven't you been paying attention to infoflow?"

"Servs. CorpTroops. What's the fucking difference? They're all Parkers, right? How serious can that be?"

Subprime waves one hand toward the mainscreen. "For starters, take a goddamn look." Abercrombie reaches to pick up his latte, instead. "Before that, they took down an entire meg." Abercrombie blows then sips his hot drink, savoring its rich, coffee flavor. Not bad. He swallows loudly. "And they somehow infiltrated that ArcAir base. I'd say all that's serious as a goddamn heart attack, you jackass. Didn't you view *any* briefvids?"

"Briefings are for losers, my friend. Crisis intervention demands fresh points of view. That's why I'm here. Remember?"

"The only thing I've seen you here for, so far, is grossly underestimating an enemy. You sent out functionally dim mecs unsupported by adequate network sensors. How did you expect Strykers to be able to function in the field blind?"

"Look, chief," says Abercrombie, having put up with enough of the hooya bullshit, "we're here to panic these poor thumb-up-the-butt Wobblies back into submission—*and* to do it quietly. Or haven't *you* viewed any of the briefvids?" He's landed a solid point. "That's why I was brought in and put in charge. CorpHQ obviously didn't want a foaming-at-the-mouth, career diehard like yourself tear-assing around the IMS drawing a lot of attention to the situation out west. You know what I'm saying? Nobody needs that kind of negative pub at the moment. Got it?"

Behind his back, Subprime has placed a fist around the hilt of his killknife that's holstered on his web belt. The Netsmen at the back of the ops center clearly see this. "Listen to me, you smug and pudgy bastard. I've been Net for twenty years. You've been Net for maybe twenty fucking minutes. While I've been all over the globe thumbing eyeballs out of skulls, you've been pulling your poor excuse for a dick in cozy corp conference rooms in swank meg districts. Whatever bizsense you think you got that will work here *won't*. Simple as that, puke. We're facing asymmetrics out there. People so fucking desperate they don't have to make any sense, so they don't even fucking try. I've seen nothing but this my whole yanking career. I'm telling you right now, such people refuse to do whatever you predict they'll do. *What*ever. That's biz bottomline."

Abercrombie drops his cup in the trash. He's no longer in the mood for a relaxing latte. "Yeah," he nods, "they warned me you'd try to rambo the situation. Look chief—"

"ArCommander."

"Sure, whatever. Look, ArCommander, I sure the hell didn't ask to be pulled out of my cushy corpjob to come play soldier with you in the badlands. And I sure didn't look to be instantly advanced to the exalted rank of Big ArCheese, or whatever, like yourself. And I sure don't give two shits about your Net 'ops' and 'netcentric warfare' and 'asymmetrics'—and whatever other miljargon you want to toss around. We straight on all that?

Couldn't care less. But I *do* know my way around the Simulacrum, and I *do* know how to administer psycho-technology. That's what *I've* spent the past twenty years doing, and I'm goddamned good at it. That's why the fuck *I'm* here and that's why the fuck *I've* been put in charge of running this show—not you. We straight on all that, too? So just back the fuck off and let me do my work, okay? What I'm doing is what the big bossman himself ordered, so that's what the fuck I intend to deliver. Bend their brains, he told me, and for fuck's sake do it so nobody ever finds out about the fucking meg and base getting overrun. Therefore, if I need anything from you, chief, like, oh, say, a fucked-up military opinion, I'll let you know. Otherwise, stand back and watch a pro work."

During this speech, Subprime's killknife draws halfway out its holster, before it gets jammed back in.

"Fine. But your psychops shit just won't work on CorpTroops," Subprime says. He's confident he'll be told to slit this fucker's throat, later. "I'll tell you that right now."

"Psychotech works on everybody, eventually," Abercrombie smiles. "You just have to find the right pads to push. Sometimes that takes time."

"Scary holocasts and big mecs aren't going to intimidate CorpTroops. Doesn't look to me like they're rattling the Wobbly hardcore, either. You've been on this job almost a week, dumbass, with zero effect. Less than zero effect given the Wobblies have just wiped your first assault wave before it was even a couple hundred klicks out of base. Let's face it. You're nothing but a royal civilian fuck-up, Abercrombie, and way the hell out of your league. Time is exactly what they're hoping to gain here, shitbrain. Can't you see that? Reports of major waters riots are coming in from SaltCity. Some sectors just inside the Gater walls are unstable. Foenix is starting to have its own troubles. So's Denver. Meanwhile, what the yank have you accomplished? Hooked back up the 24/7 skychannel entertainment stream for BoiCity? Wow. That's a devastating blow. Sent them a fleet of bumper-cars to blow up in the desert for fun? Nice work. Yes, make them overconfident. Meanwhile, have you managed to counterslice their goddamn WobblyNet yet? That's what this is all about. That's what we need to get offstream."

"Hey, working on it, chief. All right? Working on it. Their slicer is good, spooky fucking good. We all know that. Your guys weren't able to freak it one damn iota. I've at least worked one foot in the door."

"Well," smiles Subprime, "speaking as someone who has worked directly for the big bossman, too, you'd better fucking work *faster*. But that's just my fucked-up military opinion."

"Awww," mewls Abercrombie, dabbing fake tears from his eyes, "did those mean CorpTroopies wreck all your pretty tonka trucks? Is that why we're being so scowly-owly today?"

Subprime gets up fast and hard in Abercrombie's face. "Listen, bizman," he's speaking low, for only the two of them to hear, "we treat CorpTroops like shit while training them up to do the most amazingly miserable dirty work you can ever imagine. Dirty work so hazardous and appalling that no one in his right mind would ever agree to do it voluntarily. Dirty work carried out under discipline so wretched that no trooper, not by any stretch of the imagination, will ever mistake the system he's in as being intended *really* to improve one bit his own miserable lot in life. Come on, fuckhead, not even Parkers are *that* dumb. Only you civilian Terds believe in fairytale corpatriotic shit like that. CorpTroops know they're totofucked. From day one they know that. But do you know what those CorpTroops give us in return for this treatment? Do you have any idea?" Subprime doesn't expect an answer. "A blind willingness to die. That's what. And do you know why they're willing to die? Have you just always assumed it's out of some kind of crazy devotion for Corp and Christ? Have you? Well, fuck that. It's for each other. They die for each other. Believe me, we've studied the shit out of this one to make sure we can keep it going. CorpTroops are willing to die in a desperate effort to try to protect one another, because they know no one else is going to make anything like that kind of effort. CorpTroop devotion is for CorpTroops. I know, it's beyond me, too. I don't pretend to understand it. All we Terds do is spend our days trying to stab one another in the back. Just take a good look at that mainscreen up there, Abercrombie. Go ahead, hotshot bizman. Take a good damn look at it. I dare you."

In spite of himself, Abercrombie does. While trying not to, he starts to notice the impossible angles and the grotesque distortions of the bodies spread over the weird, white ground.

"Do you have any honest idea what those men just faced to take out all those killbots? Do you, Abercrombie? Even the remotest fucking idea in hell?" Again, answers are a charade here. "I didn't think so. Now, you tell me. If those troopers are willing to kill and be killed serving *our* ends, can you even begin to imagine their level of motivation when all of a sudden they're killing and being killed to serve *their own*?"

Abercrombie nods. Subprime has landed some solid points. Nice speech. Lesson learned. Well done. Abercrombie had been aware that his plan wasn't exactly copasetic up to now. It's probably time to mend some fences. Honestly, he's been at a loss to pin down the Wobbly mindset. Subprime's real insights couldn't hurt. "All right, I get it, ArCommander," Abercrombie admits. "And I know I can be a big jackass at times. Comes with the biz territory. Know what I mean? But can you and I call a truce? For real? We're supposed to be working on this project together, after all. Remember? Helping one another out?" He's getting response zero from Subprime. As a matter of fact, the look on the ArCommander's face tells Abercrombie that he's somewhere else, listening to someone else. Abercrombie knows not to give up. "Look, it's only because the ceo wants this transaction done nonlethal and on the hush that I got fingered to direct it and not you. No other reason. So it's nothing personal, right? I don't mean to be stepping on your career toes, here. Soon as this job's done

I'm turning back in my ArCommander's pins. But the fact remains, real bottomline, is that I have my instructions to carry out."

"We'll see about that right now, fuckass." Subprime turns to address the mainscreen. "Yes, sir. Go ahead, Mr. Subceo."

The panorama of the burning Strykers vanishes. Replacing it is the giant face of Ponzi. He's looking down grimly at the two ArCommanders. "He's been convinced, ArCommander Subprime. Gloves off doublego. Deadcount no object. Deadcount tell no tales."

"That's a firm, sir." Subprime jerks his head at Abercrombie, who's standing slackjawed in alarm beside him. "And this sorry fuck, sir?"

"Keep him counterslice on their feed," the huge Ponzi face answers without looking at Abercrombie. "That's still Dmega priority. He's our best. Let's hope he's a match for them. If he can't deliver, list him kia. No word of any of this ever gets out."

The giant screen goes blank. The Sit-Ops room, as though long waiting for this cue, jumps to operation. Just before two burly Netsmen grab Abercrombie and lead him away to his new posting at slicestation in a modest room not too far down the hallway, Subprime reminds him, without bothering to look at him, of a TexArc truism. "ArCommander," he says, "never fuck with Net."

☆ ☆ ☆ ☆ ☆ ☆

Two days after the Stryker encounter, Mountain Home loses all contact with the Wobbly first line in the southern Sawtooth Forest. No distressig, no netword comes from those CorpTroops hidden along the mountains. No nothing, in fact. The Strike UAVs that Mountain Home had aloft vanish without a peep as well, making recon impossible. The next dawn, the flyflocks of MEMS show up along the southern and eastern base perimeters, looking like a horrible mosquito infestation flittering low among the sagebrush. Mall asks the Wing Commander, AirColonel Bacardi, an intelligent, polite, and soft-spoken Terd in her estimation, just what in the bloody hell those things are.

"MicroElectroMechanical Systems, ma'am. Sensor nanobots about a millimeter big. An awful lot of them, as you can see."

Indeed, the viewscreens in Base Ops covering those exposures are nearly black with them. Mall eyes the MEMS with dread. They obviously flock with a single purpose, a single mind.

"Are they bleeding dangerous? Can they kill you?"

"No, ma'am. TexArc uses them only as findbots—for reconnaissance." Bacardi folds his arms over his chest and shakes his head. "No, you make stuff like that lethal and you could wind up with big problems on your hands. Even the Crats aren't greedy enough not to know that. Some GNR you got to sit on tight. You know what I mean." The AirColonel strokes his small, blond mustache for a while, watching how the MEMS hang just outside the base perimeter. "You know what, though? I think I'd better scramble the Wing. Wherever MEMS show up, worse is sure to follow. I don't want the 366th getting caught with its pants down this morning."

"By all means," Mall agrees. She quotes the Fighter Wing's own motto to him, "Audentes Fortuna Juvat."

"Doublecheck that, ma'am. Let's hope Fortune favors the bold today. I got a feeling we're going to need a little luck."

Bacardi's getting the FotoFighters airborne in time will be about the only thing that goes well for the Wobblies this day.

☆ ☆ ☆ ☆ ☆ ☆

The brigade of NetExos had doubletime shuffled all night to cover the two hundred kilometers from the first line of insurgents in the mountains to the renegade ArcAir base at Mountain Home. Prime mission there is intact facilities retake, terming all insurgents in that given procedure. They'd first swung due west into scrublands that never had been inhabited. They certainly didn't want simply to track up along the T-84 corridor where they'd be easily detected. Once they reached the drybed of what had been the Clover River, they followed it northwest through desolate country, sometimes mind-numbing in its flat sameness and sometimes breathtaking in its wind and water deepcut elegance. They came upon the C. J. Strike Reservoir—the Cheney River fattened wide by a downstream dam—in the predawn light. At that point, the ArColonel in command, a notoriously strak combat veteran named Lehmanbros, sent MEMS forward to reconnoiter. When he saw the attackcraft scramble he knew he had no choice but to divide his force. After consulting with Sit-Ops back at Hill, he decided to send two of his battalions on toward BoiCity. They would travel along the south bank of the Cheney all the way up to Caldwell, about one hundred more klicks, where they'd cross the big river and attack from the west—from the Wobbly standpoint, an unlikely direction for Net to come. The ArColonel was assured by ArCommander Subprime that the remaining third battalion of NetExos would be sufficient to retake the ArcAir base. Net counterslicers, he insisted, were on the verge of a breakthrough. ArColonel Lehmanbros naturally preferred to rely on firepower rather than slicers, but needed to take Subprime at his word. Two of his battalions took off, sprinting doublego north for the rebel meg, while the third stood on one bank of the reservoir and, on his command, leapt as a unit to the far bank. At that point those thousand NetExos were on full swarm of Mountain Home.

☆ ☆ ☆ ☆ ☆ ☆

If the flyflocks of nanobots terrified Mall, her technology shock is incalculable when she sees on the viewscreens an army of men bounding, at impossible heights and distances, effortlessly over the perimeter fences and onto the base. The autodefenses are doing their job of targeting salvo after salvo of misterfire at these impossibly leaping figures, but with only the result of knocking them slightly off their vectors. This is sodding lunatic, thinks Mall. They should all be cranberry vapor. These extraordinary fighters look to be outfitted in nothing more than visored helmets and some sort of one-piece, sleek, camo coverall, but many of them wear enormous backpacks and a few carry heavy weaponry they flourish like toys. Before the Wobblies really know what's happening, the tarmacs to the southwest have all been captured and secured by these creatures, and more of them are overleaping A Street, Bomber Road, and Silver Sage in their drive to the very heart of the base. Base Ops, a long and low underground room lined by consoles and viewscreens, is in complete uproar.

"Jesus Almighty and fuck me!" shouts the opsman to Mall's right, frantically trying to manipulate shields and security armaments to keep up with the invaders. "I never really believed these fuckmothers existed!"

"And just what fuckmothers are we talking about?" Mall shouts back.

"Exoskeletons, ma'am!" The poor man screams, as though speaking in nothing but expletives. "Your basic Net asswipe in HPA—and armed to the teeth! Worst fucking nightmare!"

They hear mister bursts and smackdown fire from above.

"HPA?" Mall shouts louder.

"Human Performance Augmentation! Leap tall buildings! Shit like that!" Eyes fixated on his viewscreen, the opsman misses more of his targets and swears under his breath. "You got anything up your sleeve, ma'am, you better pull it out right now!"

Mall's at a loss what to do militarily. Not her area. Her Maneuvers fighters and Enron are still gone out there somewhere, in what all these military people around her bafflingly refer to as "the field." Mall can't help picturing pastureland. She's been desperately wishing for their return for days. And Sinalco's been holed up in the sliceroom the past forty-eight hours solid, struggling to fend off, from what Mall can gather, some cheeky ArcNet bastard who's trying to fidget his way into WobblyNet. All Mall can think to do is recommend they call for Bacardi and his FotoFighters from above. The opsman rolls his eyes and curses, but Mall turns toward comm, opposite them along the room, to suggest a request be issued. Before she can shout, every Airman and CorpTroop in Base Ops is doubled over vomiting profusely, and then falling totally off balance. In moments, everyone except Mall—and the odd Airman around the room who has plucked out his earpiece—is rolling about on the floor, groaning in his own mess. Mall has the unsettling impression that the Terds left standing know precisely what's taking place *and* were wishing now they'd never turned Wobbly. She picks up her mister. With uncanny synchronicity, three of these Exoskeleton fellows crash, boots-first, through the ceiling. They immediately begin executing the helpless Airmen and CorpTroops worming on the floor. Mall squeezes off a rushed burst in their direction, and witnesses for herself how their sleek suits promptly transform into nanoarmor to absorb the countless impacts then, just as instantly, return to dullmatt fabric. All three of them wheel and return her mister fire. For a twinkling, Mall entertains the fantastic notion that the maelstrom of burning lead pellets have all agreed to teem about her, in a kind of swirling cocoon, before tearing her to shreds. But then she realizes she *is* standing inside some manner of twisting gyre and that she's *not* being torn to shreds. A curious throbbing thums in her ears. A faint odor of petrol reaches far up her nostrils. Then Mall's personal tornado vanishes—implodes?—and Sinalco's standing beside her, propping her up. "Ça va?" she's asking. "Ça va?"

When Mall recovers enough to reply, it's in a surprisingly holiday tone. "Oui, ça va bien," she nods amiably to her companion. She notices, only peripherally, that the three superhuman Netsmen lie dead. Sinalco speaks very seriously to Mall. "On y va," she says.

"Oui, ça va bien," Mall agrees.

Pulling Mall along by the hand, Sinalco wends them through the underground passageways toward the northeast corner of the base.

Explosions and gunfire are constant aboveground. Sinalco explains the noises to Mall. “Those with their SigCaps back on now are—how do the CorpTroopers say it—still good to go and can fight.”

Mall hasn’t the faintest clue what Sinalco means. She’s still half in a daze. The pair run out of the cover of the passageways and emerge at the corner of Gunfighter Avenue and North Mellen Drive, hiding a while in a vestibule. Out in the streets, Airmen and CorpTrooper bodies lie everywhere. Vaulting Netsmen occasionally sail by overhead, gracefully firing downward. Sinalco picks Mall up in her arms, effortlessly as if Mall were without mass, and whispers words of caution into her ear. “Il faut qu’on va tellement vite maintenant.” Mall simply nods yes.

They’re out the doorway and past the housing areas along Tamarack Street in a flash. Then they’re high in the air and over the barricade fencing along Perimeter Road. Then they’re out-racing, rather readily, a full squad of Exoskeleton Netsmen in pursuit. Finally, they’re skimming, just the two of them, across the vast sage flats of the Cheney River Plain, heading directly into the climbing sun. Mall feels positively giddy, like a child, the wind pressing her face, being cradled like a baby, moving so very fast. She gets a cockeyed notion Sinalco’s feet aren’t even touching the ground. When Mall finally thinks to look down, she sees that they aren’t. Sinalco’s feet, in fact her entire legs, are like a blurring whirl. The sight only sobers her a touch. Mall cranes her head back to get a look into Sinalco’s large, kind, oval face. As chummy as a drinking companion who’s suddenly concerned for her partner’s welfare, Mall inquires: “Hey, just what the bloody fuck are you?”

Keeping her eyes fixed on the horizon, eyes unblinkingly, reflecting the orange ball of sun, Sinalco replies, “Not any thing I seem.”

☆ ☆ ☆ ☆ ☆ ☆

Their sprint north to Caldwell had taken under an hour. During that time, ArcMajor Ovobody, in command of the third NetExos battalion, received the welcome news from ArColonel Lehmanbros that Mountain Home had fallen. Wobbly attackcraft were still in the air, but they no longer had a base of ops. That made them vulnerable. ArcNet counterslice, too, had finally penetrated the enemy's net. Sit-Ops down at Hill ArcSpace not only had gained vital containment of the Wobbly slice trying to outgo the IMS, but it had triggered the nasty vestibular nerve overstimulation built into the ihear. That meant every Parker and CorpTroop in the region would be falling down puking with motion sickness. So will every turncoat Terd too stupid to pull out his earpiece. This assault suddenly had turned into mop-up.

When they swarm BoiCity from the west, both battalions go under orders to ignore the disequilibriumed shitubers in the parks and bound right for the Gater district. Taking out the Wobbly leadership is priority one. The further they get into the meg, the more unbelievable is the devastation along the river. ArcMajor Ovobody's command group leaps over mountain after mountain of rubble that used to be smogscrapers. He has to ask himself just what in the hell has been going on here. Occupying and securing the downtown is piece of cake with no live resistance to face and only the Gater autodefenses to deal with. Getting inside that Pyramid, though, will be a different story. Such structures selfdefend. Ovobody also wonders how in the hell a mob of Servs ever managed to get into this one in the first place. While his MEMS explore the exterior of the Pyramid, searching for openings, the ArcMajor tells his Netsmen to begin putting all the Wobblies strewn around the vicinity out of their misery. On allcomm, he compares the act to putting down rabid dogs, suggesting it's really for their own good. He's not certain how extensive a house-to-house they'll be told to conduct afterwards out in the parks. There'll be hundreds of thousands to democratize out there, but Net will assume anyone occupying the district is hardcore militant and needs to be termed. That's doublego for all Terds who've been "infected," as Sit-Ops calls it, by the Wobbly slice. Right there, you're talking days. May as well use this downtime, Ovobody calculates, to make a start. He orders his exec officer to jack up maxvol over comm the Netsmen's favorite psychsong, an earsplitting HeavyNano tune called "Burn, Fuckmother, Burn!" The NetExos fan out and eagerly begin their termings.

Cracking the Pyramid is first-thing-first. Ovobody and his six company ArCaptains start to review and discuss, over selectcomm, the MEMS initial data series. The nanobots aren't picking up much. Abruptly, each of the NetExos suffers a jolt, as though some giant boot has kicked them in the head. Their arms and legs start to tingle and numb. Even though their heads remain clear, their bodies lose much motor coordination. Standing becomes a concentrated effort, and walking a straight line an impossibility. Their Exosuits, it occurs to Ovobody. Something's gone wrong with them. *Like they're intoxicated?* With deepenetrate braintegrate existing between equipment and wearer, the Netsmen become prisoners inside their suits. Unlike the simple RHex units linked to CorpTroops, Netsmen can't undergo straight disconnect with the Exos. Once you're in, you're in until you're peeled back out by tech. However the suit fares, you fare along with it. Every NetExo in brigade, all five thousand of them occupying BoiCity and Mountain Home, are staggering and reeling like Groundsmen on virfurlough. What's worse, ArcMajor Ovobody sees the vestibular trip on the ihear just got switched off. All around him, and he assumes throughout the meg, Wobblies in their thousands are slowly reorienting themselves and beginning to regain their feet. This isn't going to be pretty.

☆ ☆ ☆ ☆ ☆ ☆

High and invisible over the river plain between the ArcAir base and the meg, AirColonel Bacardi reluctantly keeps his Wing in reserve, hoping for an opening and a shot at a useful groundstrike. He's also wary of TexArc aircraft coming into the area to challenge him, and puzzled by why they haven't appeared yet. The official mission of the Gunfighters, what the 366th was nicknamed decades ago, is to provide decisive combat power worldwide, on demand. *How ironic*, Bacardi has been musing while circling, t*hat worldwide has become backyard*. He saw right away that their ArcAir base would be lost. The combination of Exos and the cruel vestibular trick made that certain. Fortunately, pilots in flight don't wear the standard ihear. Otherwise, most of his planes might have plowed into the deck from the equilibrium disrupt. Even though they survived, there was nothing practical his FotoFighters could have done to prevent the base from falling, short of leveling it themselves—Bacardi's final act, he's decided, if it comes to that. His scouts are telling him it looks like another walkover is taking shape in BoiCity. Already the centermeg is occupied. Doesn't look like the 366th can do much good up there, either. Yep, he sure must have been nuts to believe the Wobbly movement could last ten minutes against Net. May as well start blowing Arc shit up before fuel becomes a problem. Just then an irregular channel crackles on his comm.

<Bacardi? You are there?>

<Ma'am?> he returns the sig. Sounds like the big woman from the outcrop accent. <Is that you, Sinalco?>

<Yes. That is me.> The siglock is crystal now.

<Are you all right? Do you need assistance?>

<Non, non. I am fine. I have with me Mall. We are out the base.>

<Where are you, ma'am? Do you need pick up?>

<Non. Never mind at all. Where you are?>

Bacardi pauses to decipher her syntax. <I'm hovering over T-84 at the moment with nothing much to do. Things on ground aren't looking good.>

<I know. But that changes now very soon. You must go help the BoiCity people. Very fast.>

<Ma'am, what's changed?>

<Our Wobblies are up now and their superman are down. Go fast.>

<I don't know what you mean, ma'am. That makes no sense.>

<I throw the logic bomb into their ArcNet. It makes the topsy-turvy. Their disrupt goes off and my disrupt goes on, but I don't know how long for. That is why you must go fast for the Wobblies.>

That sounds to Bacardi like all the opening his Wing needs. <Roger that, ma'am. The Gunfighters are on it. Good luck to you. Out.>

A tug comes on Sinalco's sleeve. Before Mall can ask her question, Sinalco jokes with her. "Tell me, ma petite, who is this Roger person these flyboys are always speaking about?"

"Did you manage as well to unblock the Wobbly align feeding outside the IMS?"

Sinalco shakes her head. "Non," she replies, "trop difficile. They have our Uncle bottled up again tight, like the genie. I don't think we are slicing our feed even as far to the SaltCity any longer."

"How did that happen?"

"Someone very clever counters me. Très habile, cet type. He knows to knapsack back into the WobblyNet to make go *paf* this ihear équilibre. Ça c'est ma faute. Je n'ai le pas vu. All Servs not wearing the SigCap fall down malade. Many Terds also. Que je suis bête to make for them the WobblyNet so comfortable."

"And this wanker cut off our taste as well?"

"I fear so, oui. He manipulates entire system behind him. Too big. Too much pour moi. I think I don't get around it any more."

Mall settles back into Sinalco's generous bosom. "Then we're stuffed," she says.

"Chérie," says Sinalco, "we were stuffed since the moment we step off the subterrenes. No one in Countermeasures or the Caucus expects you to do half so much as you do."

"Then what's been the bloody point of this whole, bloody farce?"

Sinalco never feels obligated to answer rhetorical questions. She concentrates on maintaining her various aligns and feeds, as well as her amazing velocity across the high desert. Mall has yet to bother about inquiring where they are headed, let alone anything at all about what Sinalco is. She seems to have resigned herself to this bizarre ride and to Sinalco's bizarre care.

☆ ☆ ☆ ☆ ☆ ☆

The FotoFighters work from centermeg outward. To every pilot's surprise, NetExos make easy targets. All of their amazing agility is gone, and their nanotextile armoring is functioning hit-or-miss. When attacked, random portions of their suits make the instant transformation to nanoarmor while other portions don't. The results can be eccentric and gruesome. On one pass the Netsman will lose a foot, or a portion of an arm, but on the next pass his head flies off. In some cases the extremities remain perfectly protected against the FotoFighter nosecannons, but the target's torso disappears. In still others, half the man will be left standing, but cleaved in peculiar ways—horizontally, vertically, diagonally. As Sinalco intended, there's no logic to it. The 366th picks off NetExos desperately clinging onto the sides of high buildings, hectically zigzagging down narrow streets, crawling pathetically for cover amid downtown rubble, vainly trying to roll onto their backs and return fire at attackcraft they cannot see. Bacardi's Wing soon clears the ward around the Pyramid. The Gunfighters then begin to make their sweeps outward and mainly southward, toward the Gater district walls and the edges of the parks. Along this rim they come upon a very different battlespace. Instead of the target-rich environment of the downtown, they're faced with a tangle of friendlies and hostiles locked in riot below them.

Packs of recovered Servs attack the Net forces in distinct bundles. Twenty or thirty Parkers struggle with a single NetExo, looking like fire ants trying to bring down a large beetle. They swarm and plague the Netsman inside, pulling him over if they can, dragging him along the street, poking and hacking at his suit with knives and hatchets, looking for weaknesses or fissures in the nano. From moment to moment the Netsman doesn't know what his suit can or cannot do. When the nanomuscle fiber in his gloves fires normally, he can crush the skulls of as many of his assailants as he can get his hands on, but they just keep him coming. When the nanotextile along his back won't armor, won't keep him from getting gored, he must lie down or press against a building and fight off the mob as best he can. The two battalions that invaded BoiCity are heavyarmed. Most of these NetExos carry ultralong supra-smackdowns or the massive hyper-howitzer instead of standard issue misters. That's a good thing for the Wobblies in this hand-to-hand brawling—except when one of those heavy-weapons pops back online and the Netsman, trying to use it for a club, can coordinate enough to pull off a round or two. Then great swaths of Wobblies fly into the air or are incinerated just before whole buildings go up in concussions that knock everyone flat for a two or three megblock radius. For every Netsman overpowered and killed, twenty to fifty Parkers might be mangled, kicked, clubbed, or crushed to death. It's a slow, bloody business taking down so many thousands of these bastards. Every once in a while the robotic system from the waist down will actuate, sending a Netsman arcing out of control over the crowds, sometimes hundreds of meters into the air. Often there's a Wobbly or two taken aloft with him, clinging for dear life to a backpack or a boot.

All the FotoFighters can do in this fight is fly cover over the battle-space and pick off isolated NetExos whenever possible. Looking down on the melee, stunned by the Serv tenacity, Barcardi murmers, "Good God, I had no idea." He's suddenly encouraged. If this is the extent of ArcNet plan to take back the Wobbly meg, it's not going to work. They might just hold. And if Sinalco's logic bomb can last, his Airmen just might be able to take back Mountain Home.

☆ ☆ ☆ ☆ ☆ ☆

The looming and sour face of Ponzi fills once again the mainscreen of the Sit-Ops room at Hill ArcSpace Base. It speaks loudly and just one word to ArCommander Subprime. "Urbicide."

Subprime nods once to acknowledge.

"And the civilian, Mr. Subceo?" the ArCommander asks in afterthought. "After all, he did counterslice their WobblyNet to cork it from spread. That was plus ultra. And he tripped their ihears. That handed Mountain Home to us."

"Yes, yes. But he couldn't do shit about their counter-counterslice, now could he? That logic bomb Wobbly just lobbed into Net has screwed the whole damned pooch, now hasn't it?"

"If I might say so, sir, that was one freak of a bomb, almost wrapped like a trojan horse. None of us here had ever seen anything like it."

"I don't have time for this, ArCommander. Knowledge is danger. Shoot him immediately. Call down GLASS now."

Blankscreen.

☆ ☆ ☆ ☆ ☆ ☆

GLobal Area Strike System combines space-based High-Energy Lasers and Kinetic Energy Weapons with hundreds of lowearth and high-earth-orbit surveillance satellites in order to control, indisputably, large parcels of the globe. When necessary, Trans-Atmospheric Vehicles can be sent down as well, usually for highly surgical stealth strikes. There's no escaping ArcSpace. It sees all, can do all. And it monitors tightest TexArc's own corpturf. Security begins at home. ArcSpace FarWest sector has been running mid-latitude highalert for weeks. At last, CorpHQ gives it the goahead. Permission to deal down some cosmic death. Megbarrage commences with KEW, the unnerving fléchettes and highdensity rods that descend invisibly and penetrate at hypervelocity. At a stroke, nearly thirty thousand in and around the BoiCity Gater district die, minced or skewered. Fully half the FotoFighters are shred to pieces along with them. To establish ancillary dominancy, the HEL multi-megawatt chemical laser constellation then precision targets another thirty or so Wobbly attack-craft, frying them where they cruise. Their OLED compuproject camouflage is irrelevant to ArcSpace sensor array. The terror in the streets is shared in common by Wobblies and Netsmen. All TexArcans stand transfixed, hunched and with their mouths open, peeping upward. When a second and wider-spread KEW bombardment rains down, they can only believe Armageddon has come.

Or has it?

As suddenly as the searing metal streaked down out of the clearblue bigsky, a soothing voice now comes audfeed over ArcNet milcomm and WobblyNet ihear alike, a voice sounding the opposite of the carnage all around them. A voice pleasant and optimistic. A voice appeasing and hopeful. A voice disarming and sincere, sentimental and forthright. Terd and Serv recognize it at once as that of their ceo, taking the time out of his busy schedule to break through the netraffic to speak directly to them—from the heart, off the cuff. Evidently, they are told, peace has broken out—providentially and miraculously. Netsmen are to be the special guests of the Wobblies for a time. All the hostile functions of their Exoskeleton suits are being shut down—immediately. Wobblies, please take good care of your Netsmen brothers. Tend to their wounds, provide them food, drink, and shelter. Many thanks. And everyone, please, no more fighting. Peace is here. Enjoy!

With most listeners standing spackled in blood and ankle-deep in raw flesh, what yub could be more mindfuck than this?

☆ ☆ ☆ ☆ ☆ ☆

Snug in the strongbox of the Gold Butte auxillary hardroom, the Grand Pooh-Bah of Wobbly sits at the head of a highly polished, oblong marble-topped conference table. He's got his new boots up on it. He's leaning back in his exechair with both hands resting on top of his head, fingers intertwined. He's smiling, even laughing out loud at times. He's quite at his ease. He and his top ministers are watching a full wallscreen showing the slice that's being fed, live and direct, into the Simulacrum—over *GaterNews*, to be exact. This means every Terd in TexArc is seeing exactly what they're seeing right now. On the screen, alerted in the upper left corner as SPECIAL BULLETIN and identified in the lower right corner as *ArcNet's Secret, Dirty War: the Battle for BoiCity*, a deftly edited vid, grisly and compelling and irrefutable, displays NetExos squeezing off the heads of ordinary citizens, NetExos leaping startling heights while firing heavyweapons down into primly landscaped Gatervillas, the waffling outline of near-invisible attackcraft executing strafing runs on thousands of screaming people fleeing down narrow centermeg streets, and, the pièce de résistance, a spacelaunched blitzkrieg of shard metal streaking down from above to pulverize edifices and to turn human beings into jiffysushi. No mistake about it, each image of the feed is worth more than a thousand words. Just to make sure, the gravity of these events is being confirmed by a voiceover asking hard, journalistic questions: "How can one explain such scenes of horror taking place inside our own corplands? Has ArcNet, the clandestine power behind CorpHQ, finally run completely amok? Are we witnessing the beginnings of a bloody coup de corp? Who's *really* in charge at CorpHQ? How can the topcrats stand idly by and allow such butchery to be carried out by our own CorpForces against our own innocent corpcivilians? Which meg will be targeted next: San Francisco, Greater Boston, Atlanta? Can anyone ever really feel safe again living in a Gater district? Isn't this *very* bad for business?"

The voice is that of the slice's editor, writer, and producer—Brand.

"Bad for business!" hoots Oak. "Now that'll move them Terds to tears! The Crats can't afford to let this shit feed for too much longer."

"Damn right they can't," Jip agrees.

The roguefeed has been slicing the Simulacrum for close to ten minutes. Now a new aud is heard, a booming voice rising from individual consoles around the conference table. "Hello in the BoiCity Pyramid!"

A grim face fills the small vidscreens in front of each Wobbly Minister.

"See there?" says Oak. "Now what'd I tell you, boys? Like fucking clockwork." The Grand Pooh-Bah looks down at the man on his vidscreen. "Who the fuck are you?"

"My name's Jitney," the man explains. His composure is studied. "I'm subceo boss of Security at TexArc CorpHQ and—"

"You ain't the big bossman," Oak cuts him off. "I don't need to be talking to you."

Even though the subceo manages to control his voice, the anger is conspicuous on his face. "I can assure you," he tries again to explain, "that I'm fully authorized to speak on behalf of the ceo and..."

Oak signals to Brand, who's sitting at a sidewall console out of sight from any vidscreen. She nods and pads once. The Simulacrum slice broadens its feed to include *CratLife Today*. Oak says indifferently to the vidscreen, "I'll patch it through to Serv *Vieworld*, too, if you like, Mr. Jitney. Don't make a shit to me." The conference vidscreens return blank. Oak uses this time to preen in front of his Ministers. "Only deal at the very top, fellas. Only at the very top. That's the first rule of biz."

"With whom am I speaking?"

A man with a face like a hatchet and hair like cornhusk has appeared on the conference-table vidscreens. The Wobblies can't quite believe what they see. It's the big bossman.

"Name's Oak Wat."

"Well, Mr. Wat, tell me. What can I do for you?"

"Seeing how I'm the one got you by the balls," says Oak, "I was figuring you tell me."

Bleached Wheat's eyes seem to deaden more into their icy blue. Then he grins. "That is indeed the name of the game, is it not, Mr. Wat? I can see you're a man who understands the nature of power. You're a go-getter with a can-do attitude who knows how to watch out for number one. You're a man always climbing to the top. Am I right about that, Mr. Wat?"

"Right as rain. I'd be a fool to be anything different, now, wouldn't I?"

Bleached Wheat laughs and nods. "Damn straight, Mr. Wat. Damn straight. If that's the case, perhaps the best thing for you and me to do is lunch."

"I'm listening."

"You and your top Wobblies, say, here to CorpHQ. We'll powwow, figure out how to divide this meg pie you've won. I do assume that's the point of your squeezing my balls, Mr. Wat—enlightened self interest. You're looking for a way to secure your capital gains. Am I right? Or are you pursuing some sort of pansy, libby agenda?"

Oak looks around the table at his Ministers. These days, they all seem to have a bit more of the selfoblige in mind, and a lot less of the we're all in this together. Wobbly is all fine and good, but not if you carry it too damn far.

"Could be," Oak answers vaguely, thinking that a negotiation technique. "Let's just say we got some grievances we need to get aired."

"Very good, then," Bleached Wheat nods encouragingly. "Grievances I can certainly understand. That's what I'm here for, Mr. Wat. I'm a problem solver. Please come be my guest. Air your viewpoints. Tell me exactly what it is you want."

Oak checks his Ministers. Some nod yes. Others no. Oak's leery. "Just nice as pie as that?"

"Well, Mr. Wat, of course we'll need to extend to one another the standard reassurances of deal."

"You saying a trust swap?"

"Yes, I believe that's exactly what I'm saying."

"You got something in mind?"

"As a matter of fact, I have. Something we both obviously don't want to do without. Something of value to each of us, Mr. Wat, to insure there's no raw dealing on either side."

"Like what?"

"Well," Bleached Wheat appears to be hesitating, "how many of my ArcNet special forces are still alive in your meg right now?"

"Them guys in them freaky jumpy suits?"

"Yes. Those."

Oak looks to Jiplap. Jiplap checks a lapbook beside him and says about a thousand, give or take. Oak relays that number then asks, "But what good are they to me?"

"The real question here, Mr. Wat," corrects Bleached Wheat, cordially, "is what good are they to *me*. The answer to that is: one hell of a lot. Think about it, Mr. Wat. Those Terds are quite indispensable to TexArc. They represent our most highly trained and informed Netsmen. Your holding them there in your meg as prisoners would more than insure your safe passage to and from CorpHQ."

Oak checks down the table with Jiplap, who thinks about it for a second then shrugs and nods his okay. Oak then looks at Hap, who shakes his head no. Being a former used vehic pitchman, he's smelling a rat.

"Deal," says Oak.

"Now wait a minute, Mr. Wat," Beached Wheat smiles. "I wasn't born yesterday. I'm going to need something in return from you. I'm not about to get sharped by an enterprising young Serv like yourself."

"Oh, yeah? Like what?"

"I'm entrusting to your care some of my top people. It seems only fair for you to do the same."

"I ain't handing you over no Wobblies."

"Of course not, Mr. Wat. I wouldn't ask you to, or expect that of you. Your coalition seems predicated on a profound mutual trust among its members, and I respect that. In this area we share common corporate values, you and I, Mr. Wat. Did you realize that?"

"Whatever. Just get to your damn point."

"My point is, Mr. Wat, I don't have in mind Wobblies at all, but only the outsiders among you. The non-Servs. All of the outlander EVens, for one, as well as one outstatus Terd dykebitch who I'm sure is there in the room with you."

Oak can't help nodding slightly in admiration of the big bossman's savvy as he looks across to where Brand sits. She's looking back at him, alarmed, her face turned a violent mustard.

"Sorry," says Oak, but still obviously looking across the room at something, "I don't know who you mean."

"*Sure* you do, Mr. Wat," Bleached Wheat cajoles.

Oak can't conceal a smile. He looks back at the vidscreen. "Now how'd you reckon that one?"

"Oh, please, Mr. Wat. Don't tell me you're one of those people who believes *all* Crats have their heads stuffed up their ass. Who else but her, the supreme whizbang of the Simulacrum, could slice it with such facility or, for that matter, construct so neat a little extravaganza as the one you're currently roguefeeding on our align? I mean, it's absolutely first rate, just as is your strategy to squeeze my balls with it."

"They sure must be turning a touch blue by now, Mr. Ceo. That feed's been running quite a little while."

Bleached Wheat doesn't react to Oak's little goad. Instead, after a significant and perfectly calm wait, he says, amiably, "I'm willing to bet, when it comes right down to it, Mr. Wat, we're both just commonsense joes who know a sweet deal when we see one."

Oak figures he won't get no better barter than this. Mall and them have been nothing but a pain in his side since the Wobblies took the meg. And with the sweet deal he's looking to cut at CorpHQ, he won't be needing Brand's services no more. Boy, that painted-up dykebitch must be kicking herself right about now for not risking going down to Mountain Home with them other dykebitch slits. He won't be giving up shit to hand over the whole pack of dykebitches to the big bossman. A deal don't get no sweeter than that.

"Okay by me," Oak agrees. "Most the damned EVens are dead already. Those that ain't we'll help you track down. Brand, here, we'll bring along with us when we come to your place."

"Choice," beams Bleached Wheat.

Optimism of the Will

The first night they'd stayed in something Sinalco knew used to be named the Shoshone Ice Caves—some pathetic roadside tourist stop. Nothing was left, save a dilapidated sign, and the caves themselves were catacombed holes sunk into the flat, sage-desert floor—cavities extending bigger, wider, deeper, and colder the further down they went. The first night there was no pursuit, not in a chasing sense. Mall loitered near the cave's opening, contemplating both the brilliant blaze of the Milky Way and how bloody ArcSpace was up there, no doubt probing for them that very moment. Did Sinalco have some way to mask their whereabouts? What was Sinalco capable of, and just what *was* Sinalco? That first night Mall had no heart for asking questions. She hardly spoke a word. In existentialist terms, that first night Mall pondered only the nothingness side of the philosophic formula. Her Wobblies had been overrun like they weren't even there, like they didn't even matter. Nothingness. All that work, all that signification, all that human coalition—all ground to dust by brute technology in the blink of an eye. Nothingness. She was certain BoiCity had suffered the same fate as Mountain Home—rifled and gutted by those insane jumping men. How many thousands upon thousands of Wobblies are lying dead? Where's Enron, Cardinal, Pernod, and Migros? How long before she and Sinalco are hunted down and slaughtered by some technology she can't even imagine? Ten minutes? Ten hours? Ten days? Nothingness. Persistently, Sinalco tried to buoy Mall's spirits, pointing out the rare invention and unlikely accomplishment of Uncle Wobbly. The miracle of bringing a slim glimmer of hope to a giant city of the hopeless. Such efforts against such odds were never to be dismissed. They still had tricks up their sleeve, and might well manage to slip away. Don't forego all hope, my dear—not quite yet. In short: being. Mall listened in testy silence, becoming so cold and hollow with hunger she felt a Shoshone Ice Cave herself. Well past midnight, she squelched all cheeering with a single rebuttal: a bloody peasant becoming the bloody fucking king does not render the bloody fucking kingdom sodding democratic.

Their next two days and nights were spent further east, wandering a singularly odd landscape Sinalco identified as Craters of the Moon—kilometer after square kilometer of wide volcanic craters, smaller splatter cones, deep sink holes, and sweeping lava fields so black some of the flows appear iridescent blue. Titanium magnetite crystals suspended in the glassy rock, she explained. "Like the blue serpent, n'est-ce pas?"

Mall couldn't care less about the geology or the poetry of this godawful place. "It mucks up their bleeding sensors, right?" she asked.

"Oui," Sinalco admitted. "A little."

Mall was extremely grouchy from eating only bulbs of strange plants Sinalco knew where to dig up, and sucking only on dirty ice. The bulbs were Sego Lilies, fibrous and dirt tasting, rather like masticating a waterlogged chestnut. They dared not light a small fire even to fry a snake or tiny lizard. And a jackrabbit roast, which the Wobblies had prepared back in the wilderness area, seemed a distant memory of a royal feast. Sinalco, of course, ate or drank nothing. Apparently, she had no need—not even for the salt they managed to scrounge at the licks. Stubbornly, Mall asked nothing about it. They felt pursuit those two nights, overhead. Stealth airvehics circled in the starry soup, impossible for Mall to spot, but Sinalco always knew when they got too close. Every few hours Mall would imagine hearing bootsteps approaching quietly over the granular surfaces, but no Netsman ever materialized. They'd probably just leap in on them quite unannounced, anyway. Sinalco assured her ArcNet had yet to put anyone on the ground. “They still eliminate the grids from above.”

Mall didn’t like, trust, or want the advantage she obviously enjoyed with Sinalco. Under the current circumstances, she knew that aversion made no sense, and she’d never imagined herself to be so extreme a technophobe. But Mall had been betrayed. By Countermeasures, by Caucus. By everyone. She’d been left outside the core infoloop. There was no greater duplicity. And this Sinalco thing—she/it crossed some line. Mall knew it. Whatever Sinalco was, Mall knew it wasn’t right.

Day and night they spent hiding and moving in and among the long, narrow caves formed by the hardened lava tubes. It was time marked only by stark contrasts. The searing heat of the black surfaces above ground, the sudden, cool interiors of the caves. Dry and roaring afternoon winds above ground, damp stillness below ground. Brilliant sunlight under the dome of the big sky, then the snug, dim, endless passageways below. These caves were treacherous to walk. Lava remelt and splash had left small, sharp stalactites along the low ceilings. In the deeper caves, ice could be underfoot or dripped into jagged stalagmites. Slippery and spongy lichens, mosses, and algae might cover the walls. In some tubes, sulfate compounds formed mineral deposits smelling like death. When Sinalco decided they needed to move on from this area, Mall wasn’t sorry to leave the moonscape for, once again, the more exposed desert stretches. She was sorry at being carried like a baby once more while Sinalco went at high speeds, but she knew it was necessary. The pair continued due east, putting hundreds of kilometers between them and the disasters of Wobbly.

On the fourth day after the ArcNet counterstrikes, early in the afternoon, they come to rest on the Big Southern Butte in the middle of the Arco Desert. The mountain knolls up like a 2300-meter dumpling on the level sagebrush flats. To its east are two smaller sister buttes, one a round-backed lump, the other more interestingly peaked at its northwest end. The trio is all that's left of a range long since eroded away. Sinalco keeps them constantly on the move over the butte, slipping from one combe and nook to another, lying low for a few hours, then ascending up the cover of the gulches to spend a few more hours. From what Mall can tell, they seem to be waiting for something, vaguely heading for somewhere, without seeming to have a destination in mind. Mall still refuses to let herself ask about anything, even though she's quite certain Sinalco is eager to bring her in on the scheme, to bring her in on everything. In most of the dusty bowls they find themselves in, they see evidence of prior inhabitants. Bootleggers, highwaymen, outlaws of various descriptions, Mall fantasizes, up to no good in these cubbyholes. For some reason the evidence gives Mall a bit of comfort, but why, she's not exactly sure. Resistance? Blind and pointless defiance? The next step up from nothingness? Most likely that, yes. Mall can feel herself relapsing into hopefulness, what she should realize by now is but an aggravating state of denial. They have, after all, successfully evaded both ArcNet and ArcSpace for several days now. Perhaps they can make their getaway. Her reemerging optimism piques Mall no end.

Late during their second afternoon on the Big Butte, high up into one of its longest box canyons, Sinalco and Mall are surprised by a squad of NetExos, ten of the lethal manmechs. The steep terrain makes them noisier than they might normally be, so they don't get the complete jump on the EVens. Nonetheless, Mall assumes immediately that Sinalco and she are done for—they'll be killed or captured at Net's pleasure. At that moment, Mall prefers being killed. But Sinalco disintegrates into that locust whorl once more, as she did in the operations bunker at Mountain Home, and in a flash envelops the entire squad. The screams that quickly turn to muffled silence are horrible. When Sinalco reassembles herself moments later, the Netsmen all lie dead. All of them have expressions on the lower half of their faces, all Mall can see beneath the helmet visors, that indicate violent suffocation.

Sinalco promptly gathers Mall up in her arms and whishes them both over the next ridge. They climb higher, then duck into an overhang protected by a bank of sweet-smelling, squat cedars.

"I do not know how they are coming to be so close," Sinalco whispers an apology.

They kneel in vigilant silence for several minutes before Mall risks whispering back. "Look here, Sinalco, I'll stop being such a bugger-all ingrate. If you care to tell me just what you are and just what's going on,I'd be grateful to hear."

Sinalco's smile is joyless, her eyes tired. "Not here, little Mall, not just now."

They wait in silence as the shadows lengthen in this ravine. When dusk sets in Sinalco moves them over two more ridges and even higher up the butte, almost to its roundtop summit. They face west where the sun has set, settling into a good hiding place, another of those looking well used. To one side there's a line of worn depressions where people obviously have slept over the decades. Before it gets too black to see, Sinalco pulls out a bundle of wrapped strips of deer jerky and hands the treasure to Mall. "Be prepared," she quotes what the Servs were always advising.

"Why now?" Mall asks after taking a large bite of the dried meat and beginning to work it with her molars.

"Waiting for the emergency."

Mall nods, still struggling with the first few tough chews. "Well then, go ahead and tell me what you are. Fill me in on the lot of it." She waves the jerky as though she intends to eat every string of it. "This can be my Last Supper conversation."

"Sinalco is digital matter," comes a man's voice, calmly and candidly, from out of the dark. Mall's wodge of jerky almost flies out her mouth. The man clears his throat before speaking again. "A fractal shape-shifting bot, to put it a different way, my dear."

Underminister Harrods steps out from behind some high brush toward the back of the hollow. There's just enough twilight remaining to make out the broad forehead and the narrow jaw. The moist, sad hound's eyes. He looks down impatiently at his watchwrist.

"We are late or you are early?" Sinalco addresses him.

"You are somewhat late," he says politely.

"There are Net on the mountain."

Harrods raises a concerned eyebrow. "Did you have to...?"

"Oui."

"Ah, right," he nods. "Well, then, they'll be here soon enough, won't they?"

"She's a *nanobot*?" Mall demands of Harrods. That particular bit of news is just slightly more miraculous to her than the Underminister's return from the dead, and slightly more pressing than Net's being here soon enough. Mall then turns to Sinalco, as though remembering her manners. "You're a *nanobot*?" she asks.

"Oui, chérie. Désolé." There's no apology in Sinalco's voice, nor embarrassment or regret. "The multipurpose programmable."

"Oh, don't be modest, my dear," Harrods chides her. "You're more than just that. Far more."

Mall is confused. "What do you mean?"

Harrods and Sinalco have a glance at one another. "Molecular self-assembly," he answers.

Mall is incredulous. "*Assemblers*?" she condemns him. "You've released *assemblers*?"

"Come, come, Mall. It's not as drastic as all that."

"You balmy old *bastard*!" Mall blurts out into the warm dark, without thinking first what a bad idea that is. She catches herself right away and lowers her voice to a hiss. "But that's *just* the bleeding point, now isn't it? You don't bloody well *know* if that will be drastic or bloody well *not*."

"Please spare me your hysteria, Mall, if you would," entreats Harrods impatiently. "Don't think I haven't heard it all many times over before."

"Oh, and *that's* meant to make me feel reassured?"

Harrods performs his worried frown. Mall discovered long since how that face is meant to convey the appearance of guilty reconsideration, but imparts nothing of the kind. Harrods rarely has a mind to change courses he's embarked upon, and it seems he's embarked on quite an extraordinary one in this case. Once again, Mall remembers herself. She turns her attention to her companion. Impassive and vigilant, Sinalco watches the west.

"I'm sorry, Sinalco," Mall says, "I know none of this is your fault. I don't mean to be rude about things."

There it is. Sinalco recognizes it. That "subtle" change in tone indicating how she's now being addressed as a utensil—a very advanced utensil, mind you, that might have something like feelings—but not as anything truly alive or requiring actual tact. Such displays of civility in fact tout, consciously or not, the largess of the sympathizer. The humanity the utensil implicitly lacks. "Non, mon amour," she clarifies *things* to Mall, "c'est pas du tout comme ça. C'est *completment* ma faute." Mall's not understanding. Sinalco also senses Harrods' discomfort over where this conversation is about to go. Without breaking off her scanning of the horizon, scarcely red now above and jet black below, she just comes out and says it, "Je ne suis pas artificiel."

It requires a while, but finally Mall understands that Sinalco is not about to return her stare. So she darts her gaze at Harrods. In their dimming little bowl it's become difficult to make out facial features. What stands out most about the Underminister is his shock of white hair—now cropped short, as though for military duty, as are his unruly eyebrows. Mall also notices for the first time that he's wearing what looks like a pilot's jump suit instead of the never-wrinkle muslins she'd always seen Harrods in before. These details strike her as absurd, completely incongruous.

"She can't be serious."

"It's true, Mall," Harrods is forced to admit. "Sinalco is human intelligence, not ersatz."

"But how is that possible?"

"I die two years ago," Sinalco interrupts the discussion about herself. "From the acute leukemia." She shrugs once, still looking down off the mountain. "I was top teek then. I am even better top teek now. Not so different really."

"You're conplant?" Mall asks, half in shock and half in respect.

"Oui, c'est ça."

"But that's forbidden."

Sinalco looks briefly at Mall, then turns back away. There's a set to her jaw Mall can't quite identify. An attitude or an insight she can't quite imagine.

"Indeed, very few know," points out Harrods.

"Does Natwest?" Underminister Harrods wavers, then nods. Mall lowers her voice. "Does Movënpick?"

"Administer Movënpick most certainly does *not* know," Harrods is adamant. "In fact, we've taken tremendous pains to keep it from her—from all of Caucus. The communicants would never approve of such an undertaking."

"But...how then? And...why?"

"The technology is not complex, you know," Harrods points out. "We've had the ability to implant human consciousness into some manner of nano mechanism since the mid-30's or so. The download is straightforward. Afterwards, one simply acquires vastly superior reflexes, previously unimaginable speed of thought, and, of course, an assortment of fractal capabilities. Otherwise, one's fundamental experience of the world is not altogether dissimilar."

"Apart from the superhuman feats and assembler self-replication, surely you must mean, Underminister." Mall's irony is thick. "Let's not leave out immortality, shall we?"

"Mall, really, I don't see why you have to insist upon—"

"And how do *you* feel about all this, Sinalco?" Mall steps in front of this large and robust conplant nanobot and looks up into her face. "*Do* you feel as though your fundamental experience of the world is not otherwise altogether dissimilar?"

Sinalco glances down. Her mouth becomes pinched with thought. No one has ever bothered to ask her such a thing. Before replying, she goes back to inspecting the emerging stars, looking for approaching trouble. Her voice is similarly celestial, spacious and serene. "For the one year maybe, maybe more, it is...exciting. I amuse myself aussi bien. Tu sais? Aussi bien. There are no consequences, you know."

Sinalco stops there.

"But now?" Mall prompts.

"Now not so fun," she says slowly. "Not so much exciting."

"And why not?"

Sinalco looks at Mall. She shrugs. "Il n'y a pas de conséquence." Sinalco returns to searching the sky. "Alors, now that I have one time lost all my time and I know no longer to waste it, it matters not if I do." She pauses to scrutinize some suspicious movement. It turns out only to be a passing satellite. "Compliqué, non? But is this not the heart of the tragique? Such knowledge too late?"

The night skyscape has completed itself, thick with its outwest astral glow. The three EVens stand high atop the butte, above the darkling plain, feeling more a part of those stars than of the TexArcan wasteland below. After a short while, Harrods breaks into their silence. "We haven't much time, Sinalco."

Mall can just make out Sinalco's grin. "The satirique is not ever too far away from the tragique, eh, chou-chou?" she asks.

"No," agrees Mall, giving in to her own small smile, "it is not."

The two hug. Even now, after so long and so much, Sinalco's halo of hair and milk-fair complexion can make Mall believe she's smelling strawberries. And maybe she is—the nano variety. Maybe that's something Sinalco is doing for her—has always done for her—thoughtfully indulging Mall's liking of real strawberries. That seems like something Sinalco would do. Mall pats her teek on the broad shoulder one last time then turns to Harrods. "Time for what, Underminister?" she asks.

Harrods clears his throat. He's growing fidgety. "Time to complete our errand, Mall. Undoubtedly you've surmised that much."

"I've surmised I'm buggered. I'm willing to wager that much, Underminister." Harrods won't respond. "I'm also willing to wager that my entire counter-advocacy project has been a load of rubbish."

"Indeed not, Mall," counters Harrods instantly. "Quite to the contrary, and quite beyond all my expectations, I might add, your signification work has proved extraordinarily useful. Extraordinarily. But you're correct in thinking that your Wobbly project has not been Countermeasures' main design. Rather, it's been a spectacular distraction, both back in EVe and here in TexArc. And for that, I can't thank you enough."

"But I'm still buggered, am I not, Underminister?"

"Well..." using the pale greenish indiglo, Harrods refers to his watchwrist once more, "that might be difficult for me to say just at the moment."

"Underminister, if you please, no more Countermeasures rot and nonsense now," Mall says firmly. "I can sodding well stand no more of it."

"Indeed not, Mall," Harrods concedes. "Nor have we the time. My apologies. Your role in all this, my dear, has been simply that of a means to a more important end. Cultural guerrilla warfare has never been our real purpose in TexArc."

"What has been, then?"

Harrods clears his throat. "Well, if you must know, fighting fire with fire."

"Rot and nonsense."

"The rank bullshit," Sinalco chimes in, "as Enron would say it."

"All right. All right. I'll put a more specific name to it, then. Permit me the chance." Harrods gathers himself. "Let's call it, then, mustering the courage—or the cowardice—to meet malevolence with malevolence. Let's call it forswearing the goodwill that's at the heart of alterity in order to preserve—or, I'm sure many would argue, to betray—alterity." Harrods holds up a hand to forestall from the two women more of their accusations about evasiveness. He explains, "EVe and Caucus and Marksoc are quite plainly too humane to withstand the coming onslaught from TexArc. I know you've had the same thought yourself, Mall. How *can* we withstand it? You've seen who these TexArcan Crats are and what they are capable of doing. They haven't a jot of reason or humanity cultivated in them any more. How can EVens possibly hope to negotiate with them? The really honest answer is, we can't. Nor will TexArc even suffer real negotiations to take place. You know that's true. What makes EVe good, Mall, is also precisely what makes us so vulnerable." Harrods runs one palm distractedly over the gray stubble of his head. "Please understand, Mall, that I'm dreadfully aware of how my actions will be regarded—likely as a colossal act of hubris. But I am merely someone who has decided to do something conclusive to fight off TexArc. I will be the one to transgress against alterity in an attempt to preserve it as a good and decent way of life upon this earth. I will be guilty of that contradiction."

Mall speaks circumspectly, "I don't mean to denigrate your sense of drama, sir, but I've still no idea what you've actually done."

"I'm launching a pre-emptive strike in the know war."

"But by what right do you act, Underminister?"

"By none whatever, Mall. I act solely out of opportunity. I'm under no delusions of grandeur, my dear, of possessing superior piety or of receiving special guidance from above—from Olympus, or Valhalla, or the very

Empyrean on high. I'm not even your wild-eyed purist raging against the evils of the oldways. I was simply in a position to see what might be done, and I've done it."

"Created Sinalco a conplant?"

"That's part of it."

"Feigned your own death?"

"Yes. So as to operate unencumbered at home and to deceive my opposite here."

"Here? Your opposite?"

"In ArcNet."

"So this is all spyworld intrigue, is it?"

"Mall, for a good century and more, the really telling matters have been practically nothing *but* spyworld intrigue."

"Rien encore," Sinalco reports, still vigilant in watching the skies.

Mall is more than troubled by what Harrods is saying, but troubling her most is her own visceral agreement with much of it. Since arriving in TexArc, she *has* had all those same thoughts. She would love to eradicate every last Crat. That would probably be a silver-bullet solution to many problems. Mall asks Harrods cautiously, as though worried about how much she might like his answer, "Might I be allowed to know exactly what it is that you've done—exactly what is this pre-emptive strike of yours?"

"Certainly you're more than entitled to know that," Harrods replies kindly. He clears his throat. "With the help of Sinalco, I've fashioned a nanovirus. One very specific to its task."

"A nanovirus," Mall repeats.

"Quite. That's a massively destructive nanotech device, one combined with molecular biology and infotech. The one I've constructed is exceedingly selective. Upon release, it will affect only a certain geographical area, and then only a certain group of people living within it, people who are genetically distinct."

"You can't be serious."

"Oh, I am deuced serious, Mall. This nanovirus will be triggered only by very specific circumstances and only when and if the time becomes right. There are failsafes engineered in, you know."

Mall needs a moment to take in all this information. "And who will it kill?" she asks finally.

"Caucasian males of Lower North America," says Harrods.

In disbelief, Mall looks to Sinalco for confirmation. Sinalco has time only to side glance quickly and shrug. "Ne me regard pas," she says turning back to the skies. "It is Harrods' little croisé éléphant-âne virus."

"Crossed elephant-donkey? Whatever do you mean by *that*?"

"Je comprend rien, moi. Je ne sais plus."

"Actually," Harrods clears his throat, "at the molecular level the virus is formed like a tiny donkey hanging from a *cross* of two elephants. It's not the two animals converged."

Mall stares at the Underminister in disbelief. "Either bloody way," she says, "whatever sodding for?"

Mall may well have a point, and Harrods absolutely hasn't the time to elaborate. "It's an old and somewhat private joke by now," it must suffice for him to explain. "Signifiers that have long since lost all touch with their signifieds. Don't bother about it, Mall. The shape of the nanovirus itself is in no way important."

"Only the bloody murderous ambition of it."

"Listen to me, Mall." Harrods *will* take the time to elaborate upon this concept. "If you are so disquieted by murderous ambition, you'll want to weigh carefully the past fifty years of TexArcan behavior. In the first few decades of this century, humankind faced a crossroads. Of the six billion people on the planet, four billion existed in abject poverty, as bad or worse as any you've witnessed in the BoiCity parks. As the world population swelled to nearly ten billion, and as all of those new people in the nascent-industrial nations dared to strive for a decent life, it became quite clear that the old, dirty technologies of burning massive quantities of carbon was pushing the climate toward greenhouse extremes. Equally apparent was the fact that neither fusion nor fission, for a variety of reasons—both scientific and political—were practicable as sufficient replacements for oil, gas, and coal. What was wanted by 2030—no, what was absolutely required—were new and clean technologies that could meet the world's mushrooming energy needs. Only such breakthroughs could hope to stabilize and, eventually, reverse the political and environmental calamities brought inevitably about by the penury and cupidity requisite to mammonism."

"You're talking about GNR," says Mall.

"Yes," Harrods confirms, "I'm talking about the knowledge of mass enablement. In particular, dry nanotechnology that enabled us efficiently to gather in the solar power we needed to replace carbon-based fuels, most notably oil. By the 2030s, in theory, we'd done it, Mall. We'd created a green, clean, and closed loop. KME was ready to revolutionize the world."

"But then TexArc happened."

"Yes." Harrods' tone becomes one of unqualified regret. "Then TexArc happened. It stepped in to convert the LNA from a nation state to a corporate state. Rather than spread and make possible KME, it bought and sold it. It controlled and parceled out GNR for its own profit and power. By doing so it eventually distilled smithprofitism down to its brute essence in corporate feudalism. To eliminate all challengers to its order, it captured and hoarded the world oil supply for its own use and sale. It 'democratized' all resisters with the mininuke. The past fifty years, my dear, have seen nothing but the deliberate promotion of privation, starvation, and disease. And who can say? Perhaps TexArc is the manifestation of Malthusian theory. I'd like to think we have more say in the matter, but depopulation seems to be, after all, what Corpfeud accomplishes best."

In the blackness lit only by starlight, Mall steps over to the older man to cup his elbow in her hand. He smells of sweat and subterrene. "Believe me, Underminister Harrods," she speaks gently to him, passionately and persuasively, "for the past months I've been living what you've described. The Crats and the Terds of TexArc *are* more than willing to muck up the planet for their own profit and privileged survival. I've the distinct impression, in truth, that most of them don't even know what they're up to anymore. They've become so inured to the suffering of others, they don't see it. They simply don't recognize the damage they're inflicting on everyone and everything. So I know and wholeheartedly agree with you that what you're saying is true." She gives his elbow a squeeze. "But if you release your nanobug, sir, well, don't you see it? You won't just be killing the Crats and the irredeemable Terds of TexArc. You'll be killing all the white male Servs as well—and *they* certainly don't deserve *that*. You'll be killing all the white male Terds, too, who feasiblely could be turned to alterity. And there are many, many Terds, sir, male or not, who might come over—who would embrace Marksoc willingly and happily if given half a chance. I *know*, sir. I've seen it. I've accomplished it. They just need to be properly introduced to another society. But if you release the nanovirus, sir, well, we forfeit that paxrevolutionary opportunity, and you put an end to many innocent lives."

"Of course I understand what you're telling me, Mall. Of course I took such matters into consideration. A nanovirus can be designed to perform many exacting things, my dear, but it can*not* be targeted class specific. I'm sorry."

"Then you become as bad as they are, Underminister. You become as barbarous as the Crats."

"No," Harrods shakes his head with insistence, "I most certainly do *not*. Come, Mall, that's an old and a simple-minded argument, one I'm surprised someone of your sophistication, and now of your experience, would make. I would enjoy bringing about social and economic justice in as peaceful and as civil a manner as you hope for, my dear. But if history has shown us nothing else, it has shown us that paxrevolution, howsoever well conceived and executed, is in the end quite defeatable by stupid brute force. Therefore, even were I to become 'as bad as they are,' as you put it, I frankly wouldn't care a fig. Steadily, Mall, decade by decade, TexArc systematically has killed off the world's cheap labor force, the very industrial slaves it so callously mandates and so casually exploits for such tremendous gain. Rather than recognize the suicidal ignorance of their own policies, though—and here I mean suicidal to their own bankrupt system, not to the planet as a whole—they persisted in them, even now to the point of sheer lunacy." Harrods reverses their rhetorical postures. He removes his elbow from Mall's palm and places a hand consolingly on her upper arm, his pale blue eyes seeking out hers through the darkness. "They are willing to kill off the people on this planet for the sake of their fetish after fine things. As you've seen for yourself, my dear, TexArc presently cultivates and kills its cheap labor at home. That's how small the labor pool has shrunk. Instead of enriching lives with GNR, TexArc withholds all empowering techs as a way to conserve its Corpfeudal stasis. Crats and Terds are more than willing to muck up for profit and privilege, as you put it, their very own citizens." He gives her arm a squeeze. "And now, Mall, they're coming after *ours*. Can't *you* see? These men are blindly addicted to their power, beyond all measure, beyond all reasoning, and beyond all recall. Something dreadful *must* be done to stop them."

"But—"

"There *are* no buts. Dissimilar ends disequate similar methods, Mall. TexArc uses its GNR to tyrannize and enslave, to prevent the spread of alterity. I use the same evil by-product of mammonism as a way to bring about mammonism's end, as a way to provide Marksoc with the opportunity to take hold. If it requires a nanovirus to accomplish that, then so be it."

Mall will not give over her other point. Even if stupid brute force must be met with stupid brute force, there *has* to be another way to go about it.

"But Underminister, such GNR is bloody dangerous. Inherently so. You know that for fact. Sodding KME can turn to KMD in a moment."

"Not if you properly account for the harmful amplifying factor of assemblers."

"The harmful amplifying factor?" Mall mimics. "You speak as though we're discussing crabgrass. We are talking about knowledge-enabled mass destruction. You're well aware there is no sure way to manage replicating assemblers."

"Sinalco has. Just look at her."

Sinalco tilts her head and pushes her chin slightly upward, toward one particular sector of the heavens.

"A conplant perhaps is able to contain its assemblers sufficiently," Mall counters. "Your far more rudimentary nanovirus may well not be able." Mall's thinking of those horrid MEMS she saw flocking about Mountain Home. "If its self-replication gets out of hand, we find ourselves up to our necks in gray goo."

"Voilà," Sinalco announces. "They come."

Mall and Harrods both take a look at her, then back at one another. They have minutes.

"The whole purpose of what came to be known as Harrods' Folly was to fool Caucus into agreeing to send Sinalco into TexArc. Here she could carefully tailor and concoct the virus to be altogether particular to the locale, both geographically and genetically. That will minimize any risk of accident."

"*Minimize*?" scoffs Mall. "*Minimize* the risk of the complete fucking annihilation of life on earth?"

"Well, yes...yes. That was the idea."

"It's a bloody stupid fucking idea, Underminister. Regardless of how pressing you feel the need is to wipe out sodding TexArc, leaving Sinalco behind to set loose your clever little time bomb is not the goddamned way to go about it."

"En vitesse," Sinalco adds to her original alert.

"How's that again?" Harrods says to Mall.

"Do not leave Sinalco behind," Mall says sharply.

Harrods says nothing. He looks at Sinalco, who knows she's being looked at, but she refuses to look back at him.

"See here," presses Mall, "I assume you've come in a two-per. Am I right?"

"That's right," says Harrods. "The small ones are virtually impossible to detect."

"And you're piloting the thing yourself, I hope. Correct?"

"Yes."

"Then the passenger spot should be hers. It *must* be hers."

"But—"

"No bloody buts about it, Underminister. You take Sinalco back with you to EVe and leave me here in her place. It's the better way."

Harrods thinks about this for as many seconds as he dares. "Do you know what you're saying, Mall?"

"Yes. I'm saying, sir, that with what Sinalco now knows about TexArc after being here for so long, and with what marvels I've seen she's capable of as a conplant, she'll be far more likely to help Countermeasures and Maneuvers devise new techniques to fend off these bastards than I ever can. Don't waste her, Underminister. One never knows what good might come about when provided the opportunity. I beg you, do not strand Sinalco here to set off that nanovirus. Not only is such a prospect too horrendous and too perilous to contemplate, but my way plainly affords us the better hope. You must see that to be true."

"ArcNet is about to land in numbers, Mall. You will be captured. You will then be tortured. Then you will be killed. My dear, make no mistake.

That much is certain."

Sinalco reaches out to find and clasp tightly Mall's hand.

"I've got to trust that such a thing is preferable to your nanovirus, sir."

"Very well. We'll have it your way. We must be off."

Mall presses her bundle of jerky unexpectedly into the Underminister's hands, clarifying only, "Genuine protein." From the signer's hand the teek's hand soft withdraws. Harrods and Sinalco hurry for the subterrene.

☆ ☆ ☆ ☆ ☆ ☆

ArcNet sop for detainee capture is two-part—immobilize and silence. Just like rules at elementary corpschool: no running and no talking. Both are executed with a sharp, controlled stroke of a mister butt. Dislocate a kneecap. Dislocate one hinge of the jaw. When three hundred NetExos jump out of the night onto the poz of the EVe terrorist, the closest two Netsmen to her neatly carry out sop.

☆ ☆ ☆ ☆ ☆ ☆

Two-person subterrenes are sleek and cramped, more torpedo than vessel, and able to travel at tremendous velocity when backtunneling their own glass hole. After sealing the exit cleft, nearly perfect vacuum conditions can be obtained. The risk of detection is slightly elevated over that of boring fresh earth, but expedience is everything in their escape from TexArc. The Underminister and the teek lie like two cartridges in a gun chamber, stomach-to-stomach on either half of the two-per as it speeds northeastward back toward Nixon Bay. Harrods lets Sinalco pilot. Her reflexes are, of course, amazingly better than his. She can steer the craft in such a way to allow it to glide a fourth again as fast. Within minutes they are beyond the extreme caution area of the surface site. They know, too, that ArcNet will be quite preoccupied with the capture of Mall.

"The nanovirus is ready inside her?" Harrods asks Sinalco. "She's completely planted?"

"Oui."

"How did you do it?"

"Avec le café. With it I installed the nano substructure in Fribourg. I did not make the final configuration until you memo me to in BoiCity."

"Again via the coffee?"

"Oui. Encore la même chose."

"I see." Harrods waits a suitable moment, but he has to ask. "And you're quite sure it will be released upon death?"

"Oui," says Sinalco, as clipped as their pace. "When Mall dies, the nanovirus get out. As you said to make."

They both know, at this point, Mall is as good as dead.

"I'm awfully sorry about all this, Sinalco," the Underminister offers. "There was no other way." Sinalco says nothing. "Mall's genetic heritage makes her the perfect carrier," Harrods goes on, "while her gender prevents her from contracting the virus herself." Subterrenes are beastly hot inside, the two-pers being even worse because of their extremely close quarters. Harrods adds a final thought. "And the fact that she's an abstainant doesn't hurt, either, mind you. Much less chance of her accidentally passing it along before it's time. Yes, I'm afraid she was the perfect nominee for the job."

"Except now she will be violer," Sinalco points out.

"Ah...yes," Harrods stammers, admitting that truth. "But you see, it will be so close to...well, you understand...it will not make a great difference."

"Not to you, non," the conplant confirms icily.

They travel for some minutes in this uneasy quiet. Underminister Harrods has no good options for restarting the discussion, but there are things he must find out. He'll just have to be blunt. "You're certain as well that all the other members of the foray crew are dead? There's no one else wanting removal?"

"Tout mort," says Sinalco. "Except maybe for Cardinal. She is not so easy to kill."

"What do you mean?"

"Two days ago I see her sigwave. I think I do."

"Good lord. Where? Doing what?"

"Very, very feeble, but going north. Into that big wheatland, je pense."

"We must try to—"

"Non," Sinalco preempts him, "her we let go. She has done enough for us."

They return to the stifling silence. Harrods tolerates its awkwardness a bit longer this time. "And that Enron fellow," he says at last, "what became of him?"

"Lui?" Sinalco actually smiles at the thought of Enron. "Je croix vraiment cet type *is* not possible to kill."

"What do you mean? Where is he now?"

"I don't know where is he now. He went sud into the battlespace, but I know he come back out of that big desert. He and Cardinal each." Sinalco shakes her head. "I think maybe Enron is having some big schemes lui-même. Comme toi, Underminister."

"Now what can you possibly mean by that?"

"Enron is no stupid man. He has been knowing depuis longtemps I am pas normal—not the real thing. So he ask me to make prepared again the bomb put into him by l'ArcNet—the one to blow up Maneuvers in Fribourg."

"And you *did*? You reactivated that nanostream eruptive they dispersed in his blood?"

"Oui. But only so he can call them together to make the big boom."

The Underminister isn't humored by such news, but on the other hand he can't imagine what tangible consequence Enron might initiate as a walking keg of gunpowder.

"For his sake," says Harrods, "I hope he attempts nothing stupid. I doubt it will do any good."

"Alors, tu es sûr, maintenant?"

"Nearly completely, yes. Why else do you think I would leave poor Mall behind like that?"

"So he is one in same man? You *know* this now?"

"Short of stepping up to him myself and trying to put a bullet through him, I'm all but certain of it. The eyes are a particular give away. Only now they're even more lunatic with zealotry."

"Je vois."

It's been over three years since Countermeasures managed to pull the first slices off of ArcNet showing TexArc's ceo distinctly enough to send a chill down Harrods' spine. After analyzing months of Mall's and Sinalco's memos and clips sent back from TexArc, he's more convinced than ever before, his suspicions are accurate.

"I met the same man, Sinalco, back in the spring of 2060, during the last secret negotiations EVe would ever hold with TexArc. We were in what used to be their capital meg, the year before it was satchel nuked. I can still remember the sight, and especially the smell, of all those cherry blossoms. Quite amazing."

Harrods had been a junior envoy then, part of a small Countermeasures contingent more or less sent along for show. But during their few days in Corporation he'd encountered his odd counterpart, a strident TexArcan sub-subceo of ArcNet who seemed distinctly out of step among the more progressive Crats with whom the EVe communicants were dealing at that time. This chap enjoyed drinking too much and, in private, expressing his hardline views. He was fervidly aggressionist, frighteningly pre-emptivist. One late night, the two of them wound up alone in a bar and well into their cups. He told Harrods the current negotiations would all go for naught. He kept waving a drunken hand scornfully and scoffing, saying things such as, "Doesn't mean piss in the wind, my libby friend. Your EVe Caucus is full of suckers. All these fucking libby Crats of ours you're yakking with right now will be crispy critters soon. Then, my wine-drinking and cheese-eating pal, *we* will be taking care of fucking business in TexArc. Yeah, that's right. And *we* will fucking bury you, just fucking *bury* your sorry asses." He'd bottomed-up his drink and ordered a fresh one. Then he'd declared with an eerie gleam to his eyes, "The cocksucking Glassea will seem like a picnic compared to what we're going to do to you fucking EVe gayboys." He'd clapped Harrods on the shoulder affably. "You can fucking take that one to the bank, dude."

"I was forty-one at the time, Sinalco. And give or take a year or two, so was he."

Sinalco nods thoughtfully. "I can see then."

"That's why you're here. You are my fire to fight fire."

"Okay. Yes. Only it is still too bad about Mall."

"I know."

"I should have been brave to tell her she carry the virus. And you should not take advantage comme ça to leave her behind not knowing."

"I know."

Sinalco shakes her head. "Mall would say to both us now that we are quite the shits. Tu as?"

"Yes. I'm aware that she would."

Awkwardly in his prone position, Underminister Harrods unwraps the curious petrifed meat, sniffs, and wrests off a bite with his back teeth. Once his saliva has softened it a bit, the stuff tastes splendid to him. Salty and like game. In his own mind,Harrods has always referred to his nanovirus as "affluenza." Another private joke—like the donkey and elephant business. Right at the moment, none of it strikes him as amusing.

Weird Scenes Inside the Gold Mine

"*How* did he bring them here?" Jitney's voice doesn't echo quite so much as its volume warrants in the Eye. A large ring of chairs has been set up on its deep blue floor. It's very unusual to see furnishings of any kind up here.

"Completely by ArcSpace." Ponzi keeps his own voice subdued, casual, as though they're talking biz. "TAVed them up from BoiCity—"

"Are you *shitting* me? No one's supposed to see our Trans-Atmospheric Vehicles!"

"Keep it down!" Ponzi raises his own voice slightly. "You think this is even a good idea for us to be talking like this, and now you're going to make a scene?"

Jitney adjusts his collarless denim shirt, a soft hazelnut hue. He glances around the empty Eye, empty except for all the damned chairs. "But he's been acting so yanking strange. And now he's bringing all these yanking shitubers here to yanking talk. That's just mindyank."

"Look, have you ever seen him *not* operating?"

"No," Jitney admits, seeing Ponzi's point. He'd better calm his head or else get it handed to him. "But I've never seen him doing shit like this, either. It's yanked."

"All the more reason to stay on our toes. Look, it gets worse than just the TAVs. He shuttled them around the earth for a couple orbits, and let them walk around the VIP platform of the elevator. He's got them staying above the hundred-and-eightieth story, here. He's feeding them real vit, letting them onto the turbolinks. Hell, he's even letting them dork the realhos. You'd think they're petrolexecs or something."

"Servs on the turbolinks *without* grasstrimmers?" Jitney shakes his head in astonishment. "Brother, keep that shit off Vieworld, or it's the end of corp as we know it."

Ponzi lowers his voice, "Exactly my point." He lowers his voice even more, "Who knows? Now might be the perfect time for that change."

Jitney's gonads start to tingle. He turns his face away from Ponzi but keeps him locked in a sideways stare. "You think?" he whispers cautiously.

"I think it's now or never. Look, how long have you and I been subceoing for him?"

"Five years."

"That's a long corptime, don't you think?"

"Yes, it is, but..." Jitney trails off.

"And who's been here longer than us?"

Jitney shakes his head. "No one. But top management turns over a lot. Everybody knows that."

"Why? Why does top management turn over so much?"

Jitney shrugs. "I don't know. Climbing the ladder?" he offers. "You know, keep fighting your way to the top?"

"Jitney," says Ponzi, "this *is* the top. Where do you fight to from here?"

Jitney blinks. For some reason he's never quite thought of that before. "Subs must just rotate out then," he says. "Move on to other topspots."

"Jitney, you ever met a *former* subceo?"

Jitney blinks again. "Come to think of it..." He has to shake his head no.

"Outside of the Waco Pyramid," Ponzi presses him, "you ever met anybody that ever *used* to work in the Waco Pyramid?"

Jitney concedes the quizgame. "What's your point, Ponzi?"

"I'm not sure. But I don't know how long *he's* been ceo. Do you?"

Jitney blinks several times. Yank doublemindyank. "For a long time. I know that. But..."

"But what?"

"But...hell, I don't know. For as long as I can remember."

"Isn't it just about as long as *anyone* can remember?"

Jitney supposes that's true, too. "I guess," he says. "But it's hard to keep track with everything turning over so much and spinning so fast up here. Yeah, it seems like he's just always been ceo. I don't know of anybody who can say for exactly how long, but I'm sure a lot of Crats wouldn't say that's a bad thing. I'm sure they'd say it's good for stability. For the pursuit of happiness."

"But is it good for *our* kind of stability? The Blood-in-the-Face kind?" From under his silk, tie-dyed shirt, Ponzi pulls out his TD medallion. He gives the fist clutching the club-cross embossed on the thick gold disk some devoted rubs between his fingers and thumb.

In ritual reply, Jitney brings out his medallion to do the same. "So, you have faith it's time?"

"I don't know. You tell me. Is it? Do you think we ought to be dealing with these blasphemer Wobblies like this? Do you think we ought to be pussy-footing around with EVe instead of bombing their idolatrous state back to the microchip age?" Ponzi deepens his voice to a dry whisper, "Do you think he's been heading TexArc in the right direction?"

Jitney whispers back, "Are you saying we call the question? Are you saying early retirement? Golden parachute?"

"I'm saying there's too much revolution-evolution in the corporate air, Brother. I'm saying he's gone soft and he's dealing weak. He's never believed in Rapture or the End Days. He plays at it for his own advantage when he needs to, but he hasn't been taken up by Allegiance. He's no more Born than that slacker Yupcap or that mongrel Java. How dare he taint the Blood purity of the boardroom."

"But can we takeover the topspot now?" Right away, Jitney realizes to correct himself. "Can you?"

Ponzi places a reassuring hand on Jitney's shoulder. "I'm of the Faith, Brother, that we have no choice. I'm not convinced all the Dmega spin and constant doublego up here at the top isn't misdirect—even coverup."

"Coverup? Of what?"

"I'm not certain. I want to say for all the personnel changes at CorpHQ. Waco's like a revolving door that spins topexecs around for a few years and then spits them out into who-knows-where. I don't think there's ever been subceos who've filled the position for more than five years."

"Seriously?" The information rattles Jitney.

"I've checked into it. Even the corprecords seem funny. Incomplete somehow. Hard to follow. Like they've been yanked with."

"He's up to something?"

Ponzi tilts his head down and stares at his coexec from under raised eyebrows. "When is he ever *not* up to somthing?"

"You're right," Jitney admits, "misdirect is his specialty. Almost his yanking gift." Jitney glances about the high-rising Eye, suddenly unnerved by its spaciousness. "So you figure we're up to our necks?"

Ponzi nods. "We've got to spin this Wobbly mess to Dominion's advantage. We've got to pitch it against him to convince the cratocracy that leadership changeover is long overdue. It's high time for a no-confidence vote." Ponzi kisses, then replaces under his shirt his TD medallion.

Jitney does the same. "We win over the shareholders, and we takeover the ceoship. Straightup Corpfeud, Brother."

"Amen, Brother. Straightup Corpfeud."

"Amen."

Noiselessly, the floor panel begins to slide aside for the platform lift. A party of forty delegates ascends into the Eye. Bleached Wheat stands in the midst of them, talking loudly, laughing with exaggeration, bizmingling expertly with the Wobbly leadership. The snively, weasely one they address ludicrously as the Grand Pooh-Bah stands dwarfed next to him, simpering, showing lots of bad teeth, ounce-by-ounce having all the cock-sure defiance he came armed with steadily charmed right out of him. Ponzi and Jitney instantly revert into their subceo professional mode.

"All these shitheads clear?" Ponzi asks Jitney while everyone looks for his seat.

"Yeah, sure. The cream of the Parker crop. Might as well all be mexes the yanking credgoons are after. Nothing but deadjobbers here."

"But no secrisks?"

"Hell, they're all security risks as far as I'm concerned. None of them ever should have been allowed to yanking set foot in CorpHQ. But they check harmless enough secwise." Jitney amends that assessment. "Well, all except for the one CorpTrooper in the bunch. His biometrics obviously have been dicked with. We're still trying to posID him."

"What, and you let him *up* here? Which one is it?"

"The big rambo over there. Calm down. We scanned the shit out of him. Nothing. And the ceo knows about it. He looked him over himself and told us to go ahead and let the dude up."

"That worries me even more. What about simple fotoID?"

"Yeah, that's yank. His face just doesn't pull up anywhere."

"Nowhere? That's not possible. How deep in did you go?"

"As deep as you can."

That makes zero sense. There's *no* too deep in ArcNet that can hide a simple fotoID from an official Security scan. The subceos look from one another to their ceo, now with suspicion and apprehension.

Bleached Wheat has struck a pose on the big white star inside the thin red circle centered in the deep blue floor. With his arms and his voice raised, he invites everyone to take a seat, any seat they like, around the wide ring of chairs. "Wobbly please mix with corpexec. After all, there is no upstatus or lowstatus up here in the Eye! We're all in this together! Right?" The execs are disoriented at first by the lack of hierarchy in the seating. The Wobblies don't seem to think anything of it. They've just finished gorging on a magnificent luncheon of cowbeef, not kangaroo, so tender it was hard to keep on the fork—for the Parkers who used forks. As they've been doing for the past two days, the Wobblies stuffed themselves to the point of near-stupor, a number of them puking out their feedtubes during the meal but immediately tucking back in again. Servs have never even imagined vit like this. Everything about the Waco Great Pyramid, in fact, is unimaginable to them. The sweep. The scale. The fringe package. As Jip pointed out in conversation with the big bossman, makes their own little Gold Butte back in OakCity seem about as useless as teats on a boar hog. Bleached Wheat smiled back at Jip.

Oak makes sure to sit Jip and Hap on either side of him. His belly may be full, but his head ain't empty, even if they have been sucking up to the big bossman a bit. *That's part of the bossman game*, Oak figures. *You suck my bangbone, I'll suck yours*. This visit to the Eye is the first real powwow since they got here, the one, Oak decides, where they'll finally get the hell down to things. So far the Wobblies have just been playing around at Crat highlife, getting boozebent bad, eating till they near drop over dead, hardnobbing tits-n-ass that are even *better* than vir, and flogging around on the long turbocourse thing playing some dumbass game that's got to be the biggest damn waste of time known to man. Oak's told his boys to enjoy hell out of themselves—shit, they deserve it—but also to keep their damn SigCaps on. Don't want another Mountain Home. They did trade in their coveralls for fancy Crat clothes, just so they wouldn't stick out so bad. According to Hap, when the Wobblies first got to Waco they stuck out like turds floating in a punch bowl. Now they're all swimming inside the pleats and loosefits and mutetones, looking a bit like a pack of nice-dressed clowns. Every one of them, that is, but Enron. He's keeping to himself, to his own clothes and to his own counsel. Oak knows his uncle is liable to do something CorpTroop brash and stupid. Enron ain't here for the greater glory of the sovereign state of Wobbly, so he's keeping Jip's eye on him. It's a flat risk bringing Uncle En along with his Ministers to CorpHQ, but he'd bullied his way here with them. That's never mind. Oak knows a way to make it pay off if he's got to.

"Gentlemen! Gentlemen!" Bleached Wheat calls the meeting to order after finding a seat on no particular point of the circle. "Perhaps it's time to get down to business?" The Eye quickly turns to quiet. "Before we do, however, I'd like to ask Yupcap and Java," Bleached Wheat locates his two subceos and nods once to each of them, "please to go downlift to nextlevel. There are some things for you to attend to there."

Looking confused, almost ashamed, as though they'd done something wrong, Yupcap and Java stand, nod back, and make their way to the platform lift. Jitney finds their exit amusing—and gratifying. Those two whelps have only been subceoing for a year, at most. It's time they tuck their tails between their legs and scoot, like yanking pups. Leave the real work of corp to the big dogs. Jitney catches Ponzi's attention and grins. Ponzi, though, is not so sure what to make of Yupcap and Java's being sent out of the Eye. Market Enterprise and Culture have everything to do with this current deal. Why not have them here? Bleached Wheat studiously waits until they're gone and the empty lift has re-ascended and sealed before making his opening remarks.

"First, I'd be remiss not to congratulate the Grand Pooh-Bah of Wobbly, Mr. Wat, and his many esteemed Ministers, Mr. Ball and Mr. Straw foremost among them, for having the courage and the wisdom to zero in on the name of the corp game. You are risktakers watching out for number one, gentlemen. You are obviously big-balled fucks who understand that the right time to stop climbing the heap is never. You truly have the spirit of El Capital. Gentlemen, we at CorpHQ salute you and acknowledge your achievement." Bleached Wheat emits a stage laugh. "We equally acknowledge that you drive a damn hard bargain. So we say to you, well done, Wobblies, well played! You have arrived at the top!"

Bleached Wheat begins to clap, encouraging, with a stern look, the crackling applause to rise from among the sub-subceos. After a moment, Oak stands to take a bow, then encourages his own boys to join in the clapping. They add their Parker hoots, hollers, and whistles, echoing off the pinnacle of the pointed chamber. Ponzi frowns at this asinine lovefest, clapping tepidly while keeping his eyes fixed on that CorpTrooper sitting silent and motionless opposite him on the circle—the only Wobbly still wearing his damn solidarity coveralls. This brute's meaty and scarred forearms are crossed tightly over his burly pectorals, and he looks to be concentrating hard on something. *There's your worst nightmare right there*, Ponzi reflects. *Corporate brawn interfaced with libby brain. No telling what shit that might bring*. He doesn't like the looks of any of it.

"Gentlemen! Gentlemen!" Bleached Wheat quiets the room again, "Indeed this is an occasion for celebration!" He stands and points to Oak. "So, second, and by way of paying tribute to your making it to the very top," here Bleached Wheat spreads his arms, indicating the very Eye of the Waco Great Pyramid, "I would like to break with TexArc biz-as-usual protocol to invite you, Grand Pooh-Bah, to have the first word of these arbitrations." There are audible gasps of surprise from the sub-subceos, then polite applause to mark the magnanimity of the gesture. It's unheard of to give over the first word. "Tell us, Mr. Oak Wat, newest overlord of OakCity, exactly what it is you would like from us. Why have you made this bold move to raise an army and capture a meg? Why have you taken hold and shaken the very foundations of our corporation? What is it you have in mind for the people of your fair meg? In brief, why have you called us all here today? Please, Oak—if I may be so familiar—fill us in on your bigpic."

Bleached Wheat reseats himself, relinquishing the deep blue floor to the Wobbly. Oak has remained standing from his bow. He scans the circle of faces staring at him. He pushes his hands down into the bottomless pockets of his loosefit twills, an understated barn red to compliment his thyme collarless shirt, and, without thinking, scratches at his free-hanging balls. At the same time he curls under his toes in the ends of the huge gel-sole runners they gave him, the smallest pair they could find, and when he clears his throat his feedtube burps up a little cowbeef. "Well now," he starts. A sub-subceo far down the circle asks for Oak to speak louder. They can't hear. Oak shouts out in the great space, "Well now!" Self-consciously, he has to adjust again, pitching his voice somewhere in between. "Well now," he tries, with adequate success, "I didn't rightly expect to have to make up a speech. We Wobblies ain't much for speeches."

"Oh?" Bleached Wheat interjects with theatrical surprise. "I certainly wouldn't say that about your uncle!"

Confused, Oak smiles along with the sub-subceo laughter in the hall, but sneaks in a careful look at Enron, who's sitting all stony and closed off like he's paying things no attention at all. Then Oak understands that Bleached Wheat means Uncle *Wobbly*. "Oh, no, Mr. Wheat, sir. He ain't my real uncle, not by a long shot. He was made up by them EVe ragheads."

Bleached Wheat feigns flabbergastion at this revelation. "No! A feed-hoax? That's a dirty trick to pull!"

Seeing how it's only the corps laughing, Oak figures he's being fucked with, and they all snicker whenever he calls the big bossman Mr. Wheat. Well, fine. Have your fucked-up Crat fun. It's time to get down to brass tacks anyway with their Wobbly grievances. That's why they came to CorpHQ in the first damn place. "Okay," Oak raises his voice just enough to get above the merriment, "that's a good one, Mr. Wheat—or can I call you Bleached? That okay I call you Bleached? That not too familiar?" Oak waits for the reply he guesses won't come. At least he's shut up the laughing of them damned sub-sub sons-of-bitches. “Okay then, Bleached, it’s like this.” Oak sits back down and kicks his legs straight out comfortable in front of him, like he likes to sit. In a V. Letting his cluster dangle. “This might come as some more bignews to you, Bleached, but your megcrats are a bunch of assholes. I know they sure were in our meg, and I bet you DollArcs to doughnuts they are in every other meg around corp, too.”

“My goodness, Oak,” frets Bleached Wheat. “Whatever do you mean?”

“I mean they don’t let The Market run fair. They fix it in their own favor, rig things so them and theirs all the time come out on top. That’s what I mean. It ain’t right.”

“My word, Oak. I had no idea. Are you telling me these Crats aren’t playing by The Market rules of hard work and honest competition?”

“That’s just what I’m saying, Bleached. When these bastards daytrade they got enough cap to do it with to make a goddamned difference, and they got real markstrats and insidertips that lets them all the time rake it in. Meantime, your averagejoe keeps taking the stocks-n-bonds bone up the ass. No way he can get ahead. He don’t got the readrite or the rithmetic. He don’t got the cap. He don’t got the nice clothes, or the bighouse, or the vehic that don’t get repoed every other week. Averagejoe’s got nothing, Bleached. Hell, he just keeps racking up the workcreds so’s not to starve to goddamn death.”

“Gosh. That sounds just awful. What would you have me do about this terrible situation, Oak?”

“Fix it! Make it right! Make the megcrats stop fucking us over. Hell, you’re the big cheeseburger. You head up The Market. If you don’t make it run fair so’s that everyone can play the game and anyone can get ahead, then who the fuck will?”

Bleached Wheat leans forward and inspects Oak, a pint-sized buffoon slouching in a conference chair, dressed in designer clothing likely costing a thousand times his personal networth. “My God, you’re serious, aren’t you?”

"Damn right I'm serious," answers Oak. "Why the hell else would I be here?"

"To be perfectly candid with you, Oak, I've been wondering that myself. I suppose I've been half-hoping you might have something up your sleeve."

"Up my sleeve?" Oak looks first to Jip, then to Hap. "Don't need anything up my sleeve, Bleached. I got your flying damn Netsmen, remember? About a thousand of the bastards. You haven't forgot our little confidence swap, have you?"

"Oh, definitely not, Grand Pooh-Bah. That's one of the best deals I've ever sealed."

"Then get your ass in gear and do something about these sons-of-bitches Crats running your megs. They're yanking up the whole free-maket fair and balanced way."

Bleached Wheat leans back in his chair and settles in. He makes an inviting hand gesture. "Go ahead, Oak. I'm interested to hear this," he says. "Do something like what?"

"Well, now in the case of OakCity, you can just leave things to me like they are. I'll take care of everything, and I'll play ball with you, too. You don't got to worry about that."

"That's good news." Bleached Wheat looks around to his fellow execs and nods. "And exactly what kind of 'ball' will we be playing, Oak?"

"Oh, you'll get a sizable cut of my take. I'll deal you square. You'll see."

Bleached Wheat smiles benignly. "A meg isn't an enormous casino, Oak." The sub-subceos snicker, again. "And I hardly need a cut of anything when I own the whole pie."

Feeling a bit lost, Oak backtracks. Maybe he tried to push ahead too fast. Maybe he should have waited longer before getting down to the nut-cutting of who gets what. "But you got to make The Market work like it's supposed to. You simple got to."

"Do I?" asks Bleached Wheat. "You seem to be implying an 'or else,' Oak. Or else what?"

Oak rubs then scratches at his chin. He checks all of his blank-faced Ministers. Jiplap hunches his shoulders up and gives back a stumped look. "What do you mean or else what?" Oak asks.

"What will you do if I don't agree to make The Market the marvelous, level playing field you hope it might be?"

"Well..." Oak's feeling the deal taking a definite downhill slide, "I guess I'll have to...uh...term all them NetExos of yours." He hopes this might stop the skid. "I hate to say it, but that's my or else, Bleached. Now, that'd be a real crying shame to waste them guys. They hop around real good. But I'm afraid I'd have to play hardball with you."

"Ah. All right. So that's where we are." Bleached Wheat gets it, now. Oddly, he's a little disappointed. He'd anticipated more. "You actually think I give a flying fuck about those Terds." He tilts his head in mock reflection. "Huh. I took you for cleverer than that, Mr. Wat. That's interesting in itself. I really thought the EVens would have prepared you much better for negotiations." He locates both Ponzi and Jitney on the circle and comments to them, "So much for our fears about external indoctrination."

"Now wait now," Oak protests, "I outright gave you Brand. And I helped you track down the rest of them damned ragheads."

"There was only one left to track down, Oak. A lean and spirited bitch, I grant you, and she'll do very nicely. But that's not strictly a bonanza."

"What the fuck you saying to me here, Bleached? Just what the hell's going on?"

"I guess what I'm saying to you, my rank little thick-skulled friend, is get ready for your first lesson in bigbiz, which is bend over and grab your ankles."

As though stepping out of nowhere, Pyramid Guards appear outside the circle of chairs, their misters trained.

"What the hell?" shouts Oak. "You fuck! We had a deal!"

"Of course we had a deal, Oak. A classic deal. You gave me something *you* didn't care about, and I gave you something *I* didn't care about. Deals like that get struck all the time. They're bizstandard and, at first glance, they look pretty darn good, don't they? But the trick is to look beyond the appeal of the deal, Oak. To see past the hype to focus in on the fact."

"The fucking fact of *what*?"

"Why, of leverage, of course, Oak. At who's got more leverage to swing the deal his way. In biz, what else is there, brother?" The ceo stands, stretches, and saunters lazily back to the very middle of the Eye, to the dead center of that big white star. "Deals are like High Noon, Oak," he says. "Or like those crazy medieval beheading contests. You take your best shot, and I'll take mine, and we'll just see who's left standing with a head." Bleached Wheat mugs a sad-face at Oak. "I just found out that you came here with nothing, Grand Pooh-Bah. Not a lick of real leverage to your name. Less than zero." He makes two deliberate, annoying tisking sounds. "*Very* bad bizmove, Mr. Wat. *Very* bad."

"Take that CorpTrooper over there, too!" Hap stands up shouting, pointing across the circle to Enron. "He's always thick as thieves with them damn EVe dykebitches! He can tell you all kinds of shit about 'em! Take him, too, goddamnit!"

"Now, now, Mr. Straw," Bleached Wheat turns his face to Hap, "have you not heard a thing I've just been saying?" Bleached Wheat then turns around to have a look at Enron. "You're still trying to offer me things you don't care about. That's not going to get you anywhere." Bleached Wheat turns back, pointedly, to Oak. "Besides, Mr. Straw, I already know everything there is to know about Mr. Wat's Uncle En. Absolutely everything."

Ponzi sits up straighter in his chair at the ceo's remark. He watches as well the look of concentration intensifying on the CorpTrooper's face, as though the guy's getting ready to pop a squat.

"Hold on now. We might still got something you need, big bossman," Oak offers quickly. "You never know. We might still."

"Oh, I doubt it very much, Oak. You helped me catch the EVe signer. You handed me the Terd who sliced her into ArcNet. That means both the concept and the conveyance of their Uncle Wobbly is gone, wiped off IMS feed—off of all Simulacrum feed—for good. In a week or two no one will even remember the old fart's name, let alone what he was trying to stand for."

"But we still control our own goddamned meg, you sorry son of a bitch," Jiplap defies the Crat.

"Your goddamned meg, Mr. Ball, is a colossal pile of shit. No one would even blink if it vanished off the face of the earth."

"We control the waters, don't you forget! We control the waters and we'll fight you with them! We'll fight you hard!"

"My dear Mr. Ball. No one doubts your stupid courage or your blind devotion to causes you obviously don't understand the first thing about. My God, you're Servs. That's what you're bred up to do. To fight and to die for things you're too pea-brained to grasp. Why do you think your kind make such perfect CorpTroops? Strak hooya and all that semper fi shit? You're made tough and dumb to buy it, that's why. It's stirring stuff, to be sure, but in the end nonsense, I'm afraid. Mere bravado, Mr. Ball. You live and die at Crat pleasure, at Crat manipulation. And as far as fighting us, hard or otherwise, let me pitch this at a level simple enough even for you to understand." Bleached Wheat leans forward a bit, toward Jiplap. "You can't, Mr. Ball," he states and then stands back up erect. "At any time I like, Mr. Wrangle Minister, I can have your dear little meg blasted into a giant holding pond. Waters problem solved."

"Big bossman," Oak breaks in again, "you don't got everything straight about who—"

"Oak, Oak," Bleached Wheat holds up a hand, "I admire your spunk. I really do. I admire it so much, in fact, I think I'm going to have your head stuck on a pole and put on display downlevels in the Dominance Foyer. Yes. Right next to the Petrol Extraction Tribute Fountains. That would be choice. Then lots of Crats and Terds can admire your spunk. And I think I'll have your Ministers' heads sent out on poles to all the other major Pyramids around corp, so lots and lots more consumers can admire you feisty Wobblies. Yes. That would help spread the word about your one big union, about how it's just the greatest thing on earth. That's a very nice plan."

"But you—"

"No more buts now, Mr. Wat. You never had much to deal with in the first place, and I don't think you have anything left at all in the way of leverage. In short, Oak, you're fucked. You may as well accept that."

Strangely, as though performing pantomime, Bleached Wheat reaches his arms slowly upward toward the apex of the ceiling directly above him. Then, while talking, he gradually lowers them to the point where he looks as though he's dangling from a cross. "Let me clue you in on something, my dear fellow, before you do get fucked. Something that you should have realized before you got sucked into all this Wobbly gibberish. Something you really should have known before you tried to do biz with me. The TexArcan Dream is *not* all about pluck and the honest sweat of your brow bringing you all imaginable success. No, no. The TexArcan Dream, purely and simply, is all about being the fucker and not the fucked. Oh, yes. And I'm the ultimate big bossman fucker, Oak. I'm the head yank. The grand bangbone. And that job's always going to belong to someone like me and never to anyone like you. Got that, Oak? That's just how corp works."

Bleached Wheat looks down at Oak and is somewhat taken aback by the sneering rat grin that meets him. He anticipated the Serv voiding into his no-crease cotton trousers at this point. "Yeah boy," Oak muses, "that might just be so, you sorry fuckmother." Oak suppresses a don't-give-a-yank laugh. "Hell, it probably is, too. What the fuck do I know? But one thing you for sure don't know, Mr. Head Fucker man, and one thing that might just even us up a bit in that leverage department of yours, is that it wasn't all that rawboned dykebitch Brand that did the whizbang shit to fuck up your feed. Fuck, no. It really wasn't her at all, if you want to know the honest truth. Nope. It was this bigass, scare-the-holy-piss-out-of-you, raghead sweetpuss that sliced so deep into Arc—"

☆☆☆☆☆☆

Months ago, just prior to the Fribourg fall while Enron speedslept aboard an ArcSpace shuttle, ArcNet Terds injected nanoplosives into the CorpTrooper's bloodstream—enough to take out an entire underground fortress. That was Net's plan, Ponzi and Jitney's plan, for terminating the outlander slice. The Terds attuned the nanos in such a way as to be able to cluster and fulminate them on remote command. Enron knew nothing about it until after Countermeasures had captured and medexamed him. Even then, all the EVe teeks could do was null the nanos, make sure they kept scattered harmlessly in Enron's blood. The teeks couldn't agree on a safe way to egest them.

It wasn't until Redfish Lake that Sinalco offered to evacuate the nanos from Enron. At that moment Enron put a lot of two-and-twos together and realized how this megawoman was extrahuman, something not at all close to the ordinary. He had the presence of mind to ask Sinalco, instead, to reattune the nanoplosives for him to re-assort and control. The CorpTrooper figured that might turn out to be handy. Reluctantly, admiringly, Sinalco agreed.

Throughout the powwow in the Eye of the Waco Great Pyramid, Enron has been concentrating hard on carrying out the steps Sinalco taught him to recall the nanos into critical mass. Step one is clenching his asscheeks for a pretty long time—a cute touch by Sinalco who simply adored Enron's tight butt. The clench draws the nanos up from his legs. Step two is crossing his arms over his chest and flexing tight all the muscles of his upper body. This tension collects the nanos in his lungs, where they can get the oxygen they need to ignite. While Enron sits flexing hard, his arms and legs go strangely tingly and numb, like they're being drained. The third and final step is a master comic touch that makes Enron smile. Sinalco told him that when he's ready, he needs only to pinch his nostrils together and blow down into them, very gently, like when you try to pop your ears. "Only doucement, my sweetcheeks," Sinalco had said. "Autrement, you might be doing hurting to yourself." *That was Sinalco for you. Always joking, because, hell, what the hell else was she ever going to do? Cry all the time?*

Their days at Redfish Lake have dominated Enron's thoughts while sitting, fully primed, waiting for his asshole nephew finally to get around to spilling the beans about Sinalco, selling her and Mall and the whole Wobbly movement right down the river. Stupid Oak son-of-a-bitch. Enron should have shot his ass a long time ago. And now the moment has arrived. Oak's starting to tell the ceo who really sliced way deep into fucking ArcNet. Well, Enron won't have that. He has no idea if what he's about to do will keep Wobbly hope alive, but he figures wiping all these corp fuckers in the room off the map—especially the big bossman fucker and that hardass Ponzi fucker who runs ArcNet and who right this second is staring at him so keen—just can't be a bad thing. Staring right back at that subceo fuckmother, Enron pinches his nose closed and blows softly. Quite softly. For, to tell God's honest truth, he really doesn't want to be doing hurting to himself.

☆ ☆ ☆ ☆ ☆ ☆

—Wham-bam and ka-boom!

From one downlevel below in the ceo's waiting room, the detonation feels more than it sounds. It's as though a massive weight—an enormous, ponderous, unimaginably tremendous weight—has been dropped on the floor of the Eye above, a big dead thud. Every juniorexec in the waiting room jumps, then freezes, looking up at the ceiling. After what seems like eons, the ceo's voice chirps over intercom: "Yupcap! Java! Come quickly! I need you!"

Smoke pours down through the ceiling aperture as the platform lift descends. The lift itself is covered thickly with red and blue oozy globs of flesh and long, white splinters of bone. The two subceos take a moment to wretch first, then step gingerly onto the platform. Their ceo calls. As they ascend, they see that the entire interior of the Eye is painted with inner organs and the odd, recognizable segment of person. Whole arms and legs mostly. All of these parts are dripping, sliding, or sometimes plopping down from far overhead to make a slippery, wet, sickening smack on the floor. But as the lift shudders closed, wedging and smooshing offal, they see the extraordinary sight of their ceo putting a kiss on his fingertips and bending down to plant it smack in the center of the star on which he stands. He is miraculously intact, unhurt, untouched. Unruffled, even. Both he and the big white star inside the thin red circle remain immaculate amid the carnage. It's as though no hair, no bone, no shit, no blood, no flesh dared venture inside the charmed boundary of the corp insignia.

Bleached Wheat stands now and looks at his subceos with a broad smile, a *huge* smile, on his face. He throws up his arms and shouts: "Folks! It's a miracle!" Then he strikes another pose, a thoughtful one of corp leadership, gesturing forthrightly with one hand and beseeching: "You see? If we don't fight them over *there*, we'll have to fight them *here*." Then he motions to behold the ooze all around him.

Yupcap and Java aren't sure what to do. Obviously the ceo is preparing newsbig, but the chamber smells like a smoldering meat locker.

"Come on, you ninnies," Bleached Wheat snaps at them. "Get that shit out over Vieworld pronto. Hit especially hard all the fucking UltraChrist channels. They'll eat this up with a goddamned spoon."

"Sir?" says Yupcap.

"You need a fucking engraved invitation, son? You're my new ArcNet subceo. Congratulations. And Java, you'll be taking over Security. Think you can handle that?"

"Sir—"

"And find me two more subceos to take over MarkEnt and Culture. Now. Right away. Be sure to make one of them a mex or something. How about that one sub-subceo of yours, Java? What's his fucking name? Pace?"

"Yes, sir."

"Fuck, he'll do fine. You all look the same to me, but I guess this is just one more wave of the future I'll have to get on board with."

"Sir?"

But Bleached Wheat has already called for muzak. He's already a few more steps ahead, even with the entrails of forty men slithering down the beveled walls.

☆ ☆ ☆ ☆ ☆ ☆

On upleft:

Wherever you go, there we are! [majestic sweepviews, inspiring leadmusic] See the world, be the world! [talkheads appear—stiff, grinning, perfect like adverbots] More youdecide breaking news! The newsbig of the day continues to come out of CorpHQ: conclusive evidence now linking EVe strongman Adolph Stalin with the terrorbombing of the Great Pyramid! [vidfeed: blood-smeared slanting walls, guts and quivering pulp thick across the entire floor of the Eye; flashpic inset downleft of upleft: EVe strongman Adolph Stalin—bearded, swarthy, turbaned, dark menacing eyes] Unmistakable traces found of chemical explosives used exclusively by covert and Omega elite EVe assassination squads targeting our ceo! [vidfeed: Bleached Wheat pristine amid the gore, arms spread wide like Jesus, CEO, shouting out in praise "Folks! It's a miracle!"] His miraculous salvation now known to be an act of divine intervention to preserve our corp! [vidfeed: Bleached Wheat's iceblue eyes ablaze, his tone that of patient and long-suffering reason as he looks into cam and tells us "You see? If we don't fight them over there, *we'll have to fight them* here.*"] Plus the sorrow of piecing together fallen heroes! [flashpics: official corp headshots of a smiling subceo Ponzi and a smiling subceo Jitney topscreen side-by-side; bottomscreen side-by-side stillshots of two piles of glop] The outrage! The calls across corp for an eye for an eye! Perhaps now the appeals of a patient and long-suffering ceo for a justwar to be waged against the terrorthreat of the EVe roguestate finally will be heard...*

On upright:

[happy sellmusic, vidfeed: happers at The Arcs] For a limited time only! Get your Eye of the McSlurry! Corpatriotic red, white, and blue swirled fury-slurry commemorating the tragic terrorvictims of the heroic Great Pyramid! [hardcut; ominous sellmusic, vidfeed: actual newsbig clip of street fighting in a Gater district] GaterPol, secguards, misters, and autoshields just not enough? [vidfeed: armed rabble scaling the walls of elegant yardandgarden manor only to disappear in bright flashes along its top] ClaymoreCo's got you covered! ClaymoreCo, for that little extra peace of mind! [hardcut; stirring sellmusic...

On downleft:

We humbly thank you for aligning in with Body and Bread! [soothmusic, serenesmile talkheads] We have always known ourselves to be blessed as one Corporation, under God! But with recent miraculous events confirming now more than ever our manifest corpdestiny, we must not shirk our sacred duty and heritage as Soldiers of God! [vidfeed, continued voiceover: the TD logo emblazoned across the sky as a force of Strykers and CorpTroops emerge from a pine forest to raze the thatched-roof stone houses and slaughter the fleeing inhabitants of a small village in a dell] Without reservation or hesitation, we must take up justified arms against these Godless hordes who would seek to destroy our special relationship with the Almighty! We must slay without remorse those minions of Satan who not only deny the One True Way, but who seek through vio-

lence to thwart God's inevitable march toward...

On downright:

[autovoice-flashpic: clear bluesea, clear bluesky, bump white sand island with three swaying palms, sailboat entering from left] No jobapps pending! Searchmode nogo! Recent jobhist: none! Workcreds pending: none! Current credgrades: seventytwo and onequarter percent! Jobfind likely at zero percent! Daytrade options: BlowEmUp Inc seventyfour and twothirds wayup seventeen and fiveeighths, Smithereens skyrocketing twentynine to twohundred even—[hotflash in upleft of downright]—Hottip! Hottip! Haloburton quadsplit! Buy at sevenfifty! Buy at sevenfifty! Doublego Dmega hottip at sevenfifty...

Bleached Wheat stands over Mall's naked body for some minutes watching, upside down, her eyes twitching beneath their half-closed lids. She's completely lost to the glassy. No recognition of any kind to what's going on around her, to anything beyond the feed. Not atypical for the first few days on align. Bleached Wheat smiles and nods at the semiotic justice of it: a signer swallowed whole by the Simulacrum. Choice.

He'd climbed down through the opening in the ceiling of the holding suite and then had the ladder retracted. The nanoglass cube they're in dangles several hundred meters above the turbolinks course, over the fabled 57th hole, in fact. For days now, turbogolfers trying to tee off have been distracted by what they can just make out far overhead as either sweetpuss bush or sweetpuss ham, depending on how Mall is lying at the moment, pressed against the floor of the suite. Most disconcerting to your game. Either the triangular patch or the deep crevice can really throw off your swing. Exec complaints have been pouring in. What they can't see at that distance is Mall lying in her own bloody shit and pissing herself every few hours. She's been going through a lot lately.

"Flush," Bleached Wheat says into the vacuum silence of the holding suite.

His word doesn't echo. Thick, blue liquid trickles down the walls from the seams around the ceiling for a good while before the powerwash begins, churning the room into a violent mist. Mall is pushed and spun about by the bath, scoured and soaked, but in no way revived. Bleached Wheat weathers the small tempest placidly, standing unmoved and staying dry as a bone.

"Block sig," he says once the cube has drained and blow-dried. Then, "Seal and lock. Cams down."

The six transparent sides of the suite quickly cloud into pure white, creating a kind of dimensional no place. From hanging death-defyingly in empty space over the vast links, the room has become suddenly like a sensory deprivation chamber. The change will be quite disorienting to Mall when she eventually comes free of the glassy, but that will take a minute or two yet. Bleached Wheat checks to make sure the digicam outgo is, indeed, off. He needs them to be quite alone together in this box. In fact, the ceo has been looking forward to their meeting for days. Days. In the endless course of daily events, and life is many days, there aren't many true turning points. Not many really at all, he's found. Bleached Wheat believes that starting with this EVe slit coming to, today will be one.

Finally Mall groans and rolls onto her stomach. She puts both her hands over her eyes.

"Well, Mall," Bleached Wheat says, "you sought out solidarity with the masses, so I've taken the liberty of giving it to you. I hope you don't mind."

Mall removes her hands. Dripping wet and using her elbows, she struggles to her knees. The one that was dislocated has been snapped back into place, but it's incredibly bruised, swollen, and tender. She blinks and blinks in her effort to see past her own eyeballs. "You're a sodding prick," she mumbles without moving her bruised and swollen jaw. She doesn't try to locate her interlocutor. No one's spoken directly to her since her capture. The sod-all Netsmen didn't even shout at her when they knocked her down into the thick dust. Evidently it's just her body wanting discipline. "Whoever the sodding hell you are, you're a sodding prick."

"Do all EVens speak so colorfully, Mall? That might indicate a lack of moral values."

"Fuck off."

Mall assumes the white blur coming from all around is the result of her eyes still not quite able to focus. Knowing she won't like what she finds, she reaches up blindly to touch her aching scalp. She finds she's bald. That doesn't surprise her. She remembers one of the first things was her being roughly sheared, like a sodding sheep. A fine new stubble is starting to sprout, which gives her some idea of how long she's been held, but higher up, across the very top of her skull—stretching from ear to ear—her fingertips find what it is that's clamped so tightly onto her head, squeezing the life out of her brains. It's a raised strip of metal, shockingly cold to the touch and unbearably raw along its edges. It's like the bleeding thing was stapled into place. Mall knows at once what it is.

"That's right, Mall!" Bleached Wheat narrates her discovery in the voice of a game show host. "It's your very own motor-sensory cortex band! Courtesy of TexArc and, I might point out, supplied and installed at absolutely no cost to you, the feed consumer!" The imitation is nothing overdone, or maybe just a touch. The irony, of course, must call a bit of attention to itself. "Now that's a deal, Mall, you won't find just any old day in corp!"

Why bother to swear back at this sick fucker. Are they going to torture her now with shoddy shtick?

Bleached Wheat drops his impression. "It's clumsily grafted, I'm sorry to say, Mall. But why waste a lot of valuable time on aesthetics for what will be, in essence, a temporary job? Right?"

Mall drops her arm back down to her side. She begins to move her head around, sussing out that the white she's seeing is, in fact, the walls, the floor, and the ceiling of this beastly chamber of horrors.

"And for your vidaud pleasure, we've also given you the regulation permimplant ipatch and ihear. All authentic servwear, Mall. Nothing but the worst. I knew you'd only want to experience the real raw deal."

Mall finally locates the man sort of floating in the white room. She follows his form up to his face. Even this apparently solid object still seems fuzzy to her.

"Who the bloody hell are you?"

"Bleached Wheat," the man returns.

Oh fucking brilliant, Mall says to herself. That's exactly who she was afraid it might be.

Her time as a detainee has been a horrid fog—now it's likely to have just gotten worse. The beatings have been constant. She's been punched, kicked, and smacked with objects at every turn. Her lips are permanently swollen and split, and she's certain one cheekbone is fractured, to go along with her ruined jaw. Both her wrists are probably broken, too, from all the restraints she's struggled against, and from how she's been dragged about. She's purple and green from head to toe. They must be pumping masses of paindrugs into her to keep her conscious. Or maybe they're managing her pain through the mot-sen/corband. That might also help explain why her head is so muddled. TexArcans seem fond of the sharp kidney poke in particular. That's probably why she's spitting up and shitting out so much blood. The continual canings have been minor, though, compared to the rest of her treatment, to the lack of food, water, and sleep, to her dangling dimensionless cell that doubles as her loo, to the cinemascopic feed clamor—all the bleeding time blaring in her temples and glutting her field of vision. But, most hideous of all, have been those surreal interludes that she would dismiss as appalling hallucinations were it not for the awful physical certitude of the sodding things.

At least a dozen times, Mall's been hauled out of her crystal skybox and taken somewhere to appear in front of a live studio audience. A huge one, maybe a thousand people in the round, where she's been the center of a wildly popular and a sadistically cruel entertainment. Some manner of reality game show, she assumes. For the first several episodes, she was generally knocked about by various members of the audience brought in to compete. At the end of each program, she was defecated upon by these same people to absolutely mad applause. After the fourth or fifth show, the sport became, almost exclusively, men, or the occasional woman wearing a strap-on, rogering her unmercifully up the bum as the deafening screams of spectator delight rang in Mall's ears, drowning out her own agonized rants directed at the audience—an audience, by the way, comprised exclusively of Terds. She could tell by their clothing and their manners. Mall can't be sure, but at least twice she believes she witnessed this spoliation happening live to herself over her ipatch downleft. Or maybe that was some kind of appalling out-of-body experience. She can't be certain. Her head is an absolute mess. Yet she carries strong impressions of her own screams simultaneously coming out of her mouth *and* feeding directly into her auditory nerves.

During all this time, her one revenge was early on when some bloke's stiffyanker was jammed into her mouth and she was ordered to hoover hard. Instead she bit down and started shaking her head with gusto. She was battered near to death for that one, but a second yank has yet to appear anywhere near her mouth. Unfortunately, her rectum has became the avenue of use—over and over and over again. *How much anal rape can viewing audiences crave?* But they've remained only back terrace. Nothing fore. Which surprises her no end. Why not rape her proper while they're at it? Why hold off special for her? If someone's willing to shit on you, why be modest about other violations? They certainly haven't been granting poor Brand the same consideration.

The last several shows have featured the two of them, tied down to podiums side-by-each, and a singular perverted electricity in the air. From the looks of things, if this is even possible, Brand is in worse shape than Mall. The Terd was fragile to begin with, so the ordeal is taking the greater toll. And Brand is routinely being double and, frequently, tripled-stuffed to the riotous approval of the mob, to their rhythmic chants of encouragement. Like an overly dry wishbone, Brand often appears on the verge of being snapped in two. Once Mall tried to call out to Brand to tell her at least to bite down on the son-of-a-bitch in her mouth, but Brand wasn't hearing or seeing anything at the moment. She seemed rather potently sedated. Ah, they like their women silent and obedient in TexArc. Closed minds and open holes. That could be the catchy title for their netcasts, in fact. That or *Rapefete '84*.

"What then?" Mall asks. "Is it showtime again, you debased and odious wanker sod?"

Bleached Wheat truly admires Mall's gift for the curse. And her old-world accent makes it that much more beguiling.

"No, Mall," he replies, "those are done with now. They've served their purpose of venting outrage and rallying zeal. But you might be interested to know that you and Brand starred in the highest-rated reality series ever to stream on the Simulacrum."

"You call that bleeding reality?"

"No," Bleached Wheat laughs, "but viewers do. You must admit, the shows had a really good hook and angle. Consumers love to watch contestants do anything to try to win something, the more outrageous the better. It affirms their own avarice. And each set of episodes had its own subtle message. 'Dykebitch Dump-Off,' 'Sodomize that Libby Slut,' or, my personal favorite, 'Butt-Fuck Them Back to the Stone Age.'" Mall can't detect whether Bleached Wheat is being facetious or proud. "Plus we took the unprecedented risk of live, original programming, Mall. *Very* compelling stuff, you have to give us that."

Mall's simply glad these ordeals are over, no matter what ordeal comes next. She's happy to have her sodding feed shut off and the glassy gone away, too, even if only bloody temporarily.

"So what's to be the game now? Torture and interrogation?"

"Oh, no, Mall," Bleached Wheat shakes his head. "You have no information I need. Detainees never do."

Mall finds such news oddly worrying, even though she's known for days that she's as good as dead. "So what then? You merely toy with me fiendishly to confirm that you are a warped, freak fuck? Is that hitting nearer the mark?"

"Business before pleasure, Mall. If nothing else, you should know by now that we're all about the biz here in TexArc. Everything happens for a reason. That's the name of the game." Mall makes a loud fart sound in her good cheek, scatological humor Bleached Wheat appreciates. "No, you've simply been playing a role for me, Mall. That's all. It's nothing personal."

"And which role would that be? The sodding Whore of Babylon?"

"Very close. The diabolical EVe terrorist is more like it. But as a crackerjack signer, as I believe Harrods liked to call you, I'm sure you've already guessed how we're spinning you."

Of course she has, but the sudden mention of Harrods frightens her. Throws her off kilter. Almost beyond her wits. She must track away from that topic. "I imagine, after suffering abject pain and humiliation at the hands—or really the pricks—of a relieved nation, it's high time for the anarchist bitch to die a horrible death. Am I correct?"

"As I believe you might put it," Bleached Wheat confirms brightly, "spot on."

"Let's get bleeding on with it then."

"Oh, there's a little bit more drama to perform, I'm afraid." He checks his watchwrist. "And...there it is. Yes. Oh, the horror, the horror." Bleached Wheat looks back to Mall. "You'll be interested to know that BoiCity—I mean OakCity—has just been tacnuked. Millions dead. Billions in damages. You

EVe fiends know no bounds."

"*No*! You bastard!"

"If you don't believe me I can align you back on feed, Mall, and you can take a look for yourself. Vieworld's on the all4s."

"*No*!" Mall protests again, too quickly, betraying her terror of the glassy. She slumps back to sit on her heels, folding her hands over her lap and staring down into the white, white floor. "How bloody could you?"

"Kill my own corpcitizens?" Bleached Wheat asks rhetorically. He waves his hand at the idea. "Eh. They were mostly rubes and christers anyway. Even the Terds. They'll believe any shit you feed them. Completely expendable for the greater corporate good." He lowers his voice and raises an eyebrow. "Between you and me, Mall, a good terrorstrike deep in the heart of TexArc always does the trick. Eliminates all the doubtoms, if you know what I mean, or at least it shuts them the fuck up long enough to give you time to facilitate the necessary cultural sea changes. A neat trick we learned right from the start of the new century." Playing at conspiracy, he crouches down and gives Mall a stage wink, almost whispering, "We haven't had ourselves one since the satchel nuking of D.C. way back in '61. Let me tell you, *that* purged any progressivist bullshit from the corp leadership. It also solidified the Bleached-Wheat Doctrine."

"The what?" Mall's not heard that phrase. "And what exactly does that state? 'Bugger off, World'?"

The ceo remains amused. "In effect, yes. But the exact slogan is 'Backward and Upward.'"

"Ah. 'Backward and Upward,'" Mall repeats. "Yes, I can see that."

"In fact," recalls Bleached Wheat, "just before D.C. was the last time I talked to your boss. Maybe there's some kind of mysterious fate at work here, huh? What do you think?"

Mall had *no* idea the Underminister had ever met personally with this TexArcan nutter—*none*. Why had he never mentioned such a vital fact?

But *no*—she must veer away from the subject of Harrods.

"So you sod over your citizenry in order to help them?" says Mall. "Is that the logic?"

"No. Fuck the 'citizenry,'" he apes her accent. "I sod them over in order to help myself—the investor. The only person who counts." Bleached Wheat settles down onto his knees, sits back on his heels, folds his hands over his lap, and looks very sincerely at Mall. "You see, I follow the convictions of my New Century Forefathers. They deliberately bankrupted the old LNA Republic, I mean they just fucking ran that obsolete piece of shit into the ground, just to prove to 'citizens' how biggov doesn't work. As a self-fulfilling prophecy, that was pretty simple to accomplish. Slash taxes, gut programs, stack the judiciary, instigate a perpetual foreign menace so you can military spend out the wazoo. Then when gov gets too depleted to serve anybody any more, you simply throw up your hands and say, '*See?*' Hell, most 'citizens' bought the con whole. Because we took care also to wave the flag and thump the bible, they bled out with a goddamn smile on their stupid faces. Never even knew what hit them. It took the Forefathers until the third decade to outright corporatize everything, but by hook and by crook, and by continual terroralert, they finally got the job done. By God, our corpstate was born. Now I'm just carrying on their policies to their logical conclusion."

"Beggaring the world and attacking EVe?"

"You're all that's left to attack."

Mall finds nothing, absolutely nothing, in those famous icy eyes. "You are insane," she realizes, "aren't you?"

"Well," Bleached Wheat concedes, "you never know. But right now, Mall, it feels more like winning. I am winning."

"But the Wobbly message has got out. I've severed your truth from your power. People have seen you for what you really are."

"Oh please, Mall, I seriously doubt that. You had a good run, yes, and

I'll admit it was a bit touch and go there for a while." Bleached Wheat awards her the double thumbsup. "Nice sign job. I'm sure old Harrods would have been proud. But your most ardent Wobbly supporters are atomized or glowing green at the moment. And those few million others around the IMS and into the PC, who you managed to taint with your libby bullshit, will soon be dead. We're tracking them down and having them killed, even those BoiCity Terds you let go who didn't want to defect from corp. Even they're going to have to buy the firm."

"But why? How?"

"Wobbly's good, Mall. Damn good. I'll certainly give you that. We can't risk even the memory of it lingering in corp." He pauses to smile, strictly for effect, "So we're claiming your feeds were infected, a killer stream concocted by mad EVe scientists."

"But that's not even possible."

"Hey, you're raghead fanatics, remember? In the pubeye, any fiendish act of envy and wanton destruction is possible—even ones that aren't possible. So anyone you reached out and touched in TexArc, Mall, either through your WobblyNet slice or with that fucked-up digiland taste of yours, will be termed. No exceptions. Make no mistake about *that*."

Mall sits silent.

"My power, my truth, Mall," Bleached Wheat reminds her. "Or haven't you been paying attention to Vieworld these past few days?"

Mall tries to recollect specific Vieworld reports she's seen recently, but can't. The feed is so overwhelming that it comes to her as nothing but a tangle of high-pitched adverts and darting images, any one thing essentially indistinguishable from all the rest. Seeing Mall at a loss, Bleached Wheat is happy to fill her in. "Your boy Oak sold you out and came to me to play let's make a deal. Seems he wanted the meg bossman job. I guess you can kiss Wobbly fellowshipride and EVe paxrevolution good-bye. There's just no future in being Mr. Nice-Guy. Your boy Enron did a little better. He didn't sell you out, but that ninny Harrods, and his proxy gayboy Natwest, sent him here so obviously reattuned as a suicide nanobomber I had no trouble spotting him. Three days ago he blew himself up right here in the Eye of the Waco Great Pyramid, taking Oak and his whole ministry of shitubers along with him." Bleached Wheat clucks his tongue. "Took half my ceo substaff with him, too. A truly appalling tragedy." He stands and carefully adjusts his casualwear. "Bottomline is, I've spun the incident to look like a totonasty EVe assassination attempt against me, foiled only by the providential Hand of God." The ceo's eyes sparkle. "I, alone, escaped the blast. The miracle vid is still streaming. Folks can't get enough of it." He feigns disappointment. "I can't believe you haven't seen it. You'll have to admit it's choice prime signification. Me, immaculate amid the whirlwind of blood and guts. Talk about your pregnant signifier."

"Jolly inspirational, that," Mall finally mutters.

"It is," Bleached Wheat gloats. "Much sympathy for me, the noble ceo, going about corp biz, and more hatred against you, the evil bitchspy, who corrupted—then manipulated—the predictably dim minds of loyal Servs and CorpTrooopers. Oh, you are nefarious in TexArc these days, Mall. Nefarious. It's a wonder your asshole's still intact after all that revenge-rape." He tilts his head to one side and takes two steps nearer Mall. "Best yet, though," he has to laugh, "I've turned your Wobblies into folk heroes, especially that little ratfuck Oak. They've all become yanking Serv legends. Can you believe that? What a goddamn joke. All across the parks of corp, every shituber there thinks Oak and his Boys were rags-to-riches averagejoes who, lamentably, got cut short by the cold, hard fate of you, Mall, just when they'd finally worked their way up to the top. Tragic. Your suckass, libby terrorism has fucked up their fairy tale, Mall. They were living the dream, but no more. Boo hoo. Life just ain't fair, is it?" He takes another step toward her. "As a matter of fact, only yesterday I returned from Oak's splendid memorial ceremony in downtown BoiCity, or in what you fucking EVens left of it. I officially rechristened that wounded meg OakCity in his honor. I pledged zillions of DollArcs for its complete reconstruction. What a deeply moving netevent it was, Mall, I can assure you. It set up, so very well, today's shocking nuking."

Mall's ready to get on with things. There's no point in any more of this. She asks simply, "And Brand?"

Bleached Wheat nods at the level-headedness of her question. "The turncoat Terd must suffer so all Terds can learn a lesson. She's scheduled for pubex. As a matter of fact, she'll be in the hotseat very soon."

"Me, too?"

"Yes, you, too. Though not before a few more special things I've planned for you, Mall. The corporation demands nothing less."

Mall is forced to blink, once initially, then several more times. Perhaps the aggressive whiteness of the room is playing tricks on her tired eyes, but it appears the edges around the figure of Bleached Wheat are becoming...indistinct. It's as if he were disincorporating before her eyes. White gaps appear in him here and there as he's shifting, changing, in some kind of corporeal motion. Then his clothing vanishes. More accurately, it melds into his physique, augmenting it, swelling him, making him buffer and more ripped. "Don't want to disappoint my constituents," he explains, "or fail to favorably impress yours."

Then his cock starts to grow—not just swell, but extend straight at her, like Pinocchio's nose. A full meter of it—a meter and a half. Alarmed, Mall starts to crawl backwards, but the serpent-cock pursues her, elongating and elongating. Not until her back is up against the wall and the nob of the thing hovers inches before her face does she notice how the prick's not inflating. It's flocking. She can hear the hum.

"Impressive, eh?" Bleached Wheat says from across the way. "Every guy's viagradream."

"You're sodding *nano*," gasps Mall, trying to glimpse Bleached

Wheat's face beyond the absurd, ominous tally whacker that keeps moving to block her view.

"Bioborn 2017. Bot-reborn 2062." The longcock starts to spiral itself into a lengthy corkscrew. "At age twenty-two I was taken seriously enough for management to adopt my Glassea proposal. You know, what's a mild nukewinter compared to control of global oil? After that, they kept finding ways to fuck me out of subceo status. I guess I was a little *too* hardball for them. They didn't want me climbing that far up the ladder. After D.C. disappeared in a cloud of radioactive dust, though, I became, well, undeniable. Became ceo in a flash. At age forty-five, I decided to make that permanent."

"You yanking loonies are *con*planting over here?" Mall's doing her best to ignore the antics of the long-range wank.

"Oh, my heavens, no, Mall. Such tech is outlaw. It's considered immoral and unnatural, here. Just like you wimps do over there in EVe. No, conplanting's not normally done in TexArc at all. In fact, there's only ever been just the one." Bleached Wheat straightens out, then wags his longshank up and down. "Me." He dips it towards Mall's crotch. "And now you're the only living person who knows about it."

"My god. You're completely and pathologically and pathetically yanked."

He strikes a fencer's pose. "Ha! Have at you!" The nanoprick darts into Mall. In an eye blink, it stuffs and bloats and does damage to her insides. Even before she can cry out, she's hoisted into the air, skewered, and carried back to the middle of the cell—to him.

"Just a little more showtime, darling," Bleached Wheat maneuvers her so he can speak into her ear, "and then it will all be over."

His dick contracts to near normal size. He puts them in the missionary position. Mall hears him say, "Cams on," but not to her. Her rape is protracted and savage. He spouts ludicrous maxims and slogans while at it. She kicks and punches and scratches and spits at him—without effect.

He's strong and impervious. In her agony, Mall attempts to shriek out: *He's a conplant for fuck's sake! He's a fucking nanobot! Good fucking god get your fucking heads out of your fucking arses and see what the fuck's going on!* But no words come. Something's filling her throat. The smell of oiled gears and burnt rubber penetrates her sinuses deeper then fuller. Throb fills her ears. It feels, maybe, like drowning.

When he's done with her, Bleached Wheat picks Mall up and throws her, skidding, across the white floor. He strikes a virile pose and shouts to an entire corp, at the entire world. "Sometimes a man's gotta do what a man's gotta do!"

Mall feels the mot-sen/corband tightening on her skull.

"Now watch this EVe terrorbitch taste the pubex of the traitor dykebitch! Watch her get a taste of her own deadly medicine! A taste like her own killer stream! Watch her taste what's in store for her!" He thrusts both fists up into the air and roars, "Backward and Upward!"

Mall has the briefest sensation of being Brand strapped naked to a cold metal chair. Then every nerve of her body seems to be unraveling, peeling under intense heat. She contorts across the pearly floor. Before losing consciousness, Mall shits black, vomits green, pisses orange, and, from between her thighs, gushes crimson.

☆ ☆ ☆ ☆ ☆ ☆

Mall has to force open her eyes. It could be hours later. It could be days. The memory of the pain suddenly clutches her. Her limbs jerk, but they cannot move. Mall's strapped to a cold metal chair. She's still naked but has been washed clean and dried. She sitting at the focal point of a cavernous and stately demi-amphitheater. The upward-slopping gallery seats are posh and a deep royal blue, and they rise until they're out of sight, but all of them are empty before her.

"We'll fill them in digitally with celebrities and dignitaries as we feed," she hears Bleached Wheat explain. “In here I can’t risk you blurting out anything.”

Mall knows how Simulacrum netcasts, even live ones, feed with a slight voice delay and are content filtered, rendering her sound images useless. Feebly, mustering all the volume she can at the moment, she murmurs, “Mammonism plus GNR renders shitstorm.”

A powerful hand grabs Mall under the chin. Her head is shaken until her eyes eventually focus on Bleached Wheat’s amused features. “You’re about to have every neuron in your body welded together and you still give a fuck about that shit?” He shakes his head. “Jesus shit, what are you libbies made of, anyway? Cocksucking stone?” Though loathsome to her, Mall can’t help resting the weight of her head in Bleached Wheat’s hand. He finds this funny. “You think I can’t control molecular self-assembly, Mall? I *am* nano assemblers.”

She manages to shake her head a bit. She swallows, with much distress. Her throat is unbelievably raw. “Must get out of hand,” come her dry words. “Unavoidable. Too difficult to control.”

He snaps her head still. “You forget, Mall, that GNR control has become our special talent here at TexArc. Who’s been carefully parceling out nanosol power all these decades? Who limits the gen-engineering that could revolutionize crop yields and eliminate diseases? That would be us, sweetheart. Ever since individual molecules and atoms could be turned into circuit elements, we’ve kept our thumb down hard on enablement.”

“You bloody oaf.” Mall finds enough strength to twist her chin out of Bleached Wheat’s hand. “Bleeding GGE.”

“Gray Goo Effect?” The ceo laughs at her. “You’re worried about a little gray goo? Suburban legend, Mall. Besides, that’s why it’s best to keep GNR tech firmly in the hands of a tiny elite. It’s obviously in our best interest—both from the standpoint of staying alive *and* staying solvent—to keep the gray goo at bay, now isn’t it? That incentivizes to keep everyone safe.”

"Bollocks and double bollocks." Mall has to breathe a moment after this exertion. "Sodding gluttony's all you care for."

Bleached Wheat loops and tightens a thick, leather strap around her forehead and double checks straps already wrapped snugly around her upper arms. He takes a few moments tweaking contemplatively each of her nipples between his thumb and forefinger. "So what?" he concludes. "What better regulates the world than greed? Did you seriously think we *wouldn't* exploit the energy and population crisis for profit?" He places a palm on each of her thighs and leans his face in towards hers. "Where's the bizsense in that, Mall?" She imagines she hears a scant thrumming. "Shareholders demand return on investment, and they don't give a shit how that's done. Just do it. You know what I mean?" He starts to slide his palms upward over her thighs. "We discovered global instability was the very best entrepretunity. A golden egg scenario if ever there was one. So we disencumbered ourselves from all hand-wringing and polite appearances and just let biz rip. Why not? Shareholders were thrilled—and shareholders run all Republics. Everybody knows unrestricted competition is the natural order of things." He has begun to massage her inner thighs. "Regulations and controls are for biggov gayboys and libby pencilnecks. You have to let the Market rock-and-roll." His fingertips are dangerously near to her quim. "That's just how people are, Mall. We're lusty brutes. We want it all, and we don't care who we hurt to get it."

Mall can just manage to spray enough piss to chase his hands off her. Unhappily, she hasn't the saliva to spit a wadge in his face. "Contrived rubbish," she declares, "and you sod-all good and know it is."

Bleached Wheat grins and backs away, shaking dry his hands."Maybe it is. But it's sure as hell an easy sell to Crats. Besides, you're the assholes trying to spread enablement around, that and your faggoty-ass alterity bullshit. If anybody's going to gray goo us, it'll be EVe with its fucking bleeding heart. How yanking bitch is that? You libbies started this Know War."

"You forced our hand. You offered the world nothing but blood-sucking demagoguery and financial slavery." Mall's conflicted about defending Caucus' calculated risk to walk the line between KME and KMD, but now she feels she must. She must somehow get through to this conplant, talk some right sense into him. "How else did you expect us to bleeding respond?"

Bleached Wheat's studied charm vanishes. "Gratefully, Mall. I expected you to respond fucking gratefully." His blue eyes ice over. "The old EU could have had it all right along with us, right from the start. We fucking handed it to you on a platter, and you fucking kicked the tray straight up into the goddamn air."

"I suppose we haven't your taste for bloodsport and oppression."

"Spoken like a euroloser, Mall. The simple truth is, EVe has no backbone. No vision. That's another reason I'm not too concerned about your GNR tech getting out of hand. You creampuffs certainly aren't going to push the envelop enough to do anything that might end up gooing us all. EVe just doesn't have the hardballs for that. Libbies don't know how to up a Know War into a Do War. Do you? Hell, you fucking people couldn't even stomach a plaindeal like the goddamn Glassea. Fucking unbelievable."

While Mall watches the nanoassemblers replicating a red face and throbbing temple veins, she experiences disturbing yet fascinating thoughts. *Does the conplant dictate the nanobot, or is it the other way around? Or is that too reductive a binary?* Does a sentient entity persist and continue to unfold and live in the biosense of that term, or does the hardware hamper, as it were, the software? *Once nanoencased, might one become arrested, stifled, dwindled, even locked into cognizant place? A mirror and not the lamp? And just which way would the entitlement of nanoimmortality go? Epiphany leading to empathy and magnanimity? Or do you calcify into being, quite literally, just the ghost in the machine?* Mall best find out—quickly.

"*You're* sodding upset because you can't have any of it anymore, can you?" Mall's question backs Bleached Wheat even further off than her pissing. "*You're* not a lusty brute any longer at all, are you, despite your gigantic coil of a yanker?" Bleached Wheat lifts his hands completely off the chair. "You *can't* want it all and not care who you hurt to get it—because you're *not* people anymore, not genuinely. Are you?" Mall hopes, what she glimpses, is a flicker of remorse in the conplant's eyes. "You're just going through the motions, aren't you? You may as well be mech now, frozen stiff like some bit of gadgetry, without real purpose and not subject to actual consequences."

"My purpose has always been the same. Just the one. To break your union." His conceited smile returns. "And consequences are what we all strive to be free of. Are they not, Mall?"

Just for an instant, Mall has a picture of the two of them, Bleached Wheat and Sinalco, quite by themselves on some future, distant, sterile plain, under, say, a lowery and caramel-colored sky, locked in perpetual, gyrating, utterly strange nanocombat simply because there is nothing else left to do.

"I'm quite sure that last part is not right," Mall answers his question.

Bleached Wheat approaches her again, pressing close. He inspects the deep bruising around her eyes and nose from the taste of Brand's pubex. His ironic manner has completely returned. "Nice tug on the nanoheart-strings. Very professional. But it does you no good." He puts his hands dispassionately on her breasts, as if getting ready to spin two dials. "Very soon now, my pretty, I'll be strolling down your Champs Élysées trying not to gag on the stink of cheese. Then all corp problems will be solved for good."

Mall is tired enough to consider, momentarily, simply dying in resigned agony. *Why fight this any longer?* Behind her, she hears the sound of others, backstage perhaps, making preparations for the pubex event. She wonders about shouting out to them, about recklessly attempting to reveal Bleached Wheat's identity as a nanobot to them. But she suspects, if she tries, her throat will only swell again with that nasty viscosity and odor. And she suspects, as well, that should anyone in TexArc come to realize what's actually taking place with their ceo, that person would soon be found inexplicably dead. Ignoring his hands, Mall looks past Bleached Wheat to the extensive and ornate hall behind him. The seat cushions are so deep and velour to appear almost purple. The bas-relief faux columns lining the walls have gilded fluting and Ionic volutes superimposed on Corinthian capitals. The ceiling is a jumble of odd-angled, acoustic tiling, no doubt designed to capture crisp and lively the screams of terrified agony that emanate from the hotseat she occupies. Mall sighs and summons her last bit of stamina. Idealists are what they call someone not lazy enough to stop working for a better reality. She'll talk econformation. She'll try that last-ditch. Why sodding not? That's what's led them to this godawful mess in the first place. "First off, laddiebuck, get your sodding microbits off my bloody tits. You may as well be one big prosthetic penis. You can't even rape and molest proper."

Conceding her point, Bleached Wheat complies with a smile and a nod.

"And second bloody off, your Corpfeud cannot sodding sustain itself, you bloody idiot. Biospherically. Fiscally. You sodding well name it, and it can't keep it up forever. But you already bloody well know that, don't you?"

"Do I?" the ceo says coyly. "Do I now? I'm not so sure. Profit margins have been holding up nicely, so far. It sure seems like Corpfeud marches in place. All I've really got to do is make sure Terds and Servs think their needs are being met, and they won't rock the boat."

"But you can't deliver those basic goods very much longer, and you know it."

"Oh, I disagree, Mall, because it's more a matter of lowering expectations than delivering goods, and expectations have been lowering in TexArc for a long, *long* time now. Take freedom and democracy, for example. No one wants those things anymore. Not the real McCoy, anyway. TexArcans don't even know what those concepts mean, now. And if you were to tell them, like you tried to do with your Uncle Wobbly, they'd balk at the level of collective responsibility it demands from them." Bleached Wheat cocks his head to inspect Mall's face. "People don't give a shit about collectivity. You know exactly what I mean. That's why you pitch your 'alterity' so hard all the time back in EVe." Bleached Wheat makes derisive air-quotation marks with his fingers around the renegade word. "By the way, that ad with the jerk in the cowboy hat zoomzooming around in the big gas-guzzler? That was doublechoice. I laughed my ass off. That's so us."

From backstage, someone calls deferentially to Bleached Wheat in order to ask him a series of questions. The ceo looks in that direction and listens carefully for a while, then nods yes to them all, only slightly impatient, before turning back to Mall. "As for Terds," he resumes, "just give them a high-medium level of techno-material comfort along with some little existential mission to accomplish in life, a career to pursue or a novel to write, and they're happy as stupid clams. You've got to take care that most of them are absolutely ignorant about who they're fucking over to come by such luxuries, of course, but you know how anxious privilege is to turn a blind eye towards reality. Terds really are a piece of cake. Servs, though, are a much harder sell. It'd be impossible, in fact, to make them buy in if it weren't for the fact we keep them so desperate and brainslow." Two blood-curdling shouts come from backstage. Sound level tests, evidently. "And there you were trying to educate the smelly bastards by pulling the wool back off their eyes." He pats her cheek. "Happily, that's all over with, now. I took a risk getting Harrods to make a move, and you just about made it backfire on me, Mall. You ought to be proud of yourself for that." The lights dim and flicker for a second or two then come back up to full strength. Surely, thinks Mall, that's just for show. "As *that* particular cat's out of the bag, the Servs can go back to what they do best—craving their basic needs. Vit and vid, that is, McSlurrys and the MFL. So that's exactly what we'll keep giving them. You see, Mall, there's really no need for TexArc to go anywhere."

"You know you're wrong, but you simply won't admit it. You're soon to run out of consumers and resources at about the same time. Then how's your bloody circus of a marketplace going to function?"

"I suppose you expect us to convert to public ownership of alienable productive assets?"

"Yes," fettered, Mall can barely nod, "I do. That's inevitable. Mammonism is little better than the chivalric nonsense it supplanted. Why not put an end to its brutality and despair sooner rather than sodding later while there's still something left to salvage?"

"Because I don't want to, Mall. Because I don't have to. That's why."

"No argument Marksoc's not perfect and it requires constant bloody attention. Bugger, it requires constant bloody *con*tention. You never get it absolutely right. But you suffer that chaos gladly. Pareto optimality represents all agents, each with the right to propose different allocations of communal holdings so long as that new allocation does no harm to the others."

"That's pansy bullshit right there."

"It's an administrative nightmare, yeah," Mall urges, "but it's not bullshit. It's an economic constitution. An endstate that we bloody well manage to muddle through."

"Yanking unworkable."

"It's your Corpfeud that's bloody bullshit and yanking unworkable. Not to mention sod-all unconscionable. Why let the handful of the self-seeking, well-to-do concoct their privatized version of The Good to foist off on everybody else? What else is bloody well going to happen but bare-knuckle plutocracy?"

"Oh, so you're *not* concocting your own libby version of The Good over in EVe to foist off on folks?"

"Of course we are. Humans always devise an artificial order out of the natural chaos. That's what people always must do." Mall has been experimenting with incrementally raising her voice in hopes that those backstage might overhear her. Bleached Wheat now shakes his head firmly for her to stop it. She reverts to her normal tone. "But you fabricate a grand stasis of haves and have-nots and then enforce it with thuggery and lies. We fabricate our commonwealth under perpetual debate where the general welfare is fostered by enablement and education."

"I think I'm going to cry."

"We arrange property rights with an eye for the benefits of their final outcome. We try to determine what principles would bring about fair economic growth and a heightened self-worth for everyone, and then we work to put those guidelines into productive action. Look here, there's no inherent need for anyone to get buggered by the use of resources or technology. Or for the less skilled to suffer at the hands of the more skilled—or vice versa. There's more than enough to go around. Ours is the superior system."

Bleached Wheat bats his eyes at Mall. "But gee, look who's sitting strapped to the chair."

"You know full well public ownership is not the monster you portray it to be. EVens retain control over their inalienable means of production, just as they keep hold of their private property. Different talents have the right to earn differential returns. That's the same in Marksoc as it is in Corpfeud. But in EVe no one has the right to hoard *capital* assets. No one has the right to turn individual talents and good fortune into the oppression of others by owning the bloody external means of production."

"Survival of the fittest, Mall. Survival of the fittest."

"*Fittest* means best able to adapt to circumstances, you great loon, not he with the hairiest knuckles. That's where it all goes wrong in Mammonism, in your delusion that you must overmaster and then own the sodding *external* world. Retain private ownership of the self, yes, by all bloody means. But don't let greedy brutes buy up the earth and then have their sniveling offspring literally inherit it."

"So what are you saying, little Miss Wobbly? There's no climbing the ladder? There's no getting ahead?"

"Getting ahead to sodding *where*, you sodding freak? Walled enclaves of the stunted wealthy surrounded by teeming slums of the stunted poor? The violent, competitive, and complete gutting of the natural world? Are these bloody places anyone sane really wants to go?"

Bleached Wheat shakes his head, slowly, in disgust. "You bellyaching Marksoc pussies drive me crazy," he says. "You always have. Crats are the direct producers. We take all the fucking risks. We deserve all the fucking rewards. Why penalize our leadership and initiative with regulations and taxes? Why limit *our* horizons and those of our children because we're go-getters and you're pathetic whiners?"

"Because your so-called 'leadership and initiative' are a bloody farce, that's why. They're nothing more than the inevitable by-products of your privileged upbringing, a sodding upbringing purchased at the expense of those you're too scared *really* to compete with."

"Terds and Servs are the fucking parasites. Their asses belong to us, the topcrats, who God, in His infinite wisdom, endowed with the property rights of this great Corporation."

"Oh, get off your bloody God hobbyhorse. You don't believe that tripe any more than I. Proper Christianity is based on the Sermon on the Mount, not on fucking lunatic Revelations. You employ Jesus as a bleeding mask for your robber-barony, and you bleeding well know it." Bleached Wheat smirks, arching his eyebrows. "TexArc is a sodding minstrel show where your Terds serve out of sloth and your Servs obey out of fear. All your holidays and anthems are bloody frauds."

"Hey, so long as Terds and Servs exercise their free will to know their fucking place and stay the fuck in it, everyone's spiritual needs are met."

Mall sighs out of an exasperation that has become all too familiar. How does one engage in intellectual combat against those who either believe in absurdities or else wilfully and knowingly manipulate such absurdities? "Fine. Have your bit of fun. But very soon you'll be needing a new master plan. The providence of private ownership of alienable assets already is no longer optimal for harnessing and developing the productive forces still left on the planet. You've been propping up that dinosaur artificially for too many decades now without adapting in the least. After you sack EVe, Corpfeud will explode in your face. That might take several decades, but eventually even you Crats must go under. *You* might want to go backward and upward, but history inevitably marches onward."

Bleached Wheat's eyes turn triumphant. He glances over the back of the metal chair to make certain no one is in earshot. He curls his upper lip to reveal, in a kind of contorted satyr grin, teeth pure and even as ivory. "Who fucking cares?" he says in a low, pointed whisper. Had he any breath, it would be in Mall's face. "*This* topcrat's never going under." His glee is consuming, unabashed. "I'm the crown of fucking Corpfeud creation. There *are* no consequences for me."

Just when she thought it no longer possible, Mall attains a new plateau of horror. That's been the story of her time spent in TexArc. "But that makes no sodding sense."

"Sense?" Bleached Wheat pauses a moment to chuckle. "Mall, Mall. Who ever said anything about any of this making sense?"

He backs away several steps then stops to adjust his smart cratsuit so that it hangs just right on him. After a moment he glances up, as though just noticing Mall tied, nude, and glowering at him. He shrugs and turns his palms outward in an insincere apologetic gesture.

"Golly, sorry, Mall. What can I say? For some reason it's just always been easy to make everybody buy into a bullshit dream that only really pays off for the superich few." He ruminates on his own statement for a moment. "Hm. Must be that public ignorance and private greed are an impossible combination to defeat. By the time I've sucked the Market life out of EVe, China will be ripe for the plucking. We've been letting her revive a bit recently. After China, there will be India. Then maybe Brazil. Why not? I'll give everyone a turn at being TexArc's bitch. No doubt things will cycle back around to being EVe's turn again, eventually. Don't you see, Mall? We've arrived at the end of history."

The ceo beckons. Two similarly dressed Crats appear on stage. They assume an official stance on either side of the hotseat. One of the men is a light cocoa color. Other than that, Mall doesn't bother to notice anything more about them. Run-of-the-mill bloodsucking swine, she reckons. Even if he would permit her to speak some commonsense joe to them, it wouldn't do a rat's ass bit of good. Bleached Wheat patiently explains to the pubexecutee that since she is the most notorious perpetrator of terrorist atrocities ever livecaptured in TexArc, her hotseat experience is to be special. She will undergo what's been advertized as doublejeopardy. A simultaneous digiland taste of her execution, complete with emostim and fivesensestim, while undergoing actual execution. Vir and real death at once. It's never been attempted before in the long and storied history of spectacular TexArc executions. It should redefine the art of cruel and unusual punishment.

"You live by the sign, you die by the sign, Mall. You and Brand never should have fucked around with that digiland simudisc of yours. That shit got *way* too deep into the heads of my Terds. Your hotseat doublejeopardy should deter any other clown from even thinking about using that tech again. Everyone in TexArc, but more important everyone in EVe, will watch you wishing you'd never been born."

"Piss off."

"I'm not going to make anyone else in TexArc taste your execution along with you. Not even the shithouse Servs. Everyone can just kick back and enjoy this show. I'll have you know that's an unprecedented act of largess in the post mot-sen/corband era, Mall. My people are lovin' me for it."

"Piss off."

"Oh, and Mall, when you do reach your libby-atheist hell, be sure to say hello to that loser Harrods for me. I do so regret missing out on that opportunity to gloat. Although, I must say, sometimes I almost regret having the Underminister assassinated that first time we pretended to come after you. But the old goat was smart. I'll give him that. I couldn't risk him seeing through what I was trying to get Countermeasures to do."

Must keep him off the topic of Harrods.

"We're not liberals, asshole. We're socialists."

"Oh, I'm well aware of that, Mall. But by making liberals out to be our enemy, we create the very useful illusion of that conservative outlook being wild-eyed and dangerous. Right? And that illusion acts like a buffer against your genuinely radical and threatening shit, shit like your Wobbly alterity. See what I mean? Vilifying liberals makes it infinitely easier for us to keep you socialists at bay. Over the decades it's been a masterstroke of Signification, wouldn't you say, Mall?"

"Piss off."

"I will say this, though. I'm really going to miss our little chats. I so seldom get to talk to anyone real anymore."

"You can sod off now, as well."

Mall's pubex feeds livevent over the Simulacrum all4s, of course. It surpasses her pubrapes as the highest rated netcast in TexArc history. All of these netevents are then slicedelayed onto EVeWave, a move calculated to appall and unnerve the commonweal. Mall anticipates their propaganda. For as long as she's able to maintain conscious action, she wills herself to mouth the word "conplant" again and again. Mall wagers that Sinalco will notice, surely, and be able to decipher this crucial bit of intelligence. Mall's almost comforted by the fact that Harrods has serendipitously created a human consciousness nanobot to meet the threat of....but wait....Harrods' fire with fire...he already...and the nanovirus isn't...it's in...and Sinalco *knew*...

Before such tragic thoughts long vex Mall's mind—she manages to form "conplant" three rapid and desperate times—she succumbs to the tototrauma of doublejeopardy. Bleached Wheat's digiland taste induces a doubling effect of physical and emotional agony. It produces, as it was designed to produce, an excruciating in-and-out-of-body experience at once. Knowing Mall's likely to be stressed more by intellectual than by bodily torture, Bleached Wheat stimulates into her, as well, the emotions of abject loss and profound personal failure. Against her will, through the corband riveted across the top of her head, Mall stimfeels, during her final moments on earth, that everything she has ever worked for, loved, and believed in passionately has been rendered meaningless, useless, invalid, even erased from human memory by shortcomings and blunders entirely of her own fault. It quickly becomes obvious to all witnessing the hideously protracted pubex of this EVe terrorbitch—obvious from the jerkings and the excretions of her carcass, from the contortions of torment and anguish screwing her face, from the stream of bloody tears smearing her cheeks, then running down onto her jiggling breasts—that this hotseat jockey is seriously wishing right about now that her shit-for-brains papa had never slipped the big hardnob to her slit of a mama.

☆ ☆ ☆ ☆ ☆ ☆

A day and a half following the glorious corpspectacle, subceo boss of ArcNet Yupcap comes down with the most ominous hacking cough accompanied by the most persistent case of sniffles CorpHQ docs have ever seen. Subceo boss of Security Java, in the meantime, seems to be just fine. Enjoying perfect health.

This is the End

Announced by the amusing hermetic farting sound, Bleached Wheat steps, smiling to himself, from between the sliding outer doors of the double airlock. He's always relieved to disembark a shuttle. Cramped and vile things. Their stale air gives him headaches. Or at least he pretends to his new subceos that it does. As he'd ordered, the executive platform is deserted, as he likes it for this kind of thing. On the wall to his right is the big white star inside a thin red circle against the deep blue background. In fact the whole interior of the execplat is deep blue. Walls, deck, ceiling. People like color. Dynamic color. It helps them enjoy their space. Sodding sheep. Yes, he likes these exotic curse words. He'll need to get proficient at them. He puts the kiss on the fingertips of his right hand and plants it with a brisk slap in the center of the star. Then, with anticipation in his step, Bleached Wheat makes his way across the forty meters of polished blue floor to the curved bank of observation windows.

"Top80," he says as he goes.

An agreeable and faintly militaristic tune begins to play, not too loud and not too soft. People enjoy tunes, too, he thinks. It helps them do their jobs well—or bloody else. With one hand, Bleached Wheat sweeps the lank, blond forelock from his eyes. His other hand brings his gold Rolex watch-wrist up for him to see. Time to catch Vieworld. As those talkheads constantly blurt out: *Time To Know!* Another thin smile stretches over the bluish lips. Yes indeed, he nods. How simple it is to *make* the know.

He stops a few meters short of the windows to concentrate on the little flatscreen. It's been something of a problem over the past few days, suppressing rumors of a whiteman's plague sweeping through TexArc. Suppression, though, is the name of the game. If you don't sit hard on certain things, well, you never know what might happen. The newsbig hype he's got droning 24/7 doublego directfeed all4s into their dear little heads is *Terrorattack! Terrorattack! Terrorattack!* And more *Terrorattack!*—the tried-and-true of roguestate, ragheads, and deadcount. Of assaults on Our Freedom. Of corpatriotic outrage. In a word: EVe. The mother of all evil. Time for TexArc finally to take care of biz.

Satisfied with the spectacle streaming the Simulacrum, particularly with the imagesense—a pictaste is worth a thousand words, after all—put on by the consummate professionals that are the Terds of ArcNet, Bleached Wheat buries his hands deep in his pockets and slowly takes the last few steps toward the windows. Their panes extend floor-to-ceiling, thick and convex, all but invisible. He places his toes right at their edge before allowing himself to gaze out. When he does, the base of his scrotum tingles, deliciously. All before him is the vasty zilch. And far, far below the Big Blue that, in a moment or two, when his last few cards are played right, will be his. *All* his. For a while he studies the lights that crisscross the darkened LNA landmass—their webs and the intricacy of them. Like a huge nanomicrochip. He swells with the pride of power. Oh, there's never *enough* of the selfoblige.

He swivels his head northeastward and narrows his eyes. It takes some moments, but finally there it is. The other consistently lighted area of the earth. The old bitch herself with her sagging, suckled-dry teats. Teats that are about to get suckled even a little drier and become even a little saggier and, goddamn it, used for the very last time. Bleached Wheat needs no personal codes now. All of TexArc is on board with his justwar. No more doubtoms he needs to deal with. Just good old-fashioned shock-and-awe. He speaks directly to ArcSpace command, "Both at once. Now."

"Roger that, sir."

God, he loves the miltalk.

☆ ☆ ☆ ☆ ☆ ☆

ArcSpace EastAtlantic sector, at long fucking last, scrambles Dmega doublego. From highearth-orbit over EVe, its GLASS launches a thousand deeks—decoys to act as atmospheric freaks to glut and fluster the outmoded anti-missile sys facing it below. At a go, EVe early-warn lights red across the board. These poor fuckmothers aren't going to know what hit them. Two stealth Trans-Atmospherics are already scrambled in the hostile sky. Any enemy flier patrolling too close to them gets precision grilled pronto by HEL—laser bolts from on high. Zip! Sizzles an unfriendly's ass in a super hurry. With the shit breaking all across EVe airspace, both those Arc TAVs code green gotarget at once and start their runs. EVe ground/air and air/air does its best to deal with the deek overload, plotting probable attacks, but it's swamp. Flatout overkill. Textbook Arc-assault. That means double-thumbsup, smashmouth, totoyank no contest. Too much to handle. Still, at this point in engagement, ArcSpace operates under selfdeter. Annihilate's not plan. Capitulate is—yield and submit. The standard first wave is to bring ragheads to their knees—or senses. Whichever. Just bend over, grab 'em, and, oh yeah, put a smile on your face. The weapon of choice for this strategic bitchslapping is the tacnuke, that friendly little limited-but-dirty calling card. It's amazing how lowyield collateral-damage—just a few hundred urban thousands or so—focuses so sharply an opponent's mind. It's like saying: Hey, it *easily* could have been a lot, lot worse, you know. How much more of this shit do you want? We got plenty. Next round we might go aboveground and let fly on a couple of your really *major* cities.

At firepoint, each ArcSpace TAV releases two B61-11 earth penetrators, vintage stockpile, odds being sure at least one will arrive. If both make it down to target, so much more choice with the doublewhammy.

Descending hypersonic through the thin clouds and the firestorm of high-tech flak, one B61-11 missile from each pair gets obliterated by EVeShield. Lucky shots, maybe, but that's how these obsolete sys work. Send up everything and hope. Yet anything short of ideal killrate doesn't cut it in this game. Shit hits fan. Somebody ends up as nuclear toast.

One penetrator dives vertical through the dome of the Radcliffe Camera. It pierces the standard ten meters or so down into the substructure. It detonates. Boomya! The ground shock takes the feet out from under buildings. The minutely delayed air shock blows everything aboveground away, the thermal radiation flash-frying as it goes. As that fireball breaks the surface, it brings up with it some tons of dirt and debris irradiated by the acute neutron flux of the blast. That radioactive cloud then sprawls out rapidly in the form of a narrow chimney column and a broad base surge. One of those eerie-beautiful things. From groundzero, that mass of charged particles, steam, smoke, and dust ranges out two, maybe up to three klicks, bringing with it fallout that's choice nasty glow. Meantime central Oxford, the city of dreaming spires, is turned into one huge gamma-radiation crater.

The other penetrator making it to strikepoint angles forty-five true through the roof of Saint Nicholas Cathedral, traveling chancel to narthex. That slant plows the thick-tip warhead smack into the slope of the Bourg, making ground entry shallower and the ensuing blast surge wider. Why fuck with a Maneuvers fortification just too, too deep to touch? Leave them sealed up instead in a fission tomb. In a quickflash, then, the deeply carved meander in the Sarine, with its impressive roundhouse bend of sheer cliff faces, is gone. Those sturdy stonework and wooden bridges, for so many centuries making Fribourg of such vital strategic importance, are gone. Every quaint building, with every charming and irregular red-tile roof, is gone. Every pleasant Gasthaus, each worn cobblestone, all carefully tended hanging pots of flowers, and the drifting smell of baking bread, and the calm murmur of the deep and slow-moving green riverwaters—all of these good things and so much, much more—are quite completely doublegone. All in a quickflash. Poof.

☆ ☆ ☆ ☆ ☆ ☆

In geosynch orbit, 36,000km above the surface, Bleached Wheat feels through his heels the jolt of the elevator shaft auto-detaching into massive safesections. He looks down between his feet to see the top several partitions of the colossal, glossy white shaft beginning ponderously to wheel and lift independently into higher safeorbit. They'll all nanoreassemble later, once danger has passed. It's not necessarily a disaster so much as a hefty suck on capitalserve. His shuttle, *ArcSpace One*, is forced to break dock with the exec platform as well. Standard emergency protocol. No big woof. It will be able to re-dock in a matter of minutes. In the meantime, though, the ceo must endure his Top80 overridden by the diligent and gut-rumbling baritone of the alarm claxon and, mere seconds after it starts in, the almost synchronous, anxious yapping of Java and Pace, both siging him frantically to see if he's okay. Jesus, how these peeps can talk. Afros, mexs, even slopes. He's never been around these people that much before. Fuck me dry how they can talk. On and fucking on. He might just have to get used to it. Bleached Wheat's not having shit for luck bringing up, from the ranks, two new averagejoe subceos who can stay alive overnight. There might be something to this plague. Maybe he better look into it. The ceo knew breaking colorline was an unavoidable trend. That's why he brought Java up to the show. Minorities had become the majority in large segments of TexArc—the PC and the lower span of the BHC, for example, not to mention the allmex regions extremesouth. But he'd wanted to intedoctrinate slowly. Even if, soon, a little over half of all TexArcans would be non-Blood-in-the-Face, that didn't mean CorpHQ needed a shitload of tonto topcrats running around. Just enough to maintain illusion of equal shot. Now, it looks like his hand will be forced and he might just wind up being the lone whiteman ranger. No bigdeal. The need for greed knows no color barrier. He can sell, foist, or force Corpfeud on anyone. And, over time, he'll gradually get tanner and tanner.

Bleached Wheat sigs back to his ArcNet and Security subceos to goddamn relax. He's just fine. To give them both something constructive and competitive to do, he asks for "someone" to find out exactly what's happened below. Why the fuck did they have to segment? Moments later, Java gets back to him first, as he expected Java would. This one trains up quite nicely. On his watchwrist flatscreen, Bleached Wheat examines his subceo's ultra-earnest features while he reports. It occurs to the ceo that, except for pigmentation and the slightest unfortunate thickness to this young man's lips, he could be watching himself fifty years ago. Ah, to be so simple and staunch again. The bliss of totobelief.

"EVe deepsloop, sir," Java's saying. "Probably lying up for weeks on the ocean floor."

Bleached Wheat lays on thick the anger. "Which *fucking* one?"

"Probably the *Fifth of May*, sir. Their newest and most evasive according to our latest infoflow."

"What the *fuck* did ArcSea let it do?"

"They lost track of it, sir. Real poochscrew right there. Then they never relocated it. Then, when it launched a counterattack just a few minutes ago—"

"What the *fuck* did it launch?"

"Bank of nuketip torpedoes, sir. Their new sonar deadzones. A real bitch to detect—"

"And then what the *fuck* happened?"

"Well, sir...one of them...got through."

"The *sea* platform?" Bleached Wheat snarls out his guess. "We let their *fucking* deepsloop take out the elevator's floating *fucking* baseplat?"

He's near wholesale howling at this point, veins bumping blue along his temples, cheeks and ears burning ruby red—nanoassemblers going into overdrive. "Poochscrew hardly *fucking* begins to describe it, *son*!"

A baseplat bottomlines at zillions upon zillions of DollArcs. ArcSea doesn't even have one back-up standby quite at the ready yet.

"Yes, sir. I know, sir. And the five thousand seamen lost is a terrible—"

"*Fuck* lost sailorboys, Java! Save that shit for the Simulacrum. Strategically, this is borderline ass*fuck*! We're at full tilt terrorwar now!"

Make them sweat. Always make them sweat. Especially early on.

To his credit, Java steps up to shoulder the blame. Something Bleached Wheat anticipated. This is all very positive. "Yes, sir. I know, sir. All my bad, sir." Java's voice is breaking then steadying, breaking then steadying. "As your ArcNet subceo, sir, ultimately this can only be seen as my poochscrew."

The ceo glowers and waves an angry hand for him to shut up, making a show of letting this junior pipsqueak off the hook—*this* time.

"Just dock my *fucking* shuttle on the doubledouble!" he snaps. "Thanks to you we've got some major *fucking* spin to take care of now!"

"Yes, sir! Backward and Upward, sir!"

The last watchwrist image of Java shows the poor guy looking like he's getting ready to shit a brick. Bleached Wheat can't help laughing to himself once he's gazing calmly again out the observation windows, his hands folded behind his ass as he stands at ease waiting for his shuttle to arrive. He makes the annoying alarm stop and brings back up the agreeable Top80. Freespinning safe and serene, the execplat module gradually rotates to position him looking straight down what used to be the column of the space elevator. He can make out some of its lower fragments, those segments overcome by the pull of gravity, still toppling down into the head of a giant, white cloud spreading silently out over the Atlantic—like a nuclear hurricane. He thinks, *well, well*, *World War V has begun—at last.* Bleached Wheat shifts the focus of his eyes to his own elongated face smiling distorted, fun-house-mirror-like, in the thick convex nanoglass only a few centimeters in front of his nose. This is going better than he ever could have hoped.

Glossary

abstainant: EVe term for a nonsexual person; someone who abstains from sexual activity altogether.

Administer: title and office of the elected leader of the EVe Caucus; the EVe head of state.

advocacy project: an advertisement campaign designed and performed by the Signification Committee of Eve in order to promote social justice and equality; see also"alterity."

afro: TexArc slang for persons of African descent or otherwise suspiciously dark skin; pejorative.

Airman (men): Terd(s) serving in ArcAir.

aligning in: tuning in or selecting a network stream or channel.

all4s: TexArc term referring to all four viewscreens of the ipatch.

alterity: EVe term for the communal mind set resulting from the public ownership of the means of production; an overriding public concern for social justice and equality (as opposed to the fetishistic private concern for rapacity); the opposite of "disciplinarity"; see also "Marksoc."

ArcAir: TexArc air forces.

ArcGround: TexArc land forces; see also "Corptroop."

ArcNet: TexArc internet protection and disruption forces; also, the TexArc internet system.

Arcs (The): TexArc slang for McSlurrys.

ArcSea: TexArc naval forces.

ArcSpace: TexArc space forces.

Attack Crew: EVe military term for an offensive force of fighters; see also "Maneuvers."

aud: "audio."

averagejoe: TexArc slang for an everyday person; a regular guy; see also "commonsense joe."

bangbone: TexArc slang for the erect penis.

bellyfart(s): TexArc slang for feedtube regurgitation experienced by Servs; see also "shituber."

bent: TexArc slang for drunk; sometimes also "beerbent."

BHC: "Boston-to-Houston Crescent"; the most densely populated TexArc corpent.

biggov: "big government"; TexArc term for centralized government; pejorative.

bigmac(s): TexArc slang for lies, exaggerations; formerly "whopper(s)."

bigpic: "big picture"; TexArc slang for seeing things globally; taking all factors into account.

biz: "business"; TexArc term for any money-making venture.

bizdumb: TexArc academic Terd slang for Crats; pejorative.

bodyenhance: "body enhancement"; one's idealized, fantasy avatar when having a virtual experience; see also "digiland" and "virbod."

BoiCity: in TexArc, the former Boise City; a relatively minor meg of the central IMS.

bondclass: EVe term for the underclass of other societies; a vassal or wage-slave.

bossman: TexArc slang for anyone higher up the corporate ladder than yourself; see also "ceo."

bot: "robot."

bottomline: TexArc term for that which is most important.

brainintegrated: any brain-machine interface or bio-implanted device;

cybernetics.

brainslow: TexArc slang for foolish, stupid, or mentally impaired; considered the natural state of Servs and women.

buy the firm (to): TexArc slang expression for dying in combat.

cap: "capital"; TexArc slang for money.

capitalserve: TexArc term meaning to conserve or to save money.

Caucus (the): the elected legislative body governing EVe.

ceo (the): TexArc term for the top corporate position; the big boss.

christer(s): EVe, and, oddly, TexArc Crat slang for fanatical, born-again Christians; pejorative.

closedcomm: "closed communication"; any private or secure line of communication.

clutter (the): the hype and chatter streaming over a network; news, advertisements, entertainment, and the like; that which must be broken through in order to reach an audience with any type of commercial or political message.

cokecola: a cocaine-based soda drink very popular in TexArc.

commonsense joe: TexArc slang for having a practical view on matters or for being a clear-thinking person.

communicant(s): elected representative(s) serving in the Caucus of EVe.

conplant/conplantbot: "consciousness planted robot"; a human consciousness downloaded into a superintelligent nanoassembler swarm.

constituents/constituency (the): EVe term for its citizens; the citizenry.

corpanthem: "corporate anthem"; TexArc term for the official song in praise of corporation; anthem title: "O Privatization, Deregulation, Globalization!"

corpatriotism: "corporate patriotism"; see also "jingofrenzy."

corpent(s): "corporate entity"; TexArc term for the five major regional divisions of TexArc; see also "BHC," "GLR," "IMS," "PC," and "PTA."

corpexec: "corporate executive"; TexArc term for any high-ranking position within the corporation.

Corpfeud: "corporate feudalism"; the current political-economic formation of TexArc predicated on a neo-manorial system of giant, more or less self-sufficient centers of population operating within a larger, corporate-wide free market and consumer-driven paradigm; see also "meg."

CorpHQ: "Corporate HeadQuarters"; the TexArc corporate seat of power; see also Waco Great Pyramid.

CorpTroop(s)/CorpTrooper(s): "corporate troop(s)/trooper(s)"; TexArc term for infantry soldier; see also "ArcGround" and "Groundsman."

Countermeasures: the intelligence agency of EVe.

counterpitch: TexArc term for a commercial or advertising; see also "pitch."

Crat: TexArc term for the ruling corporate class; see also "corpexec."

CratVillage: where Crats reside within the central fortified district of a TexArc meg; specifically, those areas furthest away from the outer wall that separates the Gater District from the Parks; see also "elitehood."

credgrade(s): "credit grade(s)"; TexArc term for interest rates at which workcreds are to be repaid; see also "workcred."

credhole: TexArc term for personal debt.

credscard: "credits card"; TexArc term for a workcreds card enabling Servs to purchase goods and services with labor credit; see also "workcred."

credsgoon(s): "credit goon(s)"; TexArc slang for a debt collector.

credspending: both "credit spending" and "credits pending"; virtually interchangeable TexArc terms for buying with workcreds and for how many workcreds a Serv is in debt; see also "workcred."

crewtalk: TexArc slang for the specialized vocabulary of any given job; also, job instruction or information.

crewterm: TexArc term for a workplace accident or death; see also "term."

Culture Construct: the TexArc corporate division responsible for propagating the benefits of Corpfeud over the Simulacrum; headquartered at the Yale School of Reconstruction; see also "Signification Committee."

daytrade (daytrading): TexArc term for the constant stock market transactions taking place within the corporation.

deadcount: TexArc term for death toll.

deadjobber(s): TexArc slang for a Serv working an endless line of temporary, dead-end jobs; also, Servs in general.

deepsloops: EVe deep-diving stealth submarines.

democratize (to): TexArc term for the overwhelming military conquest of an enemy; to squash, control, subdue, kill.

descend shell: ArcSpace one-man pod vehicle for inserting Corptroops from shuttle orbit to ground positions.

Die Gemeinschaft: "The Community" or "The Communion"; EVe term for a nanomorph swarm; see also "flitter nanobots."

digiland: "digital land"; TexArc term for the virtual environment in which Terds (and, to a lesser extent, Crats) prefer to work.

disciplinarity: EVe term for Foucault's concept of "Truth and Power" or the panoptic control of the mammonistic modern state; the opposite of "alterity."

Dmega: "double mega"; TexArc slang for really, really big or important.

DollArcs: TexArc currency.

doublego: TexArc slang for performing a task with extreme urgency.

doubtom: TexArc slang for a doubting Thomas; more precisely, anyone who does not buy into corporate indoctrination hook, line, and sinker.

downleft: the bottom left quadrant viewscreen (wearer's perspective) of the ipatch.

downright: the bottom right quadrant viewscreen (wearer's perspective) of the ipatch.

drone (the): TexArc slang for the never-ending talk streaming over Vieworld.

dude: TexArc slang for guy, fellow, chap; generic.

dykebitch: TexArc slang for a Terd woman with any standing or authority.

econformation: "economic formation"; EVe term for the fiscal structure of a society.

elitehood: TexArc term for the neighborhood where Crats live within the Gater District of a meg; see also "CratVillage."

emostim: "emotional stimulation"; TexArc term for the emotional impact of a bio-implant electrostimulation experience; see also "taste."

emp-grenade: "electromagnetic pulse grenade"; common EVe weapon used to disable advanced machinery.

entrepretunity: "entrepreneur opportunity"; TexArc term for life itself; all the world.

euroloser: TexArc slang for someone from EVe; pejorative.

EVe: formerly the EU or European Union; a socialistic commonwealth of erstwhile nation states extending currently from Scandinavia to the Mediterranean and from the Atlantic Ocean to the Ural Mountains; during process of consolidation the "U" was changed to the Latinate "V" and the "e" then became understood; see also "Marksoc."

EVeWave: the EVe internet system.

facetime: TexArc corpexec term for a meeting or conference.

feed (the): TexArc term for the information-entertainment stream coming over the Simulacrum.

feedhoax: any manner of sham stream over a network; misinformation.

feedtube: an exterior hose connecting directly into the stomach installed in TexArc Servs for the more efficient consumption of fast food; see also "McSlurrys."

fellowshipride: a Wobbly concept meaning solidarity among Servs.

fighter: EVe term for a Maneuvers soldier.

fivesensestim: "five sense stimulation"; TexArc term for the physical impact of a bio-implant electrostimulation experience; see also "taste" and "digiland."

flitter nanobots: flock-forming miniature robots; see also "nanomorph" and "Die Gemeinschaft."

Foenix: in TexArc, the former Phoenix.

fotoID: TexArc corporate identity cards.

freak: a computer security trap or trick designed to catch or to thwart network intrusion; also "to freak"; see also "slice," "sliceimprov," "slicer," and "trail."

freemarket: in TexArc, the holy of holies.

frenzychrister(s): TexArc term for evangelical Christian; religious fanatic; pejorative or honorific depending upon point of view; see also "holyroller" and "TDer."

fringe: TexArc slang for weird, bizarre, innovative.

Gater: TexArc slang for the educated corporate class who live within the walls of the central Gater District of a meg; see also "Crat" and "Terd."

Gater District: the central, walled district of a meg nearest to the Pyramid and heavily fortified; where the educated and ruling corporate classes of TexArc live and work; see also "CratVillage" and "TerdTowne."

GaterPol: "Gater Police"; special security forces that protect the Gater District of a meg.

gge/gray goo effect: the phenomenon of self-replicating, molecular-level nanobots potentially turning the natural world entirely into digital matter; were these "assemblers" ever to begin to self-replicate beyond human control, everything could become, in effect, a mass of inanimate gray goo.

Glassea (the): "glass sea"; generic TexArc term for Middle East oil fields after the region was democratized by tactical nuclear weapons; the allusion is to the resulting extensive plains of fused sands.

glassy (the): TexArc slang for the sparkling eyes of Servs and Corptroops caused by the ipatch; also the phenomenon of being extremely mentally distracted by the continual stream of the Simulacrum.

GLR: "Great Lakes Rim"; the TexArc corpent serving as the primary freshwater stronghold for the corporation.

GNR: "Genetics, Nanotechnology, Robotics;" the NBC (Nuclear, Biological, Chemical) of the 21st century; the new technologies that can both enable and destroy; see also KMD and KME.

Gold Butte: what Oak Wat renames the BoiCity Pyramid.

go/nogo: TexArc slang for a vital or key task.

greenery(ies): greenhouses used for food production.

Groundsman (-men): Corptroop(s) serving in ArcGround; see also "landwarrior."

happers: TexArc term for customers or consumers.

hardnob: TexArc slang for the erect penis.

highmodern: term for the 20th-century era; that is, neoclassical and capitalistic in nature.

hire education: TexArc term for Terd schooling; vocational training; see also "TerdTech."

holospoof: EVe term for holographic decoy images.

holyroller: TexArc slang for evangelical Christian; religious fanatic; pejorative or honorific depending upon point of view; see also "frenzy-christer" and "TDer."

hotseat: TexArc slang for the public execution chair; see also "pubex."

hub (the): TexArc slang for the Pyramid; the heart of power.

hume: "human."

ihear: TexArc aural bio-implant audio reception device.

imagesense/imagesensing: TexArc term for bio-implant electrostimulation experience producing in a recipient the physical and emotional state of someone else; see also "taste."

IMS: "IntraMountain Spine"; a mountainous TexArc corpent stretching between the megs of Edmonton to the north and MexCity to the south.

infoflow: "information flow"; TexArc term for strategic military intelligence.

insidertips: TexArc term for insider trading on the stock market; sanctioned cheating in stock deals carried out primarily by Crats.

ipatch: TexArc term for an ocular bio-implant video reception device; features quadrant viewscreens; see also “all4s,” “downleft,” “downright,” “upleft,” and “upright.”

jingofrenzy: TexArc term for corporate patriotism; especially, that period of fervent pride display immediately following a corpatriotic bio-implant electrostimulation experience; see also “taste.”

job-ed: “job education”; TexArc Serv training.

justwar: “justifiable warfare”; TexArc term for a legitimate or morally right military conflict; that is, all TexArc aggressor actions.

kia: “killed in action”; TexArc term for a combat casualty.

killbot: “killer robot”; any automated killing machine.

KMD: “Knowledge of Mass Destruction”; also known as “knowledge-enabled mass destruction”; the ill-advised and uncontrolled use of certain technologies that will lead to social and ecological disaster; see also “GNR.”

KME: “Knowledge of Mass Enablement”; the strategic and controlled release of certain technologies that would serve to free the world from mammonistic markets and TexArc control; see also“GNR.”

knapsack: computer term for finding a legitimate ingress to a network and surreptitiously piggy-backing one's way into it.

landwarrior(s): TexArc term for ArcGround infantrymen; see also “Groundsman.”

leadmusic: TexArc term for musical segues used on Vieworld.

legislate (to): TexArc common verb for “to perform” or “to do.”

libby: “liberal”; TexArc slang for anyone of a political persuasion left of center of Corpfeud; highly pejorative.

libflee: “liberal flee”; the brain drain of intellectuals and socialists from TexArc to EVe during the 2030s and 2040s; also sometimes referred to as “right flight.”

lowstatus: TexArc term for a Serv; the bottom rungs of the corporate classes; see also "upstatus."

macroprinciples: EVe term for macroeconomics.

MAGG: "Mutual Assured Gray Goo"; the situation of technological standoff between TexArc and EVe preventing either side from using self-replicating nanotechnology for tactical advantage; see also "gge/gray goo effect" and GNR.

Mammonism: EVe term for capitalism; see also "smithprofitism."

man dance: TexArc term for any macho, warlike display; see also "strak hooya."

Maneuvers: the EVe military.

manmech: TexArc term for any brainintegrated system of soldier combined with mechanized equipment; see also "NetExo."

manushop: "manufacturing shop"; EVe term for a small factory or manufacturing facility.

Marksoc: "market socialism"; the current political-economic formation of EVe predicated on public ownership of the means of production; see also "alterity."

markstrat: "market strategy"; TexArc term for approaches to daytrading.

massprod: "mass production."

McSlurrys: leading fast food restaurant chain in TexArc; popularly known as "The Arcs."

mech(s): TexArc term for any mechanized weapon; see also "manmech."

meg: "megalopolis"; super-huge cities in TexArc that strive to function as self-sufficient economic units; see also "Corpfeud."

megcouncilor: TexArc term for those few Crats who oversee the running of a meg; see also "topcrat."

message (to): EVe term to communicate via an electronic device.

messager: EVe term for a personal communication device.

mex: TexArc slang for all persons of Hispanic descent; pejorative.

mil-ed: "military education"; TexArc term for Corptroop training.

mil-spend: "military spending"; a TexArc permanent policy.

mindfuck: TexArc slang for a shocking thing, event, situation, or idea.

mobgov: "mob government"; TexArc term for democracy; pejorative.

mobile: TexArc term for mobile home or trailer; the primary housing unit for Servs in the Parks.

motherforce: EVe military term for the main force of a Maneuvers fighter unit.

mot-sen/corband: "motor-sensory cortex band"; TexArc bio-implant brain-machine interface and stimulation device.

moveon: TexArc term for social advancement and economic amelioration in the historical materialist sense; pejorative.

nanomorph: EVe term for a nanoparticle swarm simulator capable of taking on the shapes of various real items; see also "flitter nanobots" and "Die Gemeinschaft."

nanotech solpow: "nanotechnology solar power"; innovations in the production of solar cells that would provide the world freedom from dependance on fossil fuels; see also "KME."

NetExo(s): elite ArcNet combat force of Netsmen brainintegrated with exoskeleton HPA (Human Performance Augmentation) suits; see also "manmech."

Netsman (-men): Terd(s) serving in ArcNet.

newsbig: TexArc term for important, breaking news.

OakCity: what BoiCity is renamed after the Wobbly takeover.

outbreak bug: TexArc term for pestilence-carrying insects (such as mosquitoes) or for a virus or pandemic germ itself; any widespread contagion or epidemic.

pad (to): to key information into a computer palmbook, lapbook, or console.

ParkPol: "Parks Police"; special suppression forces that seek to prevent discord in the Parks of a meg; primary function is to keep such unrest from spreading toward the Gater District.

Parks (the): short for "trailer parks"; TexArc slang for the vast urban slums surrounding the central Gater District of megs; where Servs live and work.

paxrevolution: EVe term for the largely peaceful transition from mammonism to socialism where the knowledge workers and the body workers of a society unite to overthrow the minority money owner plutocrats; see also "alterity."

PC: "Pacific Coast"; the most politically turbulent of the TexArc corpents, stretching between the megs of Vancouver to the north and Tijuana to the south.

pedanterd: "pedant terd"; TexArc term for an academic.

picvoice: the picture and voice of a feed or network stream; see also "vidaud."

pitch: TexArc term for a commercial or for advertising in general; see also "counterpitch."

plaindeal: TexArc slang for a straightforward biz transaction; a no-brainer.

plaintalk: TexArc slang for candid statement; honesty.

poochscrew: TexArc slang for a mistake or misstep; a fuck-up.

popcult: "popular culture"; EVe term and field of sociological study.

postmod: "postmodern"; anything decentralized; without a chain of command or ultimate authority; relativity.

powersleep: TexArc term for catnaps while on the go.

poz: "position"; ArcGround military term.

profit: TexArc term for salary or pay; see also "quadprofit."

promo: "promotion"; TexArc Crat term for job advancement.

PTA: "Plains-Tundra Argiworks"; the breadbasket of the TexArc corpents, stretching north-south down the geographic center of the corporation.

pubex: “public execution”; a common form of TexArc entertainment over the Simulacrum; see also “hotseat.”

pubeye: “public eye”; TexArc term for publicity or being well known.

pullons: “pull ons”; TexArc term for any removable brain-machine interface and stimulation device that is normally bio-implant in Servs (i.e. the mot-sen/corband, ipatch, and ihear); such optional devices are the privilege of Crats and Terds.

Pyramid (the): TexArc term for the pyramid-shaped hardened fortress located at the center of all megs; the seat of local corporate authority.

Pyramid Guard: ultra-elite security force for the protection of topcrats of a meg.

quadprofit: TexArc term for extremely good salary or pay; see also “profit.”

quickeat: EVe slang for a speedy eatery.

raghead(s): TexArc slang for any opponent of the corporation or anyone living outside corporate borders; all foreigners; highly pejorative.

rapegang: TexArc term for male pleasure-seekers; boys being boys.

readrite: TexArc slang for the ability to read and write; basic literacy.

revoevo: “revolution evolution”; TexArc term for the primary threat to Corpfeud; what the corporation seeks to prevent with regard to political-economic formation; see also “alterity,” “Marksoc,” and “paxrevolution.”

rithmetic: TexArc slang for the ability to do arithmetic; basic numeracy.

safeline: EVe term for a secure communication device or stream.

SaltCity: in TexArc, the former Salt Lake City; the lake evaporated.

savtrade: “savvy trade”; TexArc slang for insightful or shrewd trading practices on the stock market; see also “insidertips.”

sec: “security.”

selfoblige: TexArc term for self-gratification or self-interest; a corporate mantra.

selfterm: “self termination”; TexArc military term for when ArcGround command intentionally kills a Corptroop via autodestruct signals so that the Corptrooper will not be captured by an enemy.

sellmusic: TexArc term for advertising jingles.

Serv(s): TexArc term for the lower corporate class; workers; also the source pool for all Corptroops.

sexpolitics: EVe term for either political sexuality or sexual politics; the civics of gender denotation and formation.

s/he: EVe gender-neutral pronoun; also, her/im, her/imself.

shituber: TexArc slang for a Serv; see also “feedtube” and “bellyfart”; highly pejorative.

shock-and-awe(d): TexArc term for crushing or overwhelming an adversary, usually militarily.

sigblock skullcap(s)/SigCaps: “signal block skullcap”/“Signal Caps”; EVe devices designed to stop the continuous video and audio stream of the Simulacrum over ArcNet to the mot-sen/corbands of Servs and Corptroopers; small, roll-down hats made of metallictextile.

Signification Committee: the EVe agency responsible for propagating the benefits of Marksoc over EVeWave; situated at Worcester College, Oxford; see also “Culture Construct.”

simu: “simulation”; computer generated; see also “vir.”

simudisc: TexArc term for small computer disk with a digiland taste on it.

Simulacrum (the): the TexArc information-entertainment stream sent out to all corporate citizens over ArcNet.

sleepspan: TexArc term for an assigned period of rest.

slice (to): computer term for gaining forced entry into a network; with firewalls so extensive as to afford no way around them, fissures or cracks must be found in order to wedge one's way through them.

sliceimprov: “slice improvisation”; to devise, concoct, or rig up an unusual or illegal procedure over a network stream.

slicer: an operator or program that gains illicit entry into a computer network; see also "slice."

slope: TexArc slang for all persons of Asian descent; pejorative.

smithprofitism: EVe term for capitalism; see also "Mammonism."

Sneak Crew: EVe military term for covert forces; special-operations fighters.

snogall: EVe slang for a hypersexual person.

solarworks: power station; a facility generating electricity.

stiffyanker: TexArc slang for the erect penis.

strak hooya: TexArc military slang (used particularly by ArcNet and ArcSpace personnel) for an extremely avid or gung-ho serviceman; see also "man dance."

stream (to)/streaming: to broadcast image and voice over a communications network; also, such a transmission itself.

subceo: TexArc term for the corporate position just below that of the ceo; a top executive administrator to the big boss; see also "ceo."

sweetpuss: "sweet pussy"; TexArc slang for a woman; see also "tit-s'n'ass"; pejorative.

T-15 (e.g.): "TexArc 15"; nomenclature by which major corporate freeways are designated.

tacnuke: "tactical nuke"; a low-yield field nuclear weapon.

talkheads: "talking heads"; Vieworld news reporters.

taste: TexArc term for experiencing the physical and emotional state of someone else via bio-implant electrostimulation; often used for corpatriotic public excitation; see also "jingofrenzy."

TDer(s): a member of the Total Dominionist movement in TexArc; the most devout and orthodox of the manifold evangelical Christian groups within the corporation; see also "frenzychrister" and "holyroller."

team: EVe military term for units or squads of fighters within a motherforce.

team guide: EVe military term for the leader of a fighter team.

tech: "technology"; often referring to technical personnel or to technical apparatus; see also "teek," "Terd," and "TerdTech."

teek: "technology geek"; EVe slang for a technology/network expert.

Terd: "technology nerd"; TexArc slang for a technology/network expert; more generally, TexArc term for the educated, non-Crat corporate class; see also "Gater."

TerdTech: TexArc term for a university; vocational training institutions for Terds; see also "hire education."

TerdTowne: where the Terds live within the central fortified district of a TexArc meg; specifically, those areas nearest to the outer wall that separates the Gater District from the Parks; see also "Gater District."

term: (to)/terming: "terminate"; TexArc common verb for "to kill" or "killing."

TexArc: formerly the oil conglomerate "TexArco"; the corporation that accomplished the hostile takeover of the outmoded U.S. republic in the 2030s; currently controls the North American continent from the Arctic Circle to the Panama Canal; see also "Corpfeud."

textsymbols: TexArc term for written letters, numbers, and words.

thinksay (to): TexArc term for any brainintegrated voiceless communication between two parties; normally via the mot-sen/corband and ihear.

thunderboomers: TexArc slang for extremely powerful and dangerous thunderstorms.

tits'n'ass: "tits and ass"; TexArc slang for a woman; see also "sweetpuss"; pejorative.

topcrat: TexArc term for the uppermost governing Crats of a meg; see also "megcouncilor."

totoblank: all four viewscreens of the ipatch going blank; to stream no images; see also "all4s."

trail (to): to track an intruder (either forward to destination or backward to origin) within a computer network in an effort to prevent unwanted entry into a system; see also "slice," "sliceimprov," "slicer," and "freak."

tubed on: TexArc slang for a Serv being provided sustenance via his or her feeding tube; see also "feedtube," "shituber," and "bellyfart."

24/7: "twenty-four-seven"; TexArc slang for around-the-clock; constant.

upleft: the top left quadrant viewscreen (wearer's perspective) of the ipatch.

upright: the top right quadrant viewscreen (wearer's perspective) of the ipatch.

upstatus: TexArc term for a Crat or a Terd; the top rungs of the corporate classes; see also "lowstatus."

urbpass: "urban pacification"; TexArc term for subduing a city militarily; see also "democratize."

vianet: "via net"; EVe term for communication over the internet.

vehic: "vehicle"; TexArc term for any manner of ground, air, or space conveyance.

vid: "video."

vidaud: "video audio"; the video and audio portions of a feed or network stream; see also "picvoice."

vidfeed: "video feed"; the visual portion of a network stream.

vidgame: "video game."

Vieworld: the TexArc news network streaming nonstop over the Simulacrum; signature slogans include: "Time To Know!"; "Wherever you go, there we are!"; "See the world, be the world!"

viewscreen(s): "viewing screens"; TexArc term for video reception equipment of any kind or size.

vir: "virtual"; computer-generated.

virbod: "virtual body"; TexArc term for one's own computer-generated body, often enhanced, during any virtual experience; see also "bodyenhance" and "digiland."

virho: "virtual hole"; TexArc term for a computer-generated woman, usually for the purposes of computer-generated sex; see also "virsex."

virsex: "virtual sex"; TexArc term for computer-generated sexual stimulation over the Simulacrum.

vit: "victuals"; TexArc slang for food.

vit and vid: "victuals and video"; TexArc version of the saying "bread and games."

Waco Great Pyramid (the): TexArc corporate headquarters; see also "CorpHQ."

watchwrist: TexArc term for an information-communication device worn on the wrist.

Wave: EVe slang for EveWave.

Wobbly(ies): the name of the Serv insurrection movement in the IMS; eventually, the name of the sovereign state declared by the Wobblies around the OakCity vicinity.

wonderboy: TexArc slang for someone who questions the corporate status quo; pejorative.

workcred(s): "work credit(s)"; a unit of currency in TexArc enabling servs to purchase goods and services for the promise of future labor to be performed; a form of indentured servitude.

yank (to)/yanking: slang for coitus or for getting fucked over.

yanker: slang for the erect penis or for someone who fucks you over.

yardandgarden manors: TexArc term for individual Crat mansions (walled and heavily defended) within an elitehood; see also "CratVillage."

yub (the): TexArc Serv and Corptroop slang for gossip, wild rumor, or bullshit in general; for example, "the yub from the hub."

zoomzoom (to): TexArc slang for driving a ground vehicle.